The Forest and the Flame

BY
S.C. WOLF

Published by Beta Dreams Production Company

ISBN: 979-8-9997949-1-8

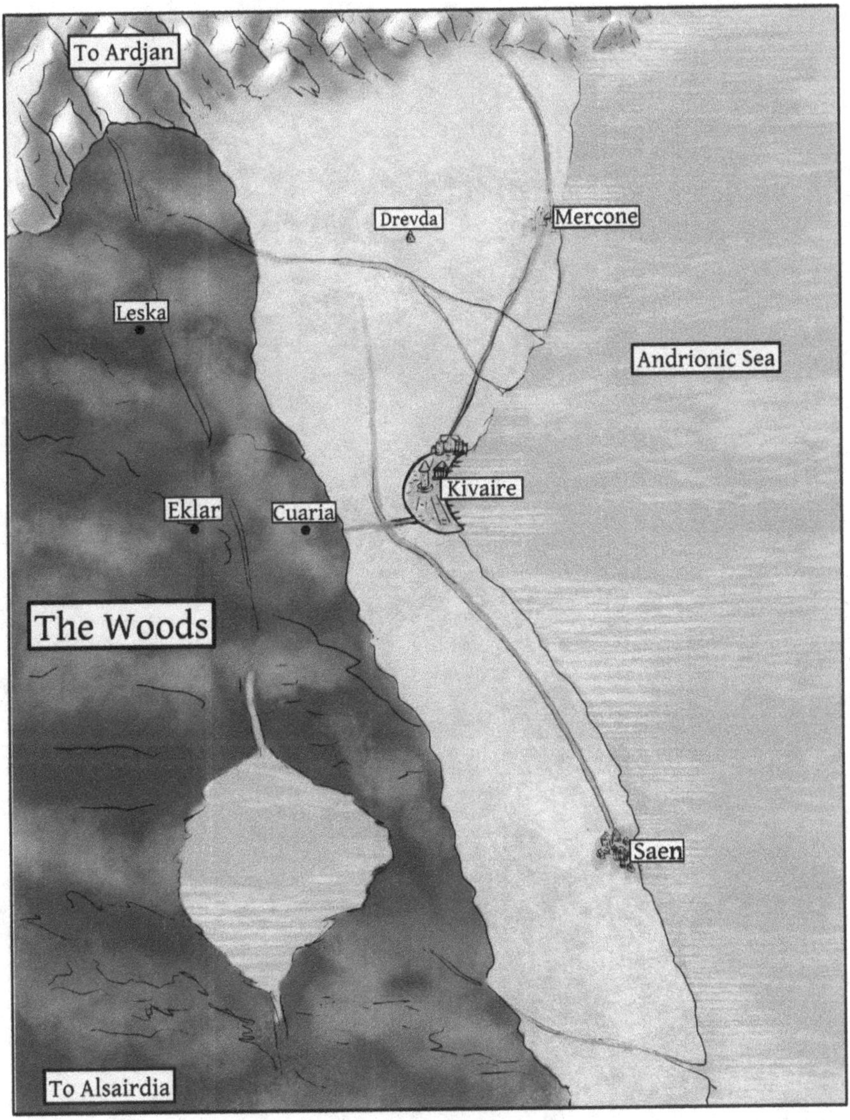

To Ardjan

Drevda

Mercone

Leska

Andrionic Sea

Kivaire

Eklar   Cuaria

The Woods

Saen

To Alsairdia

For my Poets.
Without you, none of this would exist.

Content Warnings

The Forest and the Flame includes content that may not be suitable for some readers. There is a list of these elements at the end of the book. If you have concerns, please read them so you can decide whether to continue reading. The specific list will contain spoilers for the story.

CHAPTER ONE

ALYSSIA

How many times in the last thirty-odd years of my life have I walked these Woods looking for things that aren't where they should be? Mentally, I retrace my steps while keeping an eye on my surroundings, mostly so I don't miss anything useful. There's never any danger out here, but if I've learned anything, it's that there's a first time for everything. Like finding the same spot of Woods in the same place twice.

I can hear the river to my right, just like it should be, rushing with the remnants of spring floods, carving its way to the vast lake in the Deep Woods. The trees leading to its rocky shores even larger and more wild than the rest of the Woods, creating twisted, hidden pathways and arching bridges. The sun filters through minute gaps in the leafy canopy, nearly overhead even though it was barely over the horizon when I started. It's not like this is a surprise, but still, just one time I would like to come into these tree-forsaken Woods and find the damn thing I'm looking for in the same place I left it.

The trip hasn't been totally useless. The gathering bag slung over my shoulder has a fresh stock of the Woods' more common practical bounty neatly clipped and bundled with scraps of twine, ready to be processed properly back home. But two weeks ago, I found a patch of not-quite-ready weeping widow that should be ripe for harvest now, and my window to collect it is short. I swear it has to be around the next cluster of trees at least a dozen times, but I'm foiled at every turn.

Irritated, I trip over roots and other forest detritus, mumbling to myself and plucking twigs out of my pulled-back hair like some sort of deranged forest creature. Annoyance flares every time I have to push another strand of the dirty brown-blond mess out of my face. My determination to find the flower is fading fast. I glare at my surroundings, shove an unruly tangle of branches out of my face, and as if the trees can tell I'm seconds away from starting a forest fire, I arrive at my destination. Just like that. Hours of tree cursing later than it should have been.

But it was worth it.

Weeping widow is beautiful in its haunting sorrow. The flowering vines crawl desperately along cracks in crumbling stone, dripping from walls and barely intact arches. What makes this plant so rare is that it only grows in this forest, and only on old stone. There is a large amount of folkish malarkey about the origins of these plants. Most are stories about the Otherfolk. All of them are wrong, of course, and not just because the Otherfolk are only stories themselves. But I do have to admit that deep within the green-tinged twilight of these trickster Woods, the tales could send a shiver down my spine if I was feeling fanciful. Right now, however, I'm feeling about as fanciful as a weed. So I start harvesting.

The vines flower in pairs of white, bell-like blooms, and they are ready to harvest when the stones drip with blood. It's not really blood, obviously. The flower's nectar is simply thick with dark red pollen. When the upright cups of the petals become too heavily laden, they tip and drip the viscous, red, clotted mixture down the stones. I can't help but think of the story I've always loved of an Otherfolk queen who, after being widowed young, took to wandering the forest. Some versions say she was searching for the ghost of her lost love, weeping while hunting through homes and trees and temples, the vines flowering in the wake of her tears. Other versions imply she was running from who, or what, had killed her husband. Grieving and hiding, sheltered by her people.

I shake my head with a smile and continue making quick, clean cuts with a small knife to free the blooms just beyond their base, keeping the vine intact. It isn't likely I'll ever find this place again, but it isn't right to destroy them for one year's harvest. With any luck, I'll find another dilapidated stone ruin of mysterious origin covered in ghostly foliage next year. I fill several jars with the flowers, stoppered tight and snugly fit into their pockets within the bag. Next, I remove a jar of raw spirits and begin carefully collecting flakes of the nearly resinous, blood-red nectar until the liquid in the jar takes on the desired color and opacity; roughly that of old blood. To consume the raw, sticky nectar in any great amount is typically ill-advised unless you are incredibly adventurous, have a good long time in a safe space, and don't mind separating yourself from reality for a while. Not that I would know, of course, but it's why I'm slow and careful with my scraping, catching the potent material in the relative safety of the alcohol.

The sun is quickly diving toward the horizon by the time I'm done rattling around in my own musings and collecting my second jar of expensive plant blood. Even though most of my day was spent searching through unruly forest, I still consider it well spent. This is an unusually plentiful harvest of weeping widow, a worthy prize wrested from another day of trials against the Woods.

Finally ready to turn back into the leafy abyss, a flicker of light outside one of the ruined archways stops me. Clambering out of the crumbling stones, I hum to myself on my way to a closer look, absently tucking the last jar into my bag. It wouldn't be unheard of in ruins like this for there to be some object gleaming from hidden, forgotten depths. There is a whole ledge in my shop with odd little trinkets found by me and the long line of apothecaries before me. To my surprise, that isn't the case this time. The light is definitely shining of its own accord, deep in a large knot of a massive old tree. The sun falls behind that side of the clearing and the surrounding trees are dark in shadow, except for the one I'm ambling toward.

It's a flame.

A small, leaf-green flame flickers lazily, floating in the center of its cozy nook.

With the instinct of a gatherer, my hand drifts to an empty, wide-mouthed jar, thumb and forefinger working out the cork. It likely isn't the smartest idea to bottle a mysterious, floating green fire, but part of me is certainly considering it. Who wouldn't want to see if the apparition of an impossible conflagration was something tangible, or if they may or may not have breathed in too many flakes of hallucinogenic plant byproduct while scraping it into bottles?

The air vibrates near my cheek as I hear a swish and dull thud far too close to my ear.

My head jerks to the side, shock and confusion bubbling up before I even know what interrupted my investigation. Attempting to reconcile the appearance of an oddly sparking arrow so close to my face, my head swivels wildly, searching for its origin. I've never seen anyone this deep in the trees, and I still don't despite the evidence suggesting otherwise. Someone has to be here. Someone with the audacity to shoot me with an arrow in my own damn Woods.

The gall some people have.

I sweep the flame into the vial like capturing a firefly and run headlong into the forest, putting distance between myself and my unseen assailants before another arrow can find me. One hand is gripped tightly around the glass bottle, the other fumbles the cork into place, the strangely cool, green flame flickering away inside. Belatedly, I remember fire usually goes out if you put a lid on it, but it seems the rules do not apply to green fire found floating in a tree.

If this is actually happening and is not an elaborate hallucination stealing the mysterious flame is probably a mistake, but I'm already too far to put it back. And if this *is* happening, running as fast as I can away from hidden, bow-wielding forest interlopers isn't the worst idea. I shrug off the thought and focus on not falling spectacularly onto my face. In a surprising turn of events, it's like the roots themselves are making a way for me, and the Woods blur as I leap like a deer through the undergrowth. Even though I don't know what, or who, I'm running from, I have never seen an arrow glow like that, and I doubt its proximity to my face was accidental. I simply have to trust my Woods and myself and run.

—

It's quickly apparent that bounding through the forest away from violent pursuit is an activity meant for someone much younger and in much better shape than I am. My knees ache, it feels like someone is trying to stab a knife between my ribs, and the wrenching twist of the stitch in my side takes an embarrassingly short period of time to manifest. In my defense, plants don't do an excessive amount of running, and aside from the occasional round-bottomed flask, neither does anything else in the shop. Ages pass and I find an unpleasant equilibrium of panic and physical discomfort that blends into numbness, allowing me to focus on where I'm going and why.

Eventually, enough time has passed to have circulated out whatever widow resin I may have ingested in my harvesting, allowing me to reassess my current situation without doubts about my sobriety. Trying to gather my thoughts feels like trying to catch falling leaves in a brisk autumn wind with cold-numbed hands, however; the leaves constantly out of reach and likely to shatter at a touch. Until, that is, another arrow decides to put an extremely fine point to them. Fortunately for my professional ego, it seems I didn't accidentally drug myself. Unfortunately for the rest of me, I haven't managed to outrun my regrettably real pursuers.

Well, shit.

I duck deeper into an even thicker section of trees and pass the second arrow. The head is sunken into the trunk of an old, twisted hardwood well beyond what should be naturally possible, the oddly shining shaft disappearing into the hole it bore.

Anger flashes again, this time for the forest around me. How dare these strangers come tearing through my Woods, desecrating them with their presence, let alone their weapons? This is not a place for outsiders. This is our place. Our Woods. My feet hit the earth hard for several steps as I stomp a tantrum of futility into the ground without slowing down. I can't do anything until I can see them, and I don't want to look for them before I know they can't see me.

My paring knife is the only weapon I have on me, and I long for the hefty dagger I take with me on my trips to the city. At least the little blade is sharp and, given perfect circumstances, I could probably do some damage with it. What I lack in hand-to-hand combat experience, I make up for in detailed knowledge of anatomical weak points.

When I simply can't run any further, I slow long enough to listen beyond the roar of blood rushing through my ears and the rasp of breath whistling through my airways. My steps are light, barely making a sound in the spongy undergrowth, and my eyes dart around like a nervous squirrel's. I hear men's voices, louder than I expected and freeze, breath catching in my throat painfully. They aren't loud with proximity, however; they are shouting. My breathing quiets as curiosity supersedes blind fear. The sound is too muffled by trees and distance to make out any words, but the crashing of bodies and the sound of clanging metal fades as I creep onward.

Wait. That's not right.

Why would I hear metal on metal? I'm sure I haven't been leading them toward my village. The next closest is nearly a day away and across the river. There shouldn't be anyone else out here, and it sure seems like an odd time for sword practice. The sun is nowhere to be seen beyond the leafy expanse of canopy, but the depth of full dark has not settled over the forest yet. The sun must still be above the horizon, but low and preparing for bed like I should be. The shadows of the trees crowd me as visibility drops, and soon it will be even more unpleasant to navigate. At least the same difficulty should befall my new friends. Abruptly, I realize I'm still holding the jar of green not-quite-fire, and its unearthly glow burns brightly in the growing dark. I gently wiggle the jar into its home in the bag and close the large satchel with a soft pat.

Once I am reassured of the safety of my belongings, I go against my better judgment and pick my way toward the shouting and clattering, disappearing into the blue-gray twilight of the forest. I will never forgive myself if someone I know runs into these people and gets killed. I will also never forgive myself if I waste any more energy running when I don't need to.

As the sun sinks lower and lower, the shadows amidst the soaring trees deepen and twist. I pull myself along their tendrils, climbing over and under roots, fallen logs, and worn rocks, following the darkest path towards the sounds. Surprisingly, I see a flash of light up ahead coming from a small clearing with just enough open canopy to let in some of the fading sun.

There are four figures lunging between tree shadows in such violent chaos, I have a hard time untangling what I'm seeing. Three of the figures wear vaguely familiar, uniform black coats that flutter behind them as they move, marking them as a single unit working against the fourth man. Every so often one gets stuck in the foliage and has to yank themselves free. I could have told them wearing loose clothing was a bad idea, but it looks like they are figuring it out on their own.

The fourth man wears a tight white shirt and fitted pants that let him move more freely between the trees. The bow responsible for the inciting arrow is nowhere to be seen, but two black-clad assailants have quivers at their backs and one-handed swords in their hands. The third has no quiver, but he swings a distinctly larger sword with abandon. Chunks of pale tree flesh gleam in the wake of his massive blade. He wrenches it free from a low hanging branch with a growl. I growl back at the damage they are doing.

I'm close enough to hear the heavy breathing of the men, and I turn my thoughts from the ranting tirade about harming the trees to keeping out of harm's way. I watch the dance of flashing blades with interest from the safety of the shadows. A fight in the middle of my Woods is very different from the others I have seen throughout my life. It's slower here, the combatants having to deal with obstacles at every step and swing. There's still plenty of blood, darker patches of wet splattered around and clinging to clothes, trees, and earth. The odd man out manages to break away in a feint behind a particularly wide tree root, whipping around to the unprotected side of one of the other men.

He steps in close to the man and drives the pommel into the side of his head too quickly to dodge. Disoriented, he staggers back, but the man in white catches him with his sword behind his neck. One hand on the hilt, the other midway down the blade, he pulls his weapon toward himself while kicking the other man away.

The head isn't severed, but it does hinge alarmingly as the body crumples to the ground.

As the corpse falls, the other two close in quickly. At least the man with the human skewer is in a more difficult position now, trying to herd the other man back toward the clearing instead of deeper into the dense trees.

I strangle the perfectly reasonable instinct to edge away from the slowly approaching scuffle. The man's white shirt is no longer very white, damp with sweat and blood. His dark hair is just as wet, clinging to his face in wavy clumps where it has escaped the tie holding it back. His breathing is labored, and even I can tell he's slowing. The others are also tiring, but there are still two of them to his singular person. Those odds are really not in his favor the longer this goes on. I might not make it a fair two-versus-two, but I could get it to a close one and a half.

I crouch on the curve of a root, having climbed up for a better view and look down, hugging my bag close, hunting for an opportunity to assist. Another step, and another. The dance unfolds below me. The remaining archer is down in a spray of leaves, a root poking a long tendril out of the leaf mould. The swordsman neatly punches a hole through the man's gut, flowing beneath the other man's swing into a weighty, sword-first kneel into the body on the ground.

The kneeling man springs from the entanglement of roots and corpse at his feet. Leaves fountain upward. They cover his movement as he lunges forward, inside the reach of the colossal blade. Simultaneously, the other man drops said colossal blade and brandishes a dagger instead. He also lurches forward. They collide with such force that they clutch each other in surprise. An ungainly attempt to keep their collective balance. Their unsteady embrace quickly turns into a deadly grapple, each man desperate to get the upper hand.

The mysterious hero's sword glints dully from the forest floor. He's unarmed and struggling to keep the other man's dagger from any vital spots. He snakes one arm between them, knocking the dagger to the side long enough to obtain a controlling grip on the assailant's forearm. He shakes and sweat pours in rivulets down his face.

His face. I know that face.

I skate down the slope of my root perch and land a step away from the broad expanse of the black-clad man's back. I take a white-knuckled hold on my gathering knife and surge toward him. With all my weight behind me, I swing straight for his thick, sweaty neck.

It's an inelegant move. The short blade doesn't even make it halfway in before my target reels away. White-shirt's eyes fly wide at the sight of me, revealed to him from behind a spray of blood as the man separates himself from my knife. I don't know if I managed to hit any major vessels or merely nicked him, but I have less than zero desire to stick around and find out. I book it like a scared rabbit into the undergrowth, slowing just enough to look over my shoulder at His Royal Highness, Prince Kedren D'raci, and shout.

"Well? Come on!"

CHAPTER TWO

ALYSSIA

My situation is of the good news-bad news variety, and I would really prefer it swing to the side of good at some point. At least I'm fairly certain I'm not a murderer, which could go either way really. Two out of three villainous foes causing mischief in my Woods are dead and progressing nicely into fertilizer. The threat of the potentially not dead third man leaves something to be desired, however. I do have a capable assistant on my side, but he is the unarmed, prince of the Woods-damned kingdom.

It doesn't take long for the last vestiges of adrenaline to seep from my tired, hungry body. Sooner than I'd like, the stabbing ache is back in my side, and I can feel the swelling of my knees in the most uncomfortable way. My flight is so pathetic, it doesn't cross my mind that my companion wouldn't keep up with me until I have to stop to catch my breath and I listen for sounds of pursuit. When there are none, including the ones I should hear, my flush of exertion increases with a burning wave of panic.

I turn too quickly and my vision spins uncomfortably, but thankfully the prince is not far behind me. The uneasiness doesn't leave my roiling stomach, however, as he sags against a tree in an alarming fashion, shoulders curled in, face flushed, gasping shallowly. Before I can scrounge up the energy to go to him, he pulls himself upright and takes a few unsteady steps, visibly steeling himself to keep following. He looks up and sees that I've stopped, my breath heaving in and out of my open mouth like inefficient bellows. One of his hands is clutching his chest, and I write it off as someone else who is not used to woodland sprint sessions. Then I see it, the dagger sticking out of the prince's chest beneath his collar bone and slightly out toward his shoulder.

Shit.

There isn't much blood directly around the wound, that I can tell anyway, so splashed and splattered as his shirt already is, so he must have been keeping the dagger pretty well in place. That's good. Where it is, is not as good. A large artery runs right around there, and that could cause us both some fairly significant problems.

What an awkward situation that would be. Is accidentally killing someone while trying to help them the same as killing them outright? This is really something I should know by now. Regardless, I doubt the royal family would take kindly to the news that the prince died on my watch. I guess I could always drag his body back into the trees and let a bear eat him. No one would really have to know. Unless someone *did* know where he was and came looking for him. But what could they do?

That's a plan then. I can just send anyone who comes looking on their way to get themselves lost in the Woods. Alright, it's part of a plan. Part of a bad plan. But I can't even begin to contemplate pulling the dagger out here, and I may not have to enact my plan at all if I can keep him alive. We just have to get back to my shop.

When I think I might have enough breath to speak, I wheeze out, "I don't think we are going to run into our mutual friend at this point. Do you think you can make it a little further if we slow down? I can take care of that," I nod toward the slowly oozing knife wound for pointless emphasis, "Back at my shop. We aren't far now."

And thank the trees, we are close. We're in a loose thicket of elderberry bushes that I know well, close to one of the three main roads into the village. The bushes are starting to flower, and I absently drift to the nearest bunch of fully bloomed clusters as I speak, pinching several of them off with the sharp edge of one nail and tucking them into my bag.

The prince nods, his voice surprisingly soft and deep, and only mildly breathless, "Thank you. I will be alright for a while still. I cannot say I would mind slowing down, however. The terrain here is not quite what I am used to." He tries a grin and it almost works, but comes out as more of a grimace. It's incredibly charming; blood, dirt, and leaves notwithstanding.

Despite the knife sticking out of him, he holds himself with a loose, casual grace now that he's gotten a chance to recover. Only the white knuckled grip steadying the hilt protruding from his chest, and the blood dripping slowly from his fingers spoils the illusion.

Meanwhile, I still feel like my lungs are on fire, and my legs are shaking so badly, waddling to the bushes nearly causes me to collapse. I guess dashing royalty known for adventurous carousing wouldn't become a mess after any measly fight to the death.

Show off.

"Perfect. And don't worry, I am used to it, and it's still a pain in the ass."

I tilt my head toward the twisting tunnel of roots, half-hidden behind the bushes I was fiddling with before willing my body to follow. I have absolutely no idea what small talk is supposed to sound like in this situation, so I keep my mouth shut with the excuse that all of my air is going into keeping me alive. He doesn't seem to be particularly chatty either, so I let the silence linger. My wobbly steps come easier now, back on firmly familiar ground, therefore freeing more mental resources to keep my eyes and ears tuned into my surroundings. There is no indication I need to be concerned about any flying arrows or swinging swords, but there wasn't when this day started out either, so I stay vigilant. I match my pace to the soft crunching of the prince's footsteps and scan the surrounding rough, bark surfaces for usable fungi out of habit.

The tunnel is short but curves sharply, haphazardly following the chaos of a completely natural structure. It's also dark and devoid of useful mushrooms, so I give up looking and focus on keeping just ahead of my companion. He follows in my wake until I push past a curtain of overhanging vines, and we are deposited unceremoniously onto the road leading into my village. Road being a generous description. It's barely more than a wide, mostly cleared, passage of trodden dirt and leaves leading roughly north and south. To the north the soft glow of torchlight reflects off of the bordering trees, indicating the nearness of my home; to the south is the rich dark of the forest at night. I feel a physical ache drawing me to the comfort of those torches. Everything will be better once I am back inside the village.

"Oi!"

A man's voice shouts from the firelight when we stagger into view, but I wave a hand with dramatic dismissal above my head. Belar is at the south entrance tonight and I couldn't be more pleased. He is the least likely to harass me about anything, and I can't possibly come up with a succinct and reasonable explanation for my late return, the disheveled state of my person, and the bloody guest I have with me. He recognizes me as soon as he calls out, and settles back into his knotty nook at the base of a tree next to the road, light flickering over a bemused grin. A stalwart Woodsman to his core, he is built vaguely like a tree himself: wide and tall, and dressed in browns and greens, bundled against the slight chill of the spring night air.

"Anything we should be worried about?" Belar asks, straight and to the point with minimal expectations, and no need to dig any extraneous information out of me. What a dear.

"I hope not, but maybe keep an eye open. Not sure if the owner of that knife is going to come looking for it." I nod with forced casualness to the prince. Belar won't recognize him, but I still feel nervous. Since the prince didn't immediately start proclaiming who he is, I can only assume he either doesn't want us to know, or he assumes everyone does and is being very polite about the disrespect. Erring on the side of caution, I'm going with the first option. Regardless, I certainly don't want anyone to know he's here, especially in case I accidentally kill him later.

Belar, bless his entire family line past, present, and future, grunts and nods, gesturing us into the village. There are men at the other two gates as well, and I'm confident he will tell them to be alert.

"When you can, maybe send someone out to the other villages to tell them to keep their eyes open?"

He punctuates a grunt with a curt nod so I know the matter is settled.

Before succumbing to the urge to haul myself as fast as I can to the peace of my shop, I glance back at the prince to assure myself he's still following. His eyes are wide and his lips part as we walk under the arched opening through a wall of tree, branch, root and vine that encircles the entire village. His face reminds me of the first time I entered the capital, floored with wonder and awe at the vast stone, wood, and iron of walls and gates, homes and shops. My chest bursts with pride that my home could instill that same wonder in someone. I don't remember the last time, if ever, that I have thought about what Cuaria would look like to an outsider since we get so few. I can only imagine how it looks to someone used to cities and the smaller forests in the rest of the kingdom.

The trees here are large and ancient, soaring above us. The true limits of the canopy are out of sight, even in the noon sun. The ground sees only trickles of leaf-filtered light even on the brightest of days. So large are the trees that the buildings of the village are not only built on the ground, but have grown in and around and up among the trees, whole homes tucked into knotty hollows in trunks or stacked along rises in the roots acting as ramps between stories or neighbors.

I take him through the wandering paths between homes, torches and candlelight glowing along pathways and out of windows, warming the darkness of the night. The walkways branch as endlessly as the trees, both natural and man-made structures connecting the community. We rise and fall on the most direct path leading to the village center over bridges and through the leaf strewn forest floor. Lights flicker like stars around us.

The restfulness of my village washes over me as we navigate the twists and turns. My thoughts drift to my fireplace, dinner, and how best to treat the prince when a figure drops abruptly from the sky, a twisted vine swinging in their wake. My heart stops. The prince shifts behind me, but I throw my arm up to arrest his movement.

"Inness!" The arm that isn't preventing the prince from doing anything impulsive toward my apprentice is clutching my chest, but I drop both as soon as the proverbial dust settles. "What are you doing? Where were you doing it?" The village, and Woods at large, hold many hidden nooks and crannies for young girls with streaks of mischief to find, and I swear my apprentice finds every single one.

"I was waiting for you. I finished with Da ages ago and you still weren't home." Her dark hair shines with firelight as it spills across her face as she leans to one side, looking behind me. "Who's that?"

"Just someone who needs my help." I continue on my way, catching Inness up under one arm and dragging her with me to keep her from looking too closely at our visitor. "Do you think you could stay with your Da tonight so I can take care of this?"

"But I need to start helping more with this stuff or I'll never learn," she whines. "Stop keeping me away from the gross parts."

It's true that I need to start letting her help me with the surgeon aspects of what I do for the villagers, but I can't help thinking of her as too young. I conveniently forget that I was younger than she is now when I sewed my first stitch and pulled my first bad tooth. More importantly, however, I don't want her around if I fuck up and kill the prince. Besides, I need some place to put him for the night, and its certainly not going to be in my bed.

"I promise next time, no matter how disgusting it is, you can help."

"Promise?"

"By the Trees."

She makes a satisfied little noise and twirls out of my loose embrace.

"Alright. My Da misses me, anyway. I'll be back in the morning!" With a wave, she flings herself off the edge of the bridge, catching the vine she dropped in on and uses it to swing down and on her way to her father's house.

She's truly a menace and reminds me far too much of myself at that age. I suppress a shiver thinking of my young self and all of the various, stupid things I got myself into, and out of, with too much access to substances and knowledge no teenager should have. I want to keep her safe, young and innocent as long as I can. I shake my head and keep going.

The Great Tree at the center of our village fills my vision as we duck through the warren of homes. Our few shops and meeting areas weave among its lower region, tucked into roots and hollows, the trunk lit with scattered lanterns. Gardens are tucked between and under vast, arching roots, dappled in shadow and light. And there, up and around one darkened, twisting ramp of root is home.

CHAPTER THREE

ALYSSIA

My beautiful, carved front door swings open on silent iron hinges, and I take in a deep, cleansing breath. Home. My shop, filled with its bundles and bunches of dried, fragrant herbs, flowers, and plants of all kinds, fills me with peace and a sense of calm I don't know if I've noticed this strongly in a long time. It smells like the Woods, but concentrated. Earth and green and life, bitter and sweet. The faint scent of long burned-out fires, the smallest hint of sulfur sneaking around the edges of sealed bottles. It's medicinal and mysterious, warm and rich and *mine*.

"Right then." I clap my hands together and turn toward the prince, ushering him in and closing the door behind us. "On to business."

I flow into the room, moving to the huge fireplace that occupies almost one entire wall, and shove a large cauldron on a pot hook out of my way. I hastily build a tent of wood and kindling, striking a chemical-coated splinter against the rough stone of the hearth and start the fire with the resulting small flame. The materials are difficult to come by, so I use these quick-start sticks Arty taught me to make sparingly, but it's worth it to use one now. It's been too long since he was stabbed, and I don't have time to fiddle with a flint.

I'm also not above showing off.

I can feel the prince lurking behind me, hovering over my shoulder as I light the fire, a healthy glow illuminating the room in a swelling wave of gold. I nod toward the carved wooden chair next to the fireplace.

"Sit, please"

He immediately obliges, gently collapsing into the seat with an audible sigh of relief, his legs spread casually wide.

"I'm sorry about this." He gestures toward the knife in his shoulder with sincere apology. "I was not intending to be stabbed today, but life had other plans, apparently." The smile and embarrassment is palpable, the pained strain I expect nowhere to be heard. "I have to say, I would have been quite lost without you."

"Trust me when I say we could have been quite lost with me," I mutter as I continue my work, filling a bucket with water from the pump behind my counter to boil. Mostly melted candles on the meandering, large branch that serves as a mantle are lit from the fire or off each other, generating as much light as I can. The prince is still watching me, and when I light a large candle next to a specific jar, he positively squeals.

"What is that?"

His voice cracks and I'm too tired to stifle my laugh. I rest my hand atop the large, sealed jar with affection.

"This is Arty. He will be watching over the proceedings and judging accordingly, as he always does," I say, my voice shaking with laughter.

The jar contains two, vaguely blue, heavily clouded, wrinkled eyeballs bobbing in clear liquid, their optic nerves swimming around like worms. Arty lamented that he would no longer be able to keep an eye on me once he passed, so I came up with a solution. His presence is a constant comfort and companion to me, regardless of its form, and I blatantly refuse to think of it as odd. His jar sits among other curiosities on the mantle. Additional jars of distorted organs, bones, skulls, and trinkets found in the forest. I like to think he is at home there, among the treasures of our time together.

The prince chokes, "Was Arty," he swallows visibly, "always like that?" Wide-eyed, he leans away as far as the chair allows.

"Oh no. I did that myself. A little joke between the two of us, is all." Light and teasing, I purposefully make myself sound as outrageously casual as I can. I enjoy a certain reputation of being off my hinges. I see no reason to stop just because there is a prince slowly bleeding out in my common room.

"Oh. I see," is all he can manage before he's seeing anything else.

I feel a spark of my old mischief brought on by the chaos of the day, and I lean toward him, drawing his gaze back to me with a waggle of my eyebrows.

"Maybe following a mysterious forest woman wasn't the most sensible action after all?" I wink and turn away, letting him decide what the joke is.

The rest of the shop is relatively tame, so he should have plenty of things to keep him from meeting Arty's wizened gaze while I finish preparations. Dried plants, jars of tinctures and salves, lotions, oils, and the other necessary products of my trade are stacked on shelves and tables around the room. It usually entertains my patrons, so he should be distracted. I keep the surgical implements behind the large central counter until they are needed to avoid any unwanted, or unsafe, fiddling. I'm not a recognized physician like those in the city, but I do my best for the villagers here and both of the Woods' other villages.

I wash my hands from a basin on the counter before and after selecting the tools I think I will need for the job of removing this pesky dagger from the prince's shoulder. Lint and bandages, spider silk sutures, and a long, thin, curved needle. I settle everything on a table next to him and stick my tongue out in thought, appraising the wound.

"I'm going to cut the shirt off to protect the area. It should probably be burn-"

Before I can finish the thought, the prince clutches the shirt and barks with the command I've been expecting, "No. Open the tear if you must, but nothing more."

I'm not sure what I was expecting, but such a vehement and prudish response was not it. Most young men built like him are more than eager to tear their shirts off given any opportunity. I shrug while I turn back, having forgotten my bottle of alcohol.

"Well, that isn't ideal, but I can work with it." I lean over the counter and reach down to grab the dark glass container from a shelf below. The dull clang of metal on my wood floor rings ominously.

Shit.

I rip my body back, feeling a sharp pull in my abdomen and a crack of pain as my knee slams into the wood. Leaving the bottle behind, I don't bother to stop myself from screaming as I turn around, snatching a pad of lint off of the tray.

"What are you doing?" Voice shrill, eyes wide, I take in everything at once. The dagger on the floor, his fingers slowly traveling back up to the wound now pouring, but not spurting, blood. It may still be possible he won't bleed out on my hearth.

My momentum carries me too far, too fast, and I trip over his sprawled legs. He groans as I press most of my weight into his injured shoulder, catching myself before I send both of us to the floor and staunching the bleeding in one accidentally aggressive move. The front legs of the chair teeter in the air for the blink of an eye before slamming back down with a thud. I would feel bad about it, but his stupidity warrants consequences.

With a push of extra pressure against his shoulder, I right myself and snort out a breath through my nose. The absorbent lint is already soaking through, but it really isn't as bad as it could have been.

What is wrong with men? Collectively, as a species, there is something fundamentally broken in their ability to think.

I grab another tuft of lint from the side table and quickly swap it out with the original, tossing that one in the fire.

"Keep pressure on this, you idiot." Too tired to put more than the barest hint of annoyance in my words, I resort to name calling. My body apparently had one last drop of energy left to squeeze out, and now I am spent. Wrung out.

"I was not...I simply..." The prince stutters, and he gives up trying to finish what he didn't simply do. His face is white and wet with sweat.

"Canopy Above," I whisper, looking down at my equipment and seeing the dagger out of the corner of my eye.

The edge is serrated, meaning it would have ripped at his flesh as he pulled it out. He did it quickly. I would have been pulling it out a barb at a time, trying to minimize damage, pushing and pulling the surrounding skin to see into the wound, attempting to not damage the surrounding tissue. Perhaps this *was* better for him. At least he would have died quickly instead of enduring that.

"Do you think you can stay conscious for a while longer?" I ask, amazed he has stayed with me this long.

"If I was going to lose consciousness, I would have already." He isn't sarcastic or angry or affronted; it's just a statement of fact. Like the sky is blue, or water is wet.

"Okay, then I need you to press hard for a little longer while I finish getting ready. *Someone* decided to interrupt me before I was done." I won't quite drop the fact that he did something very stupid, but I soften the delivery with a small smile.

He closes his eyes and nods, his tendons standing out more starkly in the hand pressing against his chest.

With the automatic motion of long practice, I set myself up for work. A thick ceramic mug with a sachet of pain relieving tea gets a ladle of boiling water and set aside to steep. A glass gets a heavy slug of the raw alcohol from its bottle, followed by my curved needle, threaded with a long wisp of silk. I soak a cloth with the alcohol as well and exclaim happily, going to my bag and triumphantly returning with a jar of the weeping widow tincture in hand. I've been out for months now and nearly forgot the whole point of today. It would have been better for it to steep and get mixed with the other components I usually use, but the raw form will work well enough for this. I set my treasured bottle of red goo down with the rest of my things and pour splashes of alcohol over my hands, rubbing them together vigorously until dry.

"Right then. You can let go now." The cloth soaked in alcohol in one hand, I gently pry the lint from the wound with the other. It's still wet enough that it doesn't stick too badly, but I wince as the ragged corner of the cut comes into view. It's still bleeding, but slow enough that I can see the bruises already forming around the wound and the dark, wet interior of his chest through the gaping center. The gash is long and nearly vertical, ragged and deep.

"This is going to hurt," I say, at the exact instant I press the cloth against the wound. The prince jerks away from my touch, and almost succeeds in stifling a yell that comes out as a gurgled moan instead. I keep it pressed against him, the alcohol soaking into the crusted shirt around the wound for several counts before I remove it, folding it to a clean surface and wiping away the surrounding gore.

For a moment I think he may have finally fainted.

"For the love of Kiv," he hisses, startling me.

Not unconscious, just praying. Or cursing. Or both. That's good, then. I take this opportunity of relatively blood free cleanliness to, as gently as possible, pull the wound open so I can see inside. He forces a breath through his teeth, but I hardly notice. My attention is on the bulging, sickly yellow gleam of the thin layer of fat between skin and muscle. I hunt through the torn flesh for the tell-tale sign of pink, glistening tendon or white glossy bone. The man has such nice pectorals, the dagger couldn't make it far enough to hit ribs. By the trees, he's lucky. I give his insides a final, thorough, look to be sure the vessel I feared would be damaged is whole. Satisfied that he's not going to immediately die, I sit back.

"Thank whatever sword master, training partner, or whoever it was that decided you needed to put so much work into working out. Looks like they saved you, and me, a bit of a problem."

His eyes are still squeezed shut, but the prince snorts a laugh. "He will be delighted to know."

I stop my prodding and dab at the seeping wound with lint one last time before removing the needle from the alcohol to begin the task of pulling the skin together. I've never been much for needlework or sewing clothes, but sewing a body I can do. My apprenticeship to Arty started when I was ten years old, so I never had much time for learning alternate crafts. I make quick work of the task, looping and knotting each stitch with precision.

"This is spider silk, not regular thread," I babble as I work each fine stitch, aligning the edges of the wound as best I can. "I would say the wound should scar less because of it, but this is an awful place for scarring. The spiders here are quite helpful, though, so perhaps it won't be so bad," I'm musing to myself at this point as I eye the stitching critically and snip the last thread. I open the bottle of gelatinous widow tincture and spread it thickly along the incision. The blood red of the medicine adds its own touch of horror to the scene. Tearing a piece of the lint to approximate size, I press it gently onto the sticky gel and stand up, washing my hands with hot water and another alcohol scrub.

"Alright, that will stick for a moment. Follow me, please." Without asking, I drop under his good shoulder and help him to his feet. Once he is up and steadied, I slide away to snatch the steeping tea mug from the side table and walk around the row of shelving that hides a staircase carved out of solid tree. The stairs spiral up and into the home portion of my shop, the walls golden and smooth with age, the steps just wide enough for two abreast.

They continue up to a third floor, but I duck out onto the first landing that opens into the main room and make straight for a side door after shoving the mug of tea into the prince's hand with an order to drink it. The door opens into Inness' room, simply furnished and not overly cluttered with carvings and knickknacks. She hasn't been here long enough to curate the kind of collection this house is used to. One wall is made entirely of the living bark of the Great Tree, mossy lichen adding a festive touch of green and thick mushroom shelves providing convenient spots for candles. I sweep a collection of Inness' clothes off the bed and deposit a roll of bandaging in their place. Dropping the clothes on the back of her desk chair, I start making a small fire in the much more reasonably sized fireplace, lighting it with the flint starter on the mantle instead of the quick-start sticks I left downstairs.

"You can stay here tonight," I call over my shoulder, realizing the prince hasn't followed me.

"Thank you." His voice has that rich, soft depth again as he trails into the room, sipping the tea one-handed.

I live more lavishly than most of the villagers, a perk of having a profession outside of general survival, but it's still nothing like some of the places I have seen in the capital. I can't imagine what is running through his head, comparing this place to the palace or some lord's manor. Life here may be slower and less extravagant than that in the cities, but it has a wonderful kind of calm elegance I wouldn't give up for the world.

Standing with a groan, my hand clutching the mantle above me to take some pressure off of my abused knees, I turn to the wardrobe tucked in the corner of the room and open its doors. I happen to keep some of Arty's old clothes here for circumstances such as these, and for nostalgia's sake, which irritates Inness. Rightfully, I suppose. It is her room. I dig through my apprentice's clothing to find a plain, white linen shirt. I toss it on the bed, next to the bandages I previously deposited.

"You can change into that after getting a bandage around that lint before it unsticks itself. I don't know about you but I am absolutely starving, so I'm going to go find something to eat." I pause with my hand on the door. "Do you need my help with that?" From his response to me cutting his shirt, his answer will likely be no, but I feel the need to ask anyway.

Sure enough, he shakes his head. "Thank you, but no," He pauses a moment before pushing a strand of his escaping, shoulder length, dark brown hair out of his face. "I do think I will follow your suggestion of burning this one when I am out of it though." He plucks at the shirt that is currently sticking to him with blood and sweat, and I swear I can feel the gritty crackle of it through the air between us.

"I think that's a wise choice." I shudder, half in jest. Just before shutting the door behind me, I add offhandedly, "You may feel strange for awhile. The medicine I used has some side effects, but its worth it, I promise."

I don't wait for that to register before vanishing into my kitchen.

Digging through my pantry I come up with a platter of sliced bread, hard cheese and cured meat as well as a carafe of sweet berry wine and two wooden cups. Serviceable enough. I'm just setting it out when the prince emerges from his refuge. He gave up entirely on his hair being tied back and let it fall in tangled, rakish waves around his face and shoulders. Paired with a clean, snug-around-the-shoulders shirt and generally less gore, his looks have vastly improved from sweaty, near-death vagabond. Not that his version of sweaty, near-death vagabond was particularly displeasing.

My exhausted and starved brain has to expend significant effort to prevent me from making a fool of myself, triple checking that my mouth hasn't dropped open at the sight of him. I have seen him from very far away and in painted or drawn likenesses, but I have never seen him this close. Beyond recognizing who he was, my attention has thus far been limited to making sure as much blood stayed inside his body as possible. Now that that concern has been temporarily rectified, however...

The prince is a beautiful man.

He is several years younger than me, but well into his late twenties. I forget exactly how far, but it's old enough for him to have settled firmly into his looks. Angular, high cheekbones and a long, sharp nose compliment his defined, stubble-dusted jawline. His lips turn into the slightest of soft smiles, the lines at the corners indicating it's a frequent expression. His green-brown eyes are the best part, though. They remind me of the Woods; bark and leaves with the sun shining through it all, a little wild with unnaturally wide pupils, framed by the thick lashes only men seem to be blessed with and an escaped curl of hair that is such a dark brown it's nearly black.

One of his neatly arched eyebrows quirks.

"Join me?" I ask, managing not to sputter in embarrassment at being caught out in my blatant staring.

I sit, and he follows suit, that hint of a smile still tugging at the corner of his mouth. Pouring wine, I fumble for something to say to break the awkwardness.

"You can stay as long as you need. I'd rather know you are well enough to make it back to the city."

He shakes his head while chewing, slowly, and waits until after he swallows to speak. "My horse is in that forest. I will find her in the morning and ride back to the city from there."

"Unlikely at best. Finding her would be just about impossible, especially without knowing where you came from," I pause for a long sip of wine before continuing. "I don't know how to explain it, but you'll have to trust me. You did good for the Woods today, I think, fighting those men. With any luck, they'll show your horse her way here by morning. If not, you can take mine. I'll be going to the city soon, and I can collect her then." I lean back and pop a rolled bundle of meat and cheese into my mouth, savoring its rich saltiness. With everything that happened, the last I ate was a small breakfast as the sun rose. I'm surprised I lasted this long without throwing an absolute tantrum.

"I do not understand how a forest can bring my horse to me, but if you are willing to lend me yours, I do need to get back to the city quickly." He pauses, lost in some thought that brings his mildly unfocused gaze up to meet mine for a long, dreamy moment. "All of this has been far more than I could ask for." He shifts his stare down to the table and pushes his cup around with one finger, his dilated pupils watch the swirling of the liquid intently.

If I was not so sure this was the prince, I wouldn't have guessed it by the way he is acting, hallucinogenic influence notwithstanding. I can't say I've ever put any thought into what the royal family would be like at a dinner table, but I don't think I would have said it'd look like this.

"What were you doing out here, anyway?" The reality of the day creeps in slowly now that things are quiet and I'm fed. None of it makes any sense, and worry begins to creep in over whether the village has anything to fear. "Do you think those men will come back? Find us here?"

The prince tosses his head with obvious frustration. "Honestly, I do not know. I have been following the movements of the Cult of Davor since they began clashing with the Kivarans in the city, and they led me here."

That's why they looked familiar.

Of *course* the tree-forsaken cults would be a part of this. Why not?

"I know the cults, and it doesn't surprise me that they conjured up some fool notions about these Woods. They're always poking around in things they shouldn't be. I've witnessed more than one clash over dusty tomes found in some forgotten attic or on some trading ship from the east. Always searching for more of their histories, it was only a matter of time before one of them caught wind of the ruins here. I'm not fond of the shoot first, ask questions never approach to their research, however." I pause for another sip of wine and consider the question I want to ask. "Would you be willing to send actual guards here for a while? Until they lose interest in whatever they're looking for?" His suddenly furrowed brow and pinched lips confirm my theory that he was hoping I didn't know who he was. I can tell he is about to protest, so I continue. "I've been to the city many times, Your Highness. I do a significant amount of business there. I've known who you were since that gentleman's blood finished spraying from his neck."

To his credit, the prince simply nods. "I can do my best, but I cannot promise anything. I do not have the kind of influence over my parents people think I do."

"Thank you," I say before a yawn cracks my jaw. I drain my cup and shove a last bit of bread in my mouth in an odd attempt to cover the sudden embarrassment of an act I've never been embarrassed about in my life, and am absolutely entitled to in this moment. I've been up since dawn, gotten shot at, run through forests, stitched up a prince, and I'm thirty-three. I have every right to be tired.

"I'll be upstairs. If you need anything feel free to look around or just yell. There is water in the pitcher on the counter and a kettle on a hook for your fireplace if you want to steep another round of the tea. It's just willow bark, feverfew, and a few other things. It should be helping with the pain."

His quiet voice follows me as I head to the stairs, "I do not know what magic brought me to you, but I believe it has saved my life."

My gut clenches as I try, very hard, to not think about the moment in which we locked eyes through a spray of blood, and whose blood that could've been if I hadn't been there. I wave my hand in a vague and encompassing gesture to our surroundings.

"It wasn't magic, Your Highness. Helping people is what I do."

I drag myself up the stairs to the sprawling, top room I call my own and fall into my bed without even removing my boots, vaguely wondering how much, and what, of this the prince will remember.

CHAPTER FOUR
KEDREN

My head swims as I pull myself from a dream of being lectured by a giant spider with the face of an old man. A groan escapes me as I try to move.

Everything is sore, and a fire of pain is burning across my chest, but I breathe shallowly through the shock of it and pull myself into a sitting position. The borrowed shirt clings to me with clammy sweat, a gift from the stream of unsettling dreams that chased me through the night. I still feel strange and clouded as I look around the room, faint light creeping in through shuttered windows, and I wonder if I am still dreaming.

The wall across from me is tree bark and moss and half melted candles on shelves of living mushrooms, but the rest of the room looks perfectly normal. A stone fireplace with a sturdy mantle. Dark wooden floors polished smooth with age. A wardrobe. A small desk littered with tools, vials, and scraps of parchment, the chair pushed up to it draped with a pile of clothes. A small side table holding the cold remains of bitter tea. The bed I need to get up from is larger than I expected, and has a carved headboard, the soft knitted covers still made beneath me.

Smells of cooking from the other room build on my need to return to the city. I roll myself into a standing position and test my injured side's range of motion. I ignore the black spots swirling at the edge of my vision and breathe in the outdoor, wooded scent of the room. The sound of humming and homemaking compels me to complete my grounding and lock away the pain as much as I can. I run my hand across the rough bark wall on my way to the door and smile at the wonder of a tree so large it is part of a building.

When I step into the main room, I try brushing my hair out of my face but give up when my fingers meet nothing but knots. My smile does not fade, however. The woman I feared I had conjured in yesterday's delirium stands before me, although not quite as I remember her. She is more real and less one of the legendary, magical Otherfolk I had nearly convinced myself she was.

She hums something lively, but oddly haunting, that I have not heard before and tosses sliced vegetables into a shallow pot slung over a fire. Shutters are thrown open all over the room, but the light is dim and unearthly, a greenish hue that blends with the yellow glow of the fire and creates a disorienting, magical atmosphere. The woman's hair, swinging in a straight and full tail, high on her head catches the strange light and reflects it like antique gold.

I try to take in all of the unusual sights around me, but my eyes cannot leave the woman. The longer I watch her drift ghost-like through the gloom, the more she shifts back into the Otherfolk woman of the night before. She is wearing nearly the same thing, but clean. The sleeves of her linen shirt are rolled up to reveal the smooth lines of well muscled forearms, and it is partially tucked into the high waist of dark trousers, smooth against the curve of hip and thigh and then straight and loose to the tops of her bare feet. Feet that carry her lightly through her work, dancing in time with her soft singing.

Fearing that I will be caught in my enchanted stare, I clear my throat to speak before she turns enough to see me.

"Good morning," I manage, my voice rough and low with sleep.

She yelps with a dramatic jump worthy of the stage, brandishing a wooden spoon in my direction with one hand clutching her chest.

It is as though a spell has been broken, and I can breathe again. Think again.

She shifts the threat of the spoon to a wave and chimes with forced cheer, "Good morning!"

Immediately she spins around, but not before I catch a hint of pink on her cheeks and the look of someone who has seen a ghost, or, at the very least, an unexpected house guest.

"I did not mean to startle you." I sound awkward and pretentious even to my own ears and I shift, resting the hand of my injured side on the back of a dining chair. "Can I-"

"Your horse-"

We both laugh and she turns back to face me. I nod her on.

"Your horse found its way here last night. Belar brought her by. She's outside when you're ready to leave."

"That makes no sense. We had to have been miles away in that warren."

She shrugs, scooping eggs and vegetables over toasted slices of bread.

"I told you last night. You wouldn't have been able to find her, but you did good so you got a gift." She turns fully now and slides two plates onto the table, starting to sit before changing her mind. "Two gifts really, if you count running into me." She clips the end of her sentence and turns her back to me abruptly, picking up two wooden mugs from the counter. "I just meant..." The cups are on the table and she takes her seat, waving to me with a flip of her hand. "I don't know what I meant." She finishes with a sigh.

I am not sure if the wave is a dismal of her words or an indication to sit, but I slide into the chair. I am suddenly aware that I am starving.

"This smells wonderful." I say, sounding more surprised than I intended and bury my face in the mug of tea. This, however, being the same bitter concoction from last night makes me grimace.

Her laugh is like music that rolls over me in a wave. I flush with embarrassment, but my smile answers unbidden. I could listen to that laugh all day.

"A perk of living here." She waves her hand again, this time wielding a fork. "Turns out, plants can be used for more than medicine." She winks at me, her eyes, ice-blue and wide, sparkle with teasing playfulness.

"Are there any other perks of living here?" I sound pretentious again and try to correct my tone. "I mean, the woods. The men from yesterday, do you know why they would be so interested?" I stuff a forkful of eggs into my mouth in a desperate attempt to stop embarrassing myself.

The light in her eyes sharpens to a gleaming edge and she frowns, "I don't know. I don't know what they think they are looking for out here. I don't think it's any of the plants, even though some are rare enough. Only to shoot at me and then run right by one of the most valuable makes that explanation seem unlikely."

I blink at the concept. "Someone would kill you over a plant?"

She shrugs. "It's a really good plant. And why I was out there, anyway. It's what I put on your shoulder last night. It's not as useful in its raw form like that, but I didn't have the time to make the proper salve."

"What about the ruins? Is there anything special about them?" To my surprise, I go for more of the toasted bread and egg combination and find my plate empty, so instead I sip more of the tea. Bitter as it is, it may actually be helping dull the agony of my chest.

"They are everywhere around here, and to my knowledge they just *are*. There isn't anything particularly special about them that I've ever heard of. Or special enough for me to remember, that is. But they are old, and I know both cults can whip themselves into a frenzy over something old enough to have come from before the Fall." She taps her mouth with her fork, the very tip of her tongue touching the tines. I can feel my face start to flush again gazing at the slight parting of her lips and force myself to look at the table and focus for a moment on the ache radiating from my injury. "I really don't know." She suddenly pushes up from the table, her plate also empty. "But I plan to find out."

By the last word, her voice is so soft I would not have been able to hear it if she were not leaning close to me to clean our plates away.

"Are you still planning on leaving right away?" The brightness is back as she turns to me again.

"I need to get back to the city to see if I can discover anything, and try to get men here as soon as possible." I know I should have left already, even as early as it is, but I simply do not want to. The calm and wonder of this remarkable place is disarming, regardless of my misadventure yesterday. The chaos and clatter of the palace and the capital is a distant memory in the canopy-blanketed depths of this strange, quiet village.

She nods with a slight frown. "That is against my better judgment, but who am I to keep His Royal Highness away from his princely duties?" Without allowing me to answer, she jerks her head toward the spiral stairs while turning toward them. "Follow me."

She disappears down the hollowed out tree. I follow slowly, letting my gaze linger around the space for several heartbeats, taking in the living walls and comfortable, well worn furniture, some ornately carved, some simple. A sofa piled high with pillows of every color, shape, and texture. Books and papers and dried plants littering every surface. My heart already aches to leave it, but I follow before she can wonder where I am.

I am immediately assaulted by the sights and smells of the chaos of the room below. My blurred and confused memories from the night before are both an over and under exaggeration of the space. It is less like the web-covered witch's den full of body parts and magical potions I remember, but it is very, very full of everything from drying herbs on the branches-turned-rafters above us, to entire articulated animal skeletons posed along the walls. I smell trees, the overwhelming scent of bitter green things, and something else sharp and medicinal underneath it all.

"I already tucked a few more packets of that tea into your saddlebag this morning. I always have plenty of those made up," her words rush out of her again, "But come here, quick like."

She leans against the main counter of the room as I peek out from behind the shelves hiding the stairs. Her arms are crossed, forearms still bare, the curves of her body relaxed and her voice is all casual business. I approach her, running my fingers through my hair again, a useless defense against her penetrating appraisal. She pushes off of the counter, dragging a piece of linen after her and meets me halfway, one hand reaching for my wounded shoulder.

Her touch is featherlight as she gently prods the area under the cover of bandage and shirt. I sway as she takes her hand away as quickly as it appeared, and I steady myself against the involuntary lean toward her. I must have lost more blood than I thought last night. I feel light-headed, the colors of the sunlit room swirling at the edges of my vision. The deep gold of her hair is a liquid shine in the haze. I am once against struck by the otherworldliness of her shimmering, radiant presence.

"It feels alright, not too warm, and the dressing seems good enough. You should change that and wash the wound when you get back to the city. And rest it. There is quite a bit of damage beneath the surface, and there is only so much I can do about that."

After a moment of consideration, she steps in closer than before, and I fight the reaction to finish closing the distance, following the draw of her strange magic. One hand gently shifts my injured arm against my abdomen while the other deftly loops the cloth around it, tying a sling that immediately relieves some of the ache. "This should help, especially while you're riding."

She is tall for a woman, barely tilting her head up to look me in the eyes, despite our closeness. My unbound hand raises slightly, and I am shocked to realize I am about to brush an escaped lock of her hair away from her eyes. I step back, widening the space between us in a rush.

35

"Thank you for this. For everything. I will do whatever I can to send men out here. I swear it." I bow my head awkwardly toward her and all but run for the door.

She shouts after me, "Just follow the western path out of the village and straight on to the city. You literally can't miss it."

I swing onto my golden mare, Ealyn, before I dare a look behind me, up at the beautifully carved door I assume will be closed. Instead, the woman is there, leaning against the open frame. She inclines her head to me, and the whisper of her voice carries on the breeze as I turn the horse to the west.

"Be careful, Your Highness."

—

I am well on my way to the city when my horse suddenly stumbles in a hidden divot in the road, and I jerk from a restless doze with a lurch of pain in my shoulder.

Kiv, that hurts.

However, whatever the mysterious plant the forest woman used was, I should find its name for future treatment, considering it hurts much less than it should.

I run my hand gently along the horse's neck, steadying her and myself with the touch. Thinking of names, I struggle to remember the name of the woman and find I never asked for it. At least I do not think I did. The memories of the previous night are difficult to piece together, muddled with visions I cannot separate from dreams. She saved my life, and I was so consumed by my own thoughts that I did not even ask for her name. How ungrateful.

Frustration tangles my thoughts around the uncertainties of the last several days and pulls them into tighter knots the more I try to unravel them. I try to focus on questions about the cultists. *Why are they are choosing now to act so publicly? Why would they be interested in a forgotten forest?* A forest full of tree-dark rooms and a woman who smells of sharp, green life and who's hair is a king's ransom of liquid gold. A forest full of ancient ruins and who knows what kind of forgotten secrets for the cultists to uncover.

Until recently, the Davorists have been relatively quiet, skulking in shadows and occasionally rabble rousing in an attempt to sway people to their cause with little success. The change in recent months concerns me.

I have read histories that document fully realized battles between the Kivarans and the Davorists dating back until the time of the Fall itself. Every time, the Cult of Kiv has overwhelmed that of Davor, but the threat remains. In an attempt to pacify them, my great grandparents officially recognized both cults as religions of the Kingdom and allowed the open practice of Davorism for the first time since the foundation of the nation. Their fragile peace has held until now. *Why does it crumble now?*

Darkness descends as I tread the never ending circles of my thoughts, and I have to decide to make camp and arrive at the city in the morning, or continue on and reach the gates in the dead of night. I know sleep will not find me, exposed on the road, so I tap my heels lightly into Ealyn's sides and spur her into a smooth canter. To avoid even more unfortunate questions I will have to remove my arm from its sling before I approach the gates, but I can delay that for at least a while longer.

When I reach the crossroad of the main road to the southern city of Saen, I slow Ealyn to a halt. Most people would not go beyond this road to what lays beyond in that strange forest. I certainly have not until now. Extending north and south, it is the main artery connecting the western and southern villages to the capital and Saen. Taking a few steadying breaths, I raise my injured left arm just enough to pull the sling off over my head. I feel a pang of loss as the remnants of her last touch against me are stripped away along with the relief it provided. I grind my teeth together as I lower my hand into my lap, trying to take away some of the pull the full weight of my arm exerts.

I urge Ealyn on as clammy sweat starts to break out on my face and neck. The desire to be unmoving in my bed is maddening.

As they should be, the massive, iron-inlaid, wooden gates are shut, the light from the wall's many braziers reflecting dully off of the matte metallic surfaces. As I approach, I angle my horse toward the smaller side door before the guard emerges from behind it. The passage beyond is too low for me to stay mounted so, with a hiss of breath, I swing off of my saddle and awkwardly step around Ealyn to hold the reigns with my good hand. I keep my left tucked against my side as inconspicuously as I can.

"Hold!" The guard shouts at me before I get too close. His helmet hides most of his face and muffles his voice, preventing me from identifying him at first glance.

I step wide of the horse and turn slightly side to side, showing my unarmed state. I left the empty scabbard with the woman on the off chance she, or someone else, stumbles upon the scene of the fight and picks up the sword. I have no need for its reminder of my failure, and it is just a spare from the armory, not any of mine. The guard comes closer, and even though he has no weapon drawn I know there is a longbow somewhere along the walls above us trained on me, awaiting a signal from the man.

When he is close enough to see my face clearly in the flickering light, his shoulders relax and then tighten again almost immediately.

"Your Highness? What are you doing out here?" He sounds nervous, like he missed something he should not have.

"Oh, nothing. Lost track of time enjoying some country hospitality." I wink conspiratorially and put a haughty leer into my words that makes me feel vile. The rumors of enjoying drink and women have helped explain away much of my missing time in a way that never raises additional questions, and I am very grateful for that now.

The guard laughs and mutters some agreement before turning back to the wall and gesturing to me to follow. I do so, obediently, and when he insists on coming with me as an escort to the palace, I do not protest. The city is not what I would call dangerous, despite the rising cult activity, but it is still a city and you cannot get further from the palace than the West Gate.

Whether it is the presence of the guard or simply a calm night, we make it to the palace unmolested and in good time, my need to be off my horse and in my rooms growing more desperate by the moment. We enter the grounds through a small gate frequently used by guards during shift changes that shares a courtyard with the stables, the barracks, and the palace proper. Normally I would take care of her, but I leave Ealyn with the guard and drag myself up the closest set of steps leading into the palace. Fortunately, my rooms are in this wing of the building, and I only have to navigate a short warren of corridors and servant stairways before I can finally collapse.

I am on the last stretch of my journey when I hear the click of boot heels on the smooth stone floor behind me. The hall is dimly lit, with several branching paths and shadowy alcoves. I consider ducking into one, but it is already too late. Before I can move, the sharp nails of my sister's hand dig into my bad shoulder with a squeeze that would look friendly to anyone walking by.

I bite down on my tongue so hard I taste blood.

CHAPTER FIVE
KEDREN

Well, well, little brother."

Her voice is like ground glass between my teeth. I duck away from her grasp with a twist, trying to hide the fact that I am more than half staggering, my vision going dark at the edges.

"What do you want, Daralyn?" I force the words out slowly, fighting the urge to turn and run the final distance to my rooms. I pray she didn't feel the bandages under my shirt.

"Oh my, dearest. I'm just here to make sure you're alright. We all missed you at the council meeting this morning." She smiles a reptilian grin. I take an involuntary step back from her and her flanking ladies-in-waiting, Dienna and Marlayne.

Dammit.

I forgot about the meeting this morning. She probably had someone watching for my return since then, wondering what could have kept me away. Panic rises in me like the tide, leaving me grasping at the edges of my fleeing thoughts, trying to catch something I can say to get me away from her as quickly as possible.

"Oh, you know me, sister. I just had a little too much fun yesterday and could not bear to sit through one of those boring meetings." *Please, just let it go at that.*

"I know they are tedious, brother, but can you really afford to keep missing them? Mother and father are already *so* disappointed in you." She circles me like a vulture, her fingers trace lines across my shoulders and chest. I do not move out of fear of her catching the edge of the bandage there. "And you know I will always be disappointed in you." She's hissing now, her breath ghosting against the side of my face as she leans in close. "It isn't like you to make my job of discrediting you so easy." She stops her circling and drapes her arms over my shoulders from behind, digging her chin into my bad shoulder. "I don't trust this little turn of events. Not one bit." Louder, she asks, "What do you think, my loves, does he deserve to be punished for missing the meeting without even telling me why?"

Dienna and Marlayne break into matching smiles, each one dragging their tongue along the bottom edge of their teeth.

She has to feel my sweat soaking through my shirt and dripping off of my face. I cannot stop shaking, despite my need to be ready to react. I barely hear the women respond, my awareness narrowed to my sister's arms around me, waiting for the moment the loose embrace shifts to something more.

"If you aren't careful it would simply give him an excuse as to why he wasn't there."

"She's right, love, if you get carried away it may make him a martyr."

"Although I'm certain you would make it right, regardless."

"You've always been so good about making them hear what you want them to."

Daralyn lazily drags herself off of me, laughing and brushing a strand of her black hair out of her face.

"You're right, it isn't worth my effort tonight. And I'm really quite upset with him, I don't know if I would be able to hold back." She sighs dramatically. Mockingly. "The usual narrative will have to do."

"What a waste." Dienna sneers.

"Truly a disgrace." Marlane chimes after.

"Practically a menace."

"It's a wonder we have all put up with him this long."

"Amazingly generous of our princess." Dienna finishes their disparaging tirade. The three of them smile in unison.

"He has his uses," my sister drawls, cupping Marlayne's face gently.

"Let's hope, for his sake and ours, they stay more pronounced than his failures." She releases Marlayne to brush the back of her hand down Dienna's cheek. "The kingdom doesn't really need some drunken whore of a prince, now do they?"

"Certainly not." Marlayne titters.

"It is really only we who need him."

With a last narrowing of her black, glittering eyes, Daralyn laughs sharply.

"We are nothing if not exceedingly patient with him." She turns on her heel and the other two follow with identical, dramatic twirls, giggling as they do so. "Do at least try to maintain some sort of dignity, brother. Your place here really is hanging on by a thread. We can't use you for reputable stock if you become too much of a disgrace."

I wait until I can no longer hear their shrill voices before I stagger toward my rooms, clutching my shoulder. I all but fall against my door, digging for the key kept in a small pouch on my belt. My vision sparks with embers of light, and the edges are blurred as I fumble the key into the lock and collapse inward with the swing of the door. I do not make it fully into the room before I vomit into a vase of half-dead flowers in the entryway. Each retch jerks my chest and my eyes sting with tears by the time I finish, clutching the vase between my knees as I sit curled up against the door at my back.

My breaths are ragged and my whole body shakes as I pull myself to my knees, clutching my injured arm to me. Tears fall unchecked down my face. The pain gnaws on the frayed edges of me, but the memory of Daralyn's presence, the feel of her hands on me and the sound of her lilting, taunting voice is enough to make me choke back another gag. A sob replaces it, and I throw a hand out to catch myself before I fall. Tears and bile-soured spit splatter against my skin and the wooden boards beneath me while I am blinded by a wave of tightness gripping my chest that has nothing to do with the wound there. I cannot breathe. I cannot think beyond the sharp pressure of her nails and the hot caress of her words against my cheek. Blood and burning and her grating, haunting laughter surrounds me until I cannot hear my own cries.

I do not know how, but I manage to get myself standing long enough to lock the door behind me and stumble, half blind into the next room where my vast, canopy draped bed waits for me. I sob harder in relief and fall on top of the mattress, unable to think about undressing myself, let alone dig through the pile of bedding beneath me. I curl my left arm against my stomach and burrow into a supportive nest of pillows. My thoughts are fractured and the edges of them grind together when I try to reason out why Daralyn was waiting for me and why she did nothing but taunt me once I arrived. I do try to be present for High Council meetings, but I have missed several. Most of my absences can be directly attributed to her. If she truly does not know where I was yesterday, the lack of knowledge must be eating at her and her need for control over me.

Eventually, my exhaustion overtakes the horror and dread. The tears dry in a salty smear against my skin. My breaths come slower and more smoothly, and I finally slip into sleep as the light of dawn creeps through half-closed curtains.

—

When I wake, I momentarily wish I had died instead.

The world of the living comes back to me in waves. First, the overwhelming soreness of sitting in a saddle for nearly twenty four hours in the last three days mixed with the stiffness of sleeping in one position for far too long. Then the sharp, piercing ache of my chest wound lays over the generalized discomfort, worse this morning than it was yesterday. It leaves me groaning, soft and low in the back of my throat. Finally, the events of the last several days return, flooding me with enough sense of purpose that I struggle to stand, but settle for a half-seated position propped against the pillows instead.

"You're alive, then." The light, mirth-filled voice of Envir, my valet, bodyguard, and best friend, chimes as he enters the room. "But barely, it seems." He fills a glass with water and shoves it toward me without asking, hardly waiting for me to grasp it before walking around the bed and flinging himself down on the other side. "I do wish you would stop running off on me. It makes it very difficult to do my job."

I sigh after finishing the glass of water and set it back onto the side table. "I could not take the time to find you. I found a group of cultists sneaking out of the city and needed to follow them."

He settles into the bed on his side, tucking his cheek in his hand and waits for me to continue.

"I was trying to make sure they didn't cause any trouble with the Kivaran priests leaving here after a meeting with my parents. A group of three of them, armed, ducked away from the crowd and headed west out of the city, so I followed. They went to the western woods no one ever seems to mention, and Vi, it was unreal. The trees there are bigger than the buildings of any city I have been to. They have roots like bridges and trunks that fit multiple homes. You can barely see the sky at all through the canopy above you." He snorts but I keep talking. "Anyway, I followed them there and they sort of drifted. I do not know if they knew where they were going, or if they were merely hoping to stumble across something. Regardless, they did find something. One of them started drawing a bow with one of those Kiv-forsaken spelled arrows nocked. They were aiming at a woman humming through some old stone ruins."

"Of course there was a strange woman alone in the mysterious, legendary woods. The same woods people claim steal children and eat men. The woods that everyone in this kingdom have been warned away from with ghost stories since our grandparents' grandparents were children?" Envir laces his words with disbelief and annoyance, but I ignore it.

"Anyway. I knocked him to the ground and, thankfully, the arrow missed its mark. Everyone started running, and I did not want to lose sight of the cultists, so I followed. I lost the woman but ended up getting into a bit of a scuffle with the others." I pull down the neck of my borrowed shirt to show him the bandage wrapped around my chest and he hisses in a breath, ready to speak. I, once again, talk over him. "That should have been my throat, but the woman dropped the man holding the knife in a spray of blood. Out of no where, she appeared from the curtain of gore and beckoned for me to follow."

That at least shut him up for a moment.

"I am unsure what happened after that. I was very focused on keeping as much of my blood in me as I could. She was leading me up and around and through trees until we got to one bigger than even the stories of the Otherfolk could imagine. She took me up a set of stairs carved into one of its giant, curling roots and into her apothecary. She stitched my chest back together, and I stayed in her spare room before she sent me on my way in the morning."

I decide Envir does not need to know about the old-man-faced spiders that haunted my dreams, and the fact that I am still not certain the common area of the woman's shop was not a cavernous witch den with some kind of glamour over it. Nor do I want to share my morning spent in the unbelievable peace of the strange and fanciful tree-house, or the woman laughing at my awkwardness, or the ache I feel to hear that laughter now. It is an unusual sensation, this warmth that spreads through me at the thought of her, and one I would like to keep to myself for a while longer.

He waits until he knows I am finished before rolling off the bed and shaking his head, his voice soft, "Kedren, Otherfolk apothecary aside, you could have died."

I start to protest, but he cuts me off.

"No, you *have* to stop doing this shit on your own. I know you think there is something going on with the Davorists, and I believe you. But you are the prince, and frankly the only royal child anyone, aside from your parents, actually likes. You can't just run after potentially dangerous people because you feel like it, regardless of what they may be doing." He goes to one of my wardrobes and starts pulling out clothes. "No one knew where you were for almost three days, Ked. Jyn and I have been combing the whole damn city for you. Do you know how many steps there are in this place? My calves are killing me."

He winks so I know he is glad to see me home and in mostly one piece, despite his irritation, and my cheeks heat with shame.

"I am sorry, Vi. I should have sent word back with a guard on my way through the gates, but I did not know what I could say without raising some kind of alarm." I push my hand through my dusty hair as he unlaces my boots and throws them unceremoniously to the floor with a dramatic wrinkle of his nose.

"Just promise me you aren't going to do that again. Not for a while at least. Daralyn has been prowling the castle trying to figure out why you missed the meeting yesterday, and you know how she is when she gets a stick up her ass."

With significant help from Envir, I stand and allow him to finish undressing me. I noticed the crackling of the fire in the washroom next to the bedchamber some time ago and knew this was the direction he was leading me. Envir is one of the few people who have seen me stripped bare, and in more ways than one, but even with him I am not entirely comfortable. I cling to my shirt, holding it up to drape down the front of me and let him usher me into the bath. As he fills the large tub from the elaborate, brassy, metal cauldron heating next to it, I reluctantly let the last piece of my protection fall to the floor.

The tub is large enough for me to stretch my legs out and savor the heat of the water as it pours over me, filling the space around my aching muscles. As I settle back, letting my eyes close against the bliss, Envir neatly slices through the cloth strips holding the little puff of lint padding against my wound. It is dry and crusted red with both my blood and the strange ointment the woman used. Envir soaks it with the warm water until it is wet enough to peel off without tearing at the open flesh beneath.

"Your Otherfolk physician can sew a good stitch though, can't she? I can barely see them."

"Spider silk." I say absently, my eyes closed, soaking in the heat of the water. *That* is where the spiders came from. She told me about the spider silk thread.

He makes a small noise in response and begins to gently wash the wound before he moves to my hair, scrubbing and dumping water over my head with abandon until he is satisfied. Eventually, he leaves me to the embrace of the hot, soapy water with a promise to be back with lunch and Jyn so we can all try to figure out what to do next.

CHAPTER SIX

KEDREN

I sit on the edge of my bed, breath heaving only slightly after wrestling one-armed with a pair of overly tight trousers that are both striped *and* embroidered. Envir has too much fun deciding what is fashionable these days. I find myself daydreaming of loose, well worn pants of respectable utility instead of whatever these are. That leads me to the woman, jogging confidently ahead of me through the mysterious woods, clamoring over roots and rocks whenever going around them was impossible. The roundness of her thighs that pull her trousers tight. Her ass up in the air as she bends over the counter top giving me the distraction I needed to tear the knife from my body. The curve of her hip as she leans against an empty door frame.

Of course that is when Envir opens the door, jerking me from my reverie. I glare at him, thankful I am too tired for there to be anything the clinging pants can reveal about my thoughts.

"I think I am going to finally have a word with you about what you consider in style," I say while I stand and pull the fabric of the pants around enough to feel even mildly comfortable, while I make doubly sure no trace of my wandering thoughts can be seen. How it has been only a day since I awoke in that fascinating home, to that mystifying woman, is beyond me. To be back in the castle, wearing red and thread-of-gold striped pants that are tailored within an inch of my life and giving an incredulous eye to an absolutely billowing white shirt on the bed, is disorienting.

"You just have no taste, Ked. And if you want everyone to keep believing you're some flippant miscreant, you'll wear whatever leg wear I give you."

I roll my eyes and let him help me put the shirt on, despite my deepest misgivings about the whole ensemble. I could manage on my own, but I know better than to push myself without reason. With minimal struggle, I am drowning in lace and my hands all but disappear into the ruffled falls of the cuffs. I glare at him again.

He shrugs and tucks the shirt into the high, laced waistband of the trousers with the finality of a cell door closing.

"You have crafted me a prison of linen and lace, Envir." His outfit is very similar to mine. Slightly less gold, and the stripes of his trousers are an oceanic blue instead of red. There may be even more lace, however.

"The only price you pay for my service, and you know it to be a bargain, Your Highness." He winks again and heads for the door. Jyn clinks around in the other room, likely pouring wine and setting the table, keeping himself occupied while I dress.

Jyn and Envir have been partners for over a decade. He is privy to much of my daily life, but he respects my desire for privacy in certain matters. I am sure he knows everything Envir does, but he does not pry and for that, I am grateful. I rake my fingers through my still-wet hair, glossy black with the damp, and follow Envir out to the main room of my apartment.

"So," I say, sliding into a seat at the large round table and grabbing a wine glass, "What did I miss?" I force my voice to be light, but they give each other a look that says they are deciding who is going to tell me something unpleasant.

"We don't know for certain yet, but..." Envir starts but trails off, looking to Jyn.

"I saw the High Priestess with Daralyn's ladies-in-waiting yesterday near the Davorist temple while I was looking for you. I think they were receiving their first marks." Jyn finishes with his eyes on the table, rolling his wine glass around.

"Dienna and Marlayne? Are you sure?" My face darkens thinking of last night. The deeply unpleasant trio waiting in the shadows ready to ambush me upon my return had, unbeknownst to me, contained two members of the very cult I had been stalking. And killing.

Jyn and Envir nod together, and I slide further into my seat.

"We don't know if she's involved yet, Kedren. Not for sure." Envir tries to placate me, but he knows as well as I do that if Dienna and Marlayne were receiving their Davorist tattoos then Daralyn knows. It means she wanted them to, which means she is involved in whatever the cult is doing. My sister has never been religious. She would never put her faith in anyone but herself.

I roll my eyes. "The sudden rise in activity from the Davorists and Daralyn becoming involved cannot be coincidental. Even if they are ladies-in-waiting to the future queen, it takes time for Davorists to become inducted. It could put the two events on the same timeline." The pair eye me with concern. This is what they feared when they debated telling me. I look back at them pleadingly. This is not a desperate leap. She controls everything those women do. They know that just as much as I do.

"We don't think you're wrong to suspect her, Ked. But for right now it's just a suspicion. Let's try to just find out more about what they are after, how she could use it, and what is so special about those woods. Alright?" Envir speaks now, softly, like he is talking down a snorting, wide-eyed horse. He knows what it would mean to me if we could prove Daralyn is involved in something she cannot erase by virtue of her status as the heir. Inciting religious riots and encouraging murder would certainly be a start.

My temper flashes hotly with the need to see her charged with something, anything, formally, but they are right. It is just a suspicion for now, and if I try to do anything without a proper plan she may kill me outright.

"You are both right. We will need to be cautious about this." I pull my lower lip in with my teeth and think. "I may need the time to convince my parents to send guards out to the forest. If Daralyn is involved with the cultists, she will try to stop it. But even if she is *not* involved with them, " I add hastily, cutting Envir off, "She would likely try to thwart anything I wanted to accomplish, regardless." He nods, satisfied. "Which leaves Jyn, to spend some time digging through the Library of Kiv."

Envir rolls his eyes, but Jyn looks excited. He spends most of his time in the library already, so this task should be easy for him. Sure enough, his wheels are already turning.

"We should start by finding the oldest maps we can to find out who, or what, was in those woods before everyone forgot about them. Whether they had any ties to Davor, or his followers, might be difficult to discover, but I will try my best. From what Vi told me, you didn't see anything more specific than some old ruins, right? And a mysterious woman who may or may not be an Otherfolk healer?" He winks at me.

I cough pointedly. "I think starting with the maps is a good idea. Bring me anything you can find from the Cult of Davor. I know what the Kivarans says about them, but I have never read anything from the other perspective. It could not hurt to know what they say."

He nods, and I am satisfied that at least that one part of our plan is likely to succeed. That leaves me with the next part, which is convincing my parents to protect those people.

Envir, reading my mind as always, chimes in, "I think you should start with your father, Ked. He has more sway with your mother than you do, and I think he is less certain about Daralyn."

I nod, suddenly exhausted again thinking about the politics of my own family. "I am not sure he even knows there are people out there. That alone may be enough to spur him to send a patrol. If it will be enough to counteract whatever Daralyn says, I don't know. The Queen has the final say in the business of the guard, and my sister has her bending to her every whim." I frown and drain the entire glass of wine in a swallow. Jyn refills it for me without hesitation. We all drink in heavy silence.

I consider the two in front of me to avoid thinking about speaking to my father. Envir has been by my side my entire life. We grew up together, trained together, fought and learned and stole from the kitchen together. He would be the one to find me after Daralyn was done with me and sit with me while I put myself back together. Over and over again. He was the only one who ever believed me. The only one who ever really knew. So I *know* he knows how important this is. How important it is that Daralyn is finally involved in something I can prove. Something that matters. Something that isn't just me.

We grew up and Envir found Jyn. All I have found is more and more time to sink into myself. I try to keep busy. I have been all over the world, with my family and without, filling an empty role of a meaningless diplomat. I am an ornament for my parents to dangle in front of other nations while my sister sits in meetings and twists policies to her desires. I find small ways to do things that matter, despite their best efforts to keep me stored away for only such use as they deem me worthy of.

When I look at the two men, I do wonder what it would be like to find someone to fall into. Someone who is not a political match, or looking for something my name can give them. Someone who would brush a lock of my hair out of my eyes as Envir does with an errant spring of Jyn's outrageously curly blond mess, tangled slightly in his gold rimmed spectacles. Someone who would look at all of me and know how hard I have tried to be who I am, and not who others have tried to make me. Someone, maybe, with dark golden hair and piercing blue eyes.

I stand and try to erase the vision of the woman looking up at me, so close I could feel her breath as she wrapped my arm in a sling with casual tenderness. I set the empty glass down for the third time and steady myself with a pull of fingers through my still drying hair.

"It is not going to get any easier sitting around here, so I suppose I may as well get it over with."

Envir nods and starts to stand, but I shake my head and motion for him to stay as I slide into a pair of short, black leather boots instead of the tall, shiny ones I know he wants to force on me. I am going to have one win against this outfit.

"The king should be in his office now, I think."

I nod again and head out the door, leaving Jyn and Envir behind me, their fingers laced together and matching looks of determined encouragement on their faces.

The corridors are plain stone and peaceful until I get closer to the palace proper. As soon as I was old enough, I demanded my rooms be as far away as possible from the actual royal apartments and had them carved out of the most utilitarian part of the building I could. Sooner than I would like, the stone turns to marble and wood paneling, paintings, tapestries, and bustling people. Not as busy as it could be, thankfully. The lower council is not due to be in session for another month, allowing the spring weather to clear for easier travel from some of the outlying towns. Their presence always fills the palace to the brim and makes it harder for me to do anything unnoticed. Many of the younger lords are very interested in pretending to be my friends, probably so I can put in a good word for them with my sister. That makes me bark a bitter laugh, startling a maid I pass into dropping her duster with a clatter.

I sweep it up off the floor and hand it to her with a smile. "Sorry about that, Aila."

She beams and drops a quick curtsy, but I do not slow my steady pace towards the High Council chamber and my father's office. The three chambers are stacked one on top of the other. Lower Council, High Council, and the King's office, like a block tower of bureaucracy. My head is swimming in wine, tiredness, and distant pain, but I make it to the top of the stairs without staggering which I consider a good start to the proceedings. I affect my most nonchalant posture and nod to the guards outside the door.

One of the guards dips into the room before returning and ushering me through to my father.

The king does not disappoint people's expectations. He is tall, taller than I am even, and just as wide shouldered and otherwise well built. He stands with his back to me, silhouetted by light that streams through the window overlooking the courtyard.

"Father, I-" I start, but he raises a hand, turning and making for his desk. He leans back in his chair with his hands behind his head; a pose I strike often. My feet would be on the desk, although that is probably too undignified for the king.

"So, what was so important this time, son?"

I brace for the list of rumored debauchery, ready to protest or divert as much as I can. The sting of my father's disappointment is an old wound, aggravated whenever I am in his presence.

"Helping with winter repairs? The spring planting? Handing out goods?" He is smiling, his green eyes glittering with an expression of approval so rarely turned towards me.

I am so shocked, I collapse into the seat opposite his desk, my mouth slightly ajar.

"I know you may not think it, but I do listen from time to time. And people love to talk." He leans forward with his elbows on the desk. "I have finally learned what you've been doing during your disappearing acts, or at least some of them. And I must admit, you surprised me a great deal."

I am still dumbfounded, but I close my mouth at least.

"What I want to know is, *why*?"

I swallow and push my fingers through my hair uncomfortably.

"Because I care about them. The people." I wave my hand around. "I want to help them. Since I am never heard here, in the council, I go to them directly." I shift in my seat like a child getting scolded and force myself still. "It is not as much as I *could* do here, but it is *something* and it makes me feel useful. And..." I hesitate for a beat too long.

"And Daralyn only cares about what happens in the city." My father supplies flatly.

"Yes. It has always been easier to avoid her out there." I admit. It is no secret in our family how I feel about her. It cannot surprise him that I would do anything I could to avoid her without abandoning my people entirely.

He nods and leans back again, apparently satisfied, and it is time to continue with why I actually came here.

"I went west this time, into the old forests there. And, father, there were *people* out there. A whole village of them." I hardly believe it, but he only looks mildly interested.

"I know folk live out there, but from what I understand, it is just a few backwards stragglers. Not worth the difficulty of dealing with those damn trees to get at."

"They are not isolated cases. I saw a whole village, practically a town, and heard mention of more."

"Interesting." He pauses for a moment, thinking with his bottom lip in his teeth. Like me. "What would you like me to do about it?"

I am so stunned by how easily this entire conversation is progressing, I have to completely reframe my planned pleading into a normal request. It takes me a few moments to shift my prepared words around.

"I was hoping we could send a small group of guards. The patrols and the other village units are nowhere near them. With the Davorists acting up in the city, I would feel a lot better knowing there was help for them if they needed it."

My father nods.

"You know I have to discuss guard movements with your mother and the Captain, but I don't see why we couldn't divert a unit that way or increase the range of a patrol. Livinnia can always use the tax revenue. If I can convince her there could be something to collect, she may be persuaded to invest the men." He scrubs a hand absently across his chin and nods again. "We have a meeting with Captain Wuall tomorrow anyway, I can talk to them both then."

He stands, and I follow suit immediately, bewildered and blinking dumbly. He steps around his desk and claps his hand on my uninjured shoulder, thank Kiv, before speaking again. "Try not to miss any more High Council meetings, but don't stop helping people, Kedren. It is miserably easy to lose sight of that from inside these walls."

When I leave his office, I blink back unexpected tears. I never expected him to speak to me like a man. Like a son. Like someone he could respect.

Hope tries to bloom in the wake of our meeting, and I do not know if I want to nurture it or send it back to the hell it came from. But before I can decide, the choice is taken from me.

Two days after I discover my father may give a shit about me, he is found dead in his office, slumped back, staring lifelessly at the ceiling. He was at his desk, in the same seat from which he smiled at me so sincerely, I dared to think I was finally enough for him.

I should know better than to ever have hope.

CHAPTER SEVEN
ALYSSIA

What an utterly ridiculous day.

In truth, I can hardly believe any of this happened at all, and wouldn't if I wasn't still scrubbing blood off of the stones around my fireplace. Not that this floor isn't already stained with decades, and who knows, maybe even centuries of the stuff, I like to get as much as I can up between visits. I roll onto my ass with a plop, draping my forearms over the damp patches on my pants where I've been kneeling. With an explosive huff of breath, I try to dislodge a sweaty lock of hair from my forehead to no avail and give up, throw the spent cloth into the bucket full of bloody water and flop back, my hands tucked behind my head to contemplate the half-tree, half-plank ceiling above me.

The prince slept in my house last night.

Being torn between questions about wild cultists running amok in my woods and the feeling of drowning in the prince's forest eyes exhausts me. What could the Davorists possibly want with the Woods? Why would they think anything associated with Davor would be here, ancient ruins or not? Why did they just so happen to stumble across those specific ruins that I was in? Why did I suddenly forget how to be a person whenever the prince spoke? Why didn't he want me to see him with his shirt off?

The ceiling offers me no answers, but a rustle of leaves does tell me my door has been opened. I roll up into a standing position, my knees creaking after yesterday's abuse and today's floor scrubbing.

"Ahh. Inness. It's just you." I beam at the girl and stretch. *Back to work.*

"Just me!" she chimes, closing the door behind her. "Did you get it? Did you get it?" Her eyes are scanning the room for my bag, and I'm swept out of the bin of my jumbled thoughts by her enthusiasm.

"I did. I got flowers and the resin and a bunch of other things you can help me with, too."

Inness Waerun is nearly twelve and has been my official apprentice since she turned ten. Her father brought her here from Ardjan six years ago after her mother died and he couldn't be in a place so full of her memory any longer. Despite the fact that the North is essentially an arctic desert in comparison to the Woods, she learns fast and has the instinct with both plants and people Arty taught me to look for in my successor. Inness took to the Woods like they were a part of her, and I took her in as though she were a part of me. The only part of me I would ever leave behind.

Her otherness from not being born to the Woods will always mark her as an outsider, but in my experience, being what I am does too. I may be invaluable to the villagers, but I'm also strange, progressive and educated. I offer remedies and ideas that are not always pleasant or accepted easily by them, and it separates me from many of my neighbors. Arty's lingering reputation of awe-inspiring eccentricity doesn't help my cause either. If Inness is going to be othered by the people regardless, I can at least show her how to have a little fun with it.

Months before her arrival, Arty had succumbed to the incurable curse of old age, leaving me empty and alone. After giving him back to the Woods, I left my home for a long while, hiding in the city or out to sea with my friends, trying desperately to feel whole again and dreading my return to an empty shop. I missed the arrival of the Waeruns during this time. When I returned, Inness appeared like an Otherfolk child in the middle of a hidden alcove of black cohosh with no warning or sound and vanished just as quickly, laughing at my scream. It was as if Arty had sent her to me to fill the cracks he left behind and give me a reason to stay.

"Inness?" I hang neat bundles of the flowers and herbs to dry as she hands them to me, making sure they are tied properly and the right size.

"Lys?" She asks back without missing a beat. She hands the last bundle to me and hops up to sit on the counter.

"Do you believe in magic?" I'm careful to not sound too serious. I'm fairly certain of her answer, she is still a child after all.

I jump off the step stool and slide it under a random table, but she still hasn't answered and looks at me like I'm the biggest idiot in the room. I probably am, but still.

"Lys," She says again, dramatically patient. "We are *witches*. Of course I believe in magic."

I want to laugh, but she is so serious I stop myself and push up onto the counter next to her to swing my bare feet against the solid wood front. "We aren't witches, Inness. This is just medicine. Science. I've been teaching you about it so you *wouldn't* think it was witchcraft. I've shown you the books from my friend at the library and everything."

She looks at me flatly with her large, doe-brown eyes and I'm about ready to get a dunce cap from somewhere and sit in the corner.

"Your friend from the library is also a witch."

Well she has me there. Carolyn is a Priestess of Kiv, and even I have a hard time convincing myself there isn't something odd about the things she can do.

"Okay, maybe that was a bad example. But still." I eye her seriously. "We aren't witches."

"There is magic though," she counters. "There's magic here just like there was magic at home."

That catches me off guard. Inness doesn't talk much about her time beyond the mountains, but this is not something she's ever mentioned. She elaborates without any encouragement.

"I think it's why Da stayed here instead of any other place we saw. They feel so much like the mountain did. Like they know you're here and want you to stick around."

A shiver runs down my spine. I didn't know she felt that way about the Woods. Aside from Arty, I didn't think anyone thought of the Woods like I did; an entity capable of judging your worthiness. I can't say I was bothered by it at her age, and now I'm so used to it I hardly think about it. The Woods are just the Woods. Not magic or overtly mysterious, just a collection of annoyingly opinionated trees.

"Inness," I say again, something in me convinced and making one of those unsanctioned decisions I've been making a lot of lately. "I'm going to show you something else I found yesterday."

She can tell something is up and scrambles off the counter, bursting with eagerness while trying to stay serious like she thinks an adult would. Although, the bouncing takes away from her tight-lipped mouth and slightly furrowed eyebrows. I don't leave my seat on the counter and stretch out to where I moved my gathering bag this morning. Inness is practically vibrating now. I open the bag with dramatic care and reach in, closing my fingers around the cool bottle of leafy green fire before I pull it out with both hands. The now empty bag drops to the floor with a weighty thud.

Her dark eyes go even wider, and she makes the tiniest sound of appreciative wonder I have ever heard.

The flame is perfectly tear shaped and floating in the exact center of the jar, flickering like a candle in the slightest of breezes. It's a pure, but complex, green. From one moment to the next I'm not sure if I would describe it as sunlight through leaves, or the deep green of the summer canopy, or the cool earthy green of the moss. It's all of them and none.

"What should we do with it?" I whisper.

She doesn't answer for quite some time, to the point I'm not sure she heard me, the green light reflecting in her owl-like stare. Eventually, she nods once at the jar and looks up with a smile, the spell of the flame broken.

"You are going to keep it," she says confidently, and pinches her dainty, dark eyebrows together in her favorite expression of thought. "But not in that. I'm going to make you something nicer for it." Without another word, Inness turns on her heel, swipes a small, empty glass ampule off of a shelf and is out the door, long black hair fluttering behind her.

"Hey, what about the rest of this stuff? We aren't done here!" I call after her, laughing, but the door has already slammed shut. I have plenty of time to teach her. I let her go and sit quietly, rolling the jar of fire back and forth between my palms. I wonder if this is what the Davorists are after, instead of some relic or lost knowledge, and how they would know of it when I didn't.

The rest of the day passes, and Inness doesn't return until late, loudly announcing she ate dinner with her Da and wants to go to bed, melting around questions of what she has been up to all day. Meanwhile, I spent my time split fairly evenly between staring into the depths of the forest's green fire and my work. The further the sun fell back into the night, the more I felt the itch to go. A need for answers rising in me that I haven't felt since I fled the loss of my mentor bubbles to the surface. The city held answers for me then, and I pray to the Trees it holds the answers I need now.

I feel that harsh emptiness again. A void that should be filled with the raspy old voice of my closest friend. But with Arty gone, if any place on this continent was going to have information about the fire, the ruins, or anything else, it would be the Library of Kiv.

CHAPTER EIGHT

ALYSSIA

I wake the next morning with a sense of solidity I greatly lacked the day before and roll out of bed immediately, my to-do list already rattling around in my head. The sun hasn't made its way down through the leaves, so I light candles and throw open every shutter and door I can once I make it downstairs. It's earlier in the year than usual for my spring trip to the city, but not by much, so my preparations aren't that far behind. Time to get to work.

I focus on mixing and grinding and packing so single-mindedly that Inness' face pops up under my elbow mid-muddling and I yelp, throwing the pestle onto the counter with a loud crash.

"Good morning," she beams.

"Good morning, you little hell creature." I catch my breath and scoop the mixture of dried ground herbs into a jar and pop the cork in.

"Are you going to the city?" she asks, even though she knows the answer. She can see my supplies cluttering every surface in the room just as well as I can.

"I am. Tomorrow morning before sunrise."

She wrinkles her nose. "I hate that part of the day."

Shit.

I forgot I told her I would take her with me on the next trip. The tip of my tongue curls around my upper lip.

"You don't want me to come," she pouts.

"No. I don't know if you *should* come. There's a difference."

"Well, why shouldn't I go?"

I consider it, but I can't come up with a reason to lie to her.

"Because there may be bad people coming here, and I don't know if it would be safer for you to be here with everyone, or out there with me." There had been no talk of black-coated strangers lurking about prior to, or since, the other day's debacle, but my gut tells me they won't just let this be. I want to know what they are looking for and if it has anything to do with what I found, or anything to do with the Woods at all. But I can't learn anything here, and I don't know what use I'd be if they did show up in the village. It would be ideal if the prince can manage to get guards out here soon, but I can't rely on him. He didn't seem sure he would be able to, let alone when.

My thoughts drift and I worry I missed Inness's response, but her brow is furrowed. She nods once, clearly to herself, and pats my arm.

"If there are bad people coming, I should be with Da. He'll worry if I'm not. And if you are busy being worried about protecting me, you might be less safe. I'll stay here. But you have to keep this safe." She triumphantly reveals a twine necklace from behind her back, a pendant wrapped in black cloth swinging in front of her face. The black fabric is a little drawstring bag which she unties and slides off revealing one of the most beautiful things I have ever seen.

Inness used the vial she swiped yesterday and wove the forest around it. Strands of vines, tough grass, and hearty little flowers spiral around the glass and it's lovely in the glowing light of the emerald flame that floats in the center, perfectly content to burn within the confines of its containment.

"Inness. It's wonderful." My finger traces along one line of twisted grasses. "But when did you get the fire in there?"

"Just now. You left the jar on the table, and you were very focused on what you were doing. I figured since you got it into the first one, I'd be able to get it into this one. I just sort of poured it in." She scuffs one foot into the floorboards and smiles up at me. "I'm glad you like it, Lys. I thought the fire would like to be reminded of home whenever you took it away with you, so I gave it something familiar to stay in."

I bend down when she pops up on tiptoe to slip the pendant over my neck. She tucks it back into its little bag before sliding it under my shirt.

"This way, no one will see it light up." She smiles again and rubs her hands together. "Right. Now what can I do to help?"

Eager and bright, creative, caring and full of love for everyone and everywhere around her. I would be lost without this girl.

We work together smoothly after years of learning each other's ways, and spend the morning deciding together what should be kept or sold. I separate the raw widow resin and flowers into small vials to sell more easily, and she wraps bundles of herbs in thin scraps of fabric. We pack up my special bags to keep everything safe and sound, and I set her free to gather lists of requests and things to sell from any of the villagers who have them. I use the time to hunt for Belar and talk to him about keeping a lookout while I am gone. I have been meaning to seek him out since leading the bleeding prince into the village to at least partially explain.

I find him outside the south entrance again, whittling something until he hears my steps.

"Just me," I offer helpfully as I poke my head through the irregular archway.

"Mhm?" He raises an eyebrow. "Need me to look for any more noble horses then, eh?"

I wince, but he said noble instead of royal so I'll take it. It was a really good horse and saddle. It isn't a leap to say it belonged to nobility.

"No, no. But I am going to go to the city a little early. Like, tomorrow. The people who stabbed that man..." I hate not knowing so much and feeling like I need to keep even more back.

"They might come 'round here?" Belar provides, helpfully.

"Yes. I think they are looking for something. I ran into them near some of the old ruins."

He nods again. "We'll keep an eye out."

"That man may be able to get a guard patrol out here, but he wasn't sure. I'm going to look into it when I'm in town."

"That could help, but we'll manage either way."

The man is a rock, and his stolid serenity helps unclench my stomach. I breathe easier for the first time in two days.

"Thank you, and I'm sorry. I can't explain it, but I feel like it's my fault." I'm quieter than usual as I lean back against the tangled wall of overgrown trees, brush and other flora that comprises the rough wall encircling our home. I scan the growing darkness of the Woods like I will spot lurking cultists ducking behind every shadow.

He hums again, this time resting one of his large, callused hands on my arm and giving it a squeeze.

"Good night, Belar."

"G'night, Lys."

I take my time getting back to the Great Tree, drifting along the sweeping lanes of bridge and branch and pass some of my old favorite hiding spots. Some of them are so precarious they make me nervous just to look at now, but others take willpower not to crawl into and hide. I was having a very normal, annoying, day two days ago and now I've been shot at, cleaned royal blood off of my floor, and had my view of magic upended by an impossible fire and a twelve year old girl. I try to conjure Arty for some kind of guidance, but it's no use. He would turn the pendant of flame over in his hand and murmur something incomprehensible and either experiment with it, or chalk it up to the Woods and move on. As for the cultists, what was it that he always said? *You can only do for tomorrow what you can do today.*

And well, I did for tomorrow what I could do today by giving Inness her choice and asking Belar to keep an eye on our people. I may be an oddity to them, with my organ jars, shelved skeletons and frequent disappearances into the Woods or city, but I care for the people here. Physically, of course, as their lives are frequently in my hands. But I care that they are safe and allowed to live peacefully here as well. I will keep my home safe.

By the time I close my door behind me, I feel as settled and whole as I can manage. Inness has left the village shopping list on top of my small pile of bags, and I tuck it into one of the pockets for safe keeping. Instead of going straight up to bed like I know I should, I duck off onto the second floor very quietly and try very hard to not think about what I'm doing. I float along with my body as it opens one of the small casks of wine, a payment for some service rendered, and fills a carafe. My hand hovers over a cup, but I forsake it and turn with the full container, drinking and drifting in an aimless fashion toward my top floor sanctuary.

The wide, curved wall of windows sheds murky moonlight across my messy refuge in patterns of leaves and twisting branches. I scrape my boots off and toss them next to a wardrobe, followed by my pants, letting the long hem of my shirt fall loose around my thighs. I take the wine to a desk tucked up against the windows and throw myself into the chair while taking a swig of the tart, dry liquid. I trace the path the prince and I took as far as I can before it twists away into shadow and my mind's eye takes over the roving. I picture the tousled fall of his hair in the morning that dusts his wide shoulders. The billow of linen tucked into his waistband is tantalizing, and my teeth dig into my lower lip at the thought of running my hands down the rough linen of the shirt, feeling the rasp of cloth and the solid curve of muscle beneath my finger tips. The snug fit of his trousers, hugging narrow hips and chiseled calves before disappearing into well worn boots pulls my imagined gaze along the incredible length of his body. Tall and strong and beautiful.

Just my type.

As the phantom fingers of my daydreamed self start trailing along the edges of the leather belt at his waist, I empty the wine and leave the container on the desk. I pull the image of us to the bed waiting for me and settle into the embrace of linens and pillows. One hand runs up the soft skin of my inner thigh, pushing the fabric of my shirt out of the way and fall asleep to thoughts of princes.

CHAPTER NINE

ALYSSIA

I smile in the dark as I get ready quietly, trying to avoid waking Inness. The previous night lingers with a headache and the echo of dreams that carry me through the morning in a pleasant haze.

Hauling my bags to the eastern glade we use as livestock storage, I load up my horse, Nettle, for the journey. It's still and quiet under the canopy, and I relish the sleepy sounds of animals. With a final check of straps and buckles, I swing myself up into the saddle with a sharp exhale of breath that I refuse to consider a grunt and nudge Nettle out onto the ancient track leading to the city.

Hours plod on, timed by the clatter of horse hooves on crumbling stone. Maybe this whole situation will at least lead to getting a proper road from the forest into the city again. A day's ride is close enough that we don't have to be so isolationist. Arty was always adamant that I not close myself off to the world at large, open minds and that sort of thing, but a lot of the villagers would like to remain as untethered to the city as possible.

Thoughts of Arty have my mind drifting to the past as I turn my closed eyes to the morning sun, swaying pleasantly in Nettle's saddle.

We were walking on the edge of the Woods where it looked more like the forest you would expect in the rest of the kingdom instead of the true majesty of the Woods. I had to have been twelve or thirteen at most, still early in my apprenticeship.

"What do you think of the Woods, Alyssia?"

"They're green. And everything is dirt and bark and big." I've always been painfully annoying.

"What else are they? Not just physically." He was insistent, his blue eyes boring into me, and I could sense the lecture coming.

So I thought, my feet splashing in the little pool of rainwater I found, trying to find some way to curtail the conversation before he really got going.

"They are my home, and everyone else's, of course. They take care of us and help us take care of ourselves. They are playful. They don't always stay the same, and I like that. And sometimes I think they know when we need something really bad, and they let us find it faster." I was hopeful I was on the right track because Arty was nodding instead of goading. "And I..." I remember sticking my tongue out so it touched my upper lip like I always do. "I think they're alive." He knew I didn't mean alive like a regular plant, but alive. Alive like people.

"That's better," he paused, holding a leaf in his hand. "Respect them and protect them, Alyssia. As much as you may think it now, I won't be around forever, and I need you to remember that."

I distinctly remember dismissing this conversation as a child, far more interested in the bug I found crawling on a tree trunk than the impossible thought of the world existing without Arty, but now my heart yearns for my mentor and his wisdom.

I cycle through other memories of my time in the Woods, searching through my archives for moments that didn't add up. There are more than I thought there would be. Annoyance at being lost, even though I've walked the same paths my whole life, finding myself in an entirely different area than I was expecting. Being suddenly and unexpectedly deposited back at my village. Time and time again, I see myself simply forgetting or writing off strange occurrences as some trick of memory, tiredness, or the inherent confusion of the Woods. My fingers lay against the rough surface of the amulet under my shirt in wonder. Would I have gone my whole life without questioning what power my home held? Blindly going about my business, thinking everything was normal? Mundane?

I have always known that places can have power. Certain buildings, parts of the city, areas of the sea. Different people find this sense of belonging in different spots. I never considered that the spaces may have *actual* power. I always thought they were areas where different people felt safe or connected to something greater than themselves. Like Carolyn in the library, Kyla in the Prism, Rend in the middle of the ocean. Me in my Woods.

My need for the library increases as I think of all of the history I never cared to learn as a child, my studies focused on my trade and the ways plants can help us live better, healthier lives. I still believe that is what the Woods want for us, but now I think about what else they are. What other secrets they hold. What other power. What reasons the Davorists have in stalking their leaf-shadowed depths.

The sun spins through the sky, marking the journey of my memories as I plod on, pausing briefly to eat and walk next to Nettle. I can't stop myself from pulling apart a lifetime's worth of memories and suddenly find myself at the gates to Kivaire with the sun dipping toward the horizon. I've made good time despite the thoughts churning in my head, sending me through years instead of hours. I nod at the guards, and they let me through unmolested. Despite the otherness I feel, I know I look like any other traveler from any other village more well-known by the capital.

There's plenty of time before darkness closes the streets to normal trade, and the list of supplies from the villagers is waiting in my bags along with the things I have to sell. Kivaire is a port city and the ocean runs along the entire eastern side. My final destination, the Prism, is situated a respectable distance from the city center and the docks. Nearly every spot I need to sell my wares and supply the villagers lie between me and it.

—

By the time I walk Nettle to the stables associated with the Prism, I'm nearly done with my business. Aside from the vials of widow resin I always save for Kyla, my portion of the errands are complete and only a few tasks for the villagers remain. The multi-story facade of the bar, distillery, shop and lodging house I love so dearly looms over me as I deposit my horse into the care of the stable hand.

I swing the door open and find Kyla behind the bar where she dries a glass and talks earnestly to a man who looks like no person I've ever seen. He is dressed neck to toe in black leather and long, white hair trails down his back. The bell over the door jingles as I close it behind me, and the sound triggers Kyla to look up. When she realizes who entered the bar, she squeals. I smile and brace myself as I take several steps into the room, and she leaps from the raised platform behind the counter to barrel into me. She is a head and a half shorter than I am, and I scoop her into a hug that lifts her off her feet. It has been half a year since we've seen each other, and we squeeze each other like we can erase the time that separated us if we hold on tightly enough.

"Lys!" she exclaims in pure joy and then steps back, gripping my arms. "Lys." The second address is much more pointed. I arch my eyebrow at her. "You're early," she says breathlessly, pulling me with her toward the bar and the strange man.

"I am early. I have something-"

She cuts me off with a wave of her hand. "Do you have any widow resin with you, or is it too early?"

I nod, bewildered at her interruption. It's not like her to lead with business, but then I actually look at the man she leads me to. He leans against the bar, no drink in sight. His hair isn't just pale, it's pure white and purple-red eyes bore into me when I meet them. His skin is nearly translucent where it isn't tattooed black. The ink lines his eyes, white eyelashes standing out starkly. His entire top lip is blackened, and a thick band runs through the center of the bottom. A strange symbol of curved lines tattooed under one eye completes the visible ink.

I blink rapidly. Something tugs at the corners of my mind that I try to shuffle into place. Kyla bridges the gap created by our mutual staring.

"This is the apothecary I was telling you about. You won't have to go find her after all." She beams, her red-orange curls bouncing around her face as she bounds back behind the bar.

The man nods at me, and I must look completely confused, but I try to control my features as I reach toward my bag.

"You're looking for widow resin?" I ask dumbly, fumbling for one of the vials I kept back for Kyla.

"I am." His Ayamar is heavily accented, and his voice is like spider silk at dawn, ephemeral and delicate.

I nod as I draw out a vial. I name the price, and he tilts his head in agreement even though it's rather astronomical. With the casual disregard of the small fortune I ask for, the pieces finally slide together, and I remember why his appearance is so familiar to me. He is an Edantus of Alsairdia. Rend told me about them ages ago after one of her voyages to the south. She said they were a guild that did dirty work for their Senate, or something of the sort, and they all looked eerily similar. She described them just like this man. I exchange the product for coin, but he hesitates.

He pockets the widow resin and pulls a string of strange, hollow-centered tokens from a chain around his neck. After carefully removing one, he hands it to me.

"Keep this for when you must cross into our lands." His words are flat and knowing, his unearthly eyes holding mine in a stare that digs into my bones.

And then he is gone, an unsettling blur of white-highlighted shadow vanishing through the door and into the blazing, evening sun.

Kyla bursts into laughter. "Well I never! To think one of the Alsairdians would come into my bar looking for you."

I roll my eyes. "You know exactly why he was in your bar instead of any other place in this city. You've spent too long making a name for yourself to act surprised." I've been supplying Kyla with herbs and plants to distill into odd liquors my entire adult life, including weeping widow. Anyone in the city who knows enough to look for it, knows it can be found here.

Thinking of why I knew *what* that man was, if not who, I scan the taproom quickly but already know I won't find who I'm looking for.

"Where is Rend anyway?"

Kyla doesn't hesitate at the transition and leans in against the counter, a conspirator's gleam in her eye. "She's on a mission," she pauses for dramatic effect, "For the *Crown.*"

Sybella Vangariad Rend is the most charismatic, bewildering human being I have met in my entire life, but the thought of her working for the royal family leaves me reeling. Kyla recognizes my shock and takes pity on me, sliding a golden ale my way.

"Delivering the Empress's daughter from Yadec as an ambassador," she continues blandly, going back to tidying her counter. "A right proper captain with a right proper task." She winks. "This time at least."

I choke on a swig that didn't have time to make it all the way down.

"Maybe the world really is going to shit," I say, more heavily than I intended.

Kyla gives me a long side eye, scans her bar, and then settles back on me.

"We'll get to that comment later. For now, go get yourself ready for bed. I'll be up when I kick this lot out."

I finish the beer in a long, gulping swallow and spin it on the counter.

The glass lands with the handle toward Kyla. "See you upstairs, pretty lady." I wink and slide the strap of my bag over my shoulder, looking forward to the low buzz of the patrons lulling me to sleep upstairs.

—

I'm curled pleasantly in her bed, my feet sticking out of the covers and lightly dozing by the time she closes up downstairs. Her presence rouses me as she slides under the covers, and I roll toward her drowsily.

"I met the prince."

Any sleepiness I wanted to hold onto is immediately stolen by Kyla's screech.

"You *what?*"

"I convinced myself that I had dreamed the whole damn thing, or hallucinated it, or anything other than it actually happening. But it did happen. I met him in the Woods fighting a bunch of Davorists that had been chasing me. I saved his life, and then I took him to my *house*, Kyla. I put stitches into royal flesh and discovered his eyes are the color of my forest."

"I'm sorry, *what?*"

I give her some context of the cultists, the sword fight, and my night cleaning up the prince before continuing.

"I honestly thought I made it all up. I tossed any remotely suspicious mushrooms out the window before making breakfast, just in case. I was trying my hardest to convince myself none of it had happened. My spirit absolutely left my body when he snuck up behind me while cooking and said 'Good morning.' Simple as that. Sleep mussed and completely gorgeous, standing awkwardly in my living room."

She squeals again and rolls around with laughter.

"What did you do? What did you say? Wait." She stills suddenly and looks at me seriously. "Are you okay? They didn't hurt you did they? And why were they there anyway?"

"I almost threw a spoon at him. I said 'Good morning' back like an idiot. And yes, I'm okay. Nobody hurt me, and I don't know why they were there. That's why I'm here now."

Kyla comes in close again and wraps her arm around me, laying her cheek on my chest.

"I hope you find what you're looking for."

"Me too," I yawn. "But now tell me all about you and what's happened in the city over the winter." I'm genuinely interested in what Kyla has to say, but I feel myself drifting as soon as she starts speaking. I catch only fragments about cults, Rend, and her newest beverage experiments before everything fades to the rushing silence of sleep.

—

When morning comes, I wake early with the full, unfiltered sun peaking through Kyla's curtains. I don't bother waking her before I leave, ready to finish the village errands and get to the library. Breakfast is easy to obtain among the shops and stalls as I wander from place to place. I keep an ear tuned to the street gossip for mentions of the cults but nothing comes of it.

By the time the white, gleaming walls of the Library of Kiv soar into view, the streets are fully awake. The library is at the city center, surrounded by wealthy residential districts and shopping galore. The streets branch away from it in a way that always reminds me of the Great Tree in Cuaria, and I smile.

I'm about to bound up the wide, marble steps to the library when a dress shop catches my eye. I jingle the coins in my pocket thoughtfully. Inness loves when I tell her about the clothes the women wear in the city, and I feel guilty I had to leave her at home. I'm immediately greeted by the shopkeeper upon entering. I tell her I'm after a small dress, simple but fashionable, and she directs me to several options. I thumb my way through them, thinking of what Inness would like the most. My fingers brush against the soft gray fabric of one dress, simply embroidered with deep green vines at the neck and hem, and I know this is the one. Gray for the mountains and green for the Woods. I pay for the impractical, beautiful, piece with a fraction of the money the Edantus paid for the widow resin and smile, some of my guilt assuaged.

The dress is folded neatly and tucked into my trusted leather bag slung over my shoulder as I take the library steps two at a time. Dark, wooden doors lined with gold greet me at the top, twice as tall as me and then some. They swing inward with the slightest touch of my hand, despite their size. The familiar sight of vaulted ceilings, towering stacks of books and parchments, and lines of desks tucked between them, fills me with a sense of hope. There are several white-robed cultists sitting at desks or floating among the stacks, but I don't see the severely short, sleek black hair of Carolyn. I head confidently down the main aisle, noting that a man not wearing cultist white is already here, despite the hour, pouring over an old map that looks likely to crumble into dust, weighed down at the corners by books that look just as fragile. His unruly, curled mop of blond hair falls over gold-rimmed glasses.

I aim for the door tucked into the back corner of the massive room. It leads to the small chapel, where I assume Carolyn will be at this hour. Kivaran cultists are much less focused on Kiv worship than Davorists are of their rituals for the veneration of Davor, preferring to focus on acts of service and sharing knowledge. Thus, small chapel and large library. There is a kitchen open to the poor of the city here, as well. Carolyn is extremely set in her ways and very devout, however, so she has her own rituals, even if they aren't official.

I open the door as quietly as I can. Her back is to me, kneeling on the stone floor in front of the simply made, wooden altar, head bent and black hair shimmering like oil on water in the light filtering through the one stained glass window. Kiv burns in a blaze of fire, blood dripping from a sword clutched in her fist. The Martyr in all her glory. Silently, I slip onto the pew closest to the door and wait for her to finish. I try, as I always do when I am here, to feel the same connection and devotion to Kiv as Carolyn does. It doesn't come. At least now I think I finally know why. The Woods are my saint. My protector. I have no need for the Martyr to watch over me. I'm a person of the Woods, and my heart is full with devotion to them.

Carolyn stands and slowly pulls the tips of her fingers through the candle flames on the altar, unflinching. She raises her hand and, even though I cannot see it, I know she is pressing those same fingertips to her lips. Not to soothe the burning she should feel, but to thank Kiv for her protection. She feels nothing but warmth from those flames.

She turns and redirects her smile to me.

"Lys," her voice is low and has the barest of accents from Northern Ayamar. "I knew I felt the need to pray extra hard this morning, even beyond what was already required."

We embrace, and I breathe her in. All incense and old books.

"What already needed such attention from you and your Martyr this early?"

She pulls away, eyes like cut gems boring into me.

"You have not heard?"

"I just got to the city yesterday."

"The King was found dead. The public announcement should have been made this morning."

I blink deliberately, willing the action to shuffle my thoughts back into working order.

"A failing of his heart. Found in his office. Quite dreadful for the poor girl who discovered him. We spoke with her and members of the family. No symptoms at all. "

Of course they called the Kivarans in. They have some of the city's best physicians among their ranks. Carolyn likely wasn't there in person, never having much interest in medicine and preferring to leave that to me, but she is close with many of her fellow priests and priestesses and would have found out what she could. An image of the prince smiling awkwardly at me from across my table interrupts my vision. An uneasiness settles over me, blending with the instant heartache I feel for him. I hate myself for thinking it, but the first thing on my mind is the deployment of guardsmen to my village. I'm begging the Trees it was already underway before the King passed. The reallocation of guards to a forgotten part of the kingdom would certainly not be on the palace's urgent to-do list now.

"That's awful. He was no older than my own father."

Which is true, but I know the body is a fallible thing. Death comes for us all, expected or not. Young or old. I still feel the irrational anger of a life I could have tried to save. I see the prince's tangled and sweat soaked hair clinging to his face, thanking me. Should I have tried to see the prince yesterday? Could I have helped? There are herbs to help with heart problems. Ways to get people breathing again.

Carolyn snaps my spiral back to the present with a touch to the side of my face.

"What is it?" She asks.

"I met his son three days ago."

It's Carolyn's turn to stare, mind working to catch up. I give her a more chaste retelling of the cultists, the prince, and the breakfast than I did Kyla, but I add in more about the ruins. Finally, I tell her about the green fire, my voice hushed in this chapel turned confessional.

I pull the amulet out of my shirt and remove the fabric, dangling the vine and glass pendant between us. Its flame is smaller, somehow, and dimmer here in the stained glass light of the chapel, but her eyes are wide. She leans in, the tip of her sharp, pointed nose practically brushing the flowers tucked into the weave of vines.

"It is beautiful," her voice is reverent as she pulls away, the sharp edge of her hair brushing against her jaw as it settles back into place. "And like

75

nothing I have seen."

"If you don't know what it is, then I certainly have no hope."

"Well. Let us see what we can learn together, then." She brushes her fingers against my cheek and leads me out into the stacks.

"How much do you know of where you live, Lys?" Her voice is soft, our heads bent together as she combs through the shelves.

"Apparently a lot less than I thought."

"I know it used to be a nation of its own during the time of Kiv and Davor. Ecles'culaire, it was called. There are few surviving specifics, but we have maps that outline its borders with a marker for its capital by the lake you have told me of. I have not seen mention of them since the Fall, however. Nothing of what happened to the people there or how it became absorbed into Ayamar after its restructuring."

Now that she mentions it, I do remember there being more of the old ruins closer to the lake, and something vague about the lake itself, but my recollection is hazy, clouded by the mists of memory. Carolyn distracts me by aggressively digging through a dusty corner shelf, quickly leafing through scrolls of parchment and crumbling leather tomes.

I want to ask if she is looking for something specific, but before I can, someone calls out, the voice far too loud in the rustling quiet of the Library.

"Lys?"

All at once, my stomach is both in my throat and on the floor. I scramble toward the central passage of the room, breathing fast and hard before I've made it out of the corridor of looming shelves. Carolyn, torn from her search by my abrupt exodus, rounds the corner behind me.

"Adean, what are you doing here? What's wrong?" I find myself gripping the boy's shoulders and force myself to release him.

"Kyla said you would probably be here, I went to the Prism first like my Da told me too. He thinks you will know what to do."

Belar wouldn't have sent his son to find me if there wasn't a serious problem. I curse under my breath.

"What's going on?" I fear I know, but I need to confirm the severity of the situation. I start walking toward the exit as I wait for him to tell me.

"Some strange people came to the village. They were asking questions about old jewelry and some man named Davor, but Da was really suspicious and wanted you to know."

Shit.

Part of me was hoping I was wrong, and that something else happened that would have required my attention. An illness, an injury. Anything.

Apparently not.

Just dangerous, mysterious cultists harassing my people.

Thank the Trees they are only asking questions, but how long will that last until they get bored not finding any answers?

"Carolyn, I have to go, but can you send word if you find anything? I don't know what I can do, but I have to get home. If I could get to the prince, maybe I could..." I trail off in useless frustration.

"Of course. And of course you do. I will keep looking for anything that can help." She frowns, thinking. "I do not know what I can manage, but perhaps the Order can get help to your people. It is not unreasonable to believe someone in the guard would listen to us."

"I think I could help with that."

I jump out of my skin as a deep male voice pops up behind me. Whipping around, I see that it is the blond scholar I noted earlier.

"With both problems actually." He continues like he didn't just witness my undignified yelp and hands Carolyn a roll of parchment and a book.

"Jyn! Wonderful!" Carolyn brushes his cheek in her familiar greeting and tucks the objects carefully under one arm.

A sudden spark of annoyance and confusion ignites the need to be moving away from this new distraction. My body tightens, but I'm willing to listen if the newcomer can truly help.

"I'm being a little presumptuous here, but you wouldn't happen to be the Otherfolk woman who saved the prince's life a few days ago, would you?"

I know the man is talking to me but the absurdity, coincidence, and phrasing is slightly too much for me to handle. I look at Carolyn to translate, fighting down another unnecessary noise.

"Jyn is a friend of His Highness," she explains patiently, apparently much less taken aback by his sudden appearance and knowledge of my recent escapades than I am. "He could get word to him, even now."

I take a brief moment to appreciate the intense eavesdropping this blond, statue of a man is apparently capable of before I run through several courses of action, settling on one that will hopefully be the most efficient. "Adean, do you feel comfortable going with them to explain and lead them back to the village?" I put emphasis on 'them' for Carolyn's sake. I trust only her to deliver the boy safely back home. Although, he is well into his teen years now so I know I shouldn't worry as much as I do.

He looks nervous, but nods. "I want to help."

"Thank you, all of you. Please, do what you can." My back is already at the door by the time I finish speaking. I throw myself into the street, simultaneously mapping and running the quickest path back to the Prism and my horse. The chaos of the city swells around me in a blur, the news of the King's death spreads quickly now, but I have no mind for it.

I must protect my home.

CHAPTER TEN

ALYSSIA

The road blurs around me as I ride Nettle as hard as I dare. I can't risk pushing her much more, but I'm losing horribly in my race against time. The hours drag, and I bounce between the fear of what is ahead of me and the hope for what I left behind. If the prince's friend thinks he can help, there may be reinforcements after all, but I can't help my fear that it will be too late.

That *I* will be too late.

The closer I get to the Woods, the more focused I become on what lays ahead. I scan the sky for smoke, strain to hear any sounds of distress, flight or fear. No raging wildfire, screams of terror, or clashing of swords greet me as I break into the trees. Nettle's hooves churn leaf litter in explosive sprays as we close the final distance. She is breathing hard, and the path into the village grows more difficult the further in we get. Reluctantly, I slow until we approach the entrance to her paddock. I slide off, hit the ground at a run, and leave her to find her way home.

The only firelight I see is the glow of the usual torches and tears well in relief, but my heart will not unclench. I slow as I pass through the eastern arch, but everything looks normal until I reach the center. Nearly the entire village has gathered in knots around the Great Tree. The buzz of too many voices talking at once fills my ears. The spaces in front of several houses are littered with belongings, reflecting torchlight in the darkness.

Belar sees me as I hurtle down a sweeping root, half falling, half sliding in my haste and catches me before I can crash into the ground.

"Is everyone safe?" The words are hardly audible as I gulp air.

"A few people are a little roughed up from when they started turning out the houses, nothing serious, but-"

He is cut off as Jiath, Inness' father, breaks from the crowd and clutches my arms in desperation.

"They took her!" He's shaking me as his voice cracks with anguish. I feel the burn of bile in my throat. "They took Inness. They took her."

Belar is trying to peel him away from me, but he crumples at my feet in a sob. His hands still pull the fabric of my sleeves.

"Where? When?" I ask Belar, knowing Jiath can't help me now.

"Hours ago, maybe midday. She led them out through the south."

"She *led* them?"

"Once they started searching your shop, she started yelling at them that she knew the Woods better than anyone else, and she could help them find what they were looking for."

"That's not-" I start, but he shakes his head and continues.

"We tried to talk them out of it, but more of them started showing up. They took her, saying she would be safe if she could help them. We sent people after them, of course, but none have come back."

Hours ago. Half a day ago, really. Inness does know the Woods well, better than most of the villagers who have been here their whole lives, but she's only a child. Grown adults should have found her by now.

"How many cultists were there? Why haven't the men brought her back?" I'm choked, desperate.

"A dozen armed men that I saw. I don't know how many others were still loitering out in the trees."

"Why haven't they brought her back?"

The only response to my question is a silent stare from Belar and the violent sobbing of Jiath at my feet.

No.

I will not let them have her.

I tear my shirt from Jiath's fingers and hold his face in my hands.

"I will bring her back to you."

I touch the long dagger at my belt for reassurance. I'm comforted by the familiar weight of my travel companion, even if I don't really know how to use it.

I don't let panic drive me. I know I can't afford that. Instead, I adopt a steady, ground-eating pace toward the south. The wildness, uncertainty, and surreal tirade of what-ifs that have been churning inside me for days melt down into a single, fiery purpose. Find Inness. Keep her safe. Bring her home.

I don't stop to take a torch as I pass into the forest again, instead reaching into my shirt and pulling out the fabric wrapped amulet, easing the cloth free and allowing the green glow to illuminate the Woods.

Their trail is not hard to find, and I dip into the trees where I see the crashing clumsiness of their passage. Inness moves through these Woods like a ghost by pure reflex. This is the work of the cultists, and I'm grateful she didn't try harder to hide it.

The path she blazes is twisted, and I recognize the signs of her passing the same spots more than once to get them even more lost. I have no doubt it's effective, but someone has to catch on sooner rather than later. We're both working on borrowed time.

"What was that?" The harsh bark cracks through the trees.

I curse to myself and cup the amulet in my hands, dampening its glow as I freeze in place. I spy the ruddy illumination of torches flickering across the underbelly of the canopy and duck away from their approach, hiding in shadows.

It has to be the cultists. Inness has to be with them.

A heartbeat later, her voice echoes through the dark.

"It was probably just an animal. We *are* outside after all." There is a pause in the tide of approaching light before she continues. "You're going the wrong way, anyway. I told you, I know where there are some really great old buildings, just like the ones you asked about. Trust me."

The nearness of her pains me, but I don't have the information I need to leap to her rescue yet. How many are there? Would they kill me the moment they saw me? How could I do that to her? What would she do in response?

Before I decide anything, the same voice sounds again.

"You two. Go find out what that was. The rest of us will follow the girl."

"But how will we find you again? What if it-?"

"Figure it out! Go! Girl, keep going!"

Shit.

My mind races to plot a course through the trees that will allow me to follow whatever path Inness is creating. I dig through tangled memories of the forest, trying to pick some place she may be taking them. She didn't lie. I could hear the truth in her words. She is taking them to ruins somewhere. I wonder if she saw the light of my flame and tried to give me a hint, but I have to leave that thread to dangle as the approaching torchlight now gains the accompanying beat of footsteps. My hiding spot is not good enough for them to pass me by if they get any closer.

I peel away from my shallow nook and disappear into the shadows, temporarily moving in the opposite direction of Inness to give myself time to think. If I'm honest, she probably does know these Woods better than anyone, quite possibly including myself. She always seems to have an easier time getting exactly where she wants to go. With one hand still blocking as much of the amulet's light as it can, I use the other to push my way through dense, clinging underbrush and over steep, twisting roots. I pause occasionally in the deepest shadows to assess where my pursuers may be.

Far too close.

Somehow they got lucky, or I got sloppy, and their torch is now lighting a narrow path directly in front of me.

Shit. Shit. Shit.

Before I can dodge back the way I came, the pair pop out from behind a root and let out a simultaneous cry of alarm. I bolt blindly into a thicket of brush to the sound of their riotous crashing and cursing behind me. My mind wants to panic, but I force an iron grip around it, squeezing it until I can focus again. My advantages are better than theirs. I know this ground better than they do. I can move more quietly than they can. They have light and, theoretically, weapons they know how to use, but I can do this.

I crouch low, ignoring the screaming of my knees as I move with lunging steps, deliberately snapping the occasional twig on my way to lead them along. The surroundings illuminated by their torchlight are familiar. There is a dead end ahead of us that I can use to my advantage.

I silence all noise and slink further into the brush as they stumble out onto the small deer trail leading to the clearing. Falling back, I keep pace with them as they attempt to sneak dramatically through the Woods, one with a bow ready to draw, the other with a wicked short sword reflecting the torchlight blazing from his off-hand.

Just before they break into the obvious dead end, I slide my own dagger out of its sheath and start fervently praying to the Woods that my hardly-baked plan will work, and that I won't be killed immediately. My gaze narrows to a pair of legs exposed by a woven window of greenery as they hesitate, stepping into the obviously empty clearing. I have exactly one chance, just like my last violent encounter. I take two slow, deep breaths and focus on the space of puckered trousers between the bend of the knee and the top of a dusty boot.

In an explosion of movement I didn't think myself capable of, I lash out with the dagger from my hiding place, bursting through my cover like a snake. The blade makes jarring contact. I slam the heel of my other hand against the hilt and drive the knife into flesh in a slash backed by my entire, lunging body.

Before the second man can react, I let go. I leave the blade satisfyingly deep in the tendon-heavy leg meat of my target and push myself back into the cover of the forest. My retreat is chased by a scream, and I beg anything that is listening that the other man stays to help the first instead of following me. Just in case, I bolt through the Woods like the whole Cult of Davor is after me.

Not a flicker of light is visible behind me when I slow to catch my breath. I search for the deepest burrow I can find and dive in like a gopher. I have to think. I have to know, somewhere in the recesses of my mind, where she is taking them.

Images flash of overgrown, crumbling rocks eaten by vines and weeds, buildings worn to shapeless stone and bridges of rotting logs. Inness hangs upside down from an empty window frame. Each option is possible but indistinct, unimportant. Thinking of Inness, exclusively, I grasp a memory of her jumping into the summer-calm river from a bridge of twisted branches, and my stomach drops. I dig my way out of my hiding spot before the splash of her in the water clears.

The amulet swings around my neck, any thoughts of stealth abandoned as I use both hands to propel my way through the forest. I have veered too far from the part of the river where I know, deep in my heart, she is going despite the danger of the spring flooding. Or, knowing her, because of it.

The trees and the underbrush become more and more unruly, wild and twisting as I approach the water, the roar of its current fills my chest with its rushing urgency. Despite how close it sounds, I know it runs far below, carving its way through root and stone alike.

I scrabble desperately at footholds in the eerily illuminated dark, my hands raw from scraping against bark and earth until I finally, *finally,* see the orange glow of torches ahead. I am still too far from the narrow passage they stand before. I want to cry out in frustration, but I don't waste the breath as I hurl myself in her direction.

The first scream rings out as the narrow gap comes into view, all signs of the cultists and Inness lost behind the twisting tunnel of trees. Following them through the passage would be useless, so I dodge off to the side, following the path of the gorge through the Woods. I can imagine the chaos that is unfolding within. Shouts ring out over the sound of the churning water, as the first man plunges into the current below, slipping between slick twists of branch and root. The frantic mess of them try to push passed one another, back through the gap in the trees they entered. But the terrain prevents them.

Right on time, another scream echoes over the general shouting, the heavy smack of a body onto water quickly swallowed by the din.

Halfway along the bridge, however, is an escape that I showed Inness on one of our trips here. The problem being, this route is too narrow for a grown adult to squeeze into.

Of course she would bring them here. It's the best trap anyone could have come up with without warning. I really want to waste time cursing myself for not coming here straight away, but I redouble my search for the crevice that leads to the cursed bridge, holding the glaring green flame aloft.

The shouting of men and the roar of the water hammer into me in time with the painful racing of my heart until I can't untangle the sounds. Everything around me is lost in that howling storm.

My frantic searching finally catches a flash of movement, and the tempest in my ears melts away as Inness pulls herself out of the clinging embrace of the trees and into my arms.

"I'm here. I'm here, Inness, I'm here."

My hands tangle in her hair as I hold her to me.

"I did it, Lys. I got them to follow me into the trap. I got some of them. I got some of them back for trying to hurt us. For trying to take from us. From the Woods," her voice is shaking and small but fierce, her fists clenched in my shirt. "I told you I would protect us. And I did. I protected all of us."

"You did. You did such a good job."

I slide to my knees in front of her and expect to see the reflections of tears on her cheeks, but she is smiling at me, gasping in short, ragged breaths. She wriggles a hand free from my embrace and brushes the burning amulet with her fingertips, the flame responding to her touch, flaring brightly.

"I protected Them. And now it's your turn, Lys."

Inness coughs, a gagging sound deep in her throat, and dark droplets splatter across her hand and the pale fabric of my shirt.

No.

No no no.

The sticky warmth that coats my hands finally registers, and I hunt for what I'm begging the Woods not to find. My fingers meet the splintered end of a broken arrow shaft, slick with foamy blood that bubbles with each breath. It surges in thick waves with every fluttering beat of her heart.

I am too late.

I was too late when I left her behind yesterday. I was too late when I marked her as mine and taught her the secrets of the Woods.

I was too late.

A sob wrenches from my chest, my vision blurring. Inness still holds the amulet, its light making jewels of her dark brown eyes. Reaching with her other hand, she draws my chin up into that wide and determined gaze that reflects none of the fear that chokes me.

"Do good, Lys."

She coughs again, red staining pale lips.

I nod and shake my head through snot and tears. I want to speak but there is a vice of horror around my throat. I touch her face. Smears of her own blood leave trails like the tears she does not shed. I can't stop holding her. I can't stop trying to keep her with me by touch alone.

It's not enough.

The light from the pendant dims as her hand drops away.

Her weight falls heavy into my arms.

An animalistic wail echoes from the trees around me, and I do not know if it comes from my own lungs or if the forest itself is screaming, but I feel it resonate through me, matching the vibrations of my breaking.

I'm blinded by the blur of tears and the wavering heat of a rage so deep I'm surprised I don't turn the ground around me to ash. I don't know if I would notice if I did.

I see only the face of the girl I carry, draped in my arms, her cheek tucked against me.

I don't stop. I don't stumble. Not one tree or root or branch dares to cross my path as I fulfill the promise I made.

I will bring her back to you.

I don't know how long I walk. I don't know how my path through the trees is not interrupted. All I know is that I only stop when the base of the Great Tree looms above me.

I hear voices. Close. Bodies crowd me. They're nothing but shadows.

There is nothing but the girl in my arms and the heaving ache of the sobs tearing at my chest.

I have no concept of how long I stand there, being buffeted by those around me, before one of the voices finally becomes words I can understand.

"Lys. You have to give her to her father."

The shards inside of me crumble into dust.

I am lost as she is taken from me.

CHAPTER ELEVEN

KEDREN

I am filled with the emptiness that reverberates around me. The opulent sterility of my mother's office echoes with emotionless silence and bureaucratic shuffling. The vaulted ceilings, stained glass windows, and overly-gilded furniture are as cold and impersonal as she is. Nothing like the close, warm, casualness of my father's study that spoke of a more approachable, more human, occupant. My father was not perfect, but at least he was simply a man once. My mother has been the Queen since she came of age, both of her parents dying before she was old enough to assume the throne. I am unsure if she was ever anything but a vessel for the Crown.

Even now, the day after her husband's death, she sits behind her grand desk, surrounded by papers, several scribes, and the looming shadow of my sister. Working. Her black hair falls in shining, pristine waves over her shoulders and down her back, blending into the silk of her severely cut mourning gown.

At least her dark eyes are red rimmed. Some hint of lingering humanity.

"Daralyn will be taking over all of the King's duties and obligations, effective immediately." Flat. Commanding. Official.

"I am more than capable of managing the roles that are mine by right."

"And you may, in time, but we cannot wait for you to prove yourself. A death in the royal household can create instability if not handled properly. I will not have it. Daralyn has been preparing for such a position and participating in leadership roles for years now. She has more than demonstrated herself capable of the responsibility." Her words are calm, measured, without a hint of disdain or malice. My perceived incompetence is nothing but an inconvenient fact.

I want to argue. I want to ask her or her precious daughter if they know how much physical work it takes to feed our people. How to work with, speak to, and care for those who do it. I want to ask them how they plan to manage the northern lords who will begin to siphon tax revenue and circumvent policy because only my father's northern blood and physical presence kept them in line. I want to know why my mother has let Daralyn corrupt her opinion of me since the day I was born. I want to know how my sister has been able to manipulate everyone and everything around her for decades.

I hold myself steady against the torrent of my frustration while under the beady, hawk-like stare of Daralyn. Straight backed, dressed and veiled in black like the perfect, dutiful princess. She is always eager for me to try to stand up for myself, say anything that does not fit her narrative of me. It always manages to provide her with some new way to weave lies about me.

"Of course, Your Majesty." I bow formally and turn to leave. The point of my summons was only to remind me I will continue to be of no use to them.

"A moment, brother."

Daralyn's voice scrapes down my back like nails along my spine. I shiver to a halt.

"About what father was advocating for, the guard disbursement to some backwater hamlet you found. It won't be happening."

"Excuse me? It was settled two days ago."

"Two days ago, father dearest was still alive, and we weren't in the position we are now. Really, brother, you couldn't think we would have the men to spare on such nonsense."

"There is no reason to think the death of the King would further embolden the Davorists. It is a religious debate gone too far, not a political issue, if what the council knows is true. Surely a dozen men would make little difference here."

"But we don't know what is truly motivating the cult, now do we? It isn't like we have one of their priests giving us private counsel. Not like the Kivarans," she spits the name. "I don't think it would be a good idea to underestimate what their religious differences could mean for the city." Her grin is wolfish when she continues, "Besides, there's trouble to the south and who knows what those barbarians in the north are thinking. It would be best to not spread our forces any thinner."

"The south? There is unrest in Alsairdia? How would you even know?"

"It seems someone has been throwing stones into the viper pit that is their senate, and they are getting a little hissy." She absently inspects her nails as she speaks, still grinning.

There was a twist in the word 'someone,' and I am suddenly sure she had something to do with this as well. For her to even know of it speaks volumes. First the Davorists, then my father's death, and now news from a foreign senate no one has had contact with in centuries. It is all too much of a coincidence.

"That is concerning, at best," I manage through gritted teeth.

"Quite unfortunate, yes. As you can see, we really can't go shuffling around guards for a little pet project of yours." She waves a hand at me dismissively, and turns back to my mother, peering at something on the desk. "You may go now."

Filing her teeth into points could not make her look more like a predator when she smiles at me from her place over the Queen's shoulder.

I bow again and turn for the door, my mother's voice following me as I flee, eager to escape the oily, corruption-coated luxury of this office and its inhabitants.

"The funeral will be in two weeks. Please try to be present."

Two guards close the doors behind me with resounding finality. I want to slide to the floor. Envir is outside waiting for me though, jumping up from a seat in the hallway as soon as I appear. The sight of him bolsters me.

Until he speaks.

"Your Highness, if you will come with me?" He is stiff and formal, unlike him even in the presence of the Queensguard.

"Of course." I gesture for him to lead the way, and we walk briskly through cold marble hallways.

We are nearly to my rooms, well out of range for anyone to overhear us, before he speaks.

"There's trouble with your Otherfolk."

It takes a few steps to understand what he is talking about, but when I do my stomach drops.

"What happened? Is anyone hurt? Where is-" I try to say her name, and curse myself again that I never bothered to learn it. "Where is the woman?" I jog the last several strides to my room, keeping my left arm as still as I can and wrench open the door before he has time to respond.

"Oh."

I stop in surprise. Envir has to push around me to close the door behind us.

"This is Carolyn Vintra and Adean Hult. Adean is from the village."

I push my hand through my hair to settle myself and finish stepping into the room, nodding at the group assembled at my table. Jyn is there with the strangers, a book open between him and the woman. Several bags with a mess of objects spill out across the surface. The boy, a young man really, looks like a rat deciding its best escape route. Nervous and fidgeting, his attention drifts between me and the door. I slide into a seat across from him and modulate my own anxiety.

"Adean, can you tell me what was happening when you left home?"

"There were strangers asking questions about the Woods and some other things, but my Da didn't like them, so he sent me to come get Lys. She already went back, but Jyn said he could maybe get you to help us, so I came here."

Lys must be the name of the woman who saved me. It feels right with the image of her I hold in my head, but there is no time for me to get lost in that thought. I push back from the table and stand, looking between Envir and Jyn, trying to avoid lingering on the severe looking woman between them. Her hair is somehow even blacker than my mother and sister's, reflecting blue-purple in the daylight streaming through the windows, cut harshly above thin brows and a sharp, pointed jaw. Thick lashes hide her eyes from me as she pours over the book in front of her. She is dressed in the pristine white and gold robes of a Priestess of Kiv.

"We ride out, then. Daralyn went back on the deal my father made with Wuall to get a detachment sent, but I can at least bring my detail with us. It is not much, but it could help."

"What a surprise." Envir rolls his eyes and deftly scoops errant objects from the table into the bags and settles them over his shoulder.

"Did you already pack for me?"

"For us, actually. I did yesterday in case..." His gaze flicks between the table and me, the Priestess finally looking up and interested. "Just in case you wanted to get away for a while."

He means in case my father was found to have been killed by less than natural causes, but is unsure that this is the proper company for that revelation.

"How efficient." It takes effort to not raise an eyebrow at him. "Adean, we can make sure you get back safe with us. Jyn, can you escort Priestess Vintra back to the library?"

"That will not be necessary." The woman's voice is smoky and echoes around me in a viscous caress, lilting with a faint northern accent. I have never *felt* someone speak so viscerally before. "I will be joining you. There are some things in this book Lys should know, and I promised to see Adean safe."

I cannot think of a reasonable excuse for her to not come with us, despite my misgivings toward having another person to protect.

"As long as you are prepared to leave immediately, that is fine," I try one last attempt at preventing her travel with us.

"I am always prepared to be of service." She stands and pulls a white leather satchel from the back of her chair and slides the book into it before settling it across her chest. "Shall we?"

"We shall." Envir grins and shifts away from me as I make to take my own bag, dodging over to Jyn instead.

"Be safe, my Heart," Jyn says, tilting his head up for a kiss.

"Always."

Envir plants one last kiss on Jyn's forehead before leading our perplexing little party out into the hall.

—

"I am sorry for your loss, Your Highness."

We are outside the stables, waiting for my men to finish assembling and the horses to be saddled, when the Priestess' voice calls my attention back to the present and away from the forest village.

"Thank you. We were not close. But, thank you." I am not sure what possessed me to elaborate aside from not wanting her to think will be too distracted to be of any use.

For a long moment, she holds my gaze and then nods like she

somehow expected that response. Floating away in a waft of robes, she deftly swings onto the horse presented to her. Bonyar, a large, but docile, black stallion I favor along with several others. It surprises me that she seems so comfortable on a horse, although I do not know why. I know the Priestesses of Kiv come from many ways of life, but it still seems incongruous watching her steer the horse with a slight shifting of her knees instead of rein, white leggings tucked into white and gold leather boots, exposed by long slits in her robes.

I pace restlessly until Ealyn and a horse for the boy are ready. Unlike the priestess, he makes an awkward seat, but manages well enough. I take a moment to prepare myself before I hook my boot in the stirrup and haul myself onto the saddle.

Nose to kneecap, I am reminded of what I am wearing. Fitted black silk clings to me from neck down, broken only by rows of gold buttons fastening the high waist of the pants and the brocade waistcoat. Even the sword at my hip is more ornamental than functional, and I hope it at least holds an edge. My sleeves billow and settle around me as I sink onto Ealyn, too distracted by how absurd I look to pay much attention to the burning in my shoulder.

"For the love of Kiv, Vi, please tell me you packed me real clothes."

"Hmmm. Do you really want to know what I would think to bring for you?"

I groan in mock horror and nudge Ealyn into motion, nodding at the stamping mass of riders in the courtyard to follow. There are twelve of us in total, eight of my personal guard being all that I could amass on such short notice. I left word for the rest to come if they are able to get away. It is not what it should be, but I beg Kiv it is enough.

The city is quiet for midday.

The gray stone and wooden buildings that line the streets are already draped with black cloth in remembrance of my father. My complicated feelings aside, he was a well respected king, and the subdued citizenry is a testament to that. I cannot help but wish my grief was as straightforward and detached as it is for these people who only knew him as a monarch, and not a man. Not a father.

We ride without much attention being drawn to us, but I hide within the loose circle of the guard regardless, Envir at my side and the Priestess and the boy just ahead of us. We make an ungainly group for some of the narrower streets that become even tighter as we approach the western gate.

"And here! A perfect example of the corruption rotting in the halls of Kiv!"

Our horses stop abruptly at the edge of a gathered crowd, appearing from around a tight corner, two black clad and tattooed Davorist priests at the center.

"A Priestess of the *Order*," the priest sneers, "Taking advantage of *your* resources. Your city guard! For what cause? What justification? Because they creep into the beds of the council? Whisper their *wisdom* into the ear of the Queen? Where were their priests when the King was dying? What good are their physicians, their scholars, their privilege at the palace, if they could not prevent his death? Yet they still think they have more of a right to these streets, and the protection of your guards, than any of you!"

A golden orb of light rimmed with red dances into being above the man's palm, and he starts to casually toss it into the air. Such displays of blatant, spontaneous magic are unusual at best. I cannot imagine any of the citizens here would have had the opportunity to see it before now. The crowd gasps in awe at the show of the priest's power, as simple as it is.

"They claim Kiv is the saint of protection, yet still they cower. Davor promises his people the ability to let go of fear and protect themselves!"

Our priestess shifts her horse forward casually, almost lazily, before she speaks. If I thought her words held a strange, thick power before, her voice now shifts the very tide of my blood.

"You seem to misunderstand much in this life, Davorist rat, not least of which is my position here. These men are not here for *my* protection. I am here for *theirs*."

As if on cue in a stage production, the priest hurls the orb of light toward us, but the Priestess flicks her hand as if batting away a fly.

"Please," she scoffs.

The orb splashes against an invisible barrier, disappearing into a sheet of crackling red lightning. The priest's eyes widen, and he stumbles several steps back into the crowd, clearly not expecting resistance. Displays of Kivaran magic are even more rare than Davorist. The thought of a Kivaran priestess being able to retaliate was likely nowhere on his mind. The peace of recent years and the altruistic nature of the Order leads many to believe that the followers of Kiv are pacifists. It surprises me how easy it is for some people to forget the past.

The priestess leads Bonyar through the center of the sparking light before the edges have completely faded. The crowd parts before her as she casts her gaze across them.

"If you have time to listen to this vermin, you have time to join my brethren in the Library of Kiv and learn the true depth of his lies. Learn the truth of the trials suffered by people not of the nobility under Davor's rule. The taxes. The punishments. The conscriptions. The Tyrant had no Chosen. No people. No peers. He had pawns. He had fodder for the charnel house of war. The *people* rose with Kiv at their helm and put an end to his corruption. His power will remain ash as long as the Pyre of the Martyr burns in the hearts of those people. Will you be one of them? Will you remember what they fought against? What we still fight decade after decade?"

"Remind yourselves of the reality of the past before you believe the lies of the present. Davor did not care if his tools could protect themselves. He preached destruction and domination by virtue of his actions. His followers perpetuate the same evils, despite what sweetness may coat their tongues. I have not forgotten what the Cult of Davor truly is. I have not forgotten their attempts at the crown, the continent, and the freedom of the people."

"The flames of the Martyr's death burn hot in me, and I shall raze the land with my fury to ensure the Tyrant never again holds power here. Will you blaze beside me or be ash in my wake?"

The crowd that was so enthralled by the Davorists moments ago shout their allegiance to our priestess. The priests attempt to protest, but their words are cut short by a surge of people violently pushing them back, our path through the street suddenly clear of priests and citizens alike. The priestess quirks a tiny, pleased smile.

We ride in a stunned silence until well beyond the western gate.

Envir is the first to break the quiet with a long, low whistle.

"That was one hell of a show, Priestess."

She snorts, her sharp nose wrinkling.

"Party tricks. That little light may have tingled, but it would not have done real harm. Not all of the Davorist priests are charlatans, though. It would serve us all to be wary."

Envir frowns, hesitating before he speaks, "I had no idea the cultists could wield real magic. It's all sort of legend or little theatrics, sleight of hand. That sort of thing. I feel like this is something I should have known." He glances my way suspiciously, like I have been personally holding back the secrets of the cults from him.

He has never been one to pay attention to the teachings of Kiv or her followers. He has always been much more rooted in the tangible. A participant in more earthy pursuits like swords, tailoring, and Jyn.

"We have not needed to reveal what we can or cannot do for decades, centuries even. Power. Magic. They are not our cornerstones, and The Order works very hard to maintain that. However, the Davorist scum do not follow the same ideals. They thrive on grotesque exhibition of corruption and destruction. Thankfully their relics and their minds are weak, but there is always the chance that one may rise who could cause actual damage. So many of us have stopped being vigilant against this possibility, writing the Davorists off as harmless irritants, almost as completely as the Crown. I know the official stance is that the Davorists are a religious sect and therefore have the freedom to practice. This is a mistake. They are, and have always been, a threat to the peace of our nation and should be treated as such."

I nudge Ealyn faster to ride beside the priestess.

"I have been of the same opinion much of my life. Unfortunately, my family has yet to share my concerns. But these concerns drive me now. We should make haste."

The boy, Adean, has been sawing on his reins in impatience since the gate disappeared behind us. He is the first to drive his horse to a gallop at my words. The rest of us follow and we push the horses as much as we dare, varying our pace to allow the animals rest when we must. Conversation is limited while we ride, the low voice of the priestess occasionally drifting to me on the breeze during our slower moments. She tries to comfort the boy, easing the anxiety that rises in him any time we are not at a dead run.

—

By the time we slow our mounts for the final time, the ancient forest has been nothing but a spill of ink across a moonlit sky for hours, growing larger and more ominous as the moon chases us toward its embrace. Adean is the first to enter the blackness, and we follow single-file as he makes his way with more speed than I would normally consider prudent. Soon, the trees are too dense to let in even the faintest trickle of moonlight and we dismount, carefully feeling our way along the forest road.

The child abruptly disappears into a break in the trees to our right. I follow and am rewarded with a short tunnel ending in a dazzle of moonlight and a wide open glen filled with various livestock.

"We can leave the horses here and keep going. Could someone...?"

He is hopping from foot to foot and staring longingly at the tunnel.

"Leave it, we'll take care of it." I look for a place to tie Ealyn as I speak, and move my attention to my men. "Half of you stay with the horses, for now, and half of you come with us."

Relief fills me as the light of torches begins to guide our way to the village and the flitting shadow of Adean slips beneath the arch of trees that serves as a gate. The village threatens to take my breath away again, but I focus on the task at hand and jog toward the looping streets, alert for any danger. Envir is beside me, and he struggles to contain his amazement. His mouth gapes as we duck through the twisted opening in the enormous wall of trees.

"What *is* this place?" He is breathless and wide eyed. I am intimately aware of the feeling.

"I tried to tell you."

We continue after the scrambling boy as he pops in and out of view atop rises in the path.

"You have been here before?" I ask the priestess.

She does not stare around herself in awe, but deliberately moves along the living path, her brows furrowed.

"Lys and I have been friends for an age. I have been here many times over the years."

I sense the unease rising in her just as my own washes over me. The sound of many voices builds as we near the center. It is not the casual noise of a mundane crowd. Regardless, there should not be a crowd at this hour. Without a word, we both pick up our pace and top the last rise together, the village center spilling out before us in a wash of torchlight and more people than I thought possible.

Groups of villagers and piles of scattered belongings nearly fill the open space. I search for the woman, but cannot find her. I do spot Adean under the arm of an older man I assume to be his father, and I start down the swirling root ramp toward them, the priestess and Envir close behind me.

As I approach, he seems more and more familiar, but I do not recognize him until he speaks.

"Miss Carolyn. And Lys' nobleman." He nods at us and grips his son's shoulder in a tight squeeze.

"Where is she?" The priestess asks just as I inhale to say the same thing.

"Into the trees. Been gone a few hours. Inness was taken."

"By the grace of Kiv." The priestess shakes her head, reaching out to touch the man's shoulder. "Her poor father."

My thoughts boil.

"She is out there alone? How many of the cultists were there? Was anyone else sent? Which direction did she go?" The thought of her out in that confusion of trees, hunting armed men alone, laces my words with anger.

The man holds up a hand like he wants to hold me back at the same time the priestess rests her's on my arm.

"None of the men we sent came back. No point in sending more and more in after 'em. If our best hunters can't find the girl, Lys is the best we have."

"You did not have me, or my men, before. You do now." I will not let my mistake, my failings, my sister, kill this woman.

The priestess's fingers dig into my arm.

The crowd falls silent in a wave from the west. A rippling movement like a river parting for stone passes through its center.

I feel the loss of worlds when I see her.

Everything goes still within me as the scene plays out with such wretched slowness it cannot possibly be real. People swirl around her in small eddies, colliding with her and then dispersing like ocean spray.

She does not stop until the massive tree at the village center soars above her. The light of the fire behind her throws her gruesome, many limbed shadow into exaggerated relief against its bark. The body she clutches looks painfully fragile in her arms, illuminated by a sickly, greenish light.

The priestess and I move as one. The distance passes in a haze, my vision narrowing to the woman. Distantly, I hear a man crying out in an agony I refuse to understand. I push the thought of it aside before I can name what it is and become undone with the knowing. The priestess speaks using the same low tone she used with the boy earlier, but it makes no impression on the woman. She does not make a sound, but her entire body is wracked with heaving sobs so strong I fear she will physically break. She is drenched in tears and blood. They run in rivers from her eyes and in clotted streams from the child's back, the currents meeting at her heart.

The wailing man is close enough now to enter my field of vision, and the sight of him screaming and half carried by Adean's father slams me back into myself.

He reaches for the girl, his hands stretched out, and claws at the air between them. Lys flinches back and holds the body even more tightly.

The priestess's voice is still quiet, but it holds a hint of smoky command.

"Lys, you have to give her to her father."

Before the men can take the body, her knees give way and she begins to fall.

I sweep her into my arms, holding her much like she was cradling the girl. My injured side screams in protest, but I shut myself off to it. The crushing pressure of grief threatens to tear this woman apart, but I will not see her brought to her knees by the weight of it.

The body of the girl is slack and heavy in her father's arms. He falls to his knees in the dirt, but she does not touch the ground, bundled tightly in his shaking arms. His wailing has subsided to gasping sobs that curl his body around his daughter's in convulsive waves. The love of a father breaking over the ashen, lifeless form of his child threatens to drag me into depths I do not care to explore. I turn my back to them, and let the man's devastation haunt my retreat.

CHAPTER TWELVE

KEDREN

The priestess leads the way up the winding stairs to the apothecary, the heavy wooden door already thrown open to an ominous darkness. Glass crunches under her boots as she steps into the room, and I wince at the sound. She presses one hand to her heart and throws the other out, releasing a spray of golden lights into the air above us.

The room has been eviscerated.

Glass is shattered everywhere. Liquids soak into the floorboards, and dried herbs are ground into dust at my feet. The mantle above the wall-sized fireplace has been swept clear, the proudly displayed collection thrown across the room. I shift my grip on the woman to be sure she does not see the carnage of her home, holding her close to my chest. She curls into me in response, her fists tangled in the lace of my ridiculous shirt, burying her face into the folds. I never thought I would be grateful for Envir's wardrobe choice, but, right now, it is a blessing.

I wade as carefully as I can through the debris and make my way to the hidden stairs at the back of the shop. My heart is in my throat with the hope that they went unnoticed. The priestess follows behind, her floating lights illuminating the destruction in glittering flashes. The ruination is so intense, I cannot reconcile it with the room I was in four days ago. Just as I cannot reconcile the woman in my arms with the one who was leaning against the counter with a glint of something invitingly wicked in her eye.

The floor behind the shelves is clear, and I breathe a sigh of relief. I shift her again, ignoring the pain radiating from my chest and down my arm, and continue up the spiral stairs, taking care to shield her from the walls. I hesitate at the first landing, imagining the bed I slept in and how easily it would hold the two of us before I shake the hair out of my eyes and continue upward.

The room that unfolds at the top of the stairs steals what little breath I have remaining as I stagger into the vaulted space. My gaze sweeps across the room as I turn, involuntarily, to take it all in. A wall of glass set into twisting branches and carved wood displays the village through organic windows. Whimsical, wooden furniture litters the space. The rounded edge of a large metal tub gleams in the golden light from behind a carved screen. Before I can complete a full circle, the priestess brushes past me, reminding me of my purpose and leads me to the bed taking up an immense portion of the space. Massive and created by a mixture of carved and natural curves of wood, the bed is tucked into an alcove built into the tree itself. The walls, golden and smooth with age, are carved in several different styles from fanciful swirls to detailed murals. The priestess's lights cast deep shadows around us.

When I try to lay Lys down, she clings to me, and I look to the priestess helplessly. I do not want to let her go, but this is not my place. She needs to be held together by someone who actually knows the shape of her, not some stranger dreaming of the pieces he could learn in a day.

"It will be alright, Alyssia. I will not let go. I am here." The priestess weaves her fingers beneath the grip *Alyssia* has on my clothing, prying her away gently. It is enough for me to set her down and step back, making room for the other woman to sit on the bed.

"Do you need anything?" Breaking the silence feels wrong, but so does leaving without a word.

Alyssia still takes shuddering breaths, but she has no tears left to shed. There are leaves in her hair again, but tonight they make her look lost. Hunted. None of the mischievous Otherfolk aura from the day I met her surrounds her now. I want to brush them away, smooth her hair back from her face. It is an effort to keep my hands at my side.

"We will have everything we need. Thank you, Your Highness." The priestess's eyes flash, reflecting the lights still dancing around us. "Truly. Thank you."

I bite my tongue before I say that I was the cause of this. That I could have stopped it if I would have taken action on my own, or insisted the guard be deployed immediately. If I had found out about the cult's interest in this place earlier. None of that matters now. The damage has been done regardless of the reason, and my guilt will not bring the child back. I bow my head and retreat instead.

I do not linger, even though I want to, if only to take in the wild room, cluttered with so many things I would not even know where to start looking. It does not surprise me that they will have everything they need here. I let it wash over me in a wave of woodland chaos as I disappear down the stairs and reenter reality.

With each step I take, the urgency of things left undone builds, and I start to take the stairs two at a time. My head is swimming with exhaustion and pain and overlapping images of Alyssia laughing at her dining table and clutching the body of a child to her chest like it was the only thing keeping her in one piece. I have to find Envir, my men, the murderous cultists, and the old man from the fireplace. With my hands free again, I scrub vigorously at my hair, trying to find some order to my thoughts and come up short. Envir first then. I can always count on him to make sense of me.

I make sure to add cleaning the shop to the list of things rolling around in my head as I shuffle through the dark room and toward the warm light sneaking in through the open door. Envir first. Go from there.

It does not take long for me to find him. The crowd is much smaller now, only a handful of people still sort through belongings on the ground. More has been taken than care of than should be possible, but with Envir's direction and an entire village working together, I should not be surprised. He is standing with Adean's father and my guards, the lot of them gesturing and nodding at intervals. Envir notices me first and jerks his head in invitation.

"Please tell me you have already made a plan," I try to sound less tired than I am, but I do not think I succeed.

"Of course I have. Some of us have to work for a living around here." He winks at me. "Belar here is going to set up most of our guards with a few men who know the woods to go check on the other villages. Two of our men will stay here and three at each of the others. Hopefully the rest of the unit will be able to free themselves of your sister's control so we can increase defenses a little more," he pauses to yawn dramatically, causing the rest of us to join him. "We are going to stay here and help put things to rights as much as we can until Alyssia or Carolyn can point us in a more specific direction. But we aren't going to do anyone any good if we are all falling asleep standing, so it's time to settle down for a minute or two at least."

Belar nods toward Envir and grunts in approval, but the way he looks at me, with one skeptical eyebrow raised, I know my identity has been discussed. I stop myself from shifting uncomfortably under the increased scrutiny. He turns, but pauses to look at me again, tree-bark brown eyes boring into me.

"Thank you, Your Highness."

I flinch at the title, but take a more formal posture before responding.

"Of course. The Crown has a duty to protect its citizens, whether either party considers themselves beholden to the other or not."

Belar shakes his head.

"That's all well and good, but not what I meant. Inness meant everything to Lys. She's likely to need as many hands catching her as we can find."

He walks away before I can begin to respond, and Envir leads me the other way, our men scattering behind us.

Envir leans in, wrapping his arm around me. "The villagers volunteered to house the men for however long they are here. You are going to go back to Alyssia's to wait for me. Belar said she should have enough space for all of us. I am going to get our things and show the rest of the men where they're staying."

I try to protest, but as we stand at the base of her stairs with dawn light beginning to tint the air, I know that if I have to drag myself through the village two more times, I will fall on my face. I sigh and drag myself up the steps. When I make it through the door, I realize I have to wait for Envir to show him the way upstairs, so I right the fallen the wooden chair I sat in less than a week ago and stare into the cold fireplace, trying to ignore the disaster around me and struggling to figure out why I keep thinking there is an old man I need to find.

Envir's touch to my shoulder wakes me with a jolt, taking me from another dream of the man-faced spider.

His voice is soft as he guides me up by my elbow, "Have you slept since your father died?"

"Some," I yawn widely. "There has just been so much noise up here."

I tap two fingers to my temple. "It has been hard to find enough quiet. But it has barely been two days."

He snorts his disapproval as I lead him up the stairs.

"Who would have thought a place like this existed right under our noses, eh?"

"Not me. Until we set eyes on it tonight, I had almost convinced myself I made the entire place up."

The door to the room I stayed in is slightly ajar. I push my way inside, breathing in the earthy scent of it. I can hear Envir do the same and mutter something under his breath. I feel a heavy ache as I look around, realizing that the pile of clothes outlined in shadow on the bed must have belonged to the girl. I had forgotten that I met her, however briefly, until I saw her face again. Slack in death, it held none of the vibrancy she radiated while begging Alyssia to let her help me. She was so excited.

I gather the clothing and lay it gently on the back of the chair, where it was the first time I slept here. Envir closes the door behind us and we both unceremoniously strip to nothing, preferring nakedness to travel, and in my case, bloodstained clothes. He helps without comment whenever I struggle in my one-handed attempt, and we collapse onto the bed, sleep taking Envir almost immediately. My mind cannot rest, however, trying to sharpen the memory I have of the girl. I hope, in my tired delusion, that maybe if I can bring her further into focus, full of energy and laughing with Alyssia, I can change the reality of the blood-soaked vision I left behind in the square.

CHAPTER THIRTEEN
KEDREN

I have no sense of time, or my place in it, when I wake. Even with the shutters thrown wide, the light in the room is greenish and indistinct. How anyone in this village knows what time it is without clocks is beyond me. The bed next to me is empty aside from a tiny scrap of paper with a single word written in Envir's scrawl, the only thing messy about him.

Exploring.

There are no sounds coming from the next room, and I sigh, laying still. I did not realize how badly I wanted to hear them again. Waking up in the palace is not a warm and personal affair, unless Envir and Jyn found themselves too drunk to make it down the hall to their own rooms. Even then, it is only a personal affair for them. I had never woken up to sounds of *home* like I did here.

Chill spring air wafts through the open windows, causing the hair across my body to raise in a ripple of gooseflesh, reminding me that I am naked in a stranger's home. The wound on my chest both throbs and itches beneath its bandages. Pain is always the worst in the morning, and carrying Alyssia last night did not help.

I begin to ground myself, a technique I have perfected over long years to separate my mind from my body. I breathe the scent of trees, earth, and spring. I see the green light, dark wood, and rough stone fireplace. I hear the voices in the distance, birdsong, the leaves in the wind. I touch the soft knit of the bedclothes beneath me.

I repeat my cataloging until enough of the pain is in the background to dress myself. Envir actually brought sensible clothing for me, which I am both grateful for and surprised by. The black silk is neatly folded in a pile in the corner, covered in salty tear stains and flaking, dried blood. He is likely unhappy about that turn of events, but I cannot say I am heartbroken. Without a mirror, and with only one truly functional arm, my hair will be what it is.

I expect the main room to be empty when I finally exit my safe haven, but the priestess sits at the table, frowning into a steaming wooden cup she rolls between her hands.

I have no idea what to say. Even without accounting for the the shadows under her eyes, or the pinched crease of her sharp brows, regardless of what time of day it is, the prefix of 'good' cannot describe it.

"Did she sleep?"

"She is now. With the amount of sleeping draft I just made her drink, I hope she will be that way until tomorrow." She shrugs one white-clad shoulder, still fidgeting with the mug. "The downstairs is a mess, but I have not been able to make myself start cleaning. I am not sure I even know where to begin."

She sounds as tired as I was yesterday.

"Have *you* slept?"

She flashes a small, sharp smile.

"Enough for now. It is already late in the day. I will sleep tonight."

I nod, understanding the need to be doing something.

"I was going to head downstairs, myself, if you wanted to join me. You will probably know more about anything we can save than I would."

She takes a long drag from the cup in her hands before she stands.

"I am not even certain she has a broom, but we will see what we can find."

When we arrive downstairs, the first thing the priestess does is sprinkle the twisting ceiling with her golden lights so we can see what we are working with.

"I might almost prefer the dark for this." I quirk my mouth into a smile, and I am rewarded with a short laugh.

"I think I would as well." A few of the lights flicker out as she winks at me. "A compromise."

Alyssia does, in fact, have a broom tucked into the back corner behind the shelves hiding the stairs. Cobwebs stretch to breaking when the priestess pulls it free.

"She has dried plants hanging from her rafters by the field full and still has not touched this broom in an age. I swear."

I shrug, sifting through the wreckage, careful to not cut my hands in the process, and search for any intact glassware before the priestess starts sweeping up the shards. "Adds to the atmosphere?"

That gets a genuine laugh. The sound of it is heady and low.

"She would absolutely say that."

Tension eased, we work in companionable silence, pausing frequently to stare in exasperation. I am replacing the miraculously intact skeleton of some sort of large rodent on the mantle when I am reminded of the old man by the fireplace again. I turn to the priestess, who is pouring bits of broken glass into a barrel to be melted down.

"This is not going to make any sense, but is there supposed to be a man on, or around, this fireplace?" The sentence is not completely out of my mouth before I wish I had not said it.

Silence and an odd stare are all I get back until the priestess drops the broom with a clatter.

"Artemicles!" She spins around so quickly, her hair fans out around her in a dark halo.

At least I am not as completely out of my mind as I thought.

"What are we actually looking for? Because my two options are a man watching me from the fire or a very large spider with a man's face. I cannot imagine either of those options even border reality."

That stops her frantic searching for a moment so she can look me over warily.

"What in the world did she give you?"

"I am not sure. It was a sticky, dark red substance that she spread over the wound."

A small smirk tweaks the corner of her mouth. "Ah."

Apparently this is all the explanation she needs, because she turns back to her search, crawling on hands and knees across the mostly swept floor, looking under tables and shelves, several of her lights dancing around her.

"Widow resin," she elaborates belatedly. "It is a very rare plant. Quite expensive to use in its pure form like that. Also rather hallucinogenic."

I firmly avoid examining the fact that Alyssia knowingly drugged me without telling me. At least it explains a few things.

When she stands, the priestess brushes off her knees, even though I do not see a fleck of crushed herb or dust.

"What we are looking for is a large glass jar-"

"The pickled eyes!" I wheel away from the skeleton I am arranging. "There was a jar of pickled eyeballs looking at me from the shelf. She said they were Arty's." For the briefest of moments, I think I may prefer the man-spider of my hallucinations.

"Yes, and we must find him before Lys sees this. It will already be too much. She can't lose him as well."

"Find who?"

Both the priestess and I snap our heads to the doorway where Envir is casually leaning, looking immaculate with his auburn hair pulled back into a perfect low knot. His tailored shirt and trousers are nearly identical to mine, but look somehow *more* on him. He wears his sword comfortably at his hip and has a bag slung over his shoulder. He is also holding a large, clear jar aloft, swirling it slowly so the puckered orbs inside bob around lazily.

"Arty!" The priestess snatches the jar from Envir's hand in both of hers and settles it onto the mantle in a spot clearly made for it, or rather, around it. Several large mounds of melted wax, too adhered to the wood to be removed in the ransacking, hug the jar perfectly.

"Where was that?" Unease creeps down my spine whenever one of the milky pupils floats in my direction, and yet I find it very difficult to look away.

"Outside on a bush. Whoever took him must have thought better of it and left him behind. I don't blame them. He feels rather judgmental." Envir shudders and removes himself from the doorway, closing it behind him. He gives the room a sweeping glance, nodding in satisfaction at the small collections we have made. It looks so bare compared to what it did days ago.

"You both did well. Managed it without me and everything."

"Speaking of that, where have you been?"

"Didn't you get my note? I was exploring. "

"Try not to be such an ass, Vi."

"Oh come now. Carolyn, am I being an ass?"

Her response is quick, her voice roiling with laughter just underneath.

S.C. Wolf

"Usually."

"Do the two of you know each other?" The casualness between Envir and the priestess piqued my interest, but I have been too preoccupied to ask about it until now.

"I believe we know quite a bit *about* each other, but no, we do not personally know each other. Jyn frequents the Library but struggles to instill the same academic interest in Envir." She smiles with surprising wickedness while pointlessly straightening objects around her. "Jyn is a delightful man, and we have spent much time in conversation about many things." Her gaze lingers over both of us in turn.

Envir and I laugh, knowing she must have heard plenty of Jyn's grievances about the two of us. Which, I am sure, is a long and valid list.

"Well, we have plenty to discuss that *isn't* a detailed list of my failings from my partner. Shall we?" Envir gestures to the stairs behind us and lays a hand over the priestess'. He guides her away from her futile attempt to make any more order in this chaos. With the other hand he raises his bag. "I brought dinner, as well. I have a strong feeling neither of you thought to feed yourselves."

We had not, and therefore settle into his portable feast gratefully once upstairs and seated around the table.

"Carolyn," Envir pauses for a moment to lick the buttery residue of a pastry off of his fingers, "We need to know about why the Davorists are suddenly so interested in this place."

The priestess sighs and runs one manicured finger along the rim of her wine cup.

"From how you reacted yesterday, I am going to assume neither of you know that much about how our magic works and therefore why they would be looking for anything to begin with."

Envir shakes his head, but I have paid more attention to learning than he has.

"You need relics, correct? Something to channel your faith?"

She nods, surprised.

"Mostly correct. The relics themselves hold power that our faith allows us to manipulate as long as we work within the purpose of its magic. The Order has many relics of varying potencies, depending on their relevance to Kiv. We were able to publicly gather the objects graced by her blessings more easily than the Davorists could at the time of the Fall. I have read that the Kivarans went on a mission to hide or destroy as many Davorist relics as they could."

"That brings us to this forest. When Adean told us the priests were looking for jewelry, it sparked a memory in me. Jyn and I discussed it and confirmed our suspicions in the book he found. Davor is often depicted with several very distinct objects: a crown, a ring, and a pendant. I would need to know more about them, but the consistency in which they are depicted could mean these relics hold significant power; similar to what the Sword of the Martyr could hold for a priest of Kiv if what I suspect is true. If these are, indeed, the relics they are looking for and they have come across information saying one, or all of them, were hidden here, we must find them first."

"That sounds ominous." Envir drains his wine in a long swallow and immediately begins pouring another cup.

"It is. Should these relics be as potent as suggested and they have a priest who can wield them, the Order would struggle to stop them from carrying out whatever desolation they desire. It has been over one thousand years since the Great War, and our nation has still not recovered to where it was before those battles. Cities crumbled to dust in the wake of the power they wielded. Entire towns were razed in an instant. Even with all of the relics we have, we would still have little defense against the power these could hold. I am not sure we could withstand a single one as we are now. The only relic we have to compare to them, theoretically, is the Sword, and it has been lost for centuries."

Envir hisses a breath out through his teeth, and my palms begin to sweat uncomfortably.

"So we will find the relics before they do. That is our only option." At least I sound calm, maybe even confident.

We still fall silent with the knowledge of what must be done and the ability to achieve it so unthinkably out of our grasp. How are we supposed to find a single piece of jewelry in a forest so large and willfully difficult to traverse, let alone three?

"Is there anything else you can remember, Carolyn? Anywhere we could start?" Envir sounds as desperate as I feel.

She sighs and lifts a shoulder.

"I know this place used to be a kingdom of its own during the time of Kiv and Davor. According to an ancient map, the capital was to the south around a lake. That could be somewhere to start, but I do not know if it means anything in this situation."

My hand goes through my hair again, pushing the loose strands away from my face. It is dark outside of our pocket of golden lights, and the priestess looks as though she is about to lay down on the table.

"That sounds like our best choice, given the circumstances. We can make our plan tomorrow." I have not been awake for long today, but I am so tired. My chest aches, and I look forward to throwing myself into the bed waiting for me.

"They are burying the girl tomorrow," Envir's voice is barely a whisper. He finishes his wine as he stands and disappears into the side room without another word.

The priestess's gaze flicks to the ceiling, and I wonder if we feel the same sharp pull to the woman sleeping there.

"Be with her. Sleep. We will deal with the rest tomorrow," I say to her, softly.

She vanishes in a swirl of golden lights and gleaming robes, leaving me alone in the dark to mull over what new disasters tomorrow will bring.

CHAPTER FOURTEEN

KEDREN

Belar finds Envir and me in the shop a little after mid-morning as we helplessly try to restore it however we can. The women have been gone since before either of us were awake, leaving us a note in a neat, precise hand, instructing us to not wear black, and that someone would come for us when it was time. Apparently it is time.

He practically fills the doorway with his bulk, and I wonder if he is the town's blacksmith, in addition to gate guard. It seems like the only reasonable profession for someone of his dimensions.

"Shame, this." He nods at the scene around us. "But you've done good. Good to see Arty's still with us."

Envir and I both cast uneasy smiles towards the mantle, and I look around the rest of the room, feeling a sharp pang as I do.

"There was only so much we could save, but we tried."

"Mmhm. Come on. They'll be starting soon." He beckons to us, waving green ribbons in his hand as he does so.

We start toward the door, expecting to follow him outside, but he does not move. He lifts his right elbow to indicate his own green ribbon tied in a knot around his bicep. We offer our arms to him, the green vibrant against the soft ivory of our shirts.

"Right then. Let's go."

Belar takes us north along an unusually straight path, several others bearing green arm bands joining us as we make our way through the residences and into the forest proper. The sun filters down through the dense canopy in shafts of reflected, golden-green light and dances around us like the priestess' magic. I wish I would have found this place sooner and had time to learn its ways, its secrets, like I have in other towns around the kingdom. Not like this; shrouded in death and fear.

Sunlight blinds me as we walk into a wide, open clearing. It is a lush, rolling meadow of green grass painted with swathes of small white wildflowers, its edges blurred into soft shadows created by the surrounding forest. The sense of peace here settles over me like an embrace. Like the sounds of the waves crashing against the cliff walls outside my childhood window. Like a long awaited invitation to finally rest.

The small, bell-like blooms of the flowers are enchanting and perfume the air with their sweet, floral scent as we wind our way to the gathered crowd at the edge of the shadowy border of trees. A small grave has been carved from the ground, the soil dark and heavy in a looming mound next to it.

The girl's father is standing in the grave, eyes red and heavily shadowed, but he does not weep. Alyssia and the girl are nowhere to be seen, but I spot the blue-black hair of the priestess glinting in the sun and steer us in her direction. It is quiet, even the creatures of the woods silent. I am uneasy in the intimacy of the moment, a stranger intruding into something incredibly private.

This is nothing like the funeral I will be attending for my father. The whole city will be involved in some way, and it will be lavish and dramatic with a procession more like a parade. A display of wealth and privilege ending in entombment within stone and gold. There is no theater in this moment, no pageantry, only a genuine sense of loss. A community coming together in a field of white.

A soft hum wafts across the grass from the trees, and all heads turn as one at the sound. Alyssia emerges from beneath the shadows, light playing across her in a mosaic of gold and green, until she steps into a bath of yellow sunlight. Inness is cradled in her arms again, but she is held with gentleness, the bloodied desperation of two nights ago softened into tenderness.

Her body is clothed in a gray dress the color of stone. There is green embroidery at neck and hem that reflects the midday sun in the same bright shade as the crown of woven leaves in her dark hair. Alyssia is dressed as she always is, aside from her hair falling loose in a cascade of deep gold down her back and the green ribbon around her arm. She does not cry. Her mouth and eyes are set in unsteady determination.

She stops at the edge of the grave, facing the crowd. Turning her gaze to the sky, she closes her eyes against the sun and breathes deeply. When she opens them again, they settle on the man below her.

When she speaks, her voice is soft, but clear, and resonates in the quiet of the clearing.

"I, Alyssia,"

"And I, Jiath."

"Return Inness to the embrace of the earth from which she came."

"To the mountains of the North."

"And to the Woods of the West."

"So she may tend the fire of the Mountain."

"And be one with the Trees."

Alyssia kneels and kisses Inness' forehead before she hands her to her father.

"May she be at peace and be one with the protection of this land. May she rest forever in the embrace of the forest she loved with her life." Her fingers linger on the girl's cheek as she speaks with quiet clarity.

"Rest, my girl, and find your mother safely."

Jiath also kisses his daughter's cheeks and forehead before he lays her into the soft, dark earth, arranging her into a pose clutching a sprig of the bell flowers in her small fists. With one last touch to her hair, he turns and grasps Alyssia's outstretched hand to pull himself out of the grave.

Each of them takes a spade from the mound of upturned earth in a white knuckled grip, to my shock, and begin shoveling dirt methodically. One by one, the people of the village around us approach the grave, but not to offer to take over the macabre work. They each drop a stem of flowers onto the slowly vanishing girl, turning without a word to depart from the clearing. I would never expect the bereaved to complete this dark task on their own, but no one here bats an eye.

Not much time has passed before Belar, Adean, the priestess, Envir and I are the only people remaining, holding vigil in the midday sun as the two make surprisingly quick work of the mound. When Alyssia pauses, brushing hair and sweat away from her face, Belar and Adean go to her, their flowers joining the others, I think they will finally offer to take over the work, but Belar simply pulls Alyssia and Jiath into one-armed hugs. Adean throws his arms around the woman, and then offers his hand solemnly to the man before turning and disappearing after his father.

More time passes and the priestess and Envir share a glance and a nod, each reaching down to pluck a stem of flowers to place into the rapidly filling pit. Envir looks to me, but I shake my head and the priestess nods, encouraging my choice to stay. Someone should be here when the task is finished. Someone should witness the work they have done.

Neither of them acknowledge my presence, and I do not interrupt. Instead I settle into the grass and gather handfuls of the flowers around me, braiding them into a small wreath. The sounds of nature begin to trickle back into the clearing as I wait. The songs of birds and buzz of insects weave around the soft, shuffling sound of spades in dirt.

Together, they set aside the tools when the earth has been returned to where it belongs, a dark rise of fresh soil now the only evidence of their loss. I look down at the circlet of flowers in my hands as the two clutch each other, the murmur of their voices too low for me to hear even if I wanted to.

The shuffle of boots retreat into the tall grass, and I look up to see Alyssia alone at the graveside, staring into the ground like she can see through it to the girl below. I stand and walk to her side, laying my wreath at the head of the freshly turned earth. When I straighten, I turn to her, unsure of what to say or do. Her gaze is heavy when I meet it, the blue of her eyes so vibrant surrounded by the raw red of too many tears. I think she is about to reach for me, but abruptly turns away and heads toward the path to the village.

She calls over her shoulder to me, "The others will be waiting for us back at my place. We need to get going."

"They can wait a while longer if you need more time," I raise my voice and jog to catch up, her strides taking her quickly across the glen.

When she passes into the shade of the trees, she stops and turns sharply, her loose hair whipping around her.

"The last thing I need is more time out there." She flings her hand in the direction we came from. Her voice simmers with anger and frustration.

I step close with the desire to do something, anything, to relieve some of her despair. Before I decide what to do, her arms are around me. She pulls me close. Her fingers grasp at my hair, my back, my ass. Her mouth violently seeks mine. I jerk my head to the side in surprise as her lips brush across my cheek.

"Alyssia."

Saying her full name aloud for the first time tears something inside of me. I want to speak it again and again against her cheeks, her lips, her neck. I push away from her gently to see her face tilted toward mine, tears threatening to fall from her blazing, blue-white eyes.

"I cannot do this. Not like this." I hate the words, but I have to say them.

Her hold on me tightens. Her voice drops to quiet pleading, "I just put the closest thing I will ever have to a daughter under the earth, and it was my fault. It was *my* fault. I want to forget. *Please.* Please make me forget for even a blink. A breath. I can't feel this anymore. You want to, you can't deny it. Please."

Kiv, how I want to. I am hard and ready where she presses against me. She shifts her hips in response to it. I want to tear the clothes from her. I want to twist my fingers in her golden hair and pull until I expose the flushed skin of her neck. I long to find the pulse in her throat and trace it with my lips until I reach her heart. Instead, I draw her closer to me, my mouth at her ear.

"I desire nothing more than to make you forget your tethers to this world. To forget that you exist beyond what I can make you feel." My voice is hoarse, a rough whisper against her cheek. Her breath is hot and fast on my neck. I fight the moan rising in my throat. A deep breath. Two. On the third I am able to speak again, my words as gentle as I can make them. "But not like this. I cannot make you forget this. I cannot take this sorrow from you."

Her hands fall away and she steps back, the space between us feeling like leagues. Leagues that I stretch myself across, reaching to brush strands of tear and sweat soaked hair from her cheeks. I hold my breath, desperate to see some hint that I did not just destroy any hope for this. She flinches back from my touch and rips my heart away with her.

"You're right." She sniffs loudly, scrubbing at her face with both hands. "You're right. I'm sorry, Your Highness. I'm not..."

"Please, do not apologize to me. Not about this. Not when I should be the one begging for your forgiveness."

"I think there is plenty of guilt to go around for the both of us." Her words have an edge that bites into me so deeply I wince.

We walk in silence after that, her several steps ahead of me, until I cannot stand it any longer and must speak. She seems steps away from vanishing into the shadows, and I need to keep her with me.

"I apologize for not being able to stop this."

A long silence stretches between us. How did I think she would respond? With forgiveness? Condemnation?

"And I'm sorry about your father. I heard about it before Adean came. If I had come to you sooner, I may have been able to help."

That is none of the answers I was expecting, but I hurry to reply, to engage her. "I do not think it could have been helped. There were no signs. No warnings. No reason to think there would be anything wrong."

Alyssia shakes her head, but does not say anything else, running her fingers along bark and greenery as we walk. The light plays over her in mottled shadow, rippling over her dirt stained clothes and throwing her features into dramatic chiaroscuro. She looks just like a painting of the Otherfolk we have hanging in the palace.

Another agonizing silence descends before she speaks again, her voice clinical. "How is your chest? You shouldn't have carried me last night."

Gingerly, I raise my left arm about a quarter of the way and move it back and forth, my right hand rising to cover the incision reflexively.

"It has been worse. Yesterday was uncomfortable, but," I look away from her and toward the village, "I would not change what I did."

Our arrival at the steps to her shop saves me from any further embarrassment when she takes them two at a time. She flees with a silence that speaks volumes.

CHAPTER FIFTEEN

ALYSSIA

I sigh, already tired of the argument before it starts.

"I'm not going to let those assholes destroy this place just to find something that can destroy everything else."

"I cannot ask you to come with us, we simply need directions."

The prince's argument is quiet while he stares very pointedly at the table. I want to scream at him to look at me instead of trying to dismiss me. Again.

"You aren't asking me to go with you, and I'm not asking for anyone's permission. This is a problem that could affect everyone, so if you insist on doing something about it, then we may as well go together." My tongue is a whetstone, sharpening my words.

"It is too dangerous," he bites back, still staring at his hands.

"It's too dangerous to stay here! It will be too dangerous everywhere if Carolyn is right and they get a hold of whatever they're looking for. I told you, I will protect the Woods. I will *not* rely on anyone else to do that. Not again." He has to feel the daggers I stare into him, my gaze just as cutting as my words.

At least that shut the prince up, however temporarily.

The image of Inness' dark eyes glittering in green fire rises in my mind like the tide. Those same eyes closed and ashen and collecting dirt. She is with the Woods now. I won't fail to protect her again.

I will not.

"We need to be back in the city for the King's funeral in two weeks." The prince's friend, Envir, tries a peace offering after a tense silence. "I don't think it will be wise to draw attention to the situation and our involvement by not being present. It also gives us a timeline to re-evaluate our plan if we need to."

"Is there a reason you can't call out the guard now? The cult has killed. We have proof. Witnesses." I know I can't trust anyone else to fix this, but it would go a long way to have actual soldiers combing the Woods for the Davorists while I look for the relic.

"That's...." Envir pauses and glances at the prince who sighs and takes over reluctantly.

"Complicated. I have reason to believe the princess is involved with the Davorists. With all of it. Which means, aside from my personal guard, I would not trust any man sent here. If she dispatches soldiers, it would be to help the cult, not hunt them."

I raise one eyebrow. "Everyone knows the princess isn't exactly tolerable, but that seems extreme, even for her."

"Please, trust me when I say it is not."

The prince twists his hands together on the tabletop, and I roll my eyes. If he wants to keep his distance and secrets about this, that's his prerogative. It's my responsibility to protect my home. He doesn't owe me anything.

"Fine. It's up to us then. There's no point in waiting around here if you have to be back to the city. It will take at least four days on foot to get to the lake. Another four to make it back to the village to see if any more of your men show up. Then a day to the capital. We should leave tomorrow morning. And no, it's not worth it to bring any horses with us, it isn't easy to get to where we're going with them."

I suddenly feel like I can't keep still, or breathe, or exist inside my body. Making plans like nothing happened? I feel like I'm going mad.

I close my eyes to steady myself, but the instant I do I see dirt and skin and a crown of willow branches and my lids fly open again. I shove myself away from the table and stand, turning toward my pantry, trying to find something for my hands to do.

"If either of you can use a bow, you can go to Belar for one and whatever else he thinks we may need. Tell him where we're going. Carolyn and I can stay here and go through what I have that could be useful."

I rummage through cheeses and cured sausages, plucking root vegetables out of piles I should have gone through ages ago. Too bad my pantry wasn't worth the scrutiny of power-hungry zealots. It could have used the cleaning.

"Feel free to take your time about it." I can't be bothered to be even mildly polite at this point. I want to feel bad about it, but I don't.

I hear the scraping of chairs on wood and, very deliberately, don't turn around.

"We'll take care of whatever we can and be ready to go in the morning," Envir says, followed by a suspiciously long pause before two sets of feet clatter down the stairs.

Carolyn presses two fingers to my cheek and turns my head to face her.

"It is not any of your fault. None of you." Her voice is dusky, the one she uses when lecturing or being particularly priestess-like. I try to move my head away, but she raises her other hand to hold me firm. "Not this time, Alyssia. I need you to listen to me, not run. If we are leaving tomorrow, then you need to hear these words before we go. Even if you cannot truly believe them."

I admit defeat and stop trying to pull my face away from her. She lightly brushes her thumb across my cheek and lips before going to the fire to start tea. Still lecturing, of course.

"This was not your fault. You left here to help. You could not have known they would come back when they did. You got back as soon as you could, and you went out after her immediately."

I bury myself into the sofa full of pillows and hug one of them to my chest. I feel the distinct need to protect myself from both her words and my own empty heart.

"I could have saved her, Carolyn. You weren't there. I knew where they were, but I waited. I waited for her to come to me instead of going to her," I choke on the words, but I don't sob. "She was a *child*. I was supposed to be the adult. I was supposed to save her." My face is so buried in the pillow I'm not sure if she even heard me.

Mute moments pass. I try to breathe evenly through the fabric pressing against my mouth, and Carolyn fusses with a teapot. By the time I'm ready to emerge from my makeshift hiding spot, she is standing over me, two steaming ceramic cups of tea in her hands. Handing one to me, she folds herself onto the opposite side of the sofa, tucking the ends of her pristine, white robe around her feet and settles a pillow on her lap to rest her cup on.

"How many village men went after her?" Her voice is the gentle one again, not the one that makes me think of incense. She doesn't let me respond though. "Five men. Hunters. Trackers. Excellent Woodsmen. None of them came back. None of them have been *found*. Why do you think *you* would have been able to get the two of you out of that situation?" She puts her cup to her lips, allowing me to answer this time.

"I didn't need to get the two of us out of there. I just needed to get her out. I know the Woods better than she does. Did. I could have done anything other than stand there being a coward."

"And then you would both be dead, and where would that leave the rest of us? Where would that leave me or Kyla or Rend? Where would that leave Envir and His Highness with their mission to find the Davorist relics with no one to guide them through your Woods?"

I catch myself biting the edge of my cup and force myself to take a sip before responding. My voice is so quiet, I feel my words more than hear them.

"You can't know we would both be dead. You don't *know* there was nothing I could do."

"Did you even have a weapon when you found her? They had at least a dozen armed men, at least one with spelled arrows. Who knows if any of them could use any of Davor's *other* gifts. I can make an educated guess as to how that would have played out. Do not start with me about the magic. I cannot be sure what they are and are not capable of right now, but I have some idea of how bad it can be. I know what I am capable of, and I am no longer naive enough to believe no one on the other side could match me."

I don't know what to believe about the cults and their magic anymore. I never gave it much credit beyond parlor tricks, but now I'm not so sure. I trust Carolyn. If she thinks they could be dangerous, then I can't say they're not.

"I know I cannot convince you in a day to believe me, but try to remember what I said when you get lost in blaming yourself." She nudges my foot with hers until I look up at her. "Promise me you will at least try."

I nod and speak to my tea, "I promise."

"And try not to be too terribly hard on the prince. From what I have gathered from Jyn, he really does not have much say in official matters. I do not know what was said in the clearing after we left, but I truly believe he is trying to help."

I groan and bury my face in the pillow again, trying to lock away the memories that come flooding back in a jumbled rush. Dirt. Slack, cold skin. Fierce heat. Tears. A wreath of white flowers. The rush as his words fill me with something I haven't felt in a very long time. The never ending emptiness that swallows me anyway.

"I don't blame him for anything. It had nothing to do with what happened with the cultists. But I'm begging you, Carolyn, not today. I can't talk about today yet."

Despite my unwillingness to cry anymore, tears begin to drip down my cheeks. I fold into myself like a bug and weep. I don't know what trick I've been pulling to let me talk about the night she died and make plans about what to do next, but it doesn't seem to extend to the memory of physically putting her into the ground. Carolyn has me pulled against her, stroking my hair as I babble through tears, my words catching on sharp sobs.

"She never got to see her dress. She would have loved it, and she never got to see it, and now it's covered in dirt, and I tried so hard to not get it in her eyes but I had to. We had to. And it isn't fair. She's too little. She's too little to belong to the Woods. To the Mountains. She's too young. They shouldn't have her yet. I should have her. Her father should have her. This world should still have her. And it doesn't. And she didn't even mind. She didn't even cry. She told me to do good. *Do good, Lys.* What good can I do? What good am I if I couldn't save her? I can't make this right. I can't bring her back. I couldn't stop it then. That fucking arrow went right through her heart. I don't know how she made it to me, let alone spoke to me. Comforted me. Bragged to me about keeping the Woods safe. Who am I to think I can stop anything now? What good can I do without her here? How can I stop anything else from being taken from me?"

Any other words I needed to say get lost in gasping, gut-wrenching sobs that close my throat so violently it hurts. The broken pieces of me try to stab through my chest on every emptying of my lungs. I tried so hard to pretend there was something in me other than shards, but one wrong thought and they all come slicing through my skin. I can't live with the knowledge that I had *anything* to do with the events that made me bury that bright, magnificent girl under a mound of dark, wet dirt.

Some part of me knows I have to stitch my ragged edges together enough to move. I have to find some shape that will allow me to be what I need to be for the people who are still here.

But I am a chasm. I can't even see the edges, let alone sew them back together.

I feel the slightest brushing of fingertips through the darkness. I reach for them, yearning for them to pull me from this abyss. They are so far away, and the stretching rips at my bones. I can't be lost to this.

Please.

I need to find solid ground.

Slowly. Agonizingly. My mind catches hold of something tangible. Carolyn's low voice seeps through the rushing sound of blood and grief battering my eardrums, and I can breathe again. Orient myself again.

"I am here, Lys. I am here. I am sorry. Hold on for me, darling. I will not let go."

She repeats her chant like a prayer, and her faith in me is a beacon. Her arms around me are a lighthouse in a storm. I cling to them, blinking hot, salty tears out of my eyelashes until I can see again.

"I think I'm back." My voice is ragged, and I wonder if I have been screaming as well as crying. Reluctantly, I remove myself from her embrace and sit, running an inventory of myself and my surroundings.

My head aches and everything else feels rubbed raw. Carolyn is staring at me like she's ready to sweep my broken bits back into her arms at the smallest sign of trouble. I'm overwhelmed by my love for her.

But I have to be ready to leave tomorrow, and there is still so much to do.

"First thing, I think we can agree that we won't talk about today until I have time to become a puddle." I try to sniff mucous back into my nose and untangle myself from Carolyn and the myriad of pillows all at the same time, with minimal success.

"I think that is fair."

She has a wonderful way of putting her smile into her voice. It clears the fog consuming me a little more. She stands much more gracefully than I could and helps me to my feet.

"Could you work on finding food for tonight and to take with us? I'm going to go look around for anything that might be useful."

"Of course."

"Thank you. For everything."

I wrap her in a quick hug and kiss her cheek, she brushes her hand against my face, and then I am down the stairs to my shop.

My heart threatens to break again when I reach the landing. I take a few deep breaths and remind myself that nearly everything lost here *can* be replaced once the larger task at hand is finished. A few of the odd statuettes and jewelry Arty and I had gathered from ruins are missing, but herbs can be prepared anew. Glass and pottery can be replaced, although some of my distilling equipment will be difficult unless Kyla has extra. The wreckage of my stores can be reordered. My friends, new and old, did a good job cleaning up for me, arranging things in piles for me to go through and clearing away the debris that must have been everywhere. The collection of intact or mostly intact products is where I head to now.

Miraculously, the widow resin salve I made just before leaving wasn't destroyed, and the specially designed gathering bags were with me when I went to town so I still have both of those. Rummaging through them, my fingers catch along the edge of the hollow-centered coin the Edantus gave to me. I tie the small medallion into the twine of my necklace, close to the black-swaddled pendant. With some consideration, I take the green ribbon from around my arm and weave that between the strands of twine as well.

I combine everything I may need into one of the bags, adding sutures, needles, and bandages just in case. I was already running low on suture thread before the ransacking, and guess how closely we will pass the spiders. It's out of the way, but the detour may be worth it.

I find some scraps of parchment and ink behind the counter, undisturbed, and make quick work of labeling and leaving instructions for the remaining products so the villagers know what to do with them while I'm gone. Satisfied with my travel kit of medical supplies and hasty instructions, I press a kiss to the side of Arty's jar, another miraculous survival of the destruction, and head straight up to the third floor.

Thankfully, my room is just its normal disaster instead of one created by external forces. I can find the toiletries and clothing I'm looking for quickly. From the depths of a wardrobe I pull out one of the larger canvas packs Arty and I used for our longer journeys around the Woods and strap two blanket rolls to it. I sit in the middle of my floor and hug my knees, staring out the large open bank of windows to the village beyond.

There's a pit in my stomach that says once I leave tomorrow, I won't come back to the same life. I know it won't be the same with Inness gone, but it feels like more than that. None of the cultists, their magic, or their politics were supposed to reach me here. It was always something I left behind in the city. Nothing ever really reached us here. Now everything is a mess of other people's making, and I feel like we can't go back to what we were.

I know I can't face the prince again today so I haul myself up and take the pack downstairs before they return. Carolyn has some kind of soup bubbling over the fire and an assortment of edible things and simple cookware laid out for our journey. I set the pack down on the floor near where she has everything arranged so it can be filled.

"You can use that to pack up. Can I have dinner in my room so I don't have to be around them?"

"Of course. Go back up, and I will bring you some when it is done. I will be sure everything is ready to go before I come to bed."

"Thank you. I don't know what I would do without you."

When I return upstairs, I decide to relish one last night in the privacy of my own bedroom and change into nothing but a soft, pale green shift and curl up on the bed. I have no intention of falling asleep before eating, but find myself nestled into the covers and falling victim to exhaustion within moments.

CHAPTER SIXTEEN

ALYSSIA

I see Inness, high up on a cliff's edge chipped into the side of a mountain, her arms outstretched to the sun. She laughs, poised over an endless expanse of trees. With a wink toward me, she dives into the leaves below, but I am the one who crashes through branches, feeling the blow of each against my back and limbs until darkness takes me.

Inness' black hair whips around her in a strong breeze. She smiles at me as she jumps boulders to cross the river. I stand on the bank, unable to follow, my hand stretched out to her, calling her back. She turns away and hops to the next rock. She slips and suddenly I am pulled under the water, dragged down by the current. I am drowning.

Green light dances around me, leading me somewhere I should not go. The light plays in my hair and ruffles my clothing and caresses my skin like it is tasting me. Testing me. I laugh and the sound is high-pitched and girlish. I barely recognize it as my own. The sound of Arty's deep voice echoes around me, and the lights retreat into a darkened field of green-gold stars.

I wake suddenly, reaching out into the night, searching for something I don't remember.

And that's enough of that.

I don't know what time it is, but it's time enough for me to be awake. I roll off of my bed as quickly and quietly as I can to not disturb Carolyn and pad softly over to the bank of windows framed by tree branches and boards. There are no lights flickering in the distance, and the air has the luminosity of the hours somewhere between moon-bright and sunrise that is always difficult to gauge this deep under the canopy. I have no desire to go back to bed, whatever hour it is. The more tired I am at the end of the day the better. I have no need for nightmares when we're traveling.

With a sigh, I slink away from the window and tiptoe downstairs. The fireplace in the kitchen is cold, so I quietly build a tent of kindling and start rummaging for any spare quick-start sticks I may have stashed. Finding one carelessly left in the bottom of a tin cup, I strike it and coax the small fire into life. Filling the kettle from the hand pump built into my counter, I swing it over the flame to heat.

That task accomplished, I open the shutters to the window nearest the fireplace and let the subdued blue-green glow of the pre-dawn light wash over me. I curl a lock of my hair around my finger and regret not tying it back immediately after the burial yesterday. It's now a tangled mess I'll have to address before we leave or be cursed with its unruliness for the duration of the trip.

The thin fabric of my shift doesn't hide the shadows of my nipples rising with the cool air as I stare at the black-wrapped amulet nestled between my breasts. Slowly, I strip away the fabric and let the deep green flame add its light to the dimness. I can't decide if I want to hide it, throw it away, smash it against the floor, or never let anything part me from it ever again.

Sinking into a chair, I comb my fingers through my hair with one hand and spin the pendant back and forth in the other as I wait for the water to heat.

A soft noise behind me causes me to turn curiously. Living with a twelve year old girl in a house made mostly out of a living tree numbs you to most strange sounds, so I'm not startled. The prince is there, fully clothed, with his back to me, gently shutting the door to the spare room behind him. I debate letting him know I'm sitting here, but he'll figure it out when he turns around. I shift to watch him when he does and cross my legs, exposing indecent expanses of pale skin that glows with a mixture of moonlight, firelight, and green flame.

For a dizzying moment, I'm tossed back into yesterday, the two of us pressed together, breath mingling and skin touching skin. I wrench myself free.

I'm rewarded for my silence by a sharp inhale of breath and a thud as the prince jerks back against the door. I finally remember how to be polite and stifle my laugh.

"Can't sleep?" I keep my voice pitched low and my tone neutral.

He shakes his head and joins me at the table, trying hard, and failing, to not stare at the necklace held at chest height.

"Too busy." He taps his temple twice in quick succession in a way that makes me think it's something he does without thinking, like running his hands through his hair.

"I know the feeling," I exhale heavily and try the prince's method of ruffling my fingers through the top of my own unruly strands. It does feel strangely thought-clearing to toss the front of my hair back like that, but I have the distinct feeling I look significantly less rakish in doing so.

The prince inclines his head at the spinning pendant.

"I saw that when...the other night." He shifts uncomfortably at the near mention of my dead apprentice. "What is it?" He doesn't sound anything other than mildly curious. Like the appearance of whatever this is, along with the Davorists, and everything else, isn't some massive upheaval of normal proceedings.

I stop fidgeting with it, pinching the plant and glass container between my fingers, and stare into its brightness.

"Honestly, I don't know." I let it fall back to its place between my cleavage and prop both elbows up on the table, pressing my palms into my forehead. "I have absolutely no idea what it is or what it means. It isn't anything like what Carolyn has seen from the magic of either cult. Maybe if I had ignored it, none of this would be happening. Maybe the Davorists would have found my village regardless, and nothing would be different. Inness..." I pause to make sure I won't fall apart. When I seem solid enough, I continue, "Inness thought it was special. She was so sure of it, but I don't know. It just seems like a mistake to me."

"Until someone finds the power to turn back time, unfortunately, entire lives can be looked at as a collection of what-ifs, should-haves, or would-nots. I have never found it particularly useful to look at how we could have done things. All that we can do is decide to work with what we have."

He settles back into the chair, his legs spread wide in relaxation, his chin tilted toward the ceiling. I notice him favoring his left arm in his lap, but I don't say anything. I take the opportunity to really look at him. The lines of him are strong, but softened by the glow of moonlight and loose fitting clothing. He certainly looks less physically tense than when I first met him, but being a few days out from a major stabbing would probably explain that. There is a tightness to his features though, like he really does have too much going on in his head and doesn't know what to make of it.

Without a word, I slide off my seat and tend to the kettle, pouring leaves and hot water into the teapot. I know I should feel some kind of shame or embarrassment about how I behaved yesterday, but that is in the walled off part of me, so I don't. And I know I should feel offended, embarrassed, shocked, or indecent, standing here practically naked, outlined by dim light through edges of thin fabric, but I don't feel anything about that either. In my thirty-three years on this earth, many people have seen me naked, known my body intimately. What's one more, even if it is a prince?

We sit together with hot, herbal tea clutched in our hands, not looking at each other and not saying a word, until the light of true dawn filters through the room, dulling the green glow from my necklace. I hope he recognizes this quiet moment for the apology I mean it as: an attempt to soften the jagged edges I let escape me yesterday.

Without a word, I set my cup on the table and slip upstairs to change and prepare myself for whatever may lay ahead of us.

———

That turns out to look a lot like the same irritations that lay behind me in these Tree-cursed Woods, only now with the extra spice of world peril to flavor them.

I wouldn't exactly say I'm lost yet, but we should have reached the river by now. I can hear it faintly, whooshing away in the distance, but I can't see it. I, at least, know we are still headed south from the brief glimpses of sky I catch and the overall quality of light, so I'm not worried. Not yet, anyway.

Half of my hair has already escaped its meager confines so I stop to shake it out and retie it, scattering a few leaves and probably bugs, as I do so. Apparently, the forest's love for invading my personal space is still strong, even with my current misgivings towards it. Meanwhile, Carolyn is as crisp as ever, not a hair out of place or a spot of dirt marring her white robes.

"How are you still so clean?"

My boots and pants are splattered in mud, and even the usually pristine Envir is slightly bedraggled.

"Kiv protects her followers from a multitude of ill effects."

I squint at her with a frown. I can never tell if she's joking when she adopts her priestess voice. She winks at me.

Fine then.

"We should reach the river soon, and from there we can more or less follow it south." I'm stalling to catch my breath, and to work out where we might be.

"Do you mean more or less follow, or more or less south. Because those two things seem very different." Envir has one foot kicked back against a tree, leaning with his arms crossed, and looks very skeptical.

"Ah. Well. Both, I suppose. It's a river so it doesn't exactly believe in due south."

He rolls his eyes. "And?"

"And, well," my hands flap around me, encompassing our surroundings, "What have you seen so far that would indicate anything around here would be as simple as 'walk along the riverbank'?"

Sighing dramatically, Envir peels himself away from his support. "A man can have hope, even in the most unlikely of times."

It's my turn to sigh. "Maybe it will be easier than I remember."

When I turn, picking a direction to continue, the prince's voice is soft and likely meant only for Envir's ears.

"And now she has cursed us."

My fingers wrap around the amulet tucked under my shirt, and I can't help but wonder if I already have.

CHAPTER SEVENTEEN

KEDREN

The rushing of the river becomes a pleasant roar as we push through a curtain of leaves the size of my face and follow Alyssia down the sloping bank of roots and earth. Once we reach level ground, she spins and throws her arms wide, a rare smile tugging at the corners of her mouth.

"The River Clair, everyone!"

She slips on the stone in her spin and, despite the fact that she is nowhere near the river's edge, she steps back toward us with a wary eye on the rushing current.

The path around the river is wide here, strewn with rocks from pebbles to decently-sized boulders. They shift beneath us as we make our way, the sound and sensation of them crunching under my feet not unpleasant. It reminds me of the rocky beaches on Envir's family estate, but instead of ocean spray and soaring cliffs, I am surrounded by gently sloping valley walls. Rock mixes with roots until the trees and undergrowth have enough soil to take over and crown the gorge we walk within.

The rock of the slopes is dark and striated with the passage of years and water levels long forgotten. Overhead, the rare, naked sky greets us, clear blue and blazing with the spring sun. Ahead of us at the bend, an impossibly large weeping willow drapes itself over the water, branches dragging with the current, hinting at a shady cave beneath its leaves. Birdsong, the buzzing of insects, and the croaking of frogs, serenade us as we walk. I beam a smile toward my friend.

He is just as lost in the wonder of this place and smiles back at me briefly before continuing to gape, wide-eyed at our surroundings. We weave over the stones together, bouncing from the water's edge to the mossy, root-laced stone walls. Envir runs his hand along the rough surface, staring up at the edge of overhanging canopy.

"These trees are amazing. I've never seen anything like it. I've never even heard of anything like it. Not outside of stories, anyways." He looks over his shoulder, back at the women who trail behind us hand-in-hand. "I know I have joked about her being one of the Otherfolk, but this is really incredible. The longer we're out here, the more I start to believe it." He trails off, tugging at a vine that is thicker than my forearm.

I think he is contemplating climbing it, glancing up its length speculatively. He must think better of it, however, because he moves on after one last experimental pull.

"It would take very little to convince me the stories are real." My words are hushed, quieted by my awe and what might be a lingering sense of childhood hope.

I loved reading about the Otherfolk when I was young, and he knows that. Their stories were an escape from my life in the palace before I was old enough to actually leave. I want to go back and tell myself these woods exist and they are everything I ever dreamed of. I want to tell the younger me that adventures and magic and kind, gorgeous women exist where the trees grow taller than the palace. Taller, even, than the cliffs down to the sea. That the stories of human princes walking into massive doors set into the trunks of trees and being spirited away to the lands of the Otherfolk may not be as unrealistic as they seem.

"Who knows," Envir's bright voice sparkles like the river in the sunlight and breaks me from my reverie. "maybe you will prove at least one of them true." He winks at me before attempting to skip a rock across the water.

The stone makes two jumps before it is lost to the current.

"Do you actually hear what I am thinking, or have we really just known each other for that long?"

"Ked, I can read you better than I can read a book."

"That is not saying much." I laugh and jump out of his way before he can land a reflexive hit on me.

"And you call me the asshole," he scoffs, jogging a few steps to catch up. "I can read you better than I can dress you, and that *is* saying something." He snatches up a stick caught between larger stones and gives it a few experimental swings. "I have read that story though, the one about the prince and the Otherfolk princess. You told it to me so many times when we were younger, it felt like a part of you. When you were missing and I couldn't think of anything else to do or anywhere else to search, I read it. While you were here, actually, which is rather funny now that I think about it."

The thought of Envir opening my favorite book, its pages falling open to the beginning of my favorite story, makes my heart clench and my stomach drop.

"I did not mean to distress you so much it drove you to *read*, my friend. That was horrible of me." I drape my arm around his shoulders.

"I thought you were dead. Imagining you as the prince in that story was a better alternative." He rests his head against mine as he speaks. His words are hardly audible over the sound of the water and woods.

I grip him tighter and turn so our foreheads touch. "I am not going anywhere."

He clasps my shoulder in return, and we hold each other like that for a long moment before he jabs me in the thigh with his stick and I jerk back, yelping. The girls laugh behind us.

"You better not." He wipes at the corners of his eyes with one hand as he turns away from me, his laugh joining the girls', the solemnity of the moment broken. "You deserved that though."

I shove him hard enough that he stumbles over the loose rock and my chest twinges, but we both keep laughing and slip back into our bewitched exploration. Sparing a glance behind me, I catch a glimpse of the women. Their hair, burnished gold and blue-black, shines in the sunlight, framed by the silver river and the rich brown of the earthen wall. If I had any talent for painting I would capture this moment in pigment and brush strokes. The movement of the priestess' robes in the breeze, the swooping of birds to the surface of the water, the waving of the massive leaves overhead. The bright, fleeting smile illuminating Alyssia's face. I will have to settle with committing this scene of peaceful beauty to memory, storing it with the other moments of calm I keep within me.

The sun dusts the tops of the trees with gold by the time Alyssia veers away from the river, picking her way carefully up an uneven path carved into the rock wall. I would not have noticed it among the striations and plant life, but she spotted it easily.

"We should find a place to camp with some cover. It'll be easier up there," she calls out, already halfway up the wall.

The rest of us follow, but she is lost to the trees before we top the rise. The priestess and Envir take the lead, weaving through the dense, snagging undergrowth, searching for the path Alyssia took into the depths. By the time the three of us stumble into her chosen campsite, she already has a wide space cleared for us and small fire started.

"Well this is perfect." Envir is already unburdening himself of our gear, looking around the site.

It is an excellent camp. A fence of smaller trees and scrubby underbrush encircles the open side of a bowl-shaped alcove created by two sweeping roots, taller than I am, and a trunk that could easily fit both Envir and I with our arms spread wide.

I collapse back against one of the roots as the efficient creation of camp unfolds around me. Envir insisted he carry my bag, but my body is exhausted regardless. The neatly stitched gash aches across my chest and into my shoulder. I cradle my arm in an attempt at looking casual while trying to relieve some of the pressure. The persistent nag of throbbing pain makes it difficult to organize my thoughts. I want to offer to help but one quick exchange of looks with Envir tells me he would not let me if I tried.

Before I simply slide to the ground where I stand, I peel myself away from the tree and take my place in the space Envir set up for me in front of the fire.

"I can take first watch," I offer, knowing, despite my tiredness, sleep will not come.

"That will not be necessary," the priestess responds quickly, surprising all of us. Even Alyssia's attention snaps to her friend, pulling her away from tending the pot of stew now bubbling over the fire. "I have an ability that I believe will serve us well here."

"What ability?" Alyssia quirks an eyebrow at the priestess, leaning back from the fire.

Light pink blooms across her sharp cheekbones, and I am jealous over how subtly perfect it is, my own blush much less endearing.

"I can set a ward that alerts me when it is crossed, even if I am asleep." She fidgets nervously and glances toward Alyssia from beneath lowered eyelashes. "I was trying to find a way to stop people from startling me in the chapel. After I managed that, it became something of a project." She lifts a shoulder in a shrug, the gold on her pristine white robes catching the firelight.

"Only you can hear it?" Envir is leaning forward, cross-legged and propping his chin on his hands in interest.

"Hearing is not quite the correct way to describe it. I can feel it in the same place I always feel the presence of Kiv. That feeling is strong enough to wake me from even the deepest of sleeps." Her hand goes to her heart, and her gaze drifts downwards before she looks back up to Envir, continuing in a rush. "I have tested it. And I can wake you just as quickly as anyone on watch could. We only need to make sure the ward is set far enough to prevent arrows from reaching us."

"We can do that," Envir says thoughtfully. "There's so much cover here, it shouldn't be an issue to make a pretty tight perimeter." He unfolds himself in a fluid movement that makes my body ache just watching. "I can chart a course first if you want to rest for a bit. Eat."

The priestess is already standing and brushing invisible dust off of her robes.

"No, I think it will put my mind at ease to have it done. The ward lasts for nearly half a day unless it is triggered."

Envir nods and the two of them vanish into the dark.

"That's news. The little sneak." Alyssia pulls a stack of wooden bowls from the supply pack and sets them just far enough away from the fire to be safe, grabbing one for herself and filling it with steaming stew.

"She does not tell you about her magic? I know the Kivarans do not speak of it often, but I assumed since you two were close, you might know more about it." I reach over to fill my own bowl, careful in my movements and delicately keeping my tone neutral. Our early morning meeting feels like a dream, but I do not want to ruin the progress we made toward some kind of easiness between us.

"There were a few times, when we were younger, that she tried showing me things she could do. The lights, little things like that, but I never thought much about them. For a long while I wrote them off as some kind of science or illusion. As we got older, she became a lot more private about that side of herself. She has access to the biggest library this side of the Andrionic, though, so she would show me books instead. Engineering, anatomy, mathematics, philosophy, language. Anything she thought might interest me. Arty didn't mind me slacking on our work as long as I was learning something." She swirls her bowl and takes a delicate sip, making a face and setting the bowl back into her lap.

"How long have you known each other?" Noting her reaction to the supper, I leave my bowl on the ground next to me.

She sits quietly for a moment, the tip of her tongue peeking out between her lips in her already familiar expression of thought.

"Almost twenty years, I think. She was the first friend I made in the city. When I was young, I spent a lot of time in the library. Arty would drop me off there before going out to take care of the business side of our work. I didn't start learning that until later. One day, she was just there. A girl about my age, already dressed in the white of the Order, reading at the desk I usually sat at. I rudely asked her to move, she didn't, and we've been friends ever since."

I hazard a taste of the stew but it is still far too hot to actually consume. I set it back down before responding.

"Your first friend in the city." I risk looking up at her and catch her watching me. "Do you have many there?"

"More than I have in the village, but not many, no. Storing your mentor's eyes on your mantelpiece doesn't always endear you to your neighbors, and constantly being a stranger in the city doesn't lend itself to many bosom companions there, either." Voice quiet, her gaze drifts back to the fire with an unreadable expression.

I get lost in watching the wavering light illuminate her soft, gently sad features, and I wrestle with my own heart before I can respond to her truthfully. "I understand. Vi and Jyn are the only two people I have ever considered friends."

She looks up, obviously surprised.

"Really?" She asks, clearly disbelieving. "I mean, I assumed you would have a lot of friends, given who you are."

I snort a laugh. "I know hundreds, maybe thousands of people at this point. Nobles, merchants, foreign royalty, and common citizens alike. However, it is because of who I am that none of them can truly be my friends. Not really. I am always Your Highness, and never Kedren, except to Vi and Jyn. People always want something from me, or want me to be what they think I am." My mind drifts to my mother and sister, and my voice drops to a near whisper. "Or nothing at all."

She opens her mouth to speak, but Envir and Carolyn reappear into our circle of light, the priestess leaning heavily against him.

"Carolyn?" Alyssia's voice is sharp with fear.

"I am alright. Just tired," the priestess responds. "I have not set a ward that covered that much distance before. It was more tiring than I thought it would be."

Envir settles her next to Alyssia, and she pushes her cooled soup to her friend, ladling more for herself and Envir afterwards.

"I hope you didn't insult my character too thoroughly while I was gone." He laughs, flopping down on his makeshift bed next to mine, significantly more relaxed than he was before they left.

"Only enough to warn her away from your apparent charms." I quip, grinning at him as he takes his bowl from Alyssia.

"He's enough, Your highness," she says, glancing between the two of us. "You only need a few good ones."

The new arrivals look at her, confused, but I smile and bow my head in a quick nod. She is right, of course. I have never felt as though I was lacking in friends with Envir by my side.

He rolls his eyes at both of us, and conversation drifts to talk about soup and the description of the ward's path through the trees. I let the sound wash over me, responding noncommittally when it seems appropriate. A smile twists the corner of my mouth as I watch Alyssia drift to sleep, curled protectively around the priestess.

CHAPTER EIGHTEEN

ALYSSIA

Carolyn rips me from sleep with a shake of my shoulder. I'm on my feet in a heart-stopping instant.

"What is it?" I hiss, blinking rapidly in the darkness, trying to orient myself.

Memories of a dream tug at the corners of my mind. I push them away.

"My ward. I already woke the men. They are searching the line." Her voice is low, and I scan the murky, fire-less darkness with little success.

One hand is on Carolyn's robe as I slink back into the narrowest curve of the tree, preventing anyone from getting behind or beside us. There is no sound aside from breeze-rustled leaves and my own breathing.

A scream echoes from the darkness. A clang of reverberating steel. Another. A rippling flash of lightning sparks across my night vision. It nearly blinds me to the arrow that falls harmlessly to the ground. Carolyn has one hand on my upper arm and the other twists her robes near her heart in a white-knuckled fist. Her lips move in silent prayer. Another scream pierces the night, but I can't see anything in the dark. I don't know the men's voices well enough to know if it's them. I shift from foot to foot, gaze darting in every direction, but nothing is visible. Not that I would have any idea what to do if it was.

I let go of Carolyn and clutch the amulet around my neck, my own mouth moving in a silent prayer to the Woods.

Another scream.

A sliding, shuffling sound comes closer. Through the stars still dancing in my vision, I see the prince stumble into our shelter, sheathing his sword. Heartbeats later Envir follows, one arm locked around the neck of a man. He drags him, stumbling and scrabbling against the forest floor, his other hand still gripping the hilt of his sword.

He kicks out the captive's legs and drives him into the ground. Carolyn scatters a handful of small, dim lights to hover over the leaves. Envir's sword shines a breath away from the man's throat. He is down on one knee, pinning his prisoner beneath him.

"How many are there?" All hints of the Envir I've known until now are gone. His words cut the air.

"Dozens. Hundreds." The man gasps under Envir's weight but still tries to sneer. "We are combing this cursed place in droves. This will not go unpunished." His last words are cut short as Envir leans more heavily onto his chest.

"How many were here. Now."

The man under his knee spits. The faint flash of the sword edges closer to his throat.

"Answer me."

"Why does it matter? You cannot stop the divine will of Davor."

"How. Many."

The scrape of the man's legs against the earth is grating as he kicks at leaves and dirt, looking for some purchase to escape the crushing weight of Envir's body.

"Six," he rasps. "There were six of us." Desperation creeps into him, and the choking gasps take on the air of begging. Not many stay composed in the face of death, natural or otherwise. It's no different here.

"My thanks." For the briefest of moments, Envir's casual, flippant tone returns, and then the golden edge of his sword ripples. A gurgle and the soft sound of wetness dripping against leaves follows.

"Ked, how many?"

"Two. You?"

"This makes three."

They both curse in unison.

"More will be coming."

"But when? Do we move now, or wait until light?"

"We should move now." I don't need to think about the answer. "If one was left from this group, he'll be back with others, but we should be able to lose them in the trees."

I break away from the shelter of my bark-covered alcove and snatch my bag from its place beside my temporary bed. I quickly start rolling up my blanket, the others following suit. Moments later we are ready. The corpse slowing oozing blood makes any attempt at hiding the campsite pointless. Instead I send them in the correct direction while I make as much of a false trail as I can that fades into the undergrowth. I follow a path of dim golden orbs left by Carolyn to catch up to them in the darkness.

—

The noise of the river is barely audible over the sound of my own ragged breathing. I weave us between the dense underbrush like a snake, but I still feel watched. Hunted.

Whenever I find a space open enough, we run. We make too much noise and leave too clear of a trail, but I don't have time to be overly particular. I rely on speed and, eventually, knowledge.

The trees lose some of their wildness as we distance ourselves from the water, and I blessedly begin to recognize landmarks. A shapeless mound of rock that could have once been part of a building. A strange tree with small purple leaves somewhere between a willow and a birch that I have only ever seen in one precise spot.

For some infuriating reason, I can't shake the men following us. I can't see or hear them, but I can feel them. It's like I can track their presence through the very ground beneath my feet. It feels like a taunt. A promise.

A threat.

The wildlife track I'm looking for is near enough that I'm comfortable slowing down. Carefully squeezing through the last remnants of dense thicket, the four of us tumble out onto the narrow path. The prince and Envir automatically flank Carolyn and I, searching the trees around us. Neither of them are breathing hard, but I catch the sight of blood blossoming across the prince's shirt. He must have pulled the old wound open fighting in the night.

I dig through my bag, groping for the ceramic jar of the widow resin ointment.

"Put some of that over the cut. It should stop the bleeding until I have time to look at it again." I hand the prince the jar as I push past him, but he grabs my sleeve.

"If that is going to do what it did to me before, I am not using it. Not now." His hold on my shirt is tight but he doesn't look at me, his attention on the Woods around us.

"It's safe like this."

So he did notice and make the correct correlation. Or someone told him.

He looks at me, still skeptical.

"I swear. It won't do anything to you."

"Fine."

He releases me and takes the jar. I scurry past him and Carolyn, taking my spot at the lead.

I turn my mind back to the forest. The weight of unseen eyes pushes back against me. I walk faster, still trying to catch my breath.

Carolyn sidles up next to me, handing me the jar she must have plucked from the prince on her way.

"You seem like you know where you're going," her voice is quieter than a whisper.

I nod. "I do, but I have a feeling none of you are going to like it." I frown enough to indicate that I also don't care for the idea. "But it's our best chance with no notice and being outnumbered." I shake my head to clear it and prevent Carolyn from asking questions I don't have the answers to. Questions like how do I *know* that we are so outnumbered it's worth taking this risk? I wave my hand to indicate that she should continue down the path before I drop back to Envir.

"If you see any game to shoot, do it."

"Now?" he hisses, confused and exasperated, still watching the trees.

"Now." My response is firm. I wait for him to string the bow before I squeeze past the prince and resume the lead.

As we continue, I try not to draw attention to the increasing frequency of gauzy spider webs that cling to low hanging branches.

—

"Are you going to tell us what this is about, or do I have to start guessing?" Envir lifts the string of three rabbits he managed to kill on our

144

brisk walk along the game trail. I'm honestly surprised there were that many this close to the beginning of the path.

The prince and Carolyn both eye our location warily. I can't blame them, I've led us into a trap. An old, crumbling wall of weather-worn, stony earth towers above us, dripping with moss and defaced by craggy ledges and dark fissures. Dense forest surrounds all other sides. I spot the wispy sheen of spider webs edging the widest sliver of black void.

"We're going to go into a cave." I try to make myself sound confident, but even my words want to escape from this plan. My voice shakes.

"Does this cave go somewhere else?" Envir impatiently swings the rabbits back and forth, and the way their limp bodies undulate makes bile rise in my throat.

Before I can respond, or puke, Carolyn groans. "Lys, no."

I look away from the boneless rabbit garland to Carolyn. Following her eye line, I see the shimmer of the web again.

"I would rather die, thank you," she chokes out.

"Well that's likely the only alternative. If I have to live through this, then so do you."

She winces. Before she can protest further, the prince interjects without taking his attention off of the Woods.

"What in the name of Kiv are you two talking about?"

"I thought it would be a good time to get some reinforcements."

Both of the men stare at me in annoyed confusion. Carolyn won't take her attention away from the narrow cave mouth, her face ashen.

I snatch the string of rabbits from Envir, raising it for emphasis, keeping my voice just loud enough to be heard. "This will hopefully be enough incentive for my friends to not eat us before the main course arrives. Then we either sneak or fight our way out the way we came. If there are any stragglers, maybe Carolyn can try blocking the cave mouth until they are taken care of."

"What *friends* can you possibly have that would eat us?" Envir backs down the trail, but the prince grabs his arm and puts a finger to his lips.

We fall silent immediately and listen. The snap of twigs echoes through the trees from far too many directions.

No time for further explanations. It will be uncomfortably obvious soon enough.

I duck into the entrance of the cave, being sure to not disturb the web at the corner and indicate for the others to do the same. Almost immediately, the passage turns sharply and we're cut off from the direct sunlight. I slow down, creeping along in the darkness, letting my eyes adjust to the gloom as I go. The thick, stringy webs get more difficult to avoid as they grow larger, sweeping between the walls in erratic sheets.

Another turn in the tunnel and the ground starts to slope downward. Here I dangle the rabbits in front of me with one hand, reaching the other behind me to gesture my companions closer, only to hit Carolyn's chest. The three of them are already practically on top of me. The light from the distant exit is just bright enough to make out the most basic of shapes. Far enough to keep us from being immediately discovered, but not as far in as I would like to be. I worry there will not be enough time, however. It will have to do.

I slowly drag the rabbits across a line of webbing. The soft, dappled fur sticks as it skips and dances against the tacky thread.

A heartbeat. Two.

All three of my companions tense, two of them going so far as to grab my shirt, when the rasping skittering of too many legs emerges from deep within the blackness. Forcing my breaths to stay even, I wait, still holding the string of rabbits in one hand. I'm not afraid for myself, but I've never been in the caves with anyone but Arty. I never even brought Inness here.

The rabbits twitch in my grasp as the web beneath them vibrates. One of the hands at my back starts to shake. I take a half-step forward, releasing the rabbits as the first spider emerges from the dark. I pull back enough to let the spider examine my offering, but keep my hand reaching toward it.

If it stretched out its legs, the spider would easily be my height. Its black, hairy body is impossibly thick for such spindly supports, its groping pedipalps searching along the rabbits before guiding a thin stream of webbing around and around the small bodies. The spider makes quick work of cocooning the meal. I thank the Trees one of the yearlings was the first to greet us. One of the older, larger spiders would have likely eaten them whole and been much less impressed.

With the rabbits preserved for later, the spider now turns its attention toward my still outstretched hand. The stiff, bristly hairs tickle as they explore my skin. Tasting me. Smelling me. Seeing me.

"Hello," I speak low in my chest, more vibration than audible sound. "Do you remember me?"

In response, the spider nudges its head against my hand, and I pet it. It scrambles away from me suddenly, clawing up the wall so it looms over us, its jaws scraping together with an audible hiss.

The tension of my friends thrums against my back. The indistinct murmur of people further away reaches us from the entrance.

"It's alright. These are friends." I wiggle myself back into the knot of my people, wrapping my arms around the shoulders of all three just as the chitin scratching of two more spiders, slightly bigger than the first, reverberates up the corridor. "These are mine," I emphasize again, for the newcomers, still using the low, rumbling tone Arty taught me to use all those years ago.

They both rear up, their front legs testing the air. Some of their hairs brush my hands and Envir and Carolyn's heads as they assess the intruders who dared to enter their lair. All of my friends shiver, drawing closer together.

"There are more coming, though. Those you can have."

The spiders click their mandibles together with a last brush of their legs against the huddled mass of us and go to the rabbits, clacking and chittering.

I'm confident in our momentary safety and start to edge us deeper into the cave, heading for the cavern where I collect the silk I use. I may as well get some while I'm here, although I worry that I'm asking too much of my industrious cohorts. Taking both suture silk and tricking them into fighting for us doesn't seem worth their reward to me, but I have a feeling they place a higher value on eating humans than I do.

I wind up strands of silk onto a thin, smooth stick from my bag when snatches of voices bounce off the tunnel walls in such a way, they sound as if their owners stand next to us.

"We are not going in there."

"We can be rid of them and be on our way. It's just a cave."

"Something isn't right."

"By Davor's Power, what are you afraid of?"

"Stop wasting time. I want to get out of these fucking trees before I die of old age."

Each voice comes from a different person. The echoes fade as they shift away from that perfect spot carrying their words. I yank my half-spun spool of spider silk away from the wall, dropping it into my bag. Looking for some reasonable spot to hide or make a stand, I see the faintest spark of green from the corner of my eye, deep in the recesses of the caverns. As soon as I turn to investigate the distant, flickering glow, the cave devolves into chaos.

An explosion of bulbous bodies ricochets around us, hurtling toward the sudden sound of screams emanating from the cave mouth. The hum of wildly vibrating webs builds in a low crescendo under the sound of their legs and pinching jaws.

I want to duck back, toward that familiar pulse of green, but both my two- and eight-legged friends surge away from me. The men fall into running step with the spiders, their swords already bared. Carolyn also sprints, but I don't know if it's towards the fight or away from the spiders. Possibly both.

For the spiders, it's a feast.

I'm carried out with the tide until we crash into a tangled mass of too many cultists and towering arachnids. Blades and fangs clash all around me. I duck low, weaving between the sticky snares of grasping webs. I comb the ground for a discarded weapon between stomping feet and corpses.

One of the bodies has a short sword partially plastered to it with webbing that I tear free and hold awkwardly in front of me in a one-handed grip. Above, flashes of golden light arc through the air, some edged with red as they crackle like heat lightning. They illuminate scenes of gore in short lived stills that hang before me like paintings. Blood splatters down on me as I crawl through the mess. I dodge wildly around the sharp, barbed points of spider legs. I stab into thighs, groins, and feet whenever I'm sure the person attached is not one of my companions.

How are there so many of them?

I get confused in the melee after counting over twenty of the Davorists. The easiest to count are the dead, but I struggle even then. The spiders have torn bodies apart and encased pieces of obviously different people in webbing to make indistinct, many-limbed mounds in the shadows.

I feel a sting of pain lance through my forearm as I scrabble along the cave floor, blade or spider, I can't tell. Another fire blazes across my thigh and I curse, throwing myself to my feet, sword braced tightly against my body like a spear as I careen through flashing lights, gnashing mandibles, ripping legs, and glinting blades. Suddenly I stumble, dropping the sword as I windmill my arms for balance, free of the buffeting current of violence keeping me upright.

When I steady myself, I squint against the light of the cave entrance, abruptly visible around the corner of the rock wall I gracelessly collide against.

We are so close to escape.

Behind me, the roar of sound is indistinguishable from the overwhelming sounds of my own body. My heart or the rhythm of swords? My rasping breath crackling in my ears or the snap of the cultists' magic flaring in gold and red? The dripping of my own blood on the rocky earth or the squelching of feet and spider paws on soaked ground and soft bodies? Do the screams come from me, or do they come from the heaving conglomeration before me? It's all one and the same, and I reel clutching at the stone under my fingers when I can no longer distinguish myself from the carnage.

I don't realize I've crumpled to the ground until a hand grabs my arm and yanks sharply as they run past me, toward the freedom of the forest. I come back to myself, blinking away the sight of writhing black legs overwhelming humans in waves of primal horror.

The prince clings to me with his off-hand, sword dripping blood in his other. Carolyn is right behind us, her robes an unrecognizable canvas of crimson, blue-black ichor, and mud. She holds one hand out in front of her, the other in a tight fist near her heart. She's staggering and panting. I try to reach for her, but the prince does not slow or release me despite my feeble struggle. We turn the final bend before I can pick Envir out of the chaos of writhing bodies. My feet meet the spongy give of leaf mould without catching sight of him behind us.

Carolyn, the prince, and I stand, swaying and gasping for one breath. Two. Three. On the fourth, Envir stumbles out into the light and Carolyn braces herself, hand outstretched like she is pressing against a wall with all her strength.

A transparent barrier stretches across the mouth of the cave, rippling with golden light as the men trapped behind it pound on the unforgiving surface with fists and sword hilts. It may prevent their freedom, but it does not stop their screams from escaping as, one by one, they are encased in shining, gray-white strands of silk.

CHAPTER NINETEEN

KEDREN

We flee blindly into the trees.

The underbrush and roots grab at us like eager hands, but we run heedless of the snagging and tearing of our clothing. The wetness of blood and ichor feels cold and clinging against my skin, and I want to peel my shirt off as I dodge between the branches of trees beneath trees.

Revulsion at the thought of stripping bare fills my steps with more panicked speed, but that is a problem for later. Now I twist, reassuring myself of my companions' presence. Envir is close by my side, as close as the dense forest allows. His sword, like mine, is sheathed now, its long, sharp edge a liability in this tight, frantic escape. The priestess and Alyssia weave in and out of sight behind us, staggering and lurching over the uneven ground, ducking clumsily under low branches. We will have to stop, or at least slow, soon or they will not be able to keep following. My own body and mind cannot be addressed yet, or I will come apart at the many seams of me. I have to keep moving. Alyssia's eyes are wide, rolling back and forth, the whites visible all the way around. I do not think she truly sees anything in her search.

I cannot fault her wildness. The primal need to be away from where we were drives me through the trees. All of us, I am sure myself included, are ashen under the gore. How we are all alive is a shock to me. The gauntlet between the dark, eerie cavern and blinding forest light is a blur of blades and blood and bodies. Pressing. Clicking. Screaming. My stomach clenches and bile floods my mouth. I swallow and then spit whatever will not go back down.

The only thing clear to me is that we need to go west to reach the river and south to reach the lake. I want to hear the rushing roar of the current again before I look for a place for us to shelter. Someplace to hide. To regroup. To be sure everyone is truly unharmed.

Envir and I slow to fight through an unavoidable thicket of underbrush. The women stumble, crashing into us. We tumble in a tripping, clinging mass through springy, new-growth twigs and leaves. When we break through, gasping and panting, Alyssia and I are a tangle of limbs, bracing each other against a quick drop to the ground.

All four of us burst into laughter, the edges sharp and crackling with hysteria I am relieved to hear in more voices than mine.

Without a word, we press on, our laughter dying abruptly. We walk now, all of us breathing hard and knocking into each other when we stagger too far from our own course. Alyssia leads again, more or less ahead of me now. Blood drips slowly from the tips of her fingers, and I pray to Kiv we can find somewhere safe, and soon.

The edges of my vision start to creep inward, blurring the periphery into shades of gray. For several racing heartbeats, I assume the rushing I hear in my ears is the call of unconsciousness, but the sound becomes clearer as we keep moving and, thank Kiv, it is the river.

Alyssia drops out of sight suddenly and my heart lurches after her. I try to shout, but my throat makes no sound. I scramble to the spot where she vanished. Envir grabs my shirt and drags me back. Directly below me is a sharp drop to the rocky river bank where I expect to see her crumpled on the ground, but her golden-brown hair and blood soaked shirt are nowhere to be seen. Until, that is, Envir turns my head toward her skipping and sliding down a gentler portion of slope, the priestess trailing behind her.

"Thanks," I rasp. Envir responds with a nod before starting after the women.

We slip and clatter down to the relatively flat ground of the riverbank in one piece. I watch Alyssia, swaying like a drunk toward the hollowed out underside of a massive tree and its roots, the river carving its way through and around creating an airy gazebo of tree parts. Its construction is far enough from a cave to prevent my mind from returning to the one we just left. A fact that I am extremely grateful for.

"Sit, Alyssia." Envir's voice is soft as he guides her to the center of the makeshift shelter.

"We need to boil water." Her words are urgent, but she does not resist his shepherding, collapsing onto the ground and scrubbing viciously at her slime-coated face. Just as quickly, she rolls up onto her knees and starts gathering anything that resembles kindling near her into a mound.

Envir and I take up firewood collection, an easy task in a shelter made of trees. The priestess unstraps the supply pack from her shoulders with an audible sigh of relief and collapses to the ground next to her friend.

Once we finally have a sufficient pot of boiling water, Alyssia sets it aside to cool and looks over the wilted collection of us. She and the priestess are leaning into each other, their hands clasped tightly and resting on their touching thighs. Envir and I are huddled on the other side of the fire. He leans forward, his arm hugging one knee close to his chest, seeming casual, but I can see the shaking of his hands even as he clenches his fists to steady them. I try to strike a similar pose, but the fact that my left arm is largely unresponsive makes it difficult. Pain, weakness, and exhaustion weigh me down with insurmountable heaviness.

"I need a damage report from everyone." She tries to sound like the confident professional I first met, but her voice is a mockery of the bright, easy way she spoke then. It shakes and cracks over the words. "Carolyn?"

The priestess shakes her head, her usually immaculate hair dull, tangled, full of leaves and twigs, and worse. "None of this is mine. Thank Kiv, I am whole, just filthy and too exhausted to think about any of this." She sighs deeply. "But not too exhausted to wash and change." With another sigh and an immense heave of effort, Carolyn gets to her feet and scoops up her once-white leather satchel, disappearing behind a curling wall of root that hides a shallow pool of the river from our spot by the fire.

"Don't get any of that water in any open skin, Carolyn, so help me," Alyssia shouts after her before turning her attention to Envir and I. "Envir, how much of that is yours?" Her hand waves at his blood covered visage.

He shrugs.

"Not sure. Not much, I don't think." Casually, he peels off his shirt, sending motes of flaking blood dancing in the air. A pang of jealousy at the easy action twists in my gut. His smooth, pale skin is marred only by patches of muddy gore, tan lines and the dusting of shining auburn hair at chest and lower abdomen. A crusted line of dark red snakes up one of his biceps, but it doesn't look deep enough to be concerned about. Another, deeper slash bites into his side just above his hip. Thankfully, it does not appear to have pierced anything important.

"Come here." She snares a cloth from the boiled water, wringing it out and holding it at the ready, prepared to attack Envir's filthy cuts the moment he is in range. "Have..." her voice is so quiet I have to lean forward to hear. "Have either of you ever done anything like that before?" Her hands shake as she cleans the blood from his wounds.

We look to each other across the flames and breathe out heavily in unison.

"Nothing so spectacular," he is quiet, hardly more than a continuation of breath. "We know how to fight. We've been trained, of course. Stopped a half-hearted assassination attempt or two. But never that much. Never fighting alongside spiders and magicians."

"Sparring, a few tavern brawls, the occasional unfortunate incident like Envir mentioned, but he speaks for both of us. Such a press of bodies. The rasping and crashing of the spiders. The magic." I clench my own fingers into a fist to stop their shaking. I am as ineffectual as Envir. "I know some older guards who have tried to explain it to me, veterans of some of the old skirmishes with the north, but the chaos? The blurred, primal instinct of it?" I shake my head.

"The pissing fear of it," Envir hisses as Alyssia starts to place sutures into the wound in his side.

She snorts in response. "Chaos and pissing fear seems about accurate. Add in a dash of body horror and we might just have it." Her voice shakes, but her hands are steady as she pulls the last thread in Envir's side tight. "Alright, Your Highness. Your turn."

I start to shake my head again, but she and Envir both shoot me looks so sharp, I slide myself over to her immediately. "Alright, alright." I settle before her, legs crossed and trying to sit up straight, but I slump into my elbow resting on my thigh. "You should be taking care of yourself though, Alyssia."

She waves her hand dismissively before reaching for another clean, water soaked cloth. "I already washed the cuts out. I don't want to put any stitches into myself before I finish up with the lot of you. I'd shake too much, I think." Her tone is casual, as if her own condition is an afterthought.

My eyes widen at her calmness. "You cannot be serious. If you need stitching, please let Envir do it. He has experience."

She raises one eyebrow and looks between the two of us. "Thank you, but no. I think I will trust myself with this one. It isn't that bad." She settles back on me, and the vibrating tension that consumes me fades to a dull wrenching in the back of my mind.

She is on her knees and takes my chin in one hand, tilting my face towards hers. The last of the tautness in me snaps. The blackness at the edges of my vision threatens to take the sight of her from me, but I push it back with several steadying breaths. Her eyes narrow.

"I am alright. I think." I try to laugh, but it is a thready sound.

The warmth of the cloth against my face feels wonderful even as it stings a cut on my cheek I had not noticed. I close my eyes against it as she scrubs at my skin. I breathe shallowly as drops of water roll down my face and past my jaw, my neck, pooling in the ridge of my collar bone. I keep my eyes closed as I feel her lean in, tracing the cloth along the path of the errant droplets. She holds there, the fingers of her other hand sliding up from my chin to brush damp strands of hair behind my ear, her thumb tracing the tender skin just below the shallow cut. My heart skips and my breath catches at her touch, my eyes flutter open, and I see the softness of her gaze on me. She snaps hers down to the blood crusted shirt clinging to the reopened chest wound.

"May I?" She sounds as breathless as I feel as the hand holding the now filth-soaked rag trails down, two fingers catching on the edge of my shirt.

"Just enough. Like before, please." Only the fear of her seeing me as I am is enough to freeze the heat of my need for her. I vaguely recollect the soldiers also explaining what the aftermath of battle was like. The desires they had. I did not think I had enough blood left in me for that, but I feel my face flush with the reality of it.

She nods and tosses the used cloth to the side, taking another clean one. Her fingers, lingering at my jaw, slide down with a whisper of a touch against my flushed skin to move the neck of my shirt. She shifts it just far enough to expose the length of angry, bruised flesh. Thankfully the tugging pulls enough cloth to cover the other side of my chest. Alyssia winces when she sees the torn wound, bloody, swollen and abused from nearly an entire night and day of fighting and running. At least the difficulty of raising my arm seems more justified now, looking at the partially clotted, ragged ends of shiny red meat that twitches and glistens with my curious, testing motions.

"Stop that," she glares down at me and wrings the cloth out over the injury, the flow of the water sharp against it. "Envir, come here and sit behind him." She takes the whole pot of water and starts pouring small splashes into the wound.

"Are you sure? It looks like you two have something else entirely going on over there. Three's a crowd, or so they say," Envir laughs, but he is already sliding toward me.

Alyssia glares at him, a blush rising in her cheeks.

"Lean back against him, Your Highness," she says, busying herself with the tools of her trade.

I obey without hesitation, comfortable in Envir's loose embrace, choosing to ignore his words. His presence steadies me and helps ease the overwhelming ache I have for the woman.

This is not an unfamiliar pose for us. His knees drawn up, one arm tucked around my waist, the other stretched behind him, angling me back for her to work. We have always fit together well. As soon as I have settled, she invades my temporary comfort by pouring water in such vigorous earnestness, I have the unpleasant sensation of feeling the cascading rush of it within the ragged fibers of my body. I jerk away, but Envir holds me steady, and she continues her cursed ablutions by wiping the skin around the cut clean. The wound itself is still oozing blood slowly, as it has off and on since last night. A few straggling stitches remain at either end but the majority have torn free, leaving the edges frayed.

Alyssia draws her brows together, the very tip of her tongue curling up against her top lip.

"That's a mess." I feel the rumble of Envir's voice through my back. I tilt my head to look at him.

"Of course it is. Everything else is, why wouldn't this be too?" Envir was trying to make a joke of it, but Alyssia sounds as if she is going to start crying when she speaks.

I reach out with my good arm and drag her to me, overbalancing her so she falls into us, both of us catching her in a tight embrace. I tangle my fingers in her messy hair, easing out the tie holding back remnants so it falls freely around her in a cascade of dark gold. She buries her face in my unbloodied shoulder and shakes with sobs. They are echoed by smaller vibrations behind me. Envir cries softly, trying to hide it. Before I can stop, I feel tears coming to my own eyes just as another set of arms joins our huddled mass. Clad in pure white once again, her composure restored, the priestess has returned. She hides her face in the nest of Alyssia's hair, pressing her tightly between us. Of all of us, she is the only one not taken by her emotions. Instead, she runs gentle hands over each of us in turn with a soft, caressing touch. I can hear her low, smoke-tinged voice murmuring into Alyssia's ear, the sound of it coming to me wordless, but no less soothing.

—

I blink awake to my body aching everywhere, the tingling feeling of several sleeping limbs, and the warmth of a small fire. The priestess tends the fire, the gold and white of her robes reflecting the flames, and smiles when she notices me blinking groggily at her. I contemplate trying to join her, but wonder how I can shift to minimally impact the two bodies I am entwined with. The need to force blood back into all of my extremities becomes more urgent the longer I remain trapped.

The priestess takes pity on my struggles and kneels next to our pile, her lips pursed in thought. She begins to shift Alyssia off of my chest. I want to pull her back into me, but I need to get up, so I let her go. The sleeping woman makes a small sound as we work to move her, the priestess providing a rolled up blanket as a pillow for us to settle her back onto. Finally freed after untangling myself from Envir, I pull myself to my feet and stretch cautiously. I was correct with my first assessment. Everything does hurt. A lot.

The sun has set outside of our small den, and moonlight filters through the kinks in the roots around us to blend with the firelight, creating deep shadows between the gnarled limbs.

"Any sign of trouble?" I am still cataloging what I can see of the land around us, but I turn to the priestess, my voice low.

"No. It has been quiet enough."

I nod and make my way to my pack, digging out clean clothes, ready to make for the secluded pool of the river.

"Try not to get any of the water in open wounds, it can cause them to turn," the priestess issues the soft warning just before I disappear around the screen of trees. I nod again, not understanding fully, but also not intending to argue the point. Alyssia gave the same warning to her earlier, and I have yet to see any reason to question her knowledge of medicine.

The protected alcove is screened from the sides, but open to the moon above and the silvery light reflects on the lazy current of the river, slowed here by its path through the trees and further tamed by its vast, shallow, width, the far bank barely visible. Slowly and carefully, I strip off the filthy, blood stained clothing. The shirt tears from my open flesh, having dried into the gaping hollow. I bite my tongue hard against the groan trying to escape me.

With a small effort of will, I plunge into the water, the surface rising to waist high only a few steps in. It is freezing. The complete, polar opposite to my heated baths in the palace, the steam curling around me and the warmth working its way into my bones. It is a memory from a lifetime ago, not days. Instead, my body tenses against the icy waters as it carries the grime away. Careful to keep the wound dry, I scrub as much of the crusted gore and mud off of me as I can, bending back to let the river comb its way through my hair.

When I can take the temperature of the water no longer, I wade out and sit with my back against one of the roots, legs stretched out in front of me to dry in the cool breeze. The cold and my exhaustion are a welcome distraction. Together, they prevent me from thinking about a single thing as I sit, soaking in silver moonlight and chilled, wild spring air smelling of dirt, river and wood. I close my eyes and sink into it.

A particularly violent shiver wakes me and forces me to dress as quickly as I can. I am still stomping into my boots when I duck out from behind the screen of trees to see the rest of the group awake and the fire built up, another stew simmering over it. I must have been gone for longer than I thought. I drop into the open space left for me around the fire and let its warmth seep into me, hair still dripping icy water onto my shirt.

"Your Highness, I need to sew you back together." Alyssia's face is propped on one palm as she directs her attention to me, a line of crimson already appearing on my fresh shirt.

"Did you sew yourself back together yet?" I counter, dragging my wet hair back from my face.

"I told you, after you. I'm not that bad off."

"Vi can take care of this," I let slip in my surprise.

"I would rather not if someone here is more qualified to take over," Envir says with a subtle glance at me.

"I'm fine to do it." She is already pulling a threaded needle from a jar that smells strongly of alcohol. "Just come here." We are barely out of reach of each other as it is, but we slide together until our knees touch. "You didn't get any of the river water in there did you?" She frowns, peeling the sticking shirt out of the crevice in my chest.

"Kiv," my curse comes out as a prayer and a growl. "No. No I did not. It was, in fact, quite dry." Spots flash across my vision, and I almost slip into darkness, my body swaying. A hand braces my good arm, and my eyelids flutter open again. Her wide-eyed stare meets mine with a determined strength so deep, her presence is an ocean. I beg to drown.

Envir's weight at my back is a buoy on the sea when I want to anchor myself to her, but I let myself be dragged from her depths.

"Are you with us, Ked?" His voice is warm and low in my ear as I blink the remaining faintness away.

"Yes. I am fine. Let us get this done."

Alyssia looks over my shoulder and nods at Envir, his hold on me tightening just before the first sharp prick of the needle hits. The snap of wood in the fire. Thin, milky spider silk. Bodies. Blood. Blades.

No.

The soft rush of the river. The burnished gold of Alyssia's hair still unbound and tumbling over her shoulders. The smoky scent of burning wood. The warmth of Envir's body holding mine. I repeat the mantra to myself until the last of the sutures is tied off, and the wound is covered in the strainge ointment. Envir and I work in concert to wrap a strip of linen under my shirt to cover the fresh stitching.

Satisfied with my care, she and Envir slide away from me, leaving me unmoored. I do not want to fall away again until I know she has cared for herself, so I cling to the surface of consciousness. I watch as she takes another small vial of alcohol soaked suture thread and a needle out of her bag and sets it aside before unwrapping a bloodied strip of cloth bound around her forearm. She reveals a long, but shallow, cut down the flesh of her forearm that she considers, twisting the limb experimentally and watching the edges gape. The tip of her tongue curls around her lip again. Instead of taking the needle out of the vial, she instead spills some of the liquid inside over the wound with a sharp hiss of breath.

I have collected myself enough, that the need to go to her at the first sign of distress is overridden by the reasons I should not. I content myself with angling so I can respond quickly if I feel like she will tip into the fire. The priestess is also watching her, but busies herself dividing the stew into bowls for each of us. As much as I do not want to eat, I know I need to.

"Carolyn, any theories on how they managed to follow us so easily?" Alyssia winds a new strip of cloth around her forearm as she looks to her friend.

"Not that I know of, specifically, but it would not surprise me if there was some Davorist abomination that could assist in tracking. Anything that can facilitate their rise to power is within reason."

Alyssia nods like it was the only possible explanation while rolling up her trouser leg, exposing another large stain of bloody bandage on her thigh. Before she finishes unwrapping it, I can tell this one is deeper. "They shouldn't have been able to catch up to us, so I thought it might be something like that. I have to admit, there is more to your magic than I thought."

The priestess snorts in reply and sits next to her, brushing against her uninjured leg. A gentle reminder of her presence. Her support. Her comfort. Things I cannot provide her, despite my wishes.

Alyssia leans into her, allowing herself to get a better angle at the cut, needle in hand.

"I want to know why they worked so hard to chase us down," Envir says between delicate slurps.

"We did kill several of them." I feel as though that would be enough of a reason for anyone, but Envir looks at me, thoughtful.

"If whatever they are looking for is so important, why wouldn't they keep looking for it? Why spend the time killing us?" he counters.

"They are vengeful and bitter creatures. They do not need an excuse. When we killed their brethren we gave them all the reason they needed to come after us, delay to their mission be damned," the priestess says acidly.

"Or the one who got away from us knew who I was," my words are quiet as I stare into the fire.

"Ked, we still don't know it's her."

I ignore him. Even though I know he is trying to be gentle, I hate the mistrust he has in my judgment. "I would not put it beyond my sister to allude to my death being favorable if she discovered I was involved."

"Carolyn's argument is a strong one. I have yet to meet a Davorist who wasn't a bastard." She bites her lower lip in a wince as the needle pulls at her skin before continuing deliberately, "If that wasn't the only group in this part of the Woods, it wouldn't matter if they wasted a little time for a bit of revenge murder. If they knew who we were, it would have been more prudent to follow us instead of killing us."

"Even if any of those men were involved with what happened in Cuaria, none of them would have known we were there. They were all gone before we arrived." The priestess wraps her arm around Alyssia's shoulder as she flinches against the needle.

"Except for the two that followed me through the Woods," Alyssia says. "But I doubt they would be here. Regardless, we can be sure they won't be following us now and can concern ourselves with not running across any more of them." She breathes out slowly as she smears a line of the pink salve down the cut and deftly wraps her thigh in more bandaging.

She must have filled her entire bag with first aid supplies. It should not surprise me, but her foresight in us needing so much of it is unsettling. I can only hope our demand for them runs dry before they do.

CHAPTER TWENTY
ALYSSIA

Our third day of travel is blessedly uneventful. Slow and painful as we limp along the bank of the river, but quiet and uninterrupted. The sutures pull in my thigh whenever I have to climb over something, but for the most part, the low burn of both cuts blend into the many background aches of my body. I can't thank enough trees, leaves, and bushes for the fact that my jar of fully made widow salve remained intact through the destruction of my shop. Without it, I would have a very different opinion on the state of our collective injuries.

By a unanimous consensus, we settle into camp early when we find a crumbling stone building nestled among trees with just enough wall left to create a cozy blockade against spring wind and the threat of prying eyes. This close to the lake, the slope of the river gorge has begun to mellow, the rocky shore becoming marshy as the water begins to split into a small delta.

"The frequency of the ruins has begun to increase dramatically, as you said it might." Carolyn runs her fingers along the pockmarked stone walls as she speaks.

"I told you. It didn't surprise me when you said this was the capital. It's hard to see if you don't leave the river, but it's really interesting out here." I nestle myself into a pile of last year's leaves with my blanket and look up to Carolyn. "Just not interesting enough for me to venture all this way for no reason. None of the plants here are particularly unique, although now that I think of it, I should come here when it's weeping widow season." She is too busy absorbing the awe inspiring age of the structure through a gentle caress to acknowledge my response.

"Carolyn?" Envir asks hesitantly.

I curl up into a ball, facing the fire and both the men in their customary spot opposite mine.

"Yes?" She turns from her examinations, but her hand doesn't drop from the wall.

"What is your relic, if you don't mind me asking?" When she doesn't answer immediately, he hurries on, "I've just been thinking about what we're looking for, and I was wondering what item you have that allows you to do what you do. You don't have to answer if it's private."

She laughs with a low rumble and steps away from the wall, her index and middle finger lingering on the rough stone until the last possible moment.

"It is not private. Not really." She sits between the two men, and I prop myself up to watch. "It is not an object that belonged to Kiv that I have so close to my heart." She pauses dramatically, reaching for the gold chain around her neck and removes it from the folds of her robes reverently. The glittering gold filigree of the pendant sparkles in the firelight. "It is a piece of Kiv herself."

The prince's eyes widen, while Envir's narrow in skepticism that so closely mimics my first reaction, I work hard not to laugh. Although, after seeing so much physical proof of her power, I may actually believe her now.

Carolyn spins the pendant, rolling the chain between her fingers slowly. "It is a finger bone. The Order was able to preserve at least some of the ashes of Kiv and created several relics from the remains. This is one of those."

A delicate cage of swirling gold encases the dull, mostly charred, relic. Black and deep brown with burning and age, the bone makes for a macabre jewel more precious to Carolyn than any gemstone could be.

"Why do you have that? How?" The prince is incredulous, almost rude, one hand suspended halfway to touching the dangling bone.

Carolyn rests the necklace on the outside of her robes, the gold trim framing it prettily. "So you do know more than Envir does. More than Lys does." She winks at me before I can protest.

Not that I would. I have no idea why she shouldn't have her relic. It's been hers since I met her.

"It is true that most of my brethren must earn their relics over time and develop their power as a priest of Kiv with the use of lesser objects. However, this has always been mine. I was born in Drevda, near Mercone. It is large enough to have its own temple that dates back to just after the Fall." She leans back, one hand behind her and the other fingering the necklace. "I was called to my devotion when I was very young. I discovered this relic hidden away under loose stones while exploring as a child would. I have been a full priestess since I was nine years old. The relic has been mine ever since."

"Surely the Order would reclaim it for the cult in Kivaire? The High Priest must want that for himself."

My friend barks a sharp laugh. "Oh, he has been trying to pry this away from me since I came to the library as a girl, but it is mine by rights. Technically, I am the Head Priestess of the temple from which it was found." She shrugs with one shoulder and tucks the necklace back under her robes.

The prince's mouth hangs open. Even Envir looks impressed.

"You will be the next High Priestess." The prince doesn't bother phrasing it as a question. He drags his hand through his hair and shakes his head at the same time.

"If that is the path that will allow me to best serve Kiv, I will walk it. If not, then I will not." She uses her incense and old parchment voice now, and it's a balm to me. "For now, my place is here. Thwarting Davorist machinations."

"Well, I'm certainly glad you're on our side." Envir stretches out and flops back into his own leafy bed. His well-timed levity is something I'm rapidly growing to cherish.

"Me too." My voice is sleepy and my eyelids are heavy. I reach a hand out, beckoning Carolyn to me. "With any luck, we can solve at least one part of our problem tomorrow," I yawn dramatically. "But now, sleep." She comes and settles behind me, wrapping one arm around my waist, holding me close. I breathe in the woodsmoke, leaves, and musty stone around me and almost, *almost*, feel content.

—

I dream in still images.

Carolyn, her robes stained a deep red, a sword blade held in her bloodied hands. The prince and Envir back-to-back, hands up either in defense or offense, weapons lost. Inness suspended by vines that become her flesh, green flame wreathing her like a halo. A soaring tree with leaves of gold stretching into the sky and roots plunging deep into the earth that I somehow know is me. A red void with a single point of burning black.

I wake feeling sick and spit a leaf out of my mouth, disoriented.

The fire has burnt itself down to the barest of embers, and not even moonlight illuminates the ground around me. As quietly as I can, I roll up and out of my nest, trying not to hiss as the cut on my thigh pulls against its stitches. How His Highness has been dealing with that gaping atrocity on his chest constantly moving around, is a horrific mystery.

Everyone else is still sleeping so I sneak out of the doorless frame. I remove the black cloth from my amulet and let the glow of it guide me to the river's edge. The water is a black mirror of calm this close to the winding delta, despite the season. It perfectly reflects the wavering emerald flame and my own green-limned, ghostly visage as I approach. I look more hunted than haunting though, with leaves in my hair and my sleep-deprived features thrown in deep shadows by the flame around my neck.

The mess inside of me is a shattered hive. Chaos and swarming bees stirred up again by dreams and the aches of waking. Green fire. Inness. Screaming. The shocking quiet of metal entering flesh. Pulsing walls of golden light.

It has been eight days since I bottled magic and met a prince. Four since I buried Inness under the earth she held so dear. Two since I discovered what animal fear was while trapped in a tunnel of stone and beasts and men. And if the Trees see fit to bestow any luck on me, today is the day we will figure out *something* about what's happening.

I don't want to be broken by this, but the fabric of me is unwoven. So many threads have been stolen by loss and fear, I don't know what shape I'll take when I can weave myself together again. For now, I'll leave the loom untouched and let the pieces stay as they are.

The oppressive presence of the ruined stone looms around me. There is so much made by man here, stalwart against the devouring of trees, vines and moss. Its rigidity and order feel so foreign to me, even as half-remembered shadows in the dark. But there is reverence in them as well. An appreciation for the land, and its staggering beauty, in the act of building here at all.

Sending boats made of leaves down the lazy river current, I watch the ripples of fallen tears send them bobbing on miniature waves.

CHAPTER

TWENTY-ONE

ALYSSIA

My boots make loud sucking sounds with every step as I try to make my way out of the mud and onto firmly dry land, a state of matter I'm beginning to believe doesn't exist anymore.

"I feel as though there was a miscalculation involved here," Envir laughs behind me, squelching and sinking with each step in my wake. Meanwhile, Carolyn easily traverses through the tall reeds and muck in front of us, angling toward higher ground.

"I forgot how much the spring flooding would affect things out here." The mud reeks and splatters everywhere, spraying fetid grime all over. I glare at Carolyn's sparkling white back and watch as the gunk slides off of her like water on glass.

The marshy land is so thick with water-loving trees, grasses, cattails, and insects, I can't see the lake despite its closeness. I'm desperate to get out of the mire. I long for the rocky shores and swift current of the northern reaches of the river.

Eventually, blessedly, I find earth that holds my weight when I step on it. Even the clouds of swarming bugs taper off as we return to trees, firm ground, and ruined stone. Cracked, heaving, or half-buried ancient pavers make drunken roads beneath our feet.

"How wondrous," Carolyn breathes, her fingers trailing over pitted stone laced with creeping vines. A wall towers above her, at least four stories at its highest point. Soaring, arched windows march along at ground level until they break into gaping teeth, the tops lost to time.

"This city must have been stunning." The prince is just as awed as Carolyn as he weaves in and out of decaying buildings.

"It still is." I'm at the top of a large flat stone pushed up by an invasive root. "I'm probably biased, but I think I like it better this way."

"You would think that, Otherfolk Queen," Envir laughs, bounding up next to me to pluck a leaf out of my hair.

I snatch it from his hand and place it on my palm. With a breath, I send it off into a breeze. "If only. As a Queen of the Otherfolk I could simply will all the Davorists to evaporate, or be eaten by trees, or some such, find the mysterious relic and solve all of our problems." I twirl around with my arms outstretched and wink at Envir when I spin past him.

I catch the prince looking at me, leaning against an empty archway, cradling his bad arm. I can't for the life of me decipher what his expression means, but when he sees me looking, he turns away, peeling himself from the stone.

"We *will* solve our problems." He's so serious, my fleeting smile vanishes faster than it appeared.

Envir snorts and jumps down to the other side of the rise. "Ever confident, Your Highness."

My mud-caked boots slide down the broken stone leaving a dirty trail in my wake. Envir disappears around the trunk of a tree. He lets out a low whistle.

"You're sure this is a lake, Your Otherness?" he calls from out of sight, "Not some secret ocean you've been hiding from me?"

"Almost positive." I push a branch out of my way and almost eat some of Envir's hair as I run into him.

Sun streams down from the widest expanse of open sky in the entire forest. I squint my eyes against the glare on the placid surface of the water and search for whatever it is we are looking for.

Blurry, moss-green towers pierce the sky, rising from the obsidian surface of the lake. The mist shrouded memory I have been chasing since Carolyn mentioned this place finally clears. Suddenly I'm a girl again.

An early teen, all legs and clumsy charm like a fawn, climbing a crumbling pillar jutting from the sandy shore. Another rises from the wetter sand closer to the water, and I eye the distance speculatively.

"Alyssia." Arty drags my name out with painful, reproachful slowness and I frown, squatting to sit atop my perch instead of winding myself up to jump.

"What do you think these were?" I ask, actually hoping for a lecture if it will distract him from chastising me.

He doesn't hesitate or look up from the cluster of little blue flowers he's investigating. "What do you think they were?"

I really should have expected that.

I dutifully furrow my brow and stare at the broken stone trailing into the lake toward the looming island, closer here than at any other spot on shore. I roll my eyes at myself. "It was a bridge." When I squint, I can make out similar posts on the rocky shore of the island. "Or...or docks." I jump down, landing in a crouch on the sand, satisfied with my observation. "Can I go there?"

"So you can fall through a floor and break your neck? Absolutely not. I'm too old to waste time training another apprentice."

I laugh and Envir stares at me with an eyebrow raised. Carolyn and the prince are with us as well, looking out over the lake. The south end is lost to the horizon, but the narrow channel between the off-centered island and land is visible on the western shore.

The building rising from the water is indistinct, shrouded in a misty haze, but the closer we get, the more it takes my breath away. It is easily the most intact of the ruins I have seen in the Woods. Large swathes of dark slate tiles still top the peaked roof. Crenelations, intricate stone patterns, and tall, arched, empty windows shape the walls into delicate works of towering art. Green moss and creeping ivy spill against dark gray stone like paint. It's harsh and beautiful and haunting. I know instantly, and without a doubt, that this was a place of worship. A place of reverence and supplication to the beauty those before us believed in.

"I know for sure now. This place *had* to have been built by the Otherfolk. There's no way mortal men built this." Envir runs his fingers through the tall beach grass as he walks.

We move slowly through the shifting, muddy sand, and watch the temple like it will shimmer away like an illusion. A dream.

The distance between the two sets of pillars is further than I remember, and I wish we had a boat. With falls, rapids, and the varying current, travel on the water is too impractical for us Woodsfolk to bother with, but the calm lake before us could benefit from one. Perhaps I'll talk to Rend about rummaging up a row boat in the future.

"How will we get across?" Carolyn is frowning at the water, eyes jumping between the jutting stones.

I smack my forehead with my palm. "Canopy Above, Carolyn. I forgot you can't swim." Now I *really* wish we had a boat.

The men both shoot a look her way, unbelieving.

"What use do I have for swimming in a library?" She snaps at them, another of her very rare, perfect blushes blooming on her cheeks.

"I will not be able to at present, either, if I am honest." His Highness shrugs with one shoulder careful to not disturb the other.

He has been refusing to let me put his arm in a sling on the off chance he needs to fight, but the longer he keeps treating it like this, the worse it will heal. The unofficial physician in me has been screaming for days about it. Hopefully, we can find what we are looking for here and get everyone home to rest and heal.

"You are absolutely correct. I wouldn't allow you to, even if you wanted to try. You two can keep a look out here or search the other buildings for anything suspiciously relic-like." I glance over to Envir, who is stretching dramatically, and crack a smile. "Looks like the fate of the world is on our shoulders, Envir."

"You know, I always knew I was meant for something bigger than keeping a prince alive and in good trousers." He winks and even Carolyn snorts a laugh.

The prince in question rolls his eyes. "Kiv, save us all."

I turn back to Carolyn. "I'll try to be quick, but I don't know what we'll find over there. I've never been to the island before."

She nods. "Be careful. Look for loose stones in the floors or walls if you don't see anything obvious. We will do the same here." She brushes my cheek and, not for the first time, it feels like a benediction.

The spring sun is warm on my shoulders, and I'm grateful for it. I doubt the lake is any warmer than the river, and that was unpleasant at best whenever I had to come in contact with it. The meager heat from the sun will be necessary.

"Ready for this?" I look to my partner in this adventure, both of us standing just out of reach of the slowly undulating waves.

"Not really, but unless you think the Davorists will let us wait until a nice, hot summer day, we may as well get it over with."

"Unlikely at best."

We laugh and wade into the lake. My boots slip in the sand and immediately fill with shockingly cold water. We both gasp at the first touch of the icy tendrils. Thought leaves my mind as we push against the water, steadily advancing toward the receiving set of pillars. I start swimming with long, even strokes once the water is chest high and there's no point in trying to keep any remaining part of me dry. Once I do make the switch, the passage through the lake becomes much easier, if much, much colder. It's a long swim, but I pace myself, losing track of anything outside of the rhythm of stroke and breath. The easy, buoyant motion of swimming is tiring, and the cut on my thigh twinges in protest, but it's infinitely more tolerable than all of the joint-grinding running. Or it would be more tolerable if the water wasn't threatening to turn my blood into ice.

Envir is already on the rocky shore, wringing out his soaked shirt and readjusting his sword for walking instead of swimming by the time I pull myself, splashing and sloshing, out of the water. I shiver as the first brisk breeze hits me and immediately rip off my own shirt, not willing to tolerate the prolonged wetness of wearing it. My stiff, side-laced, cropped stays are the only thing preserving my modesty, and I would consider taking them off to dry as well if they weren't such a pain in the ass to unlace when wet. Instead, I let the sun try to do its job and warm my skin while I lay out my shirt, weighed down with rocks on the shore.

"To the temple?" I ask, scanning the rocky embankment, trying to find a way up. I take the shirtless opportunity to peek at the stitched wound on his side. The edges of the thin ridge of crusted scab are already starting to show the wrinkled, glossy pink of healing, and I feel a glimmer of satisfaction. At least one of my patients is progressing nicely.

Envir nods and moves toward a worn set of stairs carved into the small bluff boarding the beach.

The ancient structure looms over us when we reach the top. Almost the entire island is consumed by it, the smallest of overgrown courtyards and narrow stretches of rocky ground outlining the sides are the only unoccupied ground. The gaping, shadowed doorway with its dramatically pointed arch and delicately carved stone trees beckons me, luring me into its immortal realm.

The light inside is dim, filtered through rotted ceilings and glassless windows. The antechamber is not what I expected, small and littered with such highly decayed wood I'm not sure what was once furniture, paneling, door or window frame. I can imagine how welcoming it must have been in its prime, though. Two curving staircases, spread like they are awaiting an embrace, lead to a shadowed second floor. The stairs are thankfully made of stone instead of wood, therefore surviving the centuries for us if we need them. Nothing I have seen compares to what lays beyond the gaping doorway centered beneath the stairs. I leave every other thought and worry behind me as I'm drawn into the chamber ahead.

The ceiling vaults above me in carved, creeping branches, the buttresses formed in the shape of the great trees of my Woods. I'm surrounded by a memorial of stone. Even in the grip of decay, I'm stunned. Woodland scenes are carved into weathered relief on every wall. Windows with the remnants of leading for stained glass make me yearn to know what used to fill them. The moss from the exterior walls creeps in through the empty spaces, and its presence here breathes life into the cold stone. I inhale deeply and am overpowered with the scents of marshy lake and moss, crisp spring air, and ancient dust.

Above all other wonders is the altar. It towers over the chamber at the end of an aisle formed by rotting wood and stone pews. I feel tears well as I wade through the debris like the waters of the lake.

The altar is a tree of stone and moss stretching and spreading above me, its canopy the entire vaulted ceiling. Its branches slip and weave between all of the others. There is a gaping, knotted hollow in the center of it, so large I could climb inside and curl around the brilliant forest-green flame burning at its heart.

I fall to my knees before it.

Now I know the feeling Carolyn has before her altar of candles and stained glass. I could give my whole being to the stone and flame in front of me and not blink; not hesitate for a heartbeat. This is my whole self. Inness. Arty. The shop. The Great Tree. All condensed into one point. One fuel-less fire. This is the shape the fabric of me will make when it's woven back together. This has always been the shape of me.

The soul of my Woods speaks to my own in this cavernous, ruinous temple. I can feel the tendrils of new growth creep through the stone and along the broken parts of me, knitting me back together. I would root myself to the earth where I kneel with no regrets if it was only my problems I would be running from. Too much relies on my ability to keep moving.

Reluctantly, I stand, snapping the tentative connections between myself and the spirit of this sanctuary.

My hands run along the pitted stone and my skin tingles at the touch with heat, need, and knowing. I trace the familiar shape of every tree I have ever touched within these Woods. The thought of any relic that isn't of this place residing here makes me physically ill. That anything tainted by Davor could be held within these walls is sacrilege. This place is a monument to life and creation, seasonal rebirth and the cyclical nature of death. Not destruction. Not murder. Not control.

When I come back to myself, I find Envir crouched on the ground behind the altar, running his hands over the stone floor, prying at the seams, checking for hidden spots like Carolyn suggested. I do the same, running my hands over the statue, feeling for anything that isn't right, but I feel no seams. No loose stone. The tree is of one piece as far as I can reach. The inside of the hollow harboring the enchanted flame feels so much like living bark, not even its stony gray coloring can convince me otherwise.

"Have you found anything?" Envir runs his hands along the walls.

"The physical embodiment of faith I didn't know I had, and the complete shape of my being. But nothing relevant, no." I try to embrace the joke, but I sound shaken. I don't want to break contact with the column, but I drag myself away to join Envir in searching the walls.

He gently bumps my shoulder with his when I join him. "I thought it may be something like that. Looked like I lost you there for a bit." He smiles and stretches up to reach a portion of the wall I can't. "You've lost a lot that can't be replaced. If what you found today can help in any way, I'm glad for it. For you." There is a profound sadness in his voice I didn't expect.

"Who was it?" I ask, quietly enough that he can pretend to not hear me.

For a moment, I think he won't answer, but he drops his questing hands and turns, leaning back against the wall. "My sister," he sighs and smiles up at the distant ceiling. "She would have loved this place. The Woods, in general, I mean. We're a coastal house so she grew up as a part of the sea, but she thrived in wildness, and I have never been anywhere as untamed as this."

"Was she buried at sea?" I rest my hand on his arm lightly as he nods. "What was her name?"

"Laenry" Her name is a prayer on his lips.

I feel my own loss swell and tilt my head toward him, buying myself a moment to be sure my voice will not break. "I will ask Rend to honor her with the others."

He turns to me, confused. "What do you mean?" His curiosity pulls some of the sadness from him, and I drop my hand to continue our search of the walls.

"My friend, Rend, is from the Ardjan islands. They bury their dead at sea, as well, and honor their spirits with prayers and shrines on their ships. I will ask her to honor Laenry of the Wild Sea as well, so her spirit may remain strong and run with the waves."

He laughs and I smile. "She would love that. *I* would love that." He rests a hand on my shoulder, and I look at him our eyes meeting. "Thank you, Alyssia." His voice is warm and serious. "Thank you."

I'm the first to reach the empty window in our search of the walls. I'm the first to see the crude raft beached in a small, rocky alcove at the base of a short cliff behind the temple. I'm the first to see the flicker of black, flapping fabric ascending the steep hill toward us.

"Shit."

CHAPTER TWENTY-TWO
ALYSSIA

"Envir. Company." I throw myself back from the window, pulling him with me before we are seen.

"What?" His hand goes for his sword immediately, his body reacting to my urgency while his mind catches up; a phenomenon I'm becoming uncomfortably accustomed to, and therefore, sympathetic toward.

I'm really going to have to consider becoming better armed if this keeps up.

"Cultists, coming up from the back. Don't know how many," I whisper, crawling on my hands and knees across the floor. Trying to stay out of sight is a difficult task when the entire chamber was built to worship the space outside of it, its walls more window than stone.

"Shit, indeed." He flattens himself against the wall and edges to the window, trying to surreptitiously spot the assailants. He roughly jerks his sword out of its scabbard, the blade sticking to the wet leather.

I press myself up against the trunk of the central tree, and bury myself in the folds of its gray bark. When my back touches the rough stone, I stifle a hysterical laugh as I realize we're both still shirtless, our clothes drying on the beach outside.

The laugh comes out as a short snort, and Envir snaps his head toward me.

"This isn't what I would normally wear if I was expecting guests."

He looks down and back up, his shoulders shaking with silent laughter.

"I suppose it would depend on the type of guest," he whispers back with a grin before stalking around the room as carefully as he can. He checks each window for movement as he makes his way to the front of the temple.

With solid, deliberate, choice this time, I uncork my pendant and edge toward the open hollow of the altar. This fire belongs here. I know, deep within me, that I should not remove it from this place. But I will not allow the cultists to take it. I know in my bones I would rather die than let that happen.

The first ringing echo of colliding metal makes me jump as I pull the necklace away from my heavy, wet hair and nearly drop it. I fumble with the jar, trying to find some angle or way to scoop the fire into it without pouring the current occupant out in the attempt. This new fire is larger than mine, larger than my pendant entirely. I start to panic. My heartbeat races faster with every clash of swords behind me, and I still don't know how to get the stupid thing to cooperate. When I finally decide to tip the pendant toward the unbound flame, the fire inside my necklace dances madly, tongues of green licking the rim, escaping toward its larger counterpart.

"Alyssia!" Envir's roar makes me drop to the ground.

A blade strikes sparks on the stone above me.

I kick back, making sharp contact with the shin of the person behind me and they falter. As they struggle to steady themselves, I push up and back. I drive my elbows into the bulk of the off-balance attacker and they stumble, slipping on the rubble strewn floor. It buys me just enough time to thrust the now empty vial into the altar. The contents of my pendant united with that of the temple and it burns like a proper fire now. Its green-yellow flames crackle within the tree of stone. With no time to decide on a better option, I cup my hand around the heatless flame and shove it toward the open mouth of the pendant. To my surprise and gratitude, it complies, coiling itself into the confines of the glass without even touching my skin.

Then I am, once again, running. Slipping on broken stones and wood,

I simultaneously try to replace the cork into the vial, put the cord around my neck, and dodge the restabilized cultist. Envir has two of them engaged in the doorway into the antechamber. I search frantically for a path to safety.

The cultist behind me will be on top of me in another heartbeat, maybe two. I have no space to backtrack to the far windows thanks to him. The side windows lead to sharp drops onto rocky cliffs and the lake below, a plunge I'm not willing to risk. The only way out is through the fight in front of me. If I can only get down to the beach, I can leave the slashing blades behind.

I rush the door, tripping and sliding. The three men are in a tight knot, defying the reach of their weapons, keeping one side of the opening clear enough for me to squeeze through. I almost get tangled in the Tree-forsaken, billowing coat of one of the cultists as they unexpectedly break away from the group. I take the opportunity to grab the offending fabric and pull with all of my momentum and my anger until I feel the give of them losing their footing. I let go before I slow down and smile when I hear the grunt of pain behind me.

The smile immediately vanishes.

Hidden behind the fight is another cultist, cast in dark silhouette waiting by the door to the outside. I have no time to stop, to think. Envir may be able to occupy all of the assholes behind me, or he may not. I may, just may, be able to get past the person at the door. It's narrower than the one I just came through, but there is only one person instead of three. I have no choice. I can't take the time to stop and consider other options, so I keep running for the sunlit courtyard. Freedom. The safety of the water and distant shore.

The safety is nothing but a delusion.

The cultist is ready for me and lunges sword-first. I'm saved only by my willingness to slam into the stone door frame to stop myself. The impact spins me. I grunt and grab the edge to stop myself from falling. Now facing the antechamber again, I see the stairs.

One more option.

The only hope I have up there is a place to hide while Envir dispatches our problems, or a nice ledge to drop a cultist off I suppose, but it's more hope than I have down here.

I fling myself away from the doorway and up the steps. I stumble out onto a massive balcony overlooking the room below. At either end of the passageway are small, dim doorways. I debate my chances of finding a respectable place to hide in either of them, but before I can make up my mind, the glint of steel flashes from the opposite stairwell, followed by its wielder. Out of options at last, I run to the edge. The railing, supports, and stone path are woven into the sculptured buttresses I saw from the ground, creating a hidden mezzanine around the entire chamber below. I have no plan. No direction. And if I had the time to be honest with myself, no hope. But I don't have time for that, so I calm my labored breathing and keep going. My footsteps erupt in clouds of centuries old dust as I make my escape, my still-wet boots making slick mud in my wake. Turning the first corner, I see the blur of my attacker between the stone branches behind me. Much too close.

Moving here feels like moving through the Woods, and I fall quickly into the same motions. The scents of earth and leaves are replaced with dust and lake, but the light strobing between pillars of stone and open windows could be the light between trees. The debris and loose, crumbling stones underfoot could be the rocks and detritus of the forest floor. The soft green light reflecting around me only adds to my conjured image. It isn't until I reach the next corner that I realize the leafy-green light is radiating from the amulet, the fabric shroud lost somewhere in my flight. The vial is solid with roiling flames, the fire filling all available space now instead of contentedly hovering in the center.

The pendant swings wildly with my slide around the bend in the path. I catch myself with one outstretched hand as something tugs on my hair. The loud ringing of a sword against stone resounds above my head. A curse and a quieter, distant clang follow. I scramble to my feet awkwardly. Rough fingertips brush my exposed skin. They grasp nothing but air as I pull away again. Thank the Trees my loose shirt is on the beach below, or I would be caught. Instead, I dart away like a fox, staying low and using my hands for several strides before straightening and making the final turn toward the front of the temple.

The entrance to the stairs and freedom are mere strides from me when my head jerks back, and I come to a sudden and painful stop. I fall, never quite reaching the ground, partially suspended by my hair in the fist of the cultist. He reaches down for my amulet. I rip myself away from him, my scalp screaming, hands grasping for the pendant. We are both off balance now. Reeling drunkenly. He lets go of my hair, and I blink watering eyes. I see, too late, that we have careened to the very edge of one of the gaping windows. He released his grip so he could brace himself against the wall.

For one agonizing, suspended eternity, I hang in the air, the twine cord biting into my neck, the pendant grasped in the meaty, tattooed hand of the cultist. I watch as the string wrapped around the vial slides off one coiled loop at a time. Then there is nothing but air beneath me and the rapidly shrinking, confused face of the man staring at my leaf-colored heart in his hand.

CHAPTER

TWENTY~THREE

ALYSSIA

I don't have time to panic about hitting the rocky cliff-side before I crash into the water, all air driven from my lungs. I can't move as I plunge into the icy depths. I can't think. The force and the cold freeze me. Even as I slam into the silty bottom of the lake, sand billowing around me, I can't react. I rebound from the bottom and lose all orientation, blinded by the cloud of muck and darkness. My lungs burn. My eyes sting with dirt. My head pounds. I want to scream, but I don't have the air.

No one is coming to save me, but I'm not done. I will not drown down here in the mud.

I gather every last ounce of strength I have and push myself back down until my boots hit the lake bed. Desperately, I launch upward. My body screams for air. My vision blurs. The surface rushes closer and the clear sight of sky taunts me. My lungs betray me and take a deep, choking breath a heartbeat before my head breaks the surface.

I emerge coughing and gagging, trying to suck in air around the half-breath of water I consumed instead. My head keeps dipping under, the coughing too strong for me to fight and stay afloat, but I can see enough between flailing and choking to spot the rocky cliffs of the island. I drag myself toward them.

My fingers scrape stone. My nails crack as I claw my way out of the water. I gag and try not to vomit. My stomach clenches painfully as I cling like seaweed to the rock. Everything hurts and my throat burns, and I'm dangerously close to falling unconscious and back into the water. But I'm alive.

When my choking abates enough for me to breathe, and I'm no longer in danger of sliding back into the lake, I drag my head up and look toward the looming island. A sheer cliff stares back at me, and I groan, my throat stinging with the effort. I shake from cold, exhaustion and delayed terror. I need to find some way to muster the strength to make it to the front of the island.

Distantly, my mind registers the sound of screaming, and I double check that it isn't coming from me. When I confirm that it isn't, I start looking around for its source. I scan the water dumbly until the sound comes to me again.

"Alyssia!"

My name echoes down to me from the cliff. I smile, weakly.

Envir is alive as well.

I try to yell back, but my voice simply doesn't want to work. A crackling, grating sound is all that comes out on my first attempt. I force a few deep breaths and swallow several times before trying again.

"I'm here!" It's still not as loud as it should be, but at least it comes out this time. I try to haul myself further onto the rock, but it is too awkwardly shaped for me to gain traction.

"Alyssia?" His shout comes again, clearer now.

One more try.

"Envir! In the water!"

His auburn hair flashes in the sun just above the edge of the cliff. Not even twice my height, without rope or strength or any place for me to get a real handhold, it may as well be taller than the temple itself. He is unreachable.

"Thank Kiv, Alyssia. Carolyn would have skinned me alive if I came back without you." His voice quavers with what I have learned over the last few days to be fear.

"Don't write off that possibility just yet." My own voice is raw, and the humor I try to convey gets lost in the cracks. "Meet me by the front beach. I can't make it up from here."

"I'll be right there." His head vanishes, and I'm very, terrifyingly, alone again.

I just have to make it to the front of the island and I won't be alone. The swim to the beach isn't that far.

"Please," my prayer is a whisper on the back of my final exhale before I push myself away from my sanctuary and plunge into the water.

It doesn't take long for me to want to give up. My muscles cramp from the abuse and the cold, but I keep kicking, propelling myself forward. I try to cut rhythmically through the water, but I'm a tangle of erratic, mismatched movements and I make agonizingly slow progress until I'm swept up suddenly. The water still comes up to my chin, but the ground is under my feet, and Envir has his arms around me, dragging me against his relatively warm body and out of the lake.

We stagger onto the beach, and I would fall to my knees if he didn't have me in a death grip. Instead, he lowers both of us down gently, rubbing my arms vigorously, trying to get me to stop shaking.

"The sun is going to set soon. We need to get back to the mainland." Sitting hurts possibly more than standing. I can't wait to see the array of bruises that are going to decorate the back half of my body.

"Alyssia..." He has me pulled up against him, one arm wrapped tightly around me. "Your necklace..."

"I'll get it back, Envir. I lost it. Not you." I know the ring of self-blame when I hear it. I've used it enough myself. "Without you it would be lost, and I would be dead." I touch the wet twine around my neck, somehow still present. The surface of the coin tied there is still dull, despite being wet, but the green ribbon is dark and shining.

"We will get it back. The four of us." He clears his throat and stands, pulling me to my feet with him. "You're right though, we do need to get back and make sure Ked and Carolyn are alright. I haven't seen any obvious trouble, but I've been a little busy."

I hadn't even considered the cultists would've found them. Urgency fills me, temporarily dampening the throbbing pain drumming against my back. I lurch out of Envir's partial embrace and begin splashing through the water.

"Hey, wait up," Envir stoops to pick something up off the ground before chasing after me.

It's my shirt.

Belatedly, I notice he is wearing his again so I take mine, sliding it over my head. My damp skin immediately makes it cling, and I'm just as cold with it on as not, but at least I won't have to carry it while I swim.

"Yell if you need any assistance."

I snort and it hurts my throat. "You know, you don't look fresh as a spring rain yourself."

His shoulders slump as we wade slower and slower through the deepening water. His shirt isn't bloodied, but I can see red nicks on his hands and one trailing down his jaw, dangerously close to his throat.

"I'm not *just* for decoration, you know," he laughs tiredly.

"I don't, actually." That did not come out at all like I intended. I try again quickly. "I mean, I don't really know who you are, aside from the prince's friend, distantly acquainted to Carolyn, and a lord from the coast."

"Oh. Right. Easy to forget we don't really know each other after all of this." He waves his hand in the air, encompassing the last week of our lives.

The water is getting too deep for me to walk through with the speed my building anxiety requires.

"When it's all settled, we'll meet at the Prism and have a good, long personal history lesson." I wink at him and dive into the water with much more vigor than I actually have left.

—

By the time I can touch the ground again, both of us are barely dragging ourselves through the water, breathing hard and leaning into each other as we splash our way to dry land.

Blood soaks the sand in long slashes of dark, muddy crimson. Carolyn and the prince are nowhere to be seen.

Envir and I lock eyes and start shouting at the same time.

"Carolyn!"

"Kedren!"

We take off at a slight angle to each other, still yelling their names.

I trip over the first body, hidden in the tall mix of grasses growing throughout the area, and land hard on my hands and knees. When I stand to look at what soft thing I kicked, I discover that I have rolled the corpse over enough to see its face. Or what's left of it. One bright eye stares at me out of the blackened, glossy ruin, the other nothing but a gaping pit rimmed with char.

If I was anyone else, I would be a lot closer to puking than I am, but even my gut churns as I lean closer, examining the damage, wondering what new facet of cult magic caused this. Envir's shouting, muffled by the trees and stone between us, reminds me what I'm about. I resume my own yelling.

Was that an answering call?

I find another corpse, this one with its throat neatly punctured, sprawled out on one of the uneven slabs of paving stone, blood trailing in sluggish rivulets down to the forest floor. A particularly large, intact leaf holds a small pool of the thick, clotting liquid, black in the shadows of the canopy. I feel a strange, disturbing urge to cup the leaf in both hands and drink from it like I would river water before tipping the rest onto the soil. It feels right. Like a ritual I have done many times before despite the revulsion I feel.

I stagger back from the vision and shake my head hard enough to replace the compulsion with the pounding of my headache.

"Carolyn!" *Please, Carolyn. Answer me.*

There it is again, a distant sound. A response or my hopeful imagination? I stumble toward it, tripping over crumbling stone and careening into trees as I propel myself through the forest. A ripple of golden light tugs at the corner of my vision, and I snap my head around to track it.

"Vi!" The prince's voice suddenly rings clearly from the same direction. I take off toward it.

"Lys?" Thank the Trees. *Carolyn.*

A small, mostly intact building pulses with golden light. I don't stop to find a doorway. I climb gracelessly through a gaping window and drop into the kind of chaos I'm beginning to find unfortunately familiar.

The prince is locked with a cultist, his sword blocking two smaller blades in the tattooed hands of the woman. The muscles of her thighs flex through the split in her coat, bulging against the thin material of her trousers. Her teeth are gritted into a snarl, and her dark eyes bore hatred into the prince.

Behind them, the golden light streaked with red flares as Carolyn and another cultist stand with their feet planted wide, several strides apart. Their hands and mouths move quickly and quietly, shaping the light around them. Without warning, the Davorist flicks his wrist, a snaking tongue of gold and red unfurling into a lashing whip. Sparks fly from its cracking tip. The cultist bursts into motion, dancing with the weapon, throwing strike after strike at my friend, advancing toward her slowly.

She is undaunted. Her eyes narrow and lips press into a thin line of concentration whenever they aren't whispering silent prayers. She has her hands outstretched, the chain of her relic woven around her fingers and wrist in a tight net, the golden pendant hanging in the center of her open palm. Her robes and shining black hair float around her as if she is suspended in water, splinters of golden light pierce the air like striking lightning from the thunder cloud she has become. The whip strikes nothing visible, but each jarring crack ends in a wave of golden light like the shattering of glass.

I have to do something. Two more bodies lay slumped on the ground, and I lunge for one, grabbing for the blade discarded at its side. When I right myself, I'm between the two struggling pairs, trying to decide who to assist.

My decision is made when the prince lets out a cry of pain, one of the woman's long daggers scraping down his forearm.

The short, curved sword in my hand is unlike any of the blades I have seen used, but I grip it tightly and charge in. I hope for nothing more than a distraction large enough to give the prince time to do something more useful. The woman is pressing her advantage against him and doesn't notice my approach from the side until its almost too late. For the quickest of heartbeats, I think I will be able to stab her and be done with it, but instead, she angles one blade to deflect mine and the other, the prince's. My bones rattle at the impact but I hold tight, backing away with a jump. The three of us stand, temporarily motionless, as we all eye each other warily. The only sound is the snapping and hissing of the magic behind us.

Apparently deciding I'm the lesser threat, the cultist turns her main focus back to the prince, keeping herself angled to watch me. His swings are wild and slow. He's soaked in sweat and blood. It's not hard to see she has the upper hand. My body tenses to move as soon as I come up with a plan.

I lunge behind her, throwing myself into a flanking position at the exact moment she has both of her blades occupied with the prince. With one low sweep of my arms, I rake the blade against the backs of her legs as hard as I can. Blood sprays in a satisfying arc. She screams. The prince stumbles to his knees. His sword drops from blood-slick fingers, physically unable to keep it raised any longer. The cultist collapses, long daggers discarded. She moans as blood soaks her clothing. The prince echoes her, clutching at his chest, blood dying his shirt red beneath his fingers.

Without hesitation, I grab a handful of her grimy, blond hair and jerk her head back. Her dark eyes are wet with tears, but full of defiance, daring me to raise my hand against her. I reverse the sword in my grip and push the blade through the exposed flesh of her throat. I saw deeply through corded muscles and stiff cartilage.

Her blood hits the ground like a spring rain.

I drop her gaping, open-mouthed like a fish, to bleed her last and turn to Carolyn. I'm rewarded with the sight of Envir, his sword plunged into the man's back to the hilt.

"It was up to us, once again, eh?" I throw the bloodied blade to the dirt and wipe my sweaty, scraped palms on my wet shirt.

"They will write songs about us, surely." He rips the sword out of the body as it crumples to the ground before diving toward the prince. He slides on his knees to his side, all his quick humor lost. "Ked, are you with me?"

The prince nods and makes a small sound I can't even categorize as a groan as he falls into his friend's arms.

We're all panting. Exhausted. Carolyn kneels in the dirt, her hands splayed to steady herself. Envir cradles the prince, one hand smoothing back sweaty tendrils of dark hair from his ashen face. I sway on my feet, afraid to sit or kneel for the pain of a bruised backside or bloodied knees. The walls of the ruin spin, and I wonder if I have a concussion from my collision with the lake on top of everything else.

The stone walls and black-clad corpses become too much all at once. I need the feel of rough bark and the scent of leaves and earth overwhelming my senses. Not blood. Retreating blindly into the forest, I collide with the embrace of a towering tree. Its roots tangle in underbrush and push stone slabs away, creating a nest of pure woodland. The gray twilight casts familiar shadows, and I breathe slow, deep breaths through my nose and out of my mouth.

I was so completely sure of my place in the world hours ago. Now everything is torn apart. I feel like I'm back in the water, stunned and unable to move or breathe. I dig my broken nails into the bark of the tree and relish the grate of it against raw skin. I need the flame of this forest to quench the burning inside of me. I need it to weave its roots through me and into the earth below. The thought of doing anything but crumbling into the dirt without it overwhelms me.

It's gone. Lost to the hands of the Davorists.

I don't realize my cheeks are wet until Carolyn is at my side, brushing tears away with a sweep of gentle fingers.

"Dear one." She holds my face. I shake with sobs. "What is it?"

"It's gone, Carolyn." I clutch desperately at the waterlogged twine at my neck. "Inness' pendant. They took it. They've taken *everything* from me."

Carolyn wraps her arms around me and squeezes tightly. "We will get it back, darling."

"I can't let them have it," my voice shakes, and I want to claw my way out of my skin, but her embrace traps my arms to my sides.

"We will get it back. I promise. We can find a way." Her voice is so gentle, so calm, I almost believe her.

"But I'm so tired. I don't know if I can do this anymore. I'm too old for this." I try to force a laugh, but I choke on despair instead.

"I know, dear one. I know. I think we are all too old for these kinds of adventures, but we started down this path, and you know we need to finish it."

I squeeze my eyes shut and dig into the crumbling bark of the tree. I don't want to exist beyond my own personal sphere of tragedies. But just because I'm dangerously close to having nothing left, doesn't mean I can give up on those around me. I struggle to conjure the image of the sweating and pale prince, collapsed on the ground. Envir swaying and staggering out of the water. Carolyn sliding to the ground with exhaustion. I try to rally myself to these immediate concerns, but it's no use. I'm too tired.

"Alyssia." It's Envir, trying to break through the void around me. "He needs you."

I need someone too.

I want to scream it until I can't scream anymore.

I can't always be the one who has to stand up and face what needs to be faced. I need sleep. I need to feel safe. I need more than half a day to grieve the child I lost.

But I'm not allowed any of that now. I don't have the privilege of letting someone else solve these problems. These are my Woods. These are my people, tired and bleeding before me. I must be enough, regardless of what I need.

I gather myself one bruised, bloody, empty section at a time and lash them all together in an attempt to not fall apart when I stand. "Take him to the building we passed this morning." *Canopy Above. Was that just this morning?* "It should be a little north of here. Carolyn and I will bring our things." The prince probably shouldn't be moved until I can check him, but I can't bring myself to go back to that house of corpses.

He nods and disappears. I remove myself from the bark slowly, reluctantly snapping the tendrils of me that try to burrow into the wood.

With Carolyn's help, I extricate myself from my haven, and we make our way to the beach and our pile of supplies. I want to throw up into the blood soaked sand and fall asleep somewhere where I can be buried in falling leaves. As a paltry compromise I spit and start shouldering bags, crossing straps over my chest until I have all of them but the large canvas supply bag digging into my bruised back. "Water, Carolyn. I'll need some to be boiled."

She nods and removes our pot from the bag before slinging it over her shoulders and going to collect water from the lake. I turn and disappear back into the Woods without her.

I find the broken paver with my muddy boot prints and follow it to the large, ruinous building with the broken teeth windows. The canopy of the trees comforts me, their trunks hiding the blackened depths of the lake from my view. I feel drunk, just ever so slightly off my axis as I unload our supplies. I dig through my bag for the packets of pain relieving tea and the container of the widow resin salve. There is only one jar of the suturing thread left, and I hope it will be enough. The new batch will not be usable for at least a week.

The thought of the spiders brings more bile to my mouth, and I spit again. I've had more than enough violence for quite awhile. I never thought this notion would cross my mind, as used to it as I am, but I'm so tired of blood.

I stack fallen wood onto an area I swept clean for a fire when all three of my companions enter through the empty doorway. Carolyn sets the pot of water down next to me and takes over making camp without a word so I'm free to turn to the prince. Envir lowers him slowly to the ground at my feet. Stifling a groan, I choose to kneel on my scraped knees instead of sit on my bruised ass.

"Alyssia, your pendant," he says roughly, his unsteady gaze locked on the empty, dangling, twine between my breasts.

"It's gone. I'm sure it will be in the hands of their High Priestess as soon as possible."

"Which means it will be in the hands of Daralyn even sooner than that," he says irritably.

I bite back a laugh. This is too much, even for the swirling unreality that is my life right now. "What *is* it between you and your sister? Did she get more toys growing up or something?" The words taste bitter in my mouth, but I wouldn't take them back if I could. His obsession with her involvement in world events is just too much for my current lack of sanity. Envir moves to step between us, his mouth open to speak, but I ignore him, leaning around him to keep hounding the prince. "You're so obsessed with all of this coming back to her. Why? What is the point of that? She's just one brat in a palace. The Davorists are more than capable of making their own problems."

I fall back with a grunt as he staggers violently to his feet. Envir tries to steady him, but is pushed away for his efforts.

"Because it's always her," he yells so loudly a crashing cloud of birds erupts from a nearby tree.

This is the first time I've heard him raise his voice.

I am incensed.

My own tired, broken anger boils to the surface, and I jump to my feet, ready to start shouting back.

Just as quickly, all that fire turns to ice.

One look at his face tells me he isn't angry.

This isn't rage.

It's despair.

A brokenness even more complete than mine.

As I watch, teeth clenched against whatever comes next, he rips his shirt off, tearing it from his useless left arm with a growl. Sweat and blood slicks his skin. But it's so much more than that.

"It is always her." The words are cracked and quiet, but his bare torso speaks them louder and louder the longer I look.

My heart breaks with the telling.

He is covered in scars.

They aren't from battles or duels. They don't make him look rugged or nobly wounded. There are the ghosts of burns and ugly ridges from poorly tended gashes that make him look as though he was ripped apart. The entire right side of his chest is a swirling mass of shiny, fibrous tissue. A glistening, churning, sea of scars. I blink back sudden tears as I see a pattern emerge. Wherever normal clothing would cover, his flesh is marred. Where it would be reasonable to see skin, it's the flawless porcelain expected of a royal. The marks are deliberate. Precise. Many are old, but some still have the faint pinkness of newer healing. The heavily bruised, bloody gash in his chest is the highest mark on his left side. Just below it are several long lines of white that look like the raking of massive claws, their edges blurred with the shadows of repeated strokes.

He turns his back to me and the assault of monochromatic brush strokes doesn't stop. Ridges of glossy flesh snake along his back and down past the waistband of his pants. Melted patches and wide, smooth lines reflect the flickering light of the fire.

"It is always her." His fist clenches at his side. His voice is no more than a breath, but I can still hear the shame in it.

I suddenly feel as though I know everything and nothing about him.

With a step forward, I reach for his ruined body without touching him. My fingers hover a hairs-breadth from the canvas of pain I can't look away from.

I've seen countless people bared in lust and professionalism, but I have never seen someone this completely naked. His adamant refusal to let me see him shirtless makes so much sense now. I feel sick with the need to take back the mere suggestion of him revealing this to me before he was ready.

He flinches away from my closeness. I drop my hand. The inflamed, red edges of his wound creep over his shoulder, and I wince. I was convinced his cavalier attitude toward the injury was just some stupid male bravado, but now I see just how wrong I was.

"Kedren," I whisper around the tightness in my throat. I chase the sound of his name with another half step forward, uselessly hoping to snatch it back before he can hear the pleading intimacy in it.

He turns abruptly, and his haunted eyes meet mine. "She is not what everyone thinks she is."

How many times have people accused him of fabricating horrors about her just like I did? If she is capable of this, what else could she be involved in?

"I believe you," I say quietly, trying not to reach for him again. "Anything you say she has done or has her hands in, I will believe you."

His breathes in small, gasping breathes as he searches my face for some lie, or trick, or thing left unsaid. He curls into himself, trying to shield his body with his arms, to hide himself from me again.

I may be a shattered ghost of myself, but even broken wood can burn. My touch against his cheek sets us both on fire.

CHAPTER TWENTY-FOUR

KEDREN

It is just a touch, a gesture in response to the sight of me. Nothing more. It cannot be anything more.

It feels like a slap. A caress. A declaration.

My labored breaths ease as her cool skin touches my burning face. I am plunged into the ice of her eyes, and the heat of my shame is quenched like a blade. My hand reaches to answer her touch with its own, but the blood dripping from my fingers catches her eye. She tears her gaze from mine and drops her hand to catch my wrist.

The thread between us breaks, and I snap back to myself painfully. Remembering what triggered my outburst, my heart breaks for Alyssia and my eyes widen as I realize what her necklace being taken means.

"Are you unharmed?" I don't wait for her response before calling out to Envir, "Vi, are you alright? What happened?" I take an abortive step toward him without breaking her hold on my wrist. I am paralyzed by the choice of who to assure myself of their safety first.

"You need to sit. You're going to fall and I can't catch you right now," she sighs. The truth of it is in her face and the betraying shake of my own knees. Neither of us are long for the vertical life.

"And you are freezing,"

She smiles with good-natured surrender and we stagger together to the edge of the fire, where the priestess and Envir sit with such studious indifference, the embarrassment of my outburst rises again.

My fingers itch to pull my discarded shirt back on, but the damage has already been done. I cannot take back this revelation. I will have to wait and see if it somehow proves itself a mistake. Aside from that, Alyssia still has a tight hold on my wrist, examining the line of red scored down my forearm.

I follow her as she kneels on the soft earth next to her ready supplies. She winces as she does.

"What happened?" I ask again, looking between her and Envir.

"Four of them showed up on a raft on the other side of the island. One of them got away," Envir replies, glancing at Alyssia before continuing to help the priestess make camp.

"That would be the one who pushed me out the window and stole the pendant, I assume?" Alyssia washes her hands in the just-boiled water, her skin reddening with the heat of it.

Envir flinches like she hit him. "I'm sorry, Alyssia."

"No, no. I didn't mean it like that. I should have been able to do something about it myself." She scrubs at my bloody forearm with, in my opinion, unnecessary vigor.

"Excuse me, you were pushed out of a window?" The priestess pauses in her allocation of dried meats and hard cheeses to look up at Alyssia with a sharp glare. "Ground floor, I trust?"

"Oh no. Somewhere near the top. I landed on the water though, instead of the rocks." She shrugs as she exchanges the wet cloth for the pink salve and a strip of bandaging.

"You could have been killed," I blurt out, stupidly, before I can stop myself.

The flat stare she gives me confirms my desire to have kept my mouth shut.

"I hate to point this out, but we all could have been. It isn't surprising that I came the closest. I seem to be the most useless in those situations." I open my mouth to speak, but she holds up a hand. "I didn't say I was useless in general, just when being chased by people with swords."

I close my mouth, not in agreement, but because I cannot think of a way to tell her otherwise without sounding placating. She has been more effective, and more courageous, than many men trained for worse.

"You have personally saved my life with a blade in your hand twice in the last few weeks. I am not sure how much more useful you want to be."

"That was luck. I can't do anything when I really need to." She turns from me. "I couldn't stop them from taking the pendant. I couldn't stop any of this."

The fact that keeping me alive does not seem to register on her list of important accomplishments stings, but does not surprise me. It wouldn't rank highly on many.

"On that note, I would like to learn how to wield a blade, Envir. If we could begin lessons, perhaps tomorrow if all goes well?" We all blink at her in confusion. "I believe you forget that Kiv was a great Sword Master in her time."

I did forget that, somehow, even though the most common image of the Martyr depicts her brandishing her bloodied sword.

"I'll do anything you ask of me, your High Priestessness. I'm certainly not going to get on your bad side." Envir grins easily and tears at a piece of dried meat with his teeth.

"If you call me that where anyone else can hear you, you will get us both in a great deal of trouble." Her tone is serious, but there is a glint in her eyes that suggests some pleasure in the title he bestowed her.

I hiss as Alyssia brings a cloth to my chest to, once again, clean away a build up of gore and grime. Miraculously, the sutures are almost all intact, but the mottled bruising around the wound has spread and deepened in color. She shakes her head and continues carefully cleaning as I dig the fingers of my other hand into the ground so deeply I find the stone floor of the ruin.

"Of course, of course, Priestess. I'll wait until you ascend, or are blessed, or whatever the process is." Envir stretches out on the ground and winks at her. "But you'll always be the High Priestess in my heart."

She tosses a handful of leaves at him with a grin. Alyssia flicks her gaze back to them, the corner of her mouth turning up a fraction. She pauses to take a sip of the tea in the wooden cup by her side, close to the fire to keep hot. It smells of the bitter, medicinal herbs she has brewed for me before. Then she resumes staring at my chest and shoulder, the tip of her tongue sneaking out in its thoughtful little curl.

"Do we agree that we'll be heading back to the city? That is the most likely destination for the necklace." Envir has pulled himself up to his elbow and takes us all in with a sweeping glance.

"We still don't have the relic they're looking for." Alyssia's voice is soft. I only hear her clearly because she is leaning close to me, wrapping my chest in overly thorough bandaging.

The priestess responds first. "I doubt they will find it before us, even if we go to the city to retrieve the vial. I do not like that we have no notion of what the flame is. It makes me very uncomfortable to think about those vermin contaminating it with their attention at all, let alone before we can discover its purpose."

Alyssia nods, frowning slightly.

"Even without horses, I think we can cut a few days off if we go straight to the city from here, instead of going all the way back to the village." I say, leaning out of Alyssia's way as she reaches for what has to be my last clean shirt, shaking off a few clinging leaves. "We can go to the southern guard tower and take a boat straight to the palace docks instead of traveling up to the west gate." I bite my tongue to keep from whimpering as she starts to pull the shirt over my left arm, raising it so I can slide into the other sleeve. Sweat drips down my face by the time I am fully clothed again, but the relief granted by the return of my thin armor outweighs the pain.

"At least there are some perks to traveling with royalty, I suppose." She flashes the smallest of smiles my way and my heart leaps.

I stand to move to the space Envir has created for me, but she grabs at my shirt and pulls herself up. I have to brace myself against her weight and grab her elbow with my good hand, steadying us both.

"No more of this," she waves her hand at my injured side dramatically, "for a while."

I am unsure what she means, but trying to reason that out with my hand still holding her arm and the heat of her so close to me is difficult. I fight the urge to bring her even closer and press my lips against hers.

She escapes my grasp and quickly ties my arm in a sling, the action complete before I can protest.

"I need to be able to fight." I start trying to untie the knot, but it is hard for me to get a good angle. One attempt to pull free without untying it sends a sharp pain through my entire side.

"Fight one handed then. Or stand behind Carolyn or Envir like I plan on doing. You are tearing yourself apart, and I won't stand for it anymore. I won't lose any more pieces of myself by watching you blatantly disregard your pain."

Her look immediately makes me drop my attempt to undo the

binding. There are tears welling in the corners of her eyes, but there is a fierceness as well. A determination I dare not defy. I raise my hand in surrender.

"Thank you." The words are clipped, and she sniffs, wiping her eyes quickly as she turns her back to me. "We'll go east tomorrow then. It shouldn't take much more than a day to get out of the Woods. Another two, maybe, to the city if I remember the distances correctly. It should save us at least two days."

Envir is grinning at me like an idiot as I finally sit next to him.

"What?" I keep my voice low, taking a piece of dried venison, and raise my eyebrow at him.

"Oh, nothing. It's just interesting to see you listen to someone for once." He smirks, also quiet.

"I do nothing but listen to people tell me what to do. What are you talking about?"

He laughs loud enough to draw the attention of the women, but he smiles them away easily. I watch them more than listen to Envir. Alyssia lays on her stomach, while the priestess massages the pink salve into her entire backside. A flash of skin from beneath her shirt reveals a sea of dark bruises. My stomach lurches at the sight of it, and I try not to imagine her falling from impossibly high windows.

"If any of the palace physicians told you to rest your arm you would have said 'Thank you, but no,' and then continued to do whatever you wanted. You also never listen to me about anything. To the point where I don't even try anymore." He waves a piece of cheese at me in emphasis. "In fact, you running away from me, despite me telling you not to, is what caused all of this in the first place." The cheese makes a pointed jab at my chest in accusation. "Meanwhile, this whole time I just needed to find an Otherfolk Queen to scold you into behaving."

"She has been through enough. If it prevents her from having one more thing to worry about?" I shrug one shoulder helplessly. "What else can I do for her? I could not save the girl. I could not stop them from taking the pendant." I take a moment to chew and watch Alyssia as she curls onto her side, nestled perfectly in the leaves, the fire creating golden highlights in her hair. If I had not seen where she lives, as unorthodox as it is, I might be tempted to think she was, indeed, a creature of this forest.

"We'll fix what we can and stop things from getting any worse." He rests his hand on my knee and squeezes gently before raising his voice and looking toward the women. "Carolyn, do you have one of your alarm wards in you tonight?"

She pauses the act of stroking Alyssia's hair and closes her eyes for a moment. "Yes, I believe I do." The priestess touches two fingers to the other woman's cheek in that familiar manner she keeps using before she stands.

Envir stands as well, stretching with a dramatic yawn. "Let's get this done then, so we can all get some sleep. I know that I've had more than enough of today."

Alyssia makes a hum of agreement and curls more tightly into her nest of blankets and leaves, her eyes already closed.

I lay back and listen to the footsteps of the other two to fade into the trees. The shadowed canopy above us hides the stars, but reflects the orange glow of the fire, and I lose myself in the shadows. Settling into my bed of leaves, I drift to thoughts of a different, deep red canopy, and the decadent softness of my bed in the palace. On the very edge of sleep, the thoughts turn to still another canopy, one of twisted branches and carved wood tucked into the hollow of a living tree, the very air around me golden and smelling of fresh cut wood, newly tilled earth and life itself, the soft heat of a sleeping woman heavy at my side.

CHAPTER TWENTY-FIVE

KEDREN

"Did Kiv fight with a longsword?" Envir stands next to me with his arms crossed, chin resting in one hand, surveying the open ground in front of him.

True to Alyssia's estimate, traveling east through the forest took us only a long day's slow walk. She and I struggled the most, stumbling over everything and nothing. We finally decided to make camp when the open plains became visible through the thinning of trees and the long shadows of the setting sun faded into moonlit dark.

With a tossing gesture, the priestess sends a spray of her golden lights into the air above the makeshift training ground she and Envir created. She frowns before replying, "I don't know. She used no shield that we know of, only the sword."

"Narrows it down a bit. Probably a two-hander of some sort, which works out considering that's what we have available." He smiles and draws his sword before also removing mine from its sheath at my waist without a word or hesitation.

Alyssia is already curled onto her side, clinging to a crumpled blanket as both pillow and covering, watching the priestess as she takes my sword from Envir and steps into the circle of light. I want to go to her, cradle her head in my lap, but I hold back, pressing against the tree behind me and focus on Envir and the priestess instead.

"The most important thing to learn is to run when you can. The second is to not die when you can't," Envir says, circling the priestess, spinning his own sword in a loose, easy hold.

"Right hand at the crossguard, thumb on the flat of the blade. Left hand just above the pommel." He slips into a low, solid stance next to her, demonstrating the grip. "Not too tight, and not too loose. Comfortable. Flexible. Ready to adapt." He punctuates his words with quick, efficient lateral movements of his sword, angling the flat of the blade like he is parrying oncoming strikes, his feet driving into the ground.

"I take it he's the one who made you put on all of that muscle of yours?" Alyssia's soft voice startles me and I run my hand through my hair.

"One of them, yes. We have had several swordmasters over the years, but he has always been there. Driving me. Making me better. Giving me someone to try, and fail, to beat," I laugh at the last.

"Oh, he doesn't let his Royal Highness win? I'd think that was mandatory." She grins up at me from her tangle of blankets and leaves.

"Absolutely not. He beats me at almost every turn. He is one of the best swordsmen in the kingdom, and the priestess could not have a better instructor if she searched the nation," my voice swells with pride for my friend, and I do not try to quell it. He deserves the praise, and more.

"They should make quite the pair, then. Carolyn is one of the best students I've ever seen, regardless of the subject."

"That does not surprise me. She seems incredibly disciplined. She would have to be, to be where she is within the Order at such a young age."

Alyssia nods and makes a small sound of agreement before rolling back to watch the others.

"I hope she doesn't need to be good at it, though," she speaks quietly, and it takes me a moment to comprehend what she said.

"I hope that for the both of you, as well. I do not want either of you to have to keep experiencing this. If I am being honest, I could be done with it too." I slide down the trunk of the tree, settling in to watch Envir correct the priestess's grip and form in the repetitive strike drills that are so familiar to me. Her movements are already clean and precise, much like everything else about her.

"Well, I'm comforted by the fact that it's been a little much even for such an experienced traveler such as yourself."

"It has certainly been one of the more exciting weeks of my life. Not the worst, but it is also not over yet. I cannot say I am looking forward to our return to the palace." I grimace at the thought of returning to stifling marble halls, the high council, Daralyn, and my father's funeral.

"I'm sorry. For a lot of things, really, but mostly that you don't get to feel good about going home," she speaks to the leaves above us, "I couldn't imagine not having that."

I sit with that for a long while. "It is not all bad. It is just," I pause, thinking how best to word it, "inevitable? All I know? There is more than losing battles against the council and..." I stop again and run my hand down my torso, not able to speak the truth of my ruined body.

"Still," she bites her lip, watching me again, "It isn't what I thought your life was like."

That makes me laugh loudly enough that both Envir and the Priestess stop their practice and look at me. "I certainly hope not. I work very hard to make sure no one thinks my life is anything like what it actually is."

I was trying to make a joke of it but she frowns, searching my face for something she apparently does not find. "That sounds very lonely."

Envir shifts his attention to Alyssia with a look suspiciously like approval before going back to throwing slow strikes into the priestess' blade, leaving me to grope for a reaction on my own.

I give up with a half-hearted, one-shouldered shrug. "I have Vi and Jyn. Books. My people. Some acquaintances from my time abroad. It is enough."

She sits up, pulling the blanket over herself like a cloak and wrapping her arms around her knees. "You have us now, too, if you want. Carolyn and I. Kyla would adore you. And *everyone* likes Rend." She chews on her lower lip for a moment. "I know that really isn't a practical offer. After this nonsense we aren't likely to cross paths again given who we are, but they are the most valuable thing I have to offer in thanks."

Kiv, save me. This woman will be my undoing.

I swallow several times before I am sure I can speak without sounding choked. "I will make sure our paths cross as often as they can."

She bends her head in the slightest of nods before hugging her legs more tightly. "I might stay in the city for awhile after this is settled. I'm not sure yet." She sighs and sets her chin on her knees. "The idea of my shop being...empty..." Closing her eyes, she shakes her head. "I just don't know."

"You do not have to know yet, dear one." The priestess, Carolyn, ruffles her hair as she walks by to hand me my sword, hilt first. "And I can continue my studies in Cuaria with you for some time, if you decide to be there."

"And then I can come and make sure she keeps up on her sword practice. Which then means His Highness has to follow, because I won't let him out of my sight ever again." Envir flashes a toothy grin and they both smile back.

"That sounds more than a little arduous, but not unwarranted, I suppose." I get to my feet and slide my sword home. "It was worth it, however."

The thought of the arrow that started this whole thing, the one meant for Alyssia, sends a shiver down my spine. I force a smile and avoid looking at anyone for fear of giving my sudden uneasiness away. Thankfully no one questions my final declaration and conversation shifts to speculations on the next two days' travel before we bank the fire and sleep.

—

None of last night's discussion of our travel included the possibility of rain, and yet by midday the sky has darkened ominously.

"I know it rains frequently here in the spring, but it really couldn't wait two more days?" Alyssia squints up at the sky like she's daring it to step out of line.

"Maybe it will wait until we have reached the city?" Carolyn looks upwards with a more hopeful expression, but Envir doesn't let her hold that hope for long.

"I doubt it will wait an hour. But we won't melt, will we?" He grins.

"Not all of us are fish people, Vi." I have to side with the women on this matter. I hate being wet.

"I won't melt, but I will most certainly chafe and be generally unpleasant." Alyssia frowns up at the sky again. "I already miss the Woods. Rain is different there."

Envir hums. "A leaky roof, as opposed to no roof?"

"That's a good way to put it." She looks from side to side. "Shouldn't there be farms here, or at least some place to take cover?"

I visualize a map of this area. "Not yet. Near the end of the day we might start seeing more fields to the southeast but they would be the furthest outfields. We would have to go out of our way to find any shelter."

"Disappointing," she huffs.

We continue in industrious silence, moving quickly with long, steady strides by unspoken consensus, covering as much ground as we can before it becomes mud beneath us.

And mud it becomes.

The rain starts slowly enough for me to ignore, but eventually the heavy, constant drops make me want to start shouting at the sky.

"Carolyn, you have to be able to do something about this." Strands of damp hair cling to Alyssia's cheeks, pink with exertion and the chill of the rain.

"Oh." Carolyn stops abruptly. "I have never tried." She scrapes tendrils of her own wet hair away from her mouth before looking up, frowning slightly against the rain. "Come closer." She waves at us absently and we oblige, huddling together behind her. I station myself between Alyssia and Envir as subtly as possible. He still grins at me slyly. I roll my eyes, but I do not switch my position.

Alyssia's laugh distracts me from our staring contest. I look toward her and then immediately up, following her line of sight. Expecting rain, I shield my eyes, but instead I drop my hand and smile. Golden light dances above us in a wash of tiny waves as the water splashes against a solidified dome of air. The protection of Kiv sparkles in response to nature's damp assault.

We walk, tightly clustered under the glittering shield, still wet and squelching through mud, but less aggravated by the sheets of spring rain pouring around us. Darkness begins to fall early because of the clouds, but we pay little attention to it, the golden light rippling around us is more than enough to travel by. Without discussing it, we continue pressing on, all of us hoping to outlast the rain.

Beyond our shield the horizon blackens, and I become uncomfortable traveling so long without any clear way to mark our direction. Becoming lost is not a concern, but if we drift too far north it will add time to our journey that Alyssia likely does not want to spare. I search the darkness for some bit of shelter; a bedraggled copse of trees, some forgotten outbuilding. Anything.

Despite my searching, it is Alyssia who calls out first. "Trees ahead and to the left. We should stop for the night."

I squint in the direction she indicates, but see nothing. She must have some kind of extra tree-sensing ability, because as we follow her, the light surrounding us reflects on the wet leaves of a small cluster of trees.

"How did you see this?" Envir voices my thoughts again.

She shrugs. "I was looking for them, so I saw them. A familiar sight for me." She smiles when she turns back to him. "I'm sure if it was a city tavern you would have spotted it just fine."

He laughs. "Fair point."

Under the trees, the reduced trickle of rain against the magic is not enough to illuminate our surroundings. Carolyn adds several of her floating golden orbs to assist our sight. The ground is not seeping water, but one would hardly call it dry, and I do not relish a night sinking into wet earth. Alyssia is, again, one step ahead of me.

Taking the knife from Carolyn's pack, she starts cutting the driest, leafiest branches, shaking excess water off as she does so. "These will help separate us from the wet ground, but I don't think we will get much of a fire out of any of it. I should have thought about storing some dry grass in my bag."

"We can always huddle together to conserve warmth," Envir laughs and follows Alyssia's example, using the duller, middle section of his sword to hack at mostly dry, leafy boughs.

"That is not the worst idea you have had," Carolyn speaks over the sound of snapping wood and her own rustling through the supplies. "I will not be able to maintain the shield while we sleep, so we may need all the heat we can manage."

Kneeling down, I focus on spreading the growing pile of branches out evenly, hiding my face before anyone can notice my reaction to the thought of all four of us sleeping so close. My chest aches with the stretching, but it does feel remarkably better after only two days of rest, and I am grateful for Alyssia's insistence. The wet fabric of the sling rubs horribly against my neck with every movement, however, and I debate taking it off.

"Kiv, I hate being wet."

Envir laughs and tosses a branch directly at me. "I'm not even going to touch that one."

The heat in my face flares even brighter, and I throw the branch back at Envir. "Since when have you not wanted to touch something?"

He snatches the projectile easily, smoothly tossing it into the perfect spot to even out the layer I have created.

The chortle that bubbles out of Alyssia, with such obvious reluctance, makes the rest of us burst into laughter, and the blush retreats from my cheeks.

Envir dips down next to me, depositing another armful of branches and speaks directly into my ear, "Almost a shame we have to go back to real life after this, isn't it?"

He is gone before I can reply, but the thought lingers.

Hardly any time has passed, but my life before all of this seems so distant. Before discovering the Davorists were actively killing innocents. Before finding whole villages in magical Otherfolk forests.

Before Alyssia.

What will my life look like after her? Without her? How can someone I have known for such a short time shape so much of my life?

The snap of fabric being shaken out brings me back to the present. Carolyn spreads the first, mostly dry, blanket onto the bed of branches we have created.

"I have a feeling this is going to be a short night." Alyssia frowns at our makeshift nest as she spreads another blanket out next to the first.

Envir finishes with ours and then immediately sprawls out across all of them horizontally. "I think you might be right."

Alyssia sighs and gets to her knees before draping herself over Envir's stomach. "I don't know, this might not be so bad."

A small whoop escapes her as Envir rolls up and neatly deposits her onto the bedding with a creak and rustle of twigs. "I don't need my liver slowly impaled by a piece of greenery throughout the night, thank you very much."

"Rude," she huffs, sticking her lower lip out in a pout. I bite my own lip in automatic response. "I can always just fix it in the morning."

"I'll leave gathering new holes to Ked, just the same."

I snort. "It is, unfortunately, one of the few things that I am better at than you."

"Speaking of," she rolls over in a crackling of twigs and ends on her knees in front of me. "How does it feel today?" She works the sling off of me gently before I respond.

"It feels much better." I wince and sigh at the same time as the sling slips off. The stinging of the raw skin on my neck is relieved, but the ache of stiff, unused joints intensifies as I stretch the arm out.

The tip of her tongue is already out, and her brow is furrowed as she softly presses around the wound before she deftly slides my shirt up, hooking the hem over my head to keep it out of her way. The damp linen clings to my mouth and nose before I huff out a sharp breath. I start to laugh but the sound dies in my throat as I feel the cold familiarity of a blade against my skin. My breathing stops. My body tenses, ready to jerk back. The edge of metal presses ever so slightly against my flesh. I cannot stop myself from flinching. A primal sound catches in my throat.

"Canopy Above, Kedren. I'm sorry." The cool pressure of the knife vanishes, and she pulls the shirt down enough for me to see. "I wasn't thinking."

I take a shaking breath, trying a smile. "It is alright. It is not something you should have to think about. I would just appreciate it if you would let me see when you hold a knife to me."

"I think that's a reasonable request," she says, smiling uneasily. "I wouldn't cut the bandages off normally, but I know the wet will make the knots a nightmare."

"It really is fine. I just need warning."

With one more long look, and a reassuring nod from me, she slides the blade under the cloth strips, barely touching my skin and deftly cuts the bindings free.

"It doesn't look too bad. The redness has gone down, and the bruising doesn't look any worse. I don't love the exposure to all this rain," she glares up at the sky, "but I think I'm going to leave it uncovered for now. Let it breathe for awhile."

She is so close to me, I can feel the heat of her exhalation. I want to lean down. Press my lips against hers. Pull her against me and take in the heat of her. Erase the fear of bare steel and blindfolds. The sheer intensity of her pale blue gaze freezes me. It reminds me of the way Envir looks at me after I have been near my sister, searching for some new hurt, looking for some new scar. The heated, possessive edge to her stare shocks me to stillness coming from someone who isn't him.

She leans in, her fingertips slipping behind my neck, and I lean down, so close I can feel the dampness of her hair against my forehead. The wet smear of that damnable pink salve traces along the skin of my neck and I sigh, cold rushing through the wound and into every other part of me.

"Hopefully that will help and we can put the sling back on in the morning without irritating your skin anymore. If this rain ever stops, that is." She frowns, glaring around her. "If my thighs rub together any more I will scream." Lazily, she slides away from me, rolling down into the makeshift bedding. "With any luck tomorrow, the skies will be clear, and we will arrive in the city. At least then we can get some dry clothes and a fire."

"I am sure I can provide both of those in the palace." I stand, stretching my aching joints before taking my place between Alyssia and Envir. "But we should probably decide where all of us will be going after we arrive tomorrow." I yawn and shiver. Envir stretches out beside me, rolling one edge of the blanket around him and curling toward me.

Alyssia's yawn follows mine. "We have a long enough day tomorrow. We can decide then." Another yawn chases her words, and she rolls onto her side, also facing me. Carolyn wraps around her in a tight embrace, the two women fitting together comfortably.

I am the only one still sitting, my head drifting from side to side. My chest aches, and I fight a gut-clenching shiver against the wet, cold, spring night, but I still smile. Even with the sharp, uneven bed of branches beneath me, I feel more at home than in any palace bedchamber or lord's estate. I have never felt this casual ease with anyone but Envir. This is so far beyond the strained relationships found in the palace, capital, and any of the other royal positions I have filled, I do not want to sleep out of fear that this is somehow a dream, and I will wake up alone within the cold, stone walls of the palace.

CHAPTER TWENTY-SIX

KEDREN

It is not yet dawn when the sharp point of a branch stabs me awake. The wet darkness disorients me and makes me shiver. I reach out, seeking warmth. It is warmer to my left, but my chest aches when I try to roll that way. I curl toward the small beacon of heat to my right. My arm drapes over the soft curve of a body in the perfect position to keep pressure off my injury. The person beneath me shifts with a small sound, writhing under me until they are tucked up against the entire line of my body.

I breathe in a deep, tired sigh and the fresh scent of rain soaked earth, the woodland scent of bark and bright, green things, and the slightest hint of tangy musk lingers pleasantly. The blanket of sleep falls over me once again, and I slip into dreams of sunlight on leaves.

When I wake again it is to an assault of barbarous twigs beneath me as Envir rolls to his feet. Dawn has arrived, and while I would not call the sky clear, it has at least stopped raining.

I am the last to leave our unruly mattress. The women are well on their way to being ready to start toward the city, and Envir is not far behind. Our makeshift camp takes very little time to break down, and before I have wiped the sleep from my eyes, we are on the move.

"Will you be going back to your apartments when we return to the city, Vi?" Finally awake and capable of thought, I venture to put together a plan.

"Just long enough to collect Jyn. We can stay in my rooms in the palace until everything gets settled." He glances toward Alyssia and then back to me.

He means until we find where her pendant is and decide how to get it back.

"Carolyn? Where do you need to be?"

"I will be going back to the library immediately. The High Priest and I will need to have quite the conversation about our encounters with the scum." She sneers at the mention of the Davorists and tosses her head, gleaming black hair catching a rare beam of sunlight.

"Of course. Send word if you need, or discover, anything." I pause, trying to find a way to keep the hope from my voice. "Alyssia? I know you have places to stay in the city but..." I trail off, unsure how to continue and sound normal. She saves me by answering the unfinished question.

"Since I can't just sneak into the Davorist temple and kill the High Priestess with my bare hands, I was hoping I could stay in the palace. If the princess is involved, I'd like to be close." She hesitates and stares deliberately straight ahead. "If that's alright, of course."

Envir starts coughing in a manner suspiciously close to laughter, and I debate the odds of my ability to kill him. With great reluctance, I decide they are not currently in my favor.

"That would be fine. There is no shortage of rooms for you to stay in." The racing of my heart betrays my ability to feel or sound nonchalant. I push my fingers through my hair and resolutely look anywhere but at Alyssia.

Will it be fine? Will any of this be fine? What if Daralyn has gotten a hold of the pendant already? What if she destroyed it? Would it be worse for it to be lost to the Davorists? My conviction that it will end up in the hands of my sister is strong, but I could be wrong. If I am, how would we find it then?

Spiraling helps nothing with so little information. I have to stay focused on what I do know until we discover more. Alyssia's fingers trail along the feathery tips of long grass. Strands of her deep gold hair frame her face, escaping from the tie holding it back as usual. I miss the strange bits of leaf and twig that usually found their way woven there. She seems so different here, in the open space of the fields. Less vibrant in the dull gray of cloudy skies instead of the soft green shadows of the woods. Less wild Otherfolk of lore and more ordinary human.

Even Carolyn seems less pristine than usual. Her robes are dusty and soft, the crisp lines of them worn away with hard wear. My sword hangs at her hip today. The black leather of the belt and sheath a jarring contrast to the white of everything else she wears. Envir insisted she carry it to become used to its presence as a part of her lessons in wielding it. Her smooth, delicate hand rests on the scabbard comfortably. I look to my own hands, covered in the myriad of tiny scars common to our aggressive training. The ridge of calloused skin on my palm is rough as I run my thumb over it. Ignoring the faint, long-healed, pucked scar on my palm, Envir's hands look much the same. I am heavy with the hope that her hands never look like ours.

Envir breaks the awkward silence like nothing happened, "We will be back before the next High Council meeting, and you know as well as I do that your mother won't postpone it for something like a state funeral." He has his thumbs hooked into his belt as he walks, his eyes meeting mine.

I groan, "How do you remember these things?" I have never been good at recalling my own schedule. "When is it?"

"Day after tomorrow." He smirks at me. "You can sleep for a while, at least."

"Thank Kiv. Unfortunately for me, that is not the worst news. It would not hurt for us to know more of what Daralyn is scheming," I take a quick breath before adding, "If anything."

"The High Priest will also be informed by then and can voice his concerns about the Davorists publicly." Carolyn frowns, her hand resting on the scabbard tightens into a white-knuckled grip. "And if he does not, I shall."

"You think there is a chance he wouldn't bring this up?" Alyssia worries the twine cord around her neck between two fingers. "They can't possibly ignore them now."

"Gremor is a doddering, bootlicking sycophant with no intention of causing a rift between the Order and the Monarchy. Or, more specifically, their money." With a quick twitch of her thumb beneath the crossguard, she pushes the sword out of its sheath, baring the metal blade for a violent moment before slamming it home again. "He will have to find something extremely distasteful before he risks that. I can only hope that my retelling of our encounters will be enough."

"I did not think that the High Priest would need convincing to be on our side. That could make it more difficult for anything to be done, especially convincing the larger populace that they pose a threat." *Kiv, I should have been paying more attention.*

Carolyn's laugh is a sharp bark. "Why else do you think the rats have infested the city as badly as they have? In no other time since the Fall have they been such an abhorrent plague. High Priest Gremor Helnic is unfit for his position."

"It isn't just the High Priest." Envir turns, walking backward as he addresses Carolyn. "The rumors about Davor's High Priestess paint an ugly picture of her. Avadavia is hardly any older than we are, and the High Priest before her died very suddenly. It has been strongly suggested that she is the one who killed him."

I blink dumbly. "How do you know any of that?"

"I listen, sometimes. Pick things up from here and there."

"He means Jyn picks things up and he listens, sometimes, to him," Carolyn snorts. "Jyn and I have spoken of the state of the cults many times."

"Ah, that sounds much more likely."

I laugh as he turns back around with a shrug. "I did still know it."

"And he is not wrong. High Priestess D'Baer is a force unlike any we have seen in the Cult of Davor in decades, perhaps centuries," Carolyn continues. "She is ruthless and beyond ambitious."

"That sounds like a dangerous combination if she really is cozying up to the princess." Alyssia's brows furrow. "I don't like the thought of that."

"Neither do I." The idea of Daralyn with access to any amount of magic makes my blood run cold.

We fall silent and walk in quiet unease for hours, cautiously approaching and passing the road to Saen, unwilling to run into anyone who may be traveling to or from the city. The road is blessedly empty, although signs of recent travel are evident. It is not long after we pass the road that the walls of the capital break the horizon.

"Finally." Envir stretches his arms overhead without slowing down.

The sun escaped the clouds some time ago, and our pace has left us all sweating despite the spring chill.

"I just want to be clean and sitting down," I sigh, relishing the thought of my bathing chamber and bed.

"I wouldn't mind laying down for approximately the rest of my life after this. I feel like I've been walking for a month." Alyssia slides her hands down her lower back gingerly. "Taking that unexpected swim didn't help either."

I wince remembering the vibrant bruising covering her back from her collision with the lake.

"It won't be long now," Envir adds, finishing his stretch.

As soon as the city breaks the horizon, the walls shoot toward the sky, stretching to their full height at our approach. The point where city meets sea gleams with reflected sun.

As we get within scouting range of the southern watch tower, I fidget with the edge of the sling, debating taking it off. The fear and the need to hide my weakness seems distant, surrounded by these friends who do not treat me as lesser because of it. I drop my hand. The guards can think what they will.

"Hold," a deep voice rings across the open space between us and the guard tower.

"I really wish I would stop having to convince people to let me into my own damned city," I murmur with irritation at the inevitable delay to my bath. So close, yet so far.

"Well if you behaved a little more like you were supposed to, maybe this wouldn't happen so much." Envir rolls his eyes at me but steps closer and in front of me, assuming his customary guard position out of habit.

"I need a flag or something," I grumble, ignoring him.

I stop when we have reached the distance safe from arrows and wait for the approaching guards to meet us. Three of them this time, reasonable considering this is not an actual entrance into the city. One of the men, at least, has his helmet off so I can see who he is. Envir beats me to addressing him, however.

"Anli! Go get a boat ready! My feet hurt, and I'm tired of walking," his voice is raised, but easy and friendly in a way I can never manage.

"Lord D'luane? What are you...Who? Your Highness," Anli drops a quick bow in my direction once he cycles through the process of recognizing Envir and I. "Your Highness, what happened? Where have you been?"

"Oh, nothing and no where, just my usual devilry, I'm afraid. We would be *very* grateful to be taken to the palace, however." I casually run my fingers through my hair as I wait the drawn out moment it takes him to reconcile our apparition.

Finally remembering himself, he jerks into action. "Trion, Fael, go ready a boat to take the prince and his companions to the palace docks." He flaps his gauntleted hand at them urgently, spurring them into a run ahead of us. "Of course we will get you home immediately, Your Highness. My Lord." His eyes go even wider as they land on Carolyn and Alyssia. "Priestess." He bows to her even lower than he did to me.

"May Kiv protect you." Carolyn uses the tone that evokes curling smoke, and I can feel the righteous intention behind her words.

Anli clearly can as well, bowing low again. "Thank you, Priestess. And may Kiv protect you, as well." He is still bowing when he turns to lead us toward the tower dock.

We follow him through an iron bound door set into the wall, framed by arrow slits, and into the open room that serves as the tower's refectory and storage space. We don't stop, passing through the opposite door in a handful of strides.

The familiar noise of the city and the harbor assaults me as the door opens. Envir and I look at each other, both of us breaking into wide grins. He takes the steps leading down to the small dock two at a time, jumping easily into the boat waiting for us. It rocks alarmingly, but he walks across the bench he landed on, settling the tilting as he goes.

I step down, carefully trying to avoid pitching the vessel. I am not unused to sailing, but I was not born to it like Envir. Still, I wait to help Alyssia and Carolyn onto the unsteady deck, only to have Alyssia vault onto the bench beside me much like Envir did, pitching us violently for the space of a breath before she and Envir correct it.

"A woman of many talents it seems," he laughs, bowing over her hand in a theatrical mockery of gentlemanly behavior.

"I told you about Rend. We've been out to sea many times during our years together. I remember a little something from it." Her pale eyes flash with her smile, the blue so bright it puts the sky to shame.

Carolyn grips my offered hand tightly as she lowers herself in after Alyssia much more gingerly.

I keep my voice for the priestess' ear only, "I take it you went on fewer sea-faring adventures?"

She flashes a quick, sarcastic smile. "Some of us had other things to do, and I had no interest in being trapped on a ship with the two of them back then."

I want to question her, but she brushes passed me with a wry smile.

The journey across the bay is not a long one. Two guards rowing, one managing the small sail, and the last manning the rudder send us cutting through the waters quickly, Envir leans back against the stern and Alyssia is balanced dangerously on the bow, one boot perched on the rail. Carolyn

S.C. Wolf

and I are seated safely on the forward bench.

"I wish you would get down from there," Carolyn's voice is tight, but Alyssia just waves her off.

"I'm not doing anything dangerous. I forget sometimes why Rend likes it out here so much. I'm just enjoying it." She looks over her shoulder and beams a smile so broad toward Carolyn that I am caught in it as well and cannot help but smile back.

Instead of sitting back with us, she is the first to jump out onto the dock as we approach it. With a practiced twist, she wraps the rope Envir tosses her around a post and ties us off blatantly ignoring the two guards that scramble to do the job suddenly taken from them.

Envir leaps up to the dock, also ignoring the men, and hooks a finger around the rope experimentally, winking at her. "Looking good, sailor. I'll have to remember you if we're down a man on any of our ships."

He grips my forearm as I climb out of the boat, steadying me as it shifts beneath my feet. Alyssia does the same with Carolyn, and in a blink we are all on solid land, heading up the stone steps carved into the cliff that supports the palace above this small, rocky alcove tucked into the larger bay.

Alyssia exhales slowly, taking in the view. "I don't think I ever knew this was here."

"We try to keep it that way." I run my hand through my hair, pushing the sweat soaked strands out of my eyes just as I reach the top, the palace looming over me. "Carolyn, Vi, are you coming inside first or going straight into the city?"

The two exchange a look.

"My apartments are on the way to the library, we can leave from here together."

"I think that would be best." The priestess pauses as Envir turns toward the path that will take them to the city. "Lys, send a message if you need anything, or come to me or Kyla directly. I will be back here in a day. Two at most." Carolyn holds Alyssia's face in both hands and kisses her forehead gently, tracing her cheek as she pulls away. "Pay attention in the High Council meeting, Your Highness. I think it is time we start finding out the true aims of the princess. Any detail could be helpful."

"Of course."

"Jyn and I will be back here in a few hours, Ked." Envir shifts his glance to Alyssia, smiling. "Please use some of your Otherfolk magic to keep him out of trouble until I get back."

Returning his smile with her own, she gives him a quick nod. "I'll do my best."

"I think we will manage to stay out of any mischief until he returns." I try to smile like he does and hide the joke behind an easy grin. I am not successful.

She laughs anyway as we turn toward one of the many small back entrances into the palace, and the sound of it puts a lightness into my tired steps. Guards posted at the small door snap to attention as I pass. One of them opens the way for us with a smart bow.

"Thank you." I return their attention with a nod and gesture for Alyssia to precede me into the relative darkness of the palace.

The door opens to a wide corridor with access to both the kitchens and a selection of store rooms, but most importantly, servant pathways that snake throughout the building unused by anyone I would rather not encounter. I stop Nemia, one of the housekeeping staff that frequently tends my own rooms and ask her to prepare a space for Alyssia and start the kettle fires for baths in both rooms.

With a curtsy and a murmured, "Yes, Your Highness." She turns to leave on her new errand. I wonder what other task I have taken her from, but the question quickly slides from my mind.

Instead, my thoughts wander in comfortable tiredness absorbing the familiar sights. The smoky scent of bright torches illuminating the dim, stone hallways. The presence of Alyssia at my side. I take us along a meandering path back to my side of the palace, both to allow time for the rooms to be prepared, and to savor this rare alone time with her.

"I never imagined being inside this place," she says softly but not awed or reverent, simply quiet. Her fingers occasionally trace the gray stone walls. "Don't you ever feel trapped here under all of this stone?"

"It is not the stone that traps me here," I reply without thinking, surprising both of us. I give her a one shouldered shrug and a small smile. "Until around two weeks ago, I didn't know there were that many other options for housing materials. If I knew Otherfolk treehouses were still in fashion, I may have felt more restricted here." She rewards me with a quick smirk and I return a smile that quickly fades as I continue, "But I feel trapped by what this place is, and what I am, sometimes."

"Do you ever wish you were just *you*?"

"Perhaps not as often as you might think." I rub at the ghostly ache of the burn scar across my chest. "Perhaps, if none of my family were who we are, my childhood may have been different. Maybe my parents would have noticed more. Maybe I would be less broken," I shrug again, "but maybe the small amount of good I have been able to do as prince would not have been done. I have to fight tooth and nail for every single thing I manage to accomplish for my people, but I honestly do not know what I would be without that work. I enjoy helping them. I enjoy meeting them. I love escaping the judgmental eyes of my family and working for the people of this horrible, beautiful, country."

"What do you mean work with them?" She steps close to me, allowing a cluster of serving girls to scurry past us and does not step away.

"I travel between villages and farms, doing what I can. Especially during planting and harvest time. It also allows me to learn what they may need. Medicines, clothing, food, whatever I can have sent. It is inadequate and frustratingly difficult because I have to go through several circuitous channels to bypass the notice of the Master of Finance. He would lick Daralyn's ass clean if she asked it of him." My temper flashes hotly and instead of slamming a fist against the wall next to me, I shift my arm enough to pull at the wound in my chest, letting the pain break the wave of anger. "But I try my hardest to make a difference."

"You are alive, and you are kind. That is more than most would be in your situation." The quiet warmth in her words quenches the remaining frustration like a bucket of water.

"Thank you. I just wish I could do more." My words are barely audible, but I am saved from having to try again by our arrival to my commandeered wing.

I swing open an indistinct door into a hallway nearly identical to the one we are in. More plain wooden doors set into plain gray stone extend in either direction. I step to the side and make a sweeping gesture.

"Ladies first."

CHAPTER TWENTY-SEVEN

KEDREN

We stop outside another unassuming door that is slightly ajar. Nemia's signal to let me know which of the rooms she had prepared.

"This will be yours for as long as you need it. Vi and Jyn are down the hall to the left. If you keep following that way, my door is the first on the right."

She nods, and I expect her to reach for the door, but she makes no move to do so. "Lead on, then. I want to make sure the wound gets cleaned properly, now that I have the opportunity."

"Oh. I can manage on my own. I do have some experience." My tongue feels too big for my mouth as I trip over my words. "You should rest, you need it just as much as I do." Suddenly the idea of the two of us alone in my room is too much. I miss the safety of Envir and Carolyn's presence.

She has already taken off down the hall.

"You have a mostly-professional at your disposal so why not take advantage of it? And also, I insist. I'm not above playing dirty to get my way, so you may as well agree before I start taking some truly below the belt shots."

I jog several paces to catch up before she disappears around the corner. "Fine, but I must insist that you do not have to feel so obligated to care for me."

She snorts a laugh. "It's quite literally my job." She tucks a lock of hair behind her ear. "I know you have more formally trained physicians here, but..." A shrug and a sigh, "My problem is, I simply can't leave someone alone if I think I can help them."

I do not think she realizes how much she has already helped me, and not just physically. "Well, I will not deprive you of such satisfaction then."

I bite my lip at the thought of how many other ways she could help me.

For a heartbeat, when I reach my door, I worry that it will be locked, my key being on the sword belt still worn by Carolyn. Nemia must have left it unlocked, however, because the door swings open at my touch.

"So this is where the prince calls home." She squeezes around me before I have even made it into the room. "I won't lie, I thought it would be much fancier."

I laugh as I slide in after her and close the door behind me, watching her as she explores. "My previous apartments were, but I escaped the residency wing as soon as I was able. My old rooms are all marble, wood paneling, and gilded fixtures, but I would rather have the relative privacy."

"I see." Still looking around, she slides her bag over her head and sets it gently down on the central table before starting to remove her boots. "I suppose that makes sense. Do you miss it?"

"Not particularly." I follow her lead and gratefully unburden myself of the boots I have been wearing for far too long. "I cannot say I care that much about decor, and I have my bed, my bath and at least some measure of peace." I step back into the bedchamber, out of sight, and start easing the sling off over my head. "I do miss hearing the crash of waves outside of my windows, sometimes." My exhale becomes a hiss of pain, and her head pops into the door frame, quickly followed by the rest of her. She is, once again, frowning at me.

"Why are you so stubborn?" She catches my stiff left arm by my wrist and helps me stretch it out more gently than I would have on my own.

"Force of habit." I wince at the ache in my elbow and shoulder as her gentle, sure hands guide me through an easy range of motion. "Until three days ago, Vi and one palace physician were the only two people I have willingly allowed to see me in any state of vulnerability, let alone shirtless and bleeding." And screaming conspiracy theories about the crown princess, but I leave that part out. "So, I am unsure if I would call it stubbornness or lack of practice."

"We'll go with both." Still holding my wrist, she takes a step closer and my heart skips. Her other hand pulls at my shirt, freeing one corner from my waistband. "I hope you can feel safe enough with someone, some day, that your first instinct isn't to be alone when something would be easier with help."

Her voice is low and warm. The shirt catches in her fingers as she traces a line up my side, her thumb brushing across the ridges of my scars. She tilts her head the barest fraction to look into my eyes and my heart races. "You have nothing to feel ashamed of. To fear. Not around me." Her voice is a whisper, a breath. "Not when I'm here."

Her words echo so loudly within me I shake with the force of them. I cannot breathe through the weight of them binding my heart and my lungs to her. Before I can pull away and cover myself again. Before I can say anything in reply, or protest, or fervent agreement, she has the shirt over my head and sliding down my injured side in a smooth, practiced movement.

The discarded garment does not touch the floor before I have one hand tangled in her hair and the other pressed against the curve of her lower back. She crashes into me.

There is nothing left except her. The soft heat of her lips against mine. The sharp dig of her fingers in my hair, pulling me closer, deeper into this kiss I have been longing for since the day we met. Her mouth opens to mine, and I press myself hard against her. I gasp for air and run the tip of my tongue against her parted lips before pulling the lower between my teeth. The feeling of her fingers dragging down my naked back nearly brings me to my knees. I trace a line along her jaw and down her neck with my lips, my teeth sinking into where her neck meets shoulder.

The sound she makes ignites me.

I dip low to secure a one-armed hold around her tight, round ass and lift her. She is heavy and solid against me, her thighs grip my hips as her hands pull my face back to hers, her tongue asking my mouth to yield to her.

But I surrendered long ago. I could not deny her if I tried.

My chest burns, but it is a distant, short burst of heat before we crash into the bed, her hips pressing into mine, our teeth knocking together with the impact. I am tearing at her shirt, the laces of her pants, trying to pull all of it off at once, while she methodically works apart the buttons on mine. Between my fumbling fingers, she slides off the edge of the bed and takes my pants with her. Her shirt remains, empty in my hands. Tossing it aside, I pull myself more fully onto the bed while she steps from the tangle of clothing in nothing but a strange, cropped set of stays. Her entire midriff is bare, and my eyes trace down the center-line of her abdomen to the perfect triangle of coarse brown hair pointing to the space between her muscled thighs. The angry red of her stitched gash fills me with a feral need to rip apart anything that has ever hurt her. Right after I let myself be destroyed by her.

I want to devour her. I want to throw her onto the bed or lift her against a wall and enter her with enough force to bruise us both. But her hands are on me, pressing her thumbs into my inner thighs, tracing a steady path up long scars. My whole body twitches under her touch. I grab her arm, urging her to me, but she resists with a wicked grin that stokes the fire in me.

A groan of unadulterated wanting escapes my throat, but is cut short by a sharp gasp. My back arches as her mouth closes over me and her tongue traces a slow line along the head of my cock. I grip the covers, ready to shred them as she slowly takes me in. Her hair falls over her face and shoulders like a curtain, allowing me tantalizing glances of her mouth and hands working in concert, stroking me with slow, steady pressure. My whole body shakes with the tension of physical pleasure so acute it borders on pain. She takes me to the very edge, then suddenly, the pressure is gone. I open my eyes to see her toss her hair back and wipe her mouth with the back of her hand.

"We shouldn't be doing this." She is breathless, straddling my legs on her knees.

The sight of her takes my soul from me.

"I can assure you, there is nothing else I would rather be doing right now."

I draw my knees up, sliding her forward until our hips meet.

She lets out a small sound and throws out her hands to steady herself, holding on to the ridges of my hip bones.

"That isn't the point." Her body betrays her words, rocking slowly against me.

"What is the point, then?" I cannot stop touching her. My hands trace her sides, cup the roundness of her ass, travel down her thighs. I can barely focus on what she is saying, let alone my response.

"To start with, you're hurt and should be resting."

A low moan escapes her as my wandering hands begin to narrow their search. I let out a short laugh.

"For fuck's sake, Alyssia. If I didn't have sex because I was in pain, I would still be a virgin."

She snorts, but I interrupt by sliding two fingers inside of her, my thumb circling its target gently. I shift my knees to support her as she arcs back against me.

I yearn to take her fully, but I will not force this on her. If she truly believes we should not continue, I will not.

But damn it, I want this with everything I am.

"Your Highness, I'm shocked." She smiles dreamily, her hands trailing the backs of my thighs. "An upstanding, unmarried, gentleman such as yourself openly admitting you have been deflowered?"

Laughing again, I add another finger to the first two, keeping the rhythm of my movements steady. My cock responds ardently to the sound that escapes her.

"I am sure *you* are not as depraved as I am. A perfect maiden still."

She shakes with silent laughter against me, and I feel it ripple through her body where we touch.

"You've got me there." She has to pause to catch her breath, pressing back against me. "And you are making an *excellent* argument for your case to continue." She rolls her hips in time with me, her lower lip caught between her teeth.

With speed I cannot fathom, she has her stays unlaced and ripped off over her head, her breasts free and hanging like pale, rounded teardrops.

With my right hand occupied, I reach for her bared chest with my left. When tearing pain cuts across my body I hiss, the steady working of my other hand losing its rhythm. Before my arm can drop back to the bed she has my hand in hers. Placing it on her breast, she leans forward until I no longer have to reach up for her. My thumb caresses the rounded tip of her nipple in time with my other thumb still stationed lower, back to its even tempo.

"I have decided to not deny myself this," her breath is hot against my neck as she speaks. Her teeth catch my earlobe like a punctuation mark.

I feel as though I have been struck by lightning.

She removes my hand from inside of her and pins it above my head. The scent of her overwhelms me. I am wild with it. I struggle beneath her, but she has my hips locked between her legs, completely in control.

It drives me mad.

"Will you make me beg?" I ask, one hand still caressing her breast, my words a whisper in her ear as she kisses my neck.

"I will only make you beg for more."

With an expert shift of her body, she takes me into her, and I lose what little of myself I had remaining. I belong to her completely. The feel of her tight, slick pressure against me and her mouth on mine overwhelms everything else.

I cannot take it.

I hook a leg around hers and roll over without separating us.

My chest burns, but it is worth it as her fists tangle in the bedclothes. I push us both as far as I can, for as long as I can, using the pain in my chest to help distract me from my own release. A very difficult task, even for such a potent distraction. Her motion matches my every stroke, surging against me with surprising force. She digs her fingers into my hair and pulls back, exposing my throat to her. Teeth scrape against the bared skin and sink into the base of it.

When she releases her hold on my neck, she pulls my ear to her mouth.

"Fuck me like you mean it, Your Highness. I will not break."

The throaty growl of her voice scours away any restraint that remained in me.

I separate us long enough to flip her, ass in the air. The impressive array of deep bruising decorating her back is almost enough to derail me, but she makes an impatient sound at my hesitation, so I grab her and thrust so hard and deep, I would not be surprised to see the lines of my hips added to the pattern. She makes a sound very close to a scream, but instead of pulling away, she presses herself harder against me. I use one hand to pull her onto me with each driving surge of my body, while the other works steadily in the space between us. I hold myself together until I feel her clenching, gasping pleasure wash over me. I pull away just as my own ecstasy tears through me with convulsive force, and I spill myself over both of us. I fall to my good side, breathless and empty, slick and sticky with sweat and the combination of our shared euphoria.

—

The gentle brush of her fingertips against my abdomen pulls me to the surface of my peaceful drowning. Moments or days have passed, and I have no desire to know which is the truth. My smile mirrors the one she wears. I did not think it was possible to find her more beautiful than I did the night I woke to her illuminated by moonlight and leaf-green flame in the peace of her home, but she is radiant with her hair in a tangled mess, the round curves of her breasts pressed against me, one long leg wrapped around mine. I would take her again immediately if it were physically possible, but I am more likely to faint than fornicate at the moment.

Before I can even brush the hair from her cheek, she slides away from me to stand. She hooks her shirt with her foot and kicks it up into her hand. I cannot think straight enough to sit up, let alone speak. I cannot ask her where she is going or why. Pushing myself up causes sharp pain to radiate from my wound. I clutch at it with a tight gasp out of reflex.

"And, I reiterate, that is one reason why we shouldn't have done that." She has her shirt on now, the hem falling along the curve of her buttocks. She sounds tired and annoyed, running both hands through her hair to shake it into some kind of order.

"One?" I'm blinking, partially to clear my watering eyes but mostly in confusion. "This is not that much worse, I just sat up wrong. Not thinking," I practically stammer in my haste to reassure her. "I really am fine, Alyssia." No worse than I was before, anyway.

She makes a noise in the back of her throat before bending to pick up the rest of her clothing and turns from me.

"Where are you going?" I ask too quickly, unwanted urgency making me breathless.

She laughs before glancing back at me, her body framed by the door to the bath. "I'm going to go find where you keep your soap and water, so I can do what I actually came in here to do."

"Oh." I run my hand through my hair and scrub my face. I think for a moment I will deny her. If she wants to be away from me so quickly, she need not bother with this, but one look at her half-dressed and and still flushed from our exertion crumbles any resolve I may have had. "It is all through there." Releasing a long, controlled breath, I drag myself to my feet and kick the pile of my clothing away from the bed. "If you would rather be elsewhere, I really can do this myself," I offer unexpectedly short and formal. As formal as I can be while naked, sweating and sticky with our combined bodily fluids, anyway. I suppose even I have some dignity left.

"No. No. I want to take care of this at least." She lets out a low whistle and runs her fingers along the edge of my bathtub. At least my bathroom impresses her, even if I do not. "I need to take notes for the house." She smiles, flipping the lever of the tap to the kettle of heated water.

I have a bar of finely milled soap and a cloth ready for her when she looks up. She fidgets with them more than necessary, lathering the cloth to within an inch of its life before looking at me again.

"You may as well get in so I don't get water all over the place." She tilts her head toward the tub.

I partially oblige her, sitting on the edge and swinging my feet in. My back is to her, and I hold my breath, staying quiet lest I beg her stay or banish her entirely. There is no sound aside from the falling water, no sensation aside from the damp warmth of the steam curling around me.

I do not know what I was expecting, but it was not the solid feel of her leaning into my back, both arms wrapped around me, pulling me into her. It was not her hair falling into my face as she bent over, examining my damage. But there she is, solid and sure behind me. Holding me gently.

I cannot understand her, but I do not need to. I lay back into her and close my eyes while she scrubs gently at the stinging cut. I do not want to look at the swollen, bruised, aching part of me, or the rest of the mangled flesh revealed by my nakedness. But she looks. She sees all of me. Her hands trace along my chest, my stomach, my arms. The sensation of rough cloth and soft skin creating shifting patterns against the parts of my body that can still feel the difference. I breathe in the scent of her. The woods still cling to her hair, and I can smell the sun and me on her skin. The water crawls up my legs, the heat of it soaking into tense, overused muscles, and it is blissful. I am sure the water is swirling with dirt, blood, and soap, but I refuse to open my eyes and let the reality impede on my current wondrous ignorance.

Her weight shifts behind me, guiding me down into the water. I let it wash over me, keeping my eyes closed. I leave the water flowing longer than I should to mask her fading footsteps.

I do not move until the sound of my door shutting cuts through the harsh buzzing of my thoughts. Only then do I open my eyes to the empty room, the blood and dirt colored water, the angry purple and red spreading like spilled paint across my chest.

Instead of allowing myself to think, I continue where she left off, scrubbing the rest of myself down quickly. Usually the one thing that can settle my mind, I feel restless and trapped by the weight of the water and step out as soon as I feel clean enough.

With a towel wrapped around my waist, I stand, dripping, before one of my wardrobes, searching for acceptable black clothing that will also be easy enough for me to get on by myself. With the help of the bed, and a complete lack of dignity, I manage to dress and make my way into my main room, draping myself dramatically over my favorite chair to frown out at the sky beyond my windows.

—

I am still brooding when Envir and Jyn arrive.

"What a pretty painting you would make, Your Highness." Envir wastes no time teasing. I do not bother responding.

I straighten in the seat and push my damp hair out of my face. Envir stands easier with Jyn at his side, their bodies touching in subtle ways as they enter the room and settle in. The routine is so familiar, but I feel a thousand worlds away from it. I continue to wrestle with the feeling of falling that keeps threatening to tear my insides out of me whenever I think of Alyssia.

"What happened, Ked?" Also dressed in all black, Envir slides onto the low table in front of me, resting his chin on an open palm.

I stare at him for a long moment. I do not want to speak of what just happened, but I also know Envir would figure it out as soon as he sees both of us in the same room. I sigh and lean back. We have always told each other everything anyway, there is no point in stopping now.

"Alyssia and I..." Even resolving to tell him, the words still stick in my throat, and I feel my face heat. "We..."

He claps his hands together, interrupting me. "You fucked finally!"

I blink, "Well, yes...but..."

"But what? This is great news! I was hoping this would happen if Carolyn and I left you alone for long enough." He looks over his shoulder to Jyn. "I told you."

"But." The word is sharper than I meant. I scrub my hand through my hair when he looks back to me, confused. "But then she got up like nothing happened. She stayed to clean out the cut..." I let out a groan of frustration, "and she was all over me again until she just...left."

"And maybe I told you." Jyn reprimands Envir, but his tone is not unkind as he squats on the ground between us. "Try to remember that a lot has been happening in a very short period of time, and she is probably feeling all sorts of very different feelings. If she doesn't know exactly what or why all of them are, it isn't because of you, or anything you are or aren't doing. Give her some time."

I sit with his words and make myself breathe. I make myself remember everything that has happened in the last several days and really think about it from her perspective instead of my own. "It really has been a mess." I sink back, staring up at the ceiling. "But I cannot help how I feel about her."

"That's fine, Kedren. As I said, time. Give *yourself* some, too. Everything will work out the way it needs to. Just deal with each step as it arrives." Jyn squeezes my hand before standing.

Envir sighs. "I suppose Jyn is right, as always. I was just excited. I've never seen you so *you* with anyone but me. But that's alright. One step at a time. And our next step is the Council meeting and finding that pendant before anything untoward happens to it."

Jyn gives a sidelong look at his partner. "I think that can all wait, my heart. All of you are exhausted and need to be ready for whatever comes. Take this respite you've been given."

"He is right. I cannot think about anything right now, and we can hardly break down Daralyn's doors to begin our search. Let us wait and see what I discover. Those damnable meetings are early enough, we will have plenty of time to make a plan afterwards." Jyn's observation opened the floodgates to my tiredness, and there is no hope to turn back that tide now. I can hear the siren song of my bed from the other room

"Fine, but I'm officially unhappy about the decision," he huffs dramatically and pushes himself off of the table.

"I'll remind you of that when you are asleep the moment your head hits your pillow, my Lord." Jyn matches Envir's drama with a courtly bow and a flourished gesture to the door.

Surprising me in the middle of a laugh at their theatrics, Envir wraps his arms around me in a tight, but careful, embrace. "I know the way she looks at you, brother, and it is the same as you look at her. Anything good takes time. In the meantime, I'll be here to remind you that you deserve more than you could ever imagine for yourself."

When the door closes behind them, I am left alone, but no longer lonely.

CHAPTER TWENTY-EIGHT

ALYSSIA

Fuck.

It takes effort to not slam the door of my borrowed rooms behind me to punctuate my escape. *Canopy Above. What was I thinking?*

I wasn't, which was my first mistake.

But I can't lie to myself for long. I *was* thinking.

I was thinking of his broad shoulders, fine features, and long, muscular legs. I was thinking of the way he pushes his hair out of his face and the soft way he looks at me. I was thinking of the emptiness in me, and the way the light that radiates from him fills me whenever I see it.

I take a deep breath and shove everything back down into a box for later so I can keep moving long enough to get clean and go to sleep.

The rooms I've been temporarily leased are smaller and even simpler than the prince's, but there is still a large, welcoming bed against one wall, an upholstered chair positioned by the window, a wardrobe that I hang my bag in, and a pleasantly crackling fire that I add a piece of wood to absently as I pass by. What I'm really interested in, though, is the slightly ajar door on one wall leading into the bathing chamber. I may dislike the feeling of being buried in rock while I'm inside this mountain of a building, but I will say one thing for the palace: their bathtubs are divine. It's a smaller kettle and tub than His Royal Highness' but it's still larger and more convenient than mine at home. The lever twists easily and releases steaming water into the waiting basin.

I kick off unlaced boots and strip out of my grimy travel clothes, very pointedly not thinking about why the fabric sticks in places, and deposit them unceremoniously into the corner of the room. I slide into the water, so hot it's on the edge of burning, and let out the longest sigh of my life. My mind churns around the jagged rocks of thoughts that would dash me apart, and I try to be as still as the water surrounding me. One problem at a time. I can't allow myself the luxury of unraveling just yet.

My aching body melts into the heat of the bath, and I scrub languorously at the days of filth caking my skin and hair, focusing on every detail of sensation. The gash down my thigh is puckered and pink thanks to the widow resin salve, the sutures ready to be removed. The cut along my forearm is itchy and irritating, but now that it is clean it looks weeks old, not days.

When the water starts to cool and I can no longer stand sitting in my own filth, I drag myself out and twist the cork-wrapped metal plug from the drain. I watch thoughtfully as the water swirls out of sight. I really do need to take notes for the house. Instead of digging through my bag to find the least dirty clothing, I forgo it entirely and wrap myself in the towel provided, rummaging around instead for the small scissors to clip the stitches out of my thigh. After sliding out the sutures and wiping away the small drops of blood left in their absence, I crawl into the luxurious bed and make an immaculate nest of pillows and blankets to cocoon myself in until very late tomorrow.

When I do finally drag myself out of sleep and into the waking world the next day, it is no longer morning. I stretch and roll off the plush mattress to further loosen my joints, stiff after a night of unbroken sleep. Opening the wardrobe to rectify my nakedness with whatever I can find in my belongings, I'm greeted by a selection of clothing that was not there the night before. It's all black and of good quality, but not fancy in any way and, for some reason, I sense Envir's hand in this. I take a flowing black top with lacing at the neck and wrists and a pair of trousers so wide and pleated that when worn they look like a full skirt. I finish the ensemble by tucking everything into a wide black belt that laces at the sides and pull on my freshly cleaned boots. The rest of my clothing is nowhere to be seen.

It's a very impractical outfit by my usual standards, but the tight lacing makes it feel like armor, and I'm suddenly much more ready to face the day. I am, however, not ready to face the prince, so there is only one thing to do.

The path to my home away from home is unfamiliar from this direction, and I actually have to pay attention lest I get turned around. But the closer I get, the easier it is to navigate, and the more leeway my mind has to wander. Which is not what I want to be doing. I try to focus on the people and buildings around me. Almost everyone I pass is wearing some amount of black, and black fabric hangs from windows in every direction. The funeral for the King is in two days and the city is certainly preparing for it. My heart aches for the prince, not because his father died, but because he wasn't ever that much of a father to him in the first place. I had two fathers really, and still have my actual parents. I can't imagine never having any of them.

By the Trees, do I wish I still had Arty. I want to be able to hand over the weight of all of this nonsense to him. Let someone who has lived more, and is more resilient to what life can bury you in, handle it. But Arty isn't here, and it's down to just me and the absolute treasures I call my friends. Maybe, just maybe, we can hold up against the weight of it together.

I push the door open to the Prism to find my first pillar of support industriously cleaning drinkware with her back to the door, humming one of her northern songs. The taproom is completely empty, which is unusual any time the door is unlocked, but it suits my purpose nicely. Her red curls swing around when I shut the door behind me, and she bursts into a smile that changes so quickly to a frown, I blink.

"Why are you back? What happened? Bar the door behind you and come here," she clips her words as she sets down the cloth she was using to clean and pours amber liquor from a dark bottle into two glasses as I follow her instructions.

"Oh, Kyla," my voice is already breaking, and I haven't even made it to the bar.

With another quick look, she expertly sweeps both glasses and the bottle into one hand and jerks her head toward the stairs. "Up you go. This needs something softer than a barstool."

I redirect and follow her up the stairs, immediately melting onto her bed.

I take a long drink of the woody, smoky liquor when she hands me the glass, and then grip it tightly in both hands. "I'm going to say something, and I'm not going to elaborate, and I really need you to not ask any questions about it yet. Alright?"

She hums her agreement and sits across from me on the bed, taking a more measured sip of her own drink and lays one hand on my knee.

"Inness was killed by Davorists. I fully intend on becoming an inhuman wreck about it as soon as possible, but we need to find something they're looking for before they do so all hell doesn't break loose. So I cannot become a mess, which is why I can't have you say anything." Tears in her eyes, she definitely looks like she wants to say something. I'm amazed I brushed past the shadow in me fast enough to not start sobbing. "What I can talk about right now is the fact that I just had sex with His Royal Highness, and I have no idea what to do about it." I take another drink while my confession sinks into Kyla.

It takes longer than I thought, the conversational whiplash more than even she can deal with. Her stupefied expression makes me giggle with a tinge of hysteria.

"I'm sorry, dear, but I thought I just heard you say you *fucked the prince*," she splutters and takes a much less measured sip of her drink.

I laugh outright. "I did. For whatever Tree-Forsaken reason, I did." I bury my face in one hand, and she refills both our glasses.

"Can you fill me in as to why that is a problem, exactly? Was it *bad*? I don't know why, but I always assumed he would be good at it. According to the rumors, he has a lot of practice."

"Oh it was very, very far from bad. But it was still a mistake." I groan and take another drink before throwing myself back onto the pillows. "The way he *looks* at me, Kyla. You'd think I was Kiv herself."

"I'm still failing to see the problem here, Lys. Having a prince worship you doesn't seem like that much an inconvenience."

"Where does it go? Nowhere, that's where. He would never leave his people. I would never leave mine. And I don't think casual consort is really something he's looking for," I sigh, "But I suppose I don't *really* know. I don't really know *him*. Despite what it feels like, we've only known each other for a few days. A few, very long days, but a few days all the same." I sit up enough to not choke on another drink and find Kyla staring at me.

"It's not like he is going to be king or anything. Why couldn't he go live in Cuaria with you?" She seems so genuinely fine with the situation, it boggles my mind.

I sit up fully with another dramatic sigh, and let myself speak the thought I have been suppressing for days. "I won't let her be Queen. Not for long, anyway." The thought turns my stomach, but I drink more and ignore it. I'm not exactly sure when I decided that, but it was somewhere between the first and second repetition of '*It is always her.*' No one who can do that to someone, to *him*, gets to be queen of anything.

Except Hell, maybe.

Kyla has gone very, very still, her voice quiet, "What are you talking about, Lys?"

"She has done terrible things. She's involved in all of this; Inness's death, whatever the Davorists are doing, and probably more. Just trust me. You don't want her on that throne." I empty my glass and stretch over to her side table to set it down, shaking my head. "And no, I don't know how, or what, or when, or if it will be me or someone else, but I know I can't let it happen. Which also means I can't have Kedren, because he's going to need to be king." His name on my lips makes my heart clench in the most uncomfortable way, especially because I know I shouldn't feel anything at all

We don't even know each other. I keep repeating it to myself.

Maybe some day I'll even believe it.

"I'm going to trust you, because I always do, and because I don't think you would say something like that unless it was really important. But maybe don't say it too loudly ever again." She smiles a tiny smile at me. "And I'm sorry. That really does put you in a pickle with the prince, doesn't it?"

"I couldn't be more in a pickle if I joined Arty in his jar." She snorts, and I laugh along with her. "It's a very big mess. I have to go back to the palace and actually face him again, and I just can't."

"Hmmm." She wiggles around on the bed and lays down next to me, depositing her own empty glass. "Will he be mad at you once his sister is eventually," she hesitates for just a moment, trying to choose a more savory word than murdered, I assume, "removed?"

"No." I don't stop to think about it. I can't fathom any way he would be upset that she died, but once again, I don't really know him. "But, I suppose I can't say for sure."

"And you obviously feel something for him." Ignoring my belated correction, she continues. I try to protest but she puts a finger on my mouth. "I know you, Lys. When was the last time you just casually slept with a *man*?" I sigh behind her finger against my lips but she doesn't move it. "Years and years. A decade even. I don't know what has been going on between you two, and obviously it's quite the story," she pauses for breath, and I hope she is deciding to stick to her promise of not asking any questions, "That you can tell me whenever you're ready. Just promise me you'll be as careful as you can physically, and maybe a little more reckless with your heart than you want to be." I want to protest even more adamantly now, but she actually pinches my lips shut, causing us both to laugh. "You don't know what is going to happen, so maybe just let it be what it's going to be, and worry about figuring it out later."

Finally, she releases me, and I stick my tongue out at her in retaliation but roll over, wrapping her in a hug. "It just feels wrong letting him think there can be anything between us."

"Don't make me shut your mouth again. You don't know what there can and can't be. I just said that."

I don't disagree, but I also don't promise anything.

"I'm afraid I won't be enough to fix all of this," I whisper into her bright curls after a long moment of silence. She squeezes me tightly.

"You don't have to be, not all on your own. You should know that by now," her words are just as quiet, her breath warm against my skin. "Can you stay today? You can help me downstairs, and maybe try to forget for a while. If you have to go, I understand."

I breathe in the scent of her soap, malt and the warm burn of alcohol, and I know this is where I want to be. I'm unsure of what I could even do in the palace today, still not ready to face the prince and unwilling to wander the halls on my own. "That sounds lovely, actually."

And it is.

I split my time behind the bar and poking around her experimental brewing, giving my unwanted opinions as I smell and taste my way through them. It reminds me of our younger days when she was just starting, and we would all spend time here, helping and getting in the way in equal measure. The memories of the ever serious Carolyn trying to keep Rend from causing too much chaos. The failed brews. The successes. Moments snuck between doing my own work, dodging Arty and responsibilities. Much like I'm doing today.

The sun has long since set by the time the last drunk patron stumbles out of the tavern, and Kyla and I collapse onto stools, giggling and more than a little tipsy ourselves.

"Canopy Above, I've missed this."

Kyla lets out a long sigh and tosses back the dregs of her last ale. "Me too, Lys. Me too."

"Does Rend still come by?"

"Whenever she's in the city. It seems less and less these days, but there will be weeks at a time when I get her here with me. For better or worse." She grins at me and I laugh. Rend for any prolonged period is always an experience.

I empty my own cup, the golden, wheaty beer, smooth and sweet. I feel old, nostalgic, sad and drunk but more whole than I have in a long while. "Thank you for asking me to stay today. I hope I get to come back soon and stay for longer."

She stands, clearing the cups from the bar and dumps them into the basin behind the counter.

I sleep even more soundly in the familiar bed, arms wrapped around my tiny friend, than I did the night before. When I wake the next morning I feel capable of facing the problems I left behind.

CHAPTER TWENTY-NINE

KEDREN

The halls are crawling with people on my way through the heart of the palace toward the waiting council chambers. I fight my rising anxiety by focusing on the mask I wear so often in public. It is harder when I do not have Envir's easy grace to mimic directly, but I conjure his image and adopt the straight-backed posture and casual stride that is his natural state. I relax my features, softening into a show of confidence I have never truly felt inside these walls.

I feel incredibly exposed dressed in striking black finery after nearly a week of nothing but dirt stained linen. Doubly so with my left arm bound to my chest in a matching swathe of silk. But, Kiv, am I thankful for it. My enthusiasm with Alyssia the day before yesterday still lingers as a constant pain at every small movement of my body. I have yet to see her again, having spent most of yesterday asleep or half-listening to Envir and Jyn murmuring in my sitting room. At some point, I think they mentioned she wasn't even in the palace. As much as that pains me, I do not need that kind of distraction before trying to match wills with my mother and sister. Not that I have stopped thinking about her since she stole from my room like a ghost.

Kiv, she drives me mad.

That cannot be my problem right now. I have to stay focused on the task at hand. My friends, and possibly the rest of the kingdom, are relying on me to learn everything I can during this meeting, and not let my sister slip anything past us. I feel more battle fear now, walking to the council chamber, than I did in the cave of spiders.

Too quickly, I reach the doors to the Lower Chamber, thrown open to the empty room, and make my way up that sweeping stair again. The memory of the last time I ascended them tries to creep in, but I push it back to the same space Alyssia currently occupies. My gaze slides from the path to my father's office as I hit the first landing, shifting to the guards outside of the High Council chamber. I slow ever so slightly, steadying myself with a deep breath before sauntering toward the men. With a nod, I stroll past them and let myself into the room.

I am not the first to arrive, but neither woman is here yet, thankfully, so I am not late. I take my place between High Lord D'luane, Envir's father, and High Priest Helnic. Across from me is the empty seat of Lord D'Guere, the sniveling Master of Finance.

"Your Highness." D'Luane's voice sounds so much like his son's, it always catches me off guard.

"High Lord D'luane." I say nothing further, but we hold eye contact for several long moments before he nods. His hand that was flat against the table curls into a fist.

He and my father were once as close as Envir and I, and he had remained as the King's closest personal council all these years. I have no doubt that he feels the loss of my father much more sharply than I do. His eyes, the same ocean blue as Envir's, flick down to my bound arm and back up, an eyebrow raised. Before either of us can speak, however, the doors open and everyone stands as my mother sweeps into the room.

Her dress is elaborate black silk that shimmers around her as she takes her place at the head of the table. She passes a look around the present members and we lock eyes. A heartbeat. Two. I will not be the first to look away. Not this time. She tilts her head to the side, and I cannot read her expression as she stares at me. Her eyebrows draw together in the slightest furrow before she snaps her attention to the door.

I have won my first skirmish of the day. Hopefully it will not be my last.

Lord D'Guere slinks in through the doors and to his place across from me. D'Laque is the last member not present, aside from my sister, and he bursts through in a flurry of official looking judiciary robes. "Apologies, Your Majesty, Apologies. The law never sleeps, as they say." The man's arrogance never ceases to astound me. Even I know no court is in session right now.

"Of course, D'laque." It is a small joy for me to experience the flat sound of disapproval coming from my mother without being its recipient, for once.

He begins lowering into his seat before catching himself and bolting back upright. The Queen still stands, and therefore the rest of us do as well.

The doors fling open one final time, and my mother's face transforms into a beaming smile as Daralyn saunters into the chamber.

Chaos erupts around me.

The Queen's face melts into a scowl. Priest Helnic shouts wordlessly into my ear, to the point I fear I will have to restrain him. Even D'Guere looks uncharacteristically affronted by something my sister has done. Captain Wuall's hand reaches for the sword he is not wearing.

"This is an *outrage!*" The priest's shouting finally resolves itself into words.

I cannot say I disagree, but at least this may be the push High Priest Helnic needed to fall fully to our side.

The doors did not close behind Daralyn. The imperious, self-possessed High Priestess Avadavia D'Brae glides into the room in Daralyn's wake like it belongs to her. She is swathed from head to toe in traditional, but decadent, black robes. A black circlet, far too similar to a crown, rests on her fine, light blond hair. The only things marring her refined, noble bearing are the harsh, black, tattoos that spill across the milk-white skin exposed at neck and hands.

My body tenses at the sight of her. The ache in my chest nags at me with the knowledge that she is the one responsible for this new scar. Helnic makes a sound unfit for a man of his status as she takes a place at the table. My *father's* place. Helnic rounds on my sister.

"I cannot stand for this, Your Highness! I will not have this *abomination* at this table," spit flies from him and lands on the back of my neck as he screams.

No one else makes a sound.

The two women have matching slow smiles that split their faces like blades.

Daralyn is practically purring, "She is the High Priestess of a cult, just as your own, High Priest Helnic, and therefore has the same right to a seat at this table as you do. Or do you suggest that our law of equal and safe practice of religion is incorrect in some way?" Her smile widens even further. "Perhaps you question your own purpose here as a representative of your people? For she is here only as a voice for those who follow the Path of Davor, as you are for those who follow the Path of Kiv." Her voice is as smooth and perfect as ice on a lake. A thin facade leading to black, frigid depths.

D'Guere and D'Laque are nodding their heads slowly, watching the priestess as their beloved princess defends her.

Helnic is not so contemplative.

"The interests of the Davorists are murder and despotism! My own-"

"Now, now. That is quite the allegation," Daralyn cuts him off smoothly, hardly raising her voice. "What evidence could you possibly have to support these claims?" Her black eyes slide to me, and she struggles to keep her features molded into polite confusion.

She must know I am involved by now, or at the very least strongly suspects it, but I am hesitant to confirm it so publicly. I try, very hard, to not react to her goading stare.

Helnic distracts her for me, still shouting, "My own priestess has witnessed the Davorists murder civilians. She has personally defended against unprovoked attacks against her person. You ask me to call into question the character of one of my most trusted devotees?"

Daralyn takes in a breath to speak, but stops short when the High Priestess raises a tattooed hand.

"Answer me, Gremor. If one of your uninitiated followers, or even a full priest, were to commit a crime, would you know of it beforehand? Would you condone the action once you learned of it?" One delicate, blond eyebrow arches. "Not even Davor and Kiv were gods, Gremor. I do not have absolute control over my people, just as you do not over yours." She smiles sweetly, her pink lips shaped like a doll's. "I do not preach murder and rebellion. As a true, modern, Davorist, I simply advocate for individual strength, and the ability to achieve one's ambitions by reasonable means. Our history is one to be learned from, not replicated without thought."

Her words are well practiced lies. Political manipulation, just close enough to reason to placate those who do not *want* to believe murderers have the support of the Crown, but transparent enough for anyone looking to see right through it.

Unfortunately, High Priest Helnic and I seem to be the only ones looking. Even D'luane seems uneasily subdued, shifting his gaze between the three women at the head of the table, waiting for some further action.

"Your Majesty! You cannot seriously be considering allowing this horror into the High Council?"

"Be wary of how you speak to me, Gremor," my mother says, sharp and cold. She glares between both cult leaders and her daughter in equal measures. "Unless High Lord D'Laque knows of some legal reason High Priestess D'Brae would be barred from sitting on the council, Her Highness is within her rights to appoint a member of the council with reasonable justification. Which she has provided." She pauses with a perfunctory glance at D'Laque. When he makes no objection, she continues. "We have several other matters to discuss, if there are no further objections?" Her words suggest a question, but the flat look she gives her audience leaves no room for a reply.

When she sits to indicate the true start of the meeting, and our permission to be seated as well, everyone I expect to sit immediately does. The members of the council fall like dominoes around the table until they reach Helnic, and shockingly, D'Maer, the High Lord of Mercone. I take my seat before either of them, deciding that now is not my time to make a stand. Helnic is still spluttering. I begin to question if he will leave altogether. D'Maer is significantly more composed, matching the queen's stare defiantly for a heartbeat longer than is proper, even for a show of dissension, before very slowly lowering into his seat. He will likely be paying for that in the near future.

"With the unfortunate passing of the King, the princess and I have been examining many of his projects, including past and current trade arrangements and his suggestions for the dispersal and arrangement of the guard." Shifting sounds and cautious glances ripple around the table at my mother's words.

D'Maer's punishment may come swifter than I thought if Daralyn has decided to take control of trade agreements without his knowledge. As the Master of Commerce, he and the King were the primary voices in drafting and negotiating new trade deals.

"That being said, the princess will be traveling to Ardjan shortly after the funeral with a small entourage to begin renegotiating. With her will be a contingent of men to be deployed throughout the north to reconcile the lack of crown-supported protection in the region."

The queen pauses to take a breath and D'Maer inserts himself before she can continue, "With all respect, Your Majesty, I have not been informed of any such journey. I do not possess the ability to arrange my affairs in such a short amount of time. Surely you would not be endeavoring to renegotiate trade without me present?"

"And I was not consulted about soldier reallocation. High Lord D'Maer and the lesser houses have no difficulties maintaining order in the north." Captain Wuall's deep voice, tinged with his own northern accent, cuts in directly after D'Maer. My mother calmly raises a hand to stop him. He has no choice but to obey.

"Gentlemen. Please. Lord D'Maer, you will be occupied here in negotiations with the emissary of Yadec. Princess Cenna will be arriving any day now, and you will be required to discuss with her new, more beneficial contracts, and of course, any other concerns she brings." The queen smiles pleasantly as the deep red flush of anger creeps past D'Maer's collar. She waits with exaggerated patience for him to acquiesce or dissent.

Through clenched teeth and tight lips, he replies, "Of course, Your Majesty. If you believe my experience would be better suited to dealing with Yadec and not the man I have significantly more rapport with, then I will stay."

Not only is the Lord of Mercone significantly more equipped to deal with King Vangariad Renvald, he is devastatingly unequal to the task of dealing with Cenna. Younger than I am, we were once engaged, and spent I two years in Ecadaes, the seat of her mother's empire beyond the Andrionic Ocean. Getting to know her, and her Empire, was nothing short of a legendary trial of wits, strength and courage.

"Excellent. And Captain Wuall, we know the north has been providing their own peace of mind for years. I believe that means they are entitled to some relief in that regard. We will be sharing the responsibility of protection more evenly throughout the kingdom. That is all."

It is all so elegantly maneuvered, and my mother speaks with such righteous clarity, I cannot believe she knows what Daralyn is truly beginning. I do not want to believe the Queen would willingly stand behind these decisions. I hope that some unseen grief for my father is clouding her judgment and ability to realize the core purpose of these machinations, and that she will come to her senses quickly enough to dismantle them. Daralyn is deliberately driving a wedge between us and the already independent northern region. Removing their autonomy by introducing royal soldiers, and setting D'Maer up to fail with Cenna by sending Daralyn north to negotiate instead is not benevolence.

Beside me, D'Luane has his fists clenched, white-knuckled, in his lap below the table. "I would beg you to reconsider, Your Majesty." He has strong connections with Ardjan as well through shipping and sea-faring. "Sol would be well-suited to bring any concerns you may have with Ardjan to King Renvald. They have a long and trusted relationship. And if you would like to reallocate Guardsmen, would Wuall not know better than anyone where they are needed?"

"We believe," Daralyn finally speaks, leaning back in her seat, "that High Lord D'Maer's relationship with the King of Ardjan is perhaps overly friendly, and that our nation would benefit from more rigorous negotiations." She leans forward, resting her elbows on the table. "As for the guard, if I find that they are truly unnecessary, we will reassess the situation upon my return. However, I believe that will be unlikely. I have examined my father's documents very thoroughly." Satisfied with her own explanation, she leans back again, casually arrogant. "After I have dealt with Vangariad, I will be sailing for Alsairdia. I have been in private correspondence with Aracles Legeas, a member of their senate and a supporter of their globalization. I will be working with them, personally, to assure a strong position for Ayamar when they open their borders to the rest of the world."

Every single person at the table, aside from the priestess, gapes at her openly. No one has had contact with a member of the Alsairdian Senate in *generations*. Her comment about unrest in their senate rushes back to me like a blow. I knew I was right to believe her involved in it. This cannot be a coincidence. None of it.

"Who will be traveling with you to the North, Your Highness?" The words are out of my mouth before I can lose my nerve to speak to her directly.

"Are you volunteering?" She tries, and fails, to keep a straight face. Laughter echoes under her words. She waves her hand dismissively, not allowing me time to respond. "Of course not. This would be far too much like responsibility for you to volunteer for it."

I grit my teeth in an attempt at a grin and slide back in my seat, trying to match her easy arrogance.

"Of course I would never volunteer for such a task." I would rather die than travel with her. Many of the people present at this table would know that, and the reason why, if they had ever bothered to listen to me when I tried to make them see what she was capable of. "I am simply curious as to who you will be taking on such an important venture." Any information I can gather could be important.

"Dienna, Marlayne, and Priestess D'Brae will be accompanying me, along with my personal guard and the detachment we will be dispersing as we travel." The corner of her mouth creeps into a smirk, her dark eyes boring into me. She expects me to be shocked at the inclusion of the priestess, but my expression does not change.

The priestess' lack of reaction to the revelation about Alsairdia confirmed my suspicions of her involvement in my sister's schemes.

"What purpose does the High Priestess serve on this journey, Your Highness?" Helnic scoffs beside me, saving me the effort of asking.

"As I am sure you are aware, D'Brae is a southern House. She will be traveling north on a pilgrimage, of sorts, to explore the role of her faith in areas of the kingdom outside of her usual patronage."

He snorts in response, but does not continue to object. Likely, he is glad she will be absent from the council for the duration of the journey and simply asked as a show of perfunctory dissatisfaction.

"Any further questions about your specific positions and assignments will be addressed individually as necessary in the coming days." My mother stands abruptly after spitting out her instructions. The rest of us rise to our feet after her. Without hesitation or acknowledging anyone, including Daralyn, she glides from the room. The doors close behind her before the rest of us can react.

A great groaning of chairs breaks the silence as the council members begin to move simultaneously, pushing away from the table and filing through the doors. Factions congregate together, whispering in low, urgent voices as they disperse. I hesitate, still debating confronting Daralyn directly until, suddenly, we are alone together, even her High Priestess nowhere to be seen. My stomach drops and I want to run, but I calmly make my way to the exit. She is closer and gets to the doors before me, leaning against them with her arms crossed. Her black mourning gown is too elegant for the way she kicks her slippered foot back against the door, the pose much more intimidating in her usual, more manly, attire.

"I must say, little brother. I am rather offended that you allowed someone else to do my job. And without even asking?" She clicks her tongue and waves one finger at me. Her smile gleams. My vision narrows to her and the doors that she bars.

Now is the moment I could confront her. Tell her that I know everything she is involved with. Make her tell me where Alyssia's pendant is. But I cannot speak. The pain in my chest burns as my muscles tense against the nightmare that is her so close to me in an empty room. I am trapped with her alone and physically vulnerable. I cannot give up my only protection of feigned ignorance by confirming I know what she has been doing and that I am trying to stop her.

"Who says anyone did this to me at all? I could have just as easily gotten drunk and fallen off a horse." It takes all of my will to prevent my voice from shaking, adding a small, one-shouldered shrug. The game of lies we play is obvious, but we play it all the same.

Her cackling laugh grates my bones, and I grimace despite my best efforts.

"A drunk who can't even sit on his horse. You really do make my job so easy." Her laughter cuts off abruptly. She shoves herself off the doors and grabs my face in one hand, yanking down so our eyes lock, her voice a low growl, "Whatever it is you and your little lackey have been doing, if it interferes with me now, *brother,* I may finally decide your usefulness is not worth my trouble. Try not to make me make that choice." As quickly as she grabbed me, she shoves me. My head snaps back and I stumble several steps.

When I steady myself, the swirl of her midnight gown disappears through the closing doors.

CHAPTER THIRTY

ALYSSIA

Sitting around the table in the prince's room, I'm no longer sure I'm up to the challenge our problems pose.

"She can't be serious. Has the Queen lost her mind?" Envir is so indigent, I think he might fall out of his chair, his fist pounding on the table. "That's war she's asking for, or least suggesting."

"I know that, and I think half the council did, but my mother was not listening. Daralyn had everything painted in the thinnest coat of reason imaginable, but it was there." The prince shakes his head. "I think D'Luane, D'Maer, and Wuall will try to stop it to some degree, but I do not have the highest hopes."

"She won't win this. Not long term. She can't," my words burns with my own indignation that this woman has so much power yet still searches for more. For worse. How many more like Inness will there be before she is satisfied? How many like the prince?

"Damn right she won't win this," Envir growls.

"What are we planning to do about it then?" Carolyn's voice of reason drifts to us from where she stands, looking out the window, her arms crossed over her once-again crisp, white robes.

"The first step is to find the pendant. We also have to find some clue as to where the relics are. That forest is too large for us to wander through aimlessly. With the disparity in our numbers, we do not have that luxury." The prince is pacing now, having given up on tilting his chair back.

"I have something that might help with that. Finding the relics, that is, but I'm not sure." It's Jyn, so quiet up until now, I forgot he was there, sitting in the shadow of Envir's fire. He dips below the table and pops back up with a book in his hand. A very, very old book. "I may have, um, borrowed this from the archives of the library when no one was looking."

"What is that? How did you even get into the Archives? Let me see it." Carolyn is across the room in a blink, reverently taking the ancient tome from him.

"I don't know, exactly. It's written in the language from before the Fall. I was hoping you would be able to translate it, as I cannot," he pauses for a moment as she slowly peels back the cover. "And as to how, I asked to see the Archives very nicely, and I was escorted on a tour of sorts. When the priest wasn't looking I snatched it and tucked it under my shirt."

"Where was this?" her question is hushed, and her stare bores into Jyn so intensely, it makes me uncomfortable from across the table.

"It was buried in a pile of trash on the floor. I only looked at it because I thought it was odd for a book to be so mistreated in a library."

"It is not simply odd, Jyn. You must have seen..." She trails off, her eyes drifting back down to the book. I can tell her hands are shaking from here, and my uneasiness drifts toward alarm.

"I did. That's why I took it."

"Saw what?" The prince stops his pacing to look over Carolyn's shoulder.

"This belonged to Kiv herself," she breathes. "It is a journal. Written in Kiv's own hand."

We all go completely still.

I don't have any particular faith in Kiv, but even I can grasp the gravity of this. Especially to my friend, someone who has been devoted to the cult her entire life. To Kiv herself. Whose own words she now holds in her hands.

"And it was just on the ground?" The prince looks past the book to Jyn.

"Half buried in scraps of paper and under a broken chest. I don't know what that means, but I couldn't just leave it there."

"I can read it, but it will take time, and I will need to go back to my study to retrieve my notes. We have so few examples from the actual time period, I am sure it will be difficult to read its variations and deviations from official teachings. I cannot believe this has just been tossed aside in a pile of rubbish this entire time." The book rests open in her hands, the pages quivering in her loose grasp. She looks afraid to move. "I do not know if it will help us now, but it is absolutely invaluable to me, Jyn. Thank you."

"Of course," he says, the hint of a soft smile at the corner of his mouth.

"So while Carolyn works on that," Envir glances at Jyn, and I feel like he didn't know about the book. "We can work on finding the pendant. Daralyn is going to be busy all day tomorrow for the funeral and the wake afterwards. As are you, Ked. So I was thinking, Alyssia and I could do a little uninterrupted sneaking while everyone was otherwise occupied. And if we find anything, I can always get to you and let you know."

The prince resumes his pacing, one hand holding his chin thoughtfully. "I will do what I can to warn you if she sneaks away. But be wary, regardless. Dienna and Marlayne could be anywhere."

"You know I'm always careful when I'm on that side of the palace. Still makes me sick to be there."

I don't want to imagine what sights could have made Envir sick in the royal apartments, but I catalouge the scars across the prince's body anyways. I start speaking just to distract myself. "That sounds like something we can manage. Do you think her rooms will be locked though?"

"Almost guaranteed, but there is always the possibility she could leave it open, or Dienna or Marlayne might have something in their rooms." The prince has moved from chin holding to hair pushing, and I fight a smile at the way the strands always stubbornly fall back into his eyes. "It will be worth trying, anyway."

"I will be with the High Priest for the duration of the ceremony, but my involvement ends before the wake. I will wait here for you when I am finished, Alyssia." Carolyn has set the book down on the table, but her hand still rests lightly on the cover. "I can begin looking through this while I wait." She pauses for a long moment before speaking again, "If you find your pendant, we may have to leave quickly. We should be ready."

I nod. That thought didn't cross my mind, but it isn't misguided. I'm sure Daralyn won't appreciate me stealing back what is mine. "I think you might be right. I don't want to be around when she finds out it is gone."

"A plan, then." The prince finally gives up his pacing and slumps back into his seat. "The start of one anyway. I will be gone early tomorrow, the procession starts across the city just after dawn. I must say, I am grateful that you will be there with me, Carolyn."

"I am glad I was chosen for the honor, so I may walk beside you." Her smile for him is soft, and she releases the book to touch his face in the same gesture she uses for her closest friends. The desire to break the easy intimacy of it ripples through me, but fades when the walls around my heart crack. "That being said, I must be awake even earlier to finish preparing for the procession, and therefore I should be back at the library already." She steps around the table to me and repeats the same motion to brush my cheek. "I will see you tomorrow. Be careful."

I lean into her touch with a nod before she sweeps from the room in a swirl of white.

Envir scrubs at his face, still trying to erase the visible anger. "If we aren't moving today, I need to go to sleep. Or pace. Or *something*." His eyes dart to Jyn. They exchange a long look before he jerks away from the table and strides out the door.

Just like that, I'm alone again with the prince, in his rooms, both of us staring awkwardly at the smooth, wooden tabletop.

"I wanted to be there with you tomorrow." I don't look up from watching my fingers dig into the edge of the table.

"It will be a better use of the time to look for your necklace, and I do not want her to know how important you are to me." He sighs and I hear the creak of his chair as he leans back again. "It would be obvious, as I would not have you anywhere but next to me."

My knuckles are white against my skin.

By the Trees, I want to go to him. Heat builds between my legs and rises to the pit of my stomach without my permission. I push back from the table abruptly. I still grip the edge, but I'm on my feet, my breaths coming faster than they have any right to. I feel him watching me. I hear the soft thud of his chair legs landing back on the floor. I smell the remnants of tonight's wine and the soap we both bathed in.

"Do you want me?" The question is a vibration I feel in my blood.

I want to be forged anew by the fire of them, but I say nothing, biting the inside of my cheek against my response. I wait for what seems like an eternity, but he doesn't move. I can't even tell if he's breathing. I want *something*, but I can't begin to describe it to myself, let alone him.

When I'm finally brave enough to look up, I'm locked into the woodland green-brown of his eyes. He must see some kind of answer in mine, because he stands and closes the space between us with determined inevitability. I tense to guard myself against a kiss or some other dramatic gesture, afraid he will take what I don't know if I'm ready to give. But he simply wraps his arm around me and pulls me close, burying his face in my hair.

"I do not need anything more than you want to give me, Alyssia."

I want to give him so much more of me, but I don't know what I have left.

Holding him tightly, I let the warmth of his body seep into mine until the solidity of his presence calms my erratic heartbeat, and my legs stop feeling as though they will give out from under me.

"I don't know what I *can* give you." Tears choke my words and sting my eyes. I'm just short enough to bury my face in his uninjured shoulder to hide my struggle to keep it together.

"You do not have to. Not now." He takes a slow breath, his cheek against my hair. "I am so, very sorry that I made you feel like you did." He squeezes me tightly once more before pulling away.

The loss of him surprises me. I wipe at my eyes to stop the tears from falling. "I'm sorry too." *For everything. And for everything to come.*

He shakes his head with a small, soft smile. "Please. It is not your fault I have fallen under your spell. The magic you wield is no more under your control than the radiance of the sun, but both shine just as bright."

I sob out a laugh, and scrub at my face again. "I'm just a mortal, Your Highness, not some magical, Otherfolk Queen despite what you two keep saying."

"*Just mortal?*" His smile grows wider, and he pushes his hand through his hair. "Just a mortal who has appeared out of nothing but tree shadows and leaves to save my life more times than I care to admit in the last three weeks? *Just* a mortal who has otherworldly creatures fight by her side?" He steps closer again, cupping my face in his hand, tilting my chin up. The intensity of his gaze steals my breath. "*Just* a mortal who has lost her entire world, and instead of running or hiding, said *fuck that* and stood to fight? No. You are not *just* anything, Alyssia." He is closer still, our bodies pressed together again. His eyes still hold mine. "You are more than I have ever seen bound together in one person. Of *course* you burn like the sun. The stars. The whole damn sky. No one body, magic or not, could contain you."

I close the distance between us and press my lips to his. It isn't the consuming fire of our first night. I kiss him gently and he responds in kind, not pressing further. When I part from him, it is reluctant. I want to stay lost in him. What do you say when someone says you are more than the entire sky?

He saves me from having to say anything by speaking as soon as I pull away. "Stay with me tonight?" His eyes are closed, and his forehead rests against mine.

My words come out in a broken whisper as I let myself be taken in by his gravity, "I think I would like that, very much, Your Highness."

CHAPTER
THIRTY-ONE
KEDREN

"Are you going to be alright without me?" Envir asks, fussing with my hair, smoothing it back into a short braid at the base of my neck. It is, thankfully, the finishing touch for this morning's dressing ritual.

"I will be fine. You have more important things to do here." I pull the hem of my coat down as I stand, straightening it for his inspection. He lingers on the only color breaking the clean lines of black and gold that adorn me. A red ribbon knotted around my upper arm wrinkles the straight lines of my perfectly tailored sleeve.

"Leave it, Vi. It is not going anywhere."

He throws his hands up dramatically. "I wouldn't dream of it."

"You are dreaming of it right now. I can tell."

"No, no. That isn't what I'm dreaming about." He grins at me before throwing himself into a chair. "Just thinking about why it's there, is all."

I turn away from him, not letting him see me smile at the thought of her. "Speaking of her, she may still be in my rooms when it is time to for you to begin your search."

"Oh?" He hums, grinning. "Anything you want to talk about?"

"Nothing happened. Neither of us wanted to be alone, that is all." I stop myself with my hand halfway to my hair and scrub my face instead.

The sky outside Envir's narrow windows is beginning to turn gray with pre-dawn light, and it is my cue to leave.

"Go back to sleep, Vi. Dienna and Marlayne will not be present for the procession, so you have time before you can do anything."

"We'll see," he yawns. "It didn't come easy for me the first time around. Maybe it will now, knowing you're properly dressed."

"You are really are the worst sometimes." I grin at him, one hand on the door. "But seriously, you may need it."

"I know." He stretches as he stands. "You could have used it too."

I shrug, pulling open the door. "I think we both know that was unlikely at best." Even without spending half the night holding Alyssia close to me, unwilling to waste time so near to her by sleeping, I would have been awake, worrying about today.

"Ked." He stops me before I am fully into the hall. "I know it was complicated between you, to say the least, but I'm sorry. I'm sorry you lost him as soon as he started treating you like a human being."

My hand tightens on the door frame, and my heart lurches into my throat. I do not speak for fear of my voice breaking, but I dip my head before disappearing into the hall.

—

I dodge the guards meant to escort me, no longer trusting any of the men not within my own unit. Since they should all be in the woods by now, I do not risk being seen by these. There is no need for bodyguards anyway. The city is quiet this early.

Black banners hang from buildings in the still, morning air as I drift through the streets. I hook my thumbs in my belt, and nod at the occasional citizen already beginning their day. Some give me lingering looks as I pass, but most do not spare a second thought. The king's funeral has drawn many lords and lesser nobility from their country estates. One more well-dressed man on the streets is not overly remarkable, even at this hour.

The pain in my chest is a constant discomfort as I walk, but I refused to let Envir bind it. This day is about my father, and I have no desire to spark gossip about my latest failings as the Whore Prince of Ayamar. Walking the length of the city next to Daralyn is going to be enough to cause comparisons, and being visibly injured is a step too far even for my limited pride.

My thoughts slide from the vision of Daralyn, not ready to deal with that nightmare yet. Instead, I dig through the sparse memories of my father as I make my way to the West Gate and his coffin.

I do not know how old I am, but I am young, looking up at the towering mass of my father. I cry fitfully, as I so often did. Our tutor had finally found me, bleeding and whimpering in a small courtyard by our nursery and had taken me to a physician, and then, my father.

"What happened this time, Kedren?" He was not unkind when he spoke to me, but he was distracted, his eyes constantly drifting toward his desk.

"Daya." I still called her by her nickname. I must have been very young. "She wouldn't s-stop. It hurt. It hurt but she wouldn't stop."

"That does not answer my question. What did she do?"

I curled into myself, sniffing and hiccuping with every breath, cradling my bandaged hand.

"She poked me with a stick. She keeped saying she wanted to know. To know what happened. Pushed and twist. She wouldn't s-stop. It hurt. It hurts." I collapsed into tears again, and he absently set his hand on my head, rubbing his thumb through my unruly hair.

The stick she had broken and sharpened against a rock had eventually burrowed straight through. I watched in screaming horror as she delighted in finding the path between bone and tendon until the makeshift spear point pierced the skin of my palm and ground into the dirt I was trapped against.

"Why would she do something like that?" he asked, disbelief tinging his words. "Nevermind, I will have your mother talk to her."

I still do not know why my father could not manage even the pretense of anger toward her on my behalf.

More memories filter through the barriers I have taken years to erect, each one twisting the knife of grief deeper into my heart. Grief that I do not have a real father to mourn today.

I was a teenager with a broken wrist, not able to join Envir in sword practice when my father came to watch us.

"What excuse is it this time?" He tilted his head, clearly disappointed.

I was frustrated enough to wave my splinted wrist in his face like he had not already seen it, even though I could feel the grating of my bones as I did.

"Your precious daughter and her friends decided to push me down the stairs. I am so sorry for the inconvenience." I snapped shut the book I was reading and stood. "I can still show you my longsword progress if you don't mind the

screaming." I had not quite reached his height yet, but it was close. I did not have to look up far to yell directly in his face.

"You fell down the stairs? Really? And you are blaming Daralyn again? You are nearly a man now, Kedren." He stepped close to me, lowering his voice. "You cannot keep expecting people to believe you when you say a woman beat you. At best, you will be laughed at, at worst they will say you are trying to undermine her right to the throne."

"Everyone already laughs at me! She has made sure of that for years! And since when has anyone ever believed me?" I shouted before throwing the book to the ground and storming away.

Envir dropped his sword and ran after me, despite the yelled curses of our instructor, picking up my book as he followed. My father didn't speak to me until I could hold a sword again.

That was the last time I tried to tell anyone what she did to me.

—

I do not think of the most recent memory of my father until I am outside of the West Gate, face to face with his gold and glass casket. I was not expecting to see him again, and the apparition of this transparent vessel stops me short. I am overwhelmed by the memory of him gripping my shoulder and telling me to remember to help people. Was that supposed to be an apology for never remembering to help me? I rest my hand on the glass, suddenly fighting the gut-wrenching need to feel the touch of an actual father for the second time in my life.

Just once more. Please.

"What the fuck are you doing?" Daralyn's voice makes me jerk away from the casket so fast my chest flairs with pain and dizziness washes over me. I stagger back a step before my vision completely returns, but she moves in close enough to grab my chin in her hand. "Are you *crying?*"

I rip away from her and force myself to breathe, to remember I am no longer a child. She cannot hurt me, physically, while we are surrounded by guards and priests. I am safe from her here.

"Why would you care if I was?" I want to sound biting or aloof, but my words come out small.

"Oh, I couldn't care about anything less, really. I was just wondering why you did."

She turns from me in a flourish of black and gold. Her dress and veil are as soft and voluminous as my suit is harsh. She could be the robed personification of death herself, swallowed by billowing blackness and just as cold.

"That man didn't give a shit about you your whole life, why should you give a shit that he's dead?"

I do not have an answer.

I watch her dress swirl around her as she saunters to her position behind the casket. Before I can follow, I catch the scent of incense and turn to find its source. Carolyn approaches from behind, removing herself from a knot of other priests, including High Priest Helnic, with an ornate censer swinging from a wooden staff.

"Your Highness." She tilts her head in a polite nod, but she smiles warmly. "Is everything as well as it can be?" She glances at Daralyn, now impatiently waiting near her position, kicking at the ground with her black slippers.

"I was not expecting this." I tilt my head toward my father's body. "It has been two weeks. He should not look like this."

"One of my brothers has been developing his own use for Kiv's protective magic. I believe he started with flowers, but it has obviously progressed further." She looks at the body thoughtfully.

I do not want to look more closely at him, but curiosity compels me.

Gray hair and deep lines age him more in death than they did when paired with his easy confidence and sheer physical presence while alive. I never thought of him as old. The King had always been such a rigid, powerful man. A pillar of strength for the Queen, but not someone to overshadow her. Now he looks like an old man asleep. Worn down and soft. Human. Flawed.

I start to turn before the grief of the father I never had can return, but I stop as a faint shimmer of gold ripples across his skin. At first, I thought it was a reflection of the gilded casket, but now I recognize it as the familiar sheen of Kivaran magic. A shiver crawls down my spine.

"It does not take a lot of power, but it is very skilled," Carolyn muses.

"Will he always be like this?" Something about the thought of my father, preserved in this way for all time, makes my skin itch.

"No. The magic needs to be maintained every few days. Nature will take its course soon enough."

I take a deep breath of relief and sneeze, having inhaled too much of the incense Carolyn carries. We both snort with partially concealed laughter.

I am still chuckling under my breath when the city gates begin to open slowly with the ominous sound of rattling chains.

My mother, framed by the towering wooden doors, leaves no question as to who the Queen of this nation is. Her dress, unlike Daralyn's, is severe. It has narrow skirts and sleeves and is made of stiff, black velvet. Her floor length veil is heavy with embroidery along its scalloped hem. The eclipsed sun of our house shines from each curve of the gauzy fabric, the metallic thread shimmering as she moves. The spiked iron crown atop her head truncates any softness the veil could have created.

If I thought Daralyn resembled death, my mother is the scythe.

She cuts through the growing crowd of guards and priests like the finest blade, neither slowing nor taking her eyes from the casket. I cannot see her face well enough to read her expression, although even without the veil, I likely would not have known what she was thinking. As she glides to my father's glass-encased body, the rest of the gathered party begins to fall into place. The High Priest will walk in front of my mother, who will be flanked by lessor priests carrying censors. Eight guards serve as pallbearers and will carry the casket behind her, a second set of men ready to seamlessly take over as needed. Daralyn and I follow behind, creating a line with two more priests on either side. Guards will also form a perimeter around our group to keep the crowds from us as we make our way through the streets.

As I take my place between my sister and Carolyn, Daralyn speaks.

"Do you have *friends,* now, little brother? More than that servant of yours?" Daralyn's voice is too low for me to make out the intonation over the clanking and shuffling of the guards in their armor and the growing crowds within the gate. If I did not know her, I would have said she was genuinely curious. The familiarity between Carolyn and I must have piqued her interest.

"Friends, sister?" I mock myself, placing a hand against my chest and pretending offense. "You know I could never possibly have friends. Not ones I did not pay, of course."

"I didn't think you would be so careless as to fall off your horse until yesterday, either. Perhaps you have other surprises for me as well."

It does not sound as though those surprises would be pleasant for either of us.

I am saved from having to respond by the mournful bray of a horn at the head of our column. As one, the pallbearers raise the casket from its temporary platform, and my mother's hand drops from the glass surface. It may be a trick of the light and shifting fabric, but I think I see her shoulders shake as she turns to face the city.

The clamoring of the crowd abruptly quiets as we pass through the gates and onto the narrow streets of the western district. The swinging of the censors mark our time as we march sedately through the city. Scraps of black cloth wave in the hands of citizens. White flowers are tossed, landing on the casket and at our feet. I try to avoid crushing the blooms as I walk, but I cannot save them all. Our path through the city will be carpeted in wilted white before the day is done.

There is wailing and weeping as we continue, interspersed with long bouts of silence. Daralyn scoffs whenever we pass a collection of more vocal mourners, and in some hateful part of me, I agree with her. My father was not some remarkable monarch for the histories. He was uncomplicated and charismatic, and always publicly advocated against raising taxes. What else could they ask for in a king? A good man? What did it matter to these people if their king never used his time to listen to his son, or to wonder why he could watch me take an unarmored hit from a dulled steel blade without flinching, or to take even one moment to tell me I would be alright when I was broken or bleeding or burning.

Why should they not mourn a man who cared more for them than his own son?

Daralyn shocks me from my rapidly rising anger by closing the distance between us, speaking so only I can hear.

"Are you realizing I was right, little brother?"

"What are you talking about?"

"That you shouldn't give a shit about the death of the man we all pretend to mourn? That all of this is playacting and pageantry?" She hisses sharply. "He was nothing. He did nothing." Her voice drops even lower. "He couldn't even save one boy from *me.*"

My hands tighten into fists at my sides, and I stretch my left shoulder back to distract myself.

As she drifts back to her position, she speaks again, even more sharply. "Some day, these people will know what it is like to have a true ruler. Someone worth their wailing."

Neither of us speak for the remainder of the macabre parade.

It is a blur of black and white and gold, my surroundings fading into a fog as I fight to not succumb to the rage that threatens to burn me from the inside. I do not need to mourn my father, but I do not want to hate him either. At the end there was hope. I had *hope* that some day he would listen to me. For two days, I had hope that I may hear him apologize to me for all of the years he could not be bothered to care. I want to hold onto that hope. Not for his sake, but for mine. I want to at least pretend there was some part of me that he could have loved.

Our path takes a indirect route. We pass the towering library, brilliant white in the morning sun, the columned theater where Jyn and I frequently drag Envir to suffer through plays, the market street just off the harbor full of colorful, cloth covered stalls. I try to focus on the city, taking in every detail that I can. The nebulous shadow of Daralyn at my shoulder is a constant reminder that I cannot take my residency here for granted. Some day soon, I am going to have to oppose her openly, and I have a strong feeling I will not be welcome here after that.

I am so tired of fighting so hard for my own place in this world without her corruption taking it from me. When will I be able to cut her rot from my life?

"Thank fuck," Daralyn mutters, twisting her back in a stretch as she stops.

I carry on several steps before I realize the rest of the column has come to a halt outside the North Gate.

The cemetery sprawls before us, spreading away from the city like an ink stain. Tombs are built into the wall, graves are dug into the ground, and mausoleums stand guard throughout. Centuries of dead are interred here, many of the markers worn to broken, featureless stone. Bodies stacked upon forgotten bodies saturate this soil with bone dust.

My mother's family's resting place has not been forgotten. White marble atop a grassy hillock, framed by a manicured garden, stands like a temple to lost gods. Family lore states that it was built before the city walls were complete, but those records are lost, and our family has not been on the throne as long as that. I am sick watching Helnic scale the stairs ahead of my parents, toward a platform awaiting the arrival of the casket within the shaded colonnade.

Carolyn abandons me to the company of my sister as she joins her High Priest on the stage for the final act of this pantomime. A ring of guards provide a buffer between us and the surging populace, gathered to hear the final rites of the King. Daralyn feigns a swoon and drapes herself over the tombstone of some distant relative. Her posture of disinterested boredom is painfully familiar to me, despite her acting.

My chest burns, my head aches, and I want to be asleep with my arms wrapped around Alyssia's body tucked tightly against mine.

I pull at the ribbon tied around my arm, thinking of the differences between this funeral and the one that inspired its addition to my wardrobe. That girl, Inness, deserved the grandness of this funeral more than my father does, but at the same time, I would not wish this on her or her family for all the stars in the sky. Her parents, surrogate and biological, laid her to rest with their own hands. They poured their love into her until the last possible moment. Until the last shovel of dirt. As soon as Helnic is done rambling platitudes, we will leave my father's body behind to be sealed into stone by nameless masons, and preside over a feast held in celebration of his life. If I did not have to watch Daralyn, I would already be planning my escape to my rooms.

Finally, after a miserable eternity of baking in the heat of late day sun reflected from pale stone, the guards behind me turn on their heels and lead us back into the city. It is slow and close and hot, and breaks down into crowded chaos quickly now that the formalities are complete. Carolyn and the other priests break from our party, heading southwest for the library while my family and the guard continue east along the wall toward the palace.

I am exhausted, dripping sweat, and I can count the blisters created by walking an entire day in stiff dress boots by the time I follow my mother and sister into the vaulted receiving room of the palace. The doors close behind us, allowing us a moment of quiet respite before the wake begins. I believe a normal family would take this time to console one another, but the three of us stand in cool silence while servants bring us food and water. Two women in my mother's service step forward to fold her veil back so she may eat, and to my shock her eyes are red with crying. Daralyn carefully avoids looking at her. I force myself to eat even though my appetite was left behind somewhere with Envir and Alyssia. I sit, huddled on a bench against a far wall until I am called back to my duty.

The flood of people released by the opening doors threatens to pull me under when combined with my worry for Alyssia and Envir. I stand to one side of my enthroned mother, Daralyn at the other, as servants direct the throng toward us to deliver their condolences.

My collar is too tight. I feel sick every time someone says how good of a man the king was. I find myself having to wrench my sore shoulder back to hide the seething rage their sentiments stir within me. Unlike the women, I do not have a veil to hide my face behind, and the expression of nauseated pain it creates is closer to the grief I should display. I sway alarmingly after an endless tirade of mourners and condolences. I must escape this and find some place I can breathe before I simply fall to the floor.

"Excuse me, Your Majesty." I bend low to speak quietly to my mother during a temporary lull in the battery of citizens. "I must step away."

She does not even look at me.

I flee into the mass of bodies, desperately seeking some kind of calm in this storm.

CHAPTER THIRTY-TWO

ALYSSIA

The vast bed is empty when I wake. I stretch this way and that, trying to find the person who was curled around me all night. When I become conscious enough to sit up and realize it wasn't Kyla or Carolyn I was reaching for, but the prince, I expect to feel horror paralyze me; some deep-rooted panic over making such a terrible mistake. I'm mildly concerned when all I find is a strong desire for breakfast.

I slide out of the velvet draped bed and distract myself with luxurious ablutions in his bathroom. When I emerge, wearing nothing but one of the prince's slightly too large shirts, Envir is in the next room, and I smell food. Briefly, I consider pants, but continue without them. The shirt hovers just above my knees and it isn't black, so I'll need to change eventually to fit the day's dress code.

"Do you always know where everyone is, or are you just really good at guessing?" I ask, shaking out my straight, freshly brushed hair and sliding into the same seat I occupied last night.

"I have a gift," he shrugs. "Buuut, he also told me you were here this morning."

"You saw him?" I reach for an interesting looking pastry with an egg cooked on top of it.

He looks at me with an eyebrow raised. "You think I'm going to let him dress himself for an official, public event? Him?"

He is so visibly, and genuinely, offended I laugh hard enough to spit out bits of the pastry I was chewing. That makes him snort as he slides into a seat opposite me.

"Honestly, I thank Kiv I didn't have to find something for you to wear too. Getting you ready to stand next to the prince is a battle I'm not sure I would win." He grins over a piece of buttered toast and it's my turn to snort.

"Just because you haven't seen it, doesn't mean I can't clean up, *Lord D'Luane.*" I toss my long, shining hair back and delicately place my hand under my chin, dramatically fluttering my eyelashes. "I've even worn at *least* one dress in my life."

It's his turn to choke on food. "I'm shocked and stand corrected, *Your Otherness.* I should have known a Queen can dress for any occasion."

He is still teasing, and I want to laugh, but I can't help thinking about what the prince said last night. I go quiet and annoyingly soft, and I'm sure I look like a dreamy idiot.

When Envir notices, he grins a slow, knowing grin, all hints of teasing erased. "What did he say?"

I hesitate, fiddling with breakfast before looking up at him. My response is tentative, quiet, as I still struggle to accept the prince's declaration. "That I burned like the whole damn sky."

He sighs loudly and dramatically. "I'm sorry if he's too much sometimes. He..." he hesitates, searching for words to explain away his friend's behavior, but I interrupt with a wave of my hand.

"I don't need apologies or explanations. He is who he is," I pause, deciding how I want to continue. "A lot of people would argue that I'm too much. Even Carolyn can be too much in her own way. *You* can certainly be too much." I smile at him. "But anyone worth knowing is too much, because it means that there is enough of them to never reach the end of. Too much is just the right amount." I start strongly, but fade by the end, not entirely sure I'm making any sense. I shove the last bite of my second egg pastry into my mouth to truncate my rambling. He stares at me like he is trying to read a book in a language he doesn't understand. "What?" I ask before I've finished chewing.

"Nothing. You're a creature of the wild, Alyssia. Never change." He shakes his head and pushes back from the table. "Except your clothes. Go get dressed. I'll meet you in your room in a bit."

He's still watching me oddly, and I don't understand why. Regardless, I unfold myself from my seat and stand, stretching and twisting. He's right; we should get moving. I want my necklace whole again.

I look back at him before I open the door and twist my face into an exaggerated version of his own. He blinks several times, clearly not understanding until, suddenly, he laughs.

"Alright, alright," he says, still laughing. "Get out of here."

I do, shaking my head with my own laugh and closing the door behind me.

A passing serving girl scurries by me with a squeak, her head lowered, and I'm reminded that I'm standing outside the prince's door in nothing but his shirt.

So much for subtly.

I probably should have changed back into what I was wearing yesterday, but it has two days of wear on it, one of those being at the Prism. I walk as quickly as I can without revealing too much of myself, and, thankfully, make it to my room with no further witnesses.

Just to spite Envir, I go straight for the black dress I saw two days ago and slip it on. It's plain, not silk but a fine, soft weave despite that. It billows loosely around my body and has the same lacing at the cuffs that the blouse did. Rummaging around in the wardrobe I find a black over-dress in the same cloth with a small amount of black, beaded embroidery that laces closed at the waist. With some quick twisting and a black ribbon, I pull my hair back into a neat knot.

When he enters, I'm stuffing my freshly laundered clothes into my bag hanging on a peg near the door, ready to grab in case of a hasty exit.

He whistles.

"I stand corrected, indeed. You *do* know how to wear a dress." He looks at me for a long moment before he tugs two strands of hair from the knot so they frame my face, and grabs the under-dress with a firm pull so its square neckline sits even with that of the over-dress. "There. Perfect."

I roll my eyes but smile. "Let's go."

I follow him through barren, stone hallways toward the center of the palace. The closer we get, the more out of place I feel. Marble and wood and gold shine around me. Servants swirl past in streams of black, preparing for the funeral feast. Vaulted ceilings loom above me like rocky caverns, and even with their soaring windows and lavish finishes, I still feel the heaviness of this place press against me. The formality. The rigid order. The obscene wealth. The sense of indistinct, but suffocating obligation. It all makes me long for the freedom of my Woods.

Find the pendant. Flee to the Woods. Find the relics.

And then what? A small voice in my head whispers.

And then I'll figure it out. I snap back, mentally glaring at myself.

Or you'll be dead. I retort helpfully.

Or we'll be dead.

"You alright over there?" Envir interrupts my internal argument, and I adjust my scowl to a mere frown.

"Just having a particularly unpleasant conversation." I wave my hand absently. "Are we getting close?" The crowd of servants has thinned now, and we only pass one or two infrequently.

"Yes, the residential wing begins just up these stairs. Daralyn has a whole hallway cordoned off for her and her ladies. It will be quickest to start there and see if we can get into any of the rooms. If we need to find keys, it could get problematic quickly." He starts up the aforementioned stairs, walking like he doesn't belong anywhere else. I follow, trying my best to emulate his confidence.

There's no one around, but I feel watched. Our boots click softly against the marble stairs and the noise echoes, the sounds of the preparations fade into a low hum behind us. A vast, painting and tapestry bedecked hall, peppered with ornate wooden doors, opens before me when I reach the top of the stairs. This is much closer to what I expected when entering the living quarters of the Royal Family, and I gawk accordingly

"All the way down until it branches to the right," his voice is low as he stalks past me, light on his feet now, on edge and determined.

I follow behind him more slowly, not trusting myself to walk quietly on polished marble. And, I admit, I'm also awestruck by the artwork and ostentatious glamor. I stop entirely when I find a particular portrait. The prince stares back at me, but he is so young it makes my heart hurt. The soft, baby curves of his face and his wide eyes catch me off-guard with their sweetness. The same magical, woodland green is captured here that I know so well, and I want to take the portrait with me. If it wasn't for the other occupant, that is. The black-haired girl, older and already rigid and cold, looms over him by several inches, gripping his shoulder. I want to reach into the painting and lead him away from her so badly I find myself actually touching the textured brush strokes.

A muffled curse from Envir snaps my attention back to the present. I hurry toward him, clicking boots be damned.

"It's Marlayne," he hisses.

I hear the woman's voice and abruptly stop breathing. I lunge for the nearest door.

It's locked. The handle rattles uselessly. Across the hall, Envir also shakes at a stubborn doorknob.

The voice at the end of the passageway gets louder, and we throw each other panicked glances. The door closest to the branching hall is the nearest for both of us. We dive for it, reaching the handle simultaneously. If it's locked, we are caught.

The door collapses open under our combined weight, and we close it as quickly as we can redirect our momentum. I swear I see a flourish of black fabric out of the corner of my eye before the door is fully closed.

"Fuck," Envir and I say together, quietly, in a burst of relieved breath.

A loud clatter and a thud precedes a second, louder repetition of the curse from within the room we have entered. A long, black braid with a familiar streak of white trails down the back of a tall, well-muscled and naked woman and the golden brown, slender legs of another are wrapped around her waist. There is a fallen wooden chair at her feet.

I would say I can't believe my eyes, but I've really become unflappable when it comes to this particular person.

"Rend!" It isn't even a question, I would know that taught, round ass anywhere.

The golden-haired head of the second woman pokes out from around Rend's shoulder. If I had any questions to begin with, her jaw-dropping beauty would be all the explanation I'd need for Rend's presence here.

"Envir?" The stranger drawls curiously in a heavily accented, honeyed tone.

"Lys?" Rend finally turns, shifting her grip on the other woman so she is on the desk instead of in her hands.

"Cenna?" Envir still leans against the door next to me, eyebrows nearly at his hairline.

I leave him behind, and in three strides I'm swept up into the arms of one of my favorite people in the entire world, my feet leave the ground as she swings me around. I bury my face in her sea salt scent and want to yell again, screaming her name with sheer joy. I hold my tongue and kick my feet instead.

The other woman, Cenna, slides off the desk, casually striding to the pile of clothing discarded on the ground, and shimmies her way into a clinging silk gown before tossing a shirt over to us. I snatch it from the air as Rend lowers me to the ground.

Reluctantly, I let her step back to tug the shirt over her head, but then my hands are on her face, pulling her back to me. Her beautiful, slightly scarred, heavily tanned face that sparkles with the metallic glint of its many piercings. It has been years since I've held her. Years since I've heard her deep, sea-weathered voice. I want to laugh and cry and forget everything else that has happened, and just be held by her. I want to tangle my fingers in the streak of white through her jet-black hair, a remnant of a scar I stitched ages ago at our first meeting. I want to lose myself in the sudden and intense feeling of wholeness she brings me.

"What are you doing here, Vi?" The other woman asks curiously, calmly, like she wasn't just naked on a desk.

Something shifts into place, connecting the ambassador-ferrying mission Kyla told me Rend was on, with Cenna, the Empress' daughter the boys were talking about yesterday. I want to question the coincidence, but I let the issue lie for now, grateful that the last pillar of my foundation has settled into place.

"I mean, technically I live here. What are *you* doing here?"

"Working, obviously."

"Ah yes, on your public *relations*, I see." They both smile, despite their sharp words.

"I always strive to make a good impression on the locals." Her smile turns playful as she glances at Rend, who laughs loudly in return.

"Ked said you were on your way to wreak havoc, but we didn't know when you were coming in." He has already made himself at home, throwing himself into a plush chair next to a grand fireplace.

I have not let go of Rend, clutching both of her hands in mine. She doesn't pull away, but looks over my shoulder to Envir. "We came in on last night's tide. I was eager to test the palace's private dock for myself. A neat little set up there, D'luane." I blink at her and twist to look at Envir, but he looks just as bewildered. "I've maybe run into D'Luane Senior a time or two in our *shared business,* and you look like he traveled in time." She grins a secretive little grin before continuing. "Putting two and two together didn't take much effort, even for me." She kisses my hands and drags me over to a sofa across from him to sit.

Cenna drifts over to her other side and drapes herself against Rend like the silk of her dress clings to the curves of her body. I'm struck with the memory of a cat that used to live in the Prism's stables.

"What are you doing in my room during your King's funeral, Envir?" Cenna twirls a long, golden curl around her fingers, looking at him flatly.

"Specifically, we needed to hide from Marlayne. More generally, we are here to break into their rooms to look for something they took from Alyssia."

She sniffs a little laugh. "That seems like a predictably terrible plan. Are you going to be rummaging through that whole wing until they get back from the feast? If the rooms are locked, what then? Have you taken up lock-picking since we last saw each other?"

"Well no. But-"

"But nothing. What are you looking for?" She leans forward and directs the question to me, around Rend.

"It's a glass vial wrapped in plants and-"

"And there is a green light inside of it?" She finishes for me quickly, a flash of eagerness in her yellow-green eyes. When I nod, she continues. "I thought that may be it. She hid it as soon as she realized it was me and not one of her people who waltzed into her room. But she was too slow." Cenna leans back, content. "Now you need not waste your time. If it is anywhere, it will be somewhere in the Crowned Bitch's quarters."

"Which will undoubtedly be locked if she is not in them," Envir sighs, slumping further into his chair. "I can't believe you just barged into her room like that."

"She was made aware of my arrival and did not greet me properly. I can be just as rude." She says, crossing her arms. "Rend, dearest, can you pick locks?"

Rend laughs again and kicks her bare feet up onto the low table, her calves flexing as she presses against the tabletop with her toes. "Princess, I am flattered that you would consider that one of my many skills. Alas, I'm afraid I must disappoint you. These hands may be dexterous, but those tools are not ones they are familiar with."

"You could never disappoint me, my oasis." She rests her hand on Rend's knee and looks back at Envir. "You will have to find some other way in. Perhaps Kedren will be able to manage it." She pauses and looks around as if just noticing something surprising. "Where is His Highness, if he isn't with you?"

"At his father's funeral where, like you so cleverly pointed out, I should be." He pulls himself straighter in the chair. "Speaking of which, why aren't you there? It seems like an ambassadorial type duty." He eyes

Rend conspiratorially.

"Our late arrival precluded me from attending the procession this morning. I will be joining them at the wake shortly." She stretches out languorously and stands in the same fluid movement. "In fact, I should be dressing for the occasion now." She kisses Rend on the forehead as she walks by and disappears through a doorway. Rend watches her until the last shimmer of silk vanishes. My heart twinges ever so slightly at the sight of it, but I brush it away.

"We may as well go down with her, and tell Ked what's going on. See if he *can* help." He rubs a hand over his face. "Worst case scenario, we could probably break in, but it would be loud."

"Let's hope it doesn't come to that." I give Rend a side-eye, who is looking thoughtful at the suggestion. "He has to be able to do something."

"Can we circle back to what *you* are doing here, Lys?" Rend suddenly changes topic, shifting on the sofa so she faces me directly. "Not that I'm not wildly grateful to see you without having to haul my ass into your Woods, but the palace is, quite frankly, the last place I would have ever expected to see you."

"I would have said the same thing about you before Kyla told me where you were, so we're even, I guess." I smirk as she shrugs in acquiescence.

"That still doesn't answer the question. And *what* are you looking for? A green light in a glass jar? What is going on?" She's frowning now, obviously confused.

"It's a long and unpleasant story that I don't want to tell right now, but what I'm looking for is important to me," I hesitate for a moment, blinking back the stinging in my eyes as Rend squeezes my thigh, "and I think it might be important to keep away from her."

"Then we'll get it back. It's that simple." She is so confident, so *her*, I can't help but feel like it could be that simple.

"That's right. We know where it is. We can get it back one way or the other." Envir pulls himself to his feet to pace around the room.

"Will you come down with us, Rend?" I ask, desperate to not lose sight of her again so soon.

"Of course. I have been hired as the Princess' personal guard. I go where she goes." She grins and tugs on my bun lightly. "And I'm not ready to say goodbye to my favorite girl just yet."

"You should probably have pants on, then." I smile and push her away playfully, trying to hide the way my heart breaks when she calls me her favorite.

"I find I am a significantly more striking figure in the buff, but if you insist." She winks and hops to her feet, jogging to the same door Cenna disappeared through, her thick braid bouncing against her back.

"She seems fun," Envir muses with suspicious blandness while picking up and setting down strange, scientific looking objects scattered throughout the room.

My eyes start to roll, but I stop myself. "She is." I stand, knowing it will not take long for Rend to be ready to depart.

"She sure is...enthusiastic," he continues his seemingly disinterested, conversational tone.

I do roll my eyes this time.

"Enough. Ask or leave it to your imagination." I laugh but I want to throw something at him. I'm afraid I'll break one of the strange brass and glass instruments if I miss him, though.

"I think I might like to leave it to the imagination, actually." His facade finally cracks into a laugh.

"What debauchery are we leaving to the imagination?" Rend is propped against the door frame, fully clothed in practical, black attire with Cenna standing beneath the archway created by her arm.

The princess is absolutely beyond words. A black, gauzy, many layered dress floats around her, anchored only by thread-of-gold embroidery at hem and plunging neckline. Her bared arms are stacked with gold bangles and a gold circlet sits perfectly on her brow, nestled in the waist length, golden waves of her hair. The only color she wears is a necklace of rubies tight around her throat. The colors of the royal family.

"Yours," I choke, coughing at the sudden tight grip around my airway. My own imagination starts to wander unbidden, and I have to close my eyes to block out the sight of the two women. I start pulling out memories at random trying to override the images of tangled of gold and black hair and soft curves. The thought of prince's steady hands working between us as I straddle him, my back pressed against his knees does nothing to help my situation.

"And yours," she laughs.

I cautiously peek through narrowed eyes, but she has moved away from the princess and the magic of their combined presence seems to have dissipated. "You don't know what I have been doing lately, Rend. You haven't been around," I snap back, still trying to match her teasing, but flustered all the same.

"You mean I don't know *who* you've been doing?" she quips. "But I think I might have a guess."

"My oasis, that is unkind. I told you the prince is uncomfortable with those kinds of activities," Cenna chimes in, ducking past Rend and heading to the door.

My retort to Rend dies on my tongue, shock widening my eyes. *Why were they talking about the prince's sex life?*

"It looks like he got comfortable with it real fast. I told you Lys was one to watch out for." Rend's hand targets Cenna's ass as she walks by. My face burns hotter. "I just didn't think the two would cross paths before our arrival. But why else would she be in the palace and giving me that look when you bring him up?"

"A magician indeed." She arches one delicate eyebrow and sounds both suspicious, and like she knows something I don't. "We were betrothed, and he would not lay with me. He would not even let me touch him."

Betrothed? Were? Who broke it off? Was it political? Did they love each other? Questions race through my mind without any particular order or necessity, but I do, at least, have one answer. Why he didn't feel comfortable sleeping with her, but was with me. Envir has gone completely still, revealing nothing, the sand of the hourglass he is holding the only thing showing he is not frozen in time.

"It has been a long and strange few weeks. That and the two idiots think I'm an Otherfolk Queen from the stories. Maybe that's it." I force myself to casually shrug and grin.

Rend laughs at that, nodding. "I'm not convinced they aren't right about that, Lys."

"Don't start, Rend. They'll never stop," I groan as I push open the door, quickly scanning the hall outside. When Cenna sweeps past me a wave of sweet spices and sharp wood hits my nose, I breathe in deeply to capture more of the scent.

"Right?" Rend nudges me with her elbow as she follows the princess through the door. "Intoxicating."

"I think Jyn would like that," Envir muses, following the pair closely.

"I can have my perfumer send you some," she chimes back. "I am always pleased to help those in need."

That gets a laugh out of all of us as I shut the door. We make our way back down the grand hall toward the stairs and the growing sounds of revelry at the center of the palace. It feels strange, retracing our steps in the company of Rend and Cenna. Absolute certainty of place radiates from the princess. Our furtive trek up to the residency has transformed to feeling like we own the entire building. A wild, delusional image of the princess simply demanding a key from Daralyn herself flutters across my vision. I stifle a laugh. I need several days without a dozen new stresses being added, or I may devolve into complete insanity.

The press of the crowd as we enter the massive, vaulting vestibule takes my breath away. The sea of people flows into the open double doors that lead to the main hall used for balls and public hearings and anything in between. It seems as though the entire city is here surging around me, and the waves of them threaten to pull me under the stones of this place. Searching for safe harbor, I grasp my friend's hand. Rend turns to me and smiles, squeezing my fingers tightly. With that one look, the waves fall back and I'm left sure-footed and confident that everything will be alright.

CHAPTER THIRTY-THREE

ALYSSIA

As we enter the throng, the crowd parts for us like they are being pushed aside by one of Carolyn's invisible walls. Bodies swirl away from the black and gold cloud that is Cenna and the towering figures of Rend and Envir. I tuck myself in the middle of them and start my search for the prince, hunting for the distinct deep brown of his hair that should be a head above the majority of the crowd.

Most of the people are congregating around tables of food and drink. Others that are brave enough, cluster in loose lines to give the veiled Queen their condolences. Daralyn is beside her, also veiled and standing primly next to her mother. Rage boils in me at the sight of her standing there like a normal, thoughtful, grieving person. I clench my fists so hard my ragged nails dig into my palms. Now is certainly not the time to draw her attention to us, so my desire to start screaming and clawing at her face like a bear is temporarily ill-advised. I satisfy myself by imagining it in great detail while I continue to look for her brother.

Cenna maintains her even, confident stroll straight through the crowd surrounding the royal women, everyone captivated by her ethereal presence. Using her as a distraction, Envir and I duck toward the walls before he can be spotted by Daralyn. As soon as we separate ourselves from the masses, I see the prince and immediately break into quiet laughter.

Obviously attempting to hide in an unused corner of the room, he is surrounded by young women of varying social status, all vying for his attention. His looks comically hunted. What I'm sure was once a sleek and tidy queue of pulled back hair, is now a ruffled mess sticking in sweaty strands to his cheeks. Envir clicks his tongue beside me as he sees it. Mussed hair notwithstanding, the prince cuts a stunning figure. A heavily structured, black coat with off-set gold buttons and matching trim at cuffs and high collar tidily frames his shoulders and waist. High-waisted pants, with mirrored rows of matching buttons and a thin line of gold tracing the outer seams, hug his thighs and disappear into tall, black, gold-buttoned boots. The only color breaking the harsh lines of his outfit is a thin, red ribbon tied around his upper arm. Tears come to my eyes unexpectedly and thoroughly unbidden.

My fingers trace the small ridge of twine hidden beneath my dress where Inness' funeral ribbon is woven into the string. I want to kiss him, witnesses be damned.

"He insisted. Absolutely ruins the lines of the jacket, but I couldn't convince him otherwise." Envir watches where my fingers fidget with the fabric and smiles softly. "Shall we go save him from his admirers?"

"If we wait any longer he's likely to bolt, and then the hunt would truly be on. He wouldn't make it out alive."

"I think you might be right," he laughs as we close the distance.

Kedren sees me first. His expression changes so completely, he practically looks like a different person. It doesn't go unnoticed. The women turn as one to assess this new development. They register Envir first, tall and striking in all black with his red brown hair catching the candlelight. An entity known to them, he is written off as nonthreatening and a ripple of relief starts among them. Then they see me. The range of violent glares that hits me rolls over me like a stampede. If only they knew how right, and how wrong, they were.

I drop into a very shaky curtsy at our approach and smile as innocently as I can at the women, but let Envir do the talking. I would like to remain as unremarkable as possible.

"Your Highness, I must apologize to you and all of these *lovely* women, but I am afraid you are needed elsewhere." He bows to the women with a look of true apology. I'm impressed once again by just how good he is at his job of managing the prince's affairs.

His Highness is not as graceful, and I'm thankful that the women are still looking at Envir and I when blatantly obvious relief floods his face. "Apologies, ladies. Thank you for your kindness and condolences. It means so much to me and my family. We are very grateful for your support at this terrible time."

He can at least follow a script, even if he can't act.

With significantly more fawning from the gathered flock than I find necessary, we extract the prince and flee into the crowd. Cenna's lilting voice weaves throughout the room, but I can't make out what she's saying. I'm grateful for her distraction, however. Everyone is far too busy watching her to notice us duck into the unadorned servant corridors.

"Did you find it?" he asks, pushing his hair back from his face as soon as we're alone.

"No, but we know where it is." I keep my voice quiet as we wander further away from the festivities. "Your rather striking former betrothed saw it in Daralyn's room."

My attempt at a jest backfires when he responds without missing a beat.

"Which one?" He winces immediately, and Envir buries his face in his hand.

I snort and shake my head, more at myself than at him. "Princess Cenna. She arrived late last night."

Envir clears his throat and stops scrubbing at his face long enough to speak. "This means we need keys."

The confusion on the prince's face is replaced with concern as the real problem settles back over him. "I will try to find Nemia. She is the most likely to know how to get in, if we can," he pauses. "Vi, can you stay down here and try to warn us, or prevent Daralyn or her ladies from coming back to their rooms?"

"Of course. Besides, it would be easier to explain why the two of you were sneaking around than the three of us." He winks. "Good luck." With a wave of mock salute, Envir turns on his heel to disappear back into the fray.

The prince and I wind quickly through the halls, looking for the woman we ran into days ago amid the steady stream of workers bustling through the corridors. We give up searching, and he asks a serving girl if she could find and send Nemia to us while we wait near the residential wing.

"They have all been arranged," he says into the dead silence that had been stretching, not unpleasantly, between us.

At first I don't understand what he's talking about, but I catch up. "It wouldn't bother me if they weren't. I have no claim over you or your past, Your Highness." I rest my head back against the wall, my arms crossed. "We all have history." I smirk wryly, "Besides, she is absolutely stunning. I couldn't fault you for sleeping with her any chance you had."

"We never-" He sounds shocked, but I put my hand up.

"Unfortunately, I know." I cough and am about to tell him that she also knows that we *have* when I'm saved by the appearance of Nemia around a distant corner.

"Nemia," he calls out as he peels himself from the wall as she approaches.

"Your Highness?"

"I need a very important, and very discreet, favor." He pushes a hand through his hair while she waits patiently for him to ask it of her. "I need a key to Daralyn's room."

The woman stares at him for a moment before coming to herself again. "I'm sorry, Your Highness. We have not been permitted to have keys to her rooms for a number of years now. We are only allowed to enter when specifically requested." She wrings her hands in her dress. I want to tell her it's fine, but helpless frustration seethes within me.

"But?" The prince is quiet and gentle, noticing what I didn't; she's holding something back.

She sighs with her eyes closed. "But Marlayne is careless with hers and leaves it in a jewelry box in her room. Which I *can* let you into."

The poor woman is wringing her dress so hard I'm afraid it's going to tear. I feel terrible asking her to do this for us, but not enough to stop.

"She will not know, Nemia. I promise she will not know," he says low and comforting, one hand outstretched. "We need to do this, or I would not ask it of you."

With a deep sigh, she nods. "Follow me."

She takes us on a twisting path through featureless halls until I'm completely lost. Stopping abruptly at a door like all of the others we've passed, she pulls a ring of small keys from her pocket and hastily unlocks the door. "I will be here to lock it when you are done. Please hurry."

She doesn't have to tell us twice. We rush through the open door and into an opulent bathing chamber that I can't begin to take the appropriate amount of time to appreciate. I jog through to the adjoining dressing room and start opening every box and drawer I see. Carefully, I sift through the contents of each, being sure to disturb as little as possible.

"I have it," his voice is hushed as he sweeps past me and back to the door we came through. I don't register his words until he waves the plain iron key in my face. I close the drawer I was searching and follow.

Another short trip through the servant's halls has us standing outside another, equally indistinct door.

"This leads to the hall outside their rooms," Nemia says quietly. "It is the closest I can get you." She hesitates for a heartbeat. "Please be careful, Your Highness. I believe you think this is necessary, but please, be careful."

He nods, and she curtsies before practically running back into the warren of halls.

Furtively, he opens the door the tiniest crack and watches for a long moment before sliding out into the hall. I take a deep breath and follow. He slinks toward the end of the passage quickly and silently. I follow, the ornate door at the end seeming further away than should be possible. My heart races and my breaths come hard and fast by the time I catch up to him at the door. My neck aches from craning my head to look behind me every other step. I can't stop my fingers from tapping against my thigh as he slips the key into the lock, and I wait, hoping against hope, that it works.

A low click is followed by the door swinging open smoothly.

We share a relieved glance before ducking in, one after the other, and shutting the door behind us. The prince locks it again with an unsettling finality.

The room isn't overly large, but tall windows frame the sea beyond like a living painting and evening light floods the room. It looks so *normal.* A large, ornate fireplace. Plush chairs. A side table full of books. There are even plants, both potted and cut blooms in vases, strewn about the room. When I realize what kinds of plants they are, I roll my eyes.

"This is too banal to be real," I mutter as I walk further into the room, hunting under and in anything I think could hide my pendant.

"What is?" The prince searches a sideboard across the room, but looks up to wait for my answer.

"Every single one of these plants is dangerous in some way. Some are also useful, but only if you know how to use them." The room is filled with everything from foxglove, to potted yews, and it's seriously difficult to not laugh. "No wonder she doesn't let anyone in here. Anyone with half a mind would be able to put two and two together." He still looks at me confused.

"What do you mean?" He takes a step back from the nearest vase of flowers, eyeing it warily.

"Several of the plants here could cause the symptoms your father experienced as he died. It isn't direct evidence, but it would certainly be enough to cause doubt if anyone found out." I'm overcome by the urge to start running through the halls waving sprigs of foxglove and oleander, screaming that the princess a murderer. "Do with that as you will."

I leave him staring at the incriminating greenery and go to explore another room. My spirits lift when I step into what has to be her study. Shelves line the walls, a large desk and a small seating area float in the center of the room, offering plenty of places for the pendant to hide. Too many. Open books and loose papers covered in scrawling notes and diagrams keep pulling my attention away from my search. Most of them look like cult texts, but I'm afraid to move anything more than absolutely necessary so I can't be sure. I don't dare to do more than the most minimal snooping. Time slips away as I rattle at locked desk drawers and peek under overturned books like the grains of sand in the hourglass Envir held. The more they bury me, the more frantic my search becomes.

I start to cry with frustration and fear which does nothing but make me more frustrated and my hunting more clumsy. Squeezing my eyes shut against the tears, I breathe deeply.

Remember the Woods.

The twisted, towering trees. The living homes of our villages. The moss painted temple in the heart of it all. The open meadow of the dead, lily-of-the-valley growing over the low mounds of my people reclaimed by the spirit of the trees.

When I open my eyes I've turned toward an ornate wooden box on one of the shelves, tucked between two rows of books. Without hesitation I reach for it. I run my fingers along the smooth, delicate inlay of the wooden lid and flick open the simple metal latch. I'm greeted by the comforting, swirling green flame of my pendant, the tiny flowers still as fresh as the day Inness gave it to me.

A cry of pain echoes from the next room and my fingers twitch into a fist around the delicate glass.

CHAPTER THIRTY~FOUR

ALYSSIA

My fear grips me so tightly I barely register the sing-song voice coming from the other room.

"I hear you, Envir, so you may as well come out. Even though I'm really not sure how you beat me here." The ringing tone of her voice is like the cracking of ice on the river.

The black dress billows around me when I jerk to a stop, my free hand clutching the doorframe, frozen by the scene I stumble into. Daralyn shuts her mouth in a tight frown, brows drawn together, before a slow, dangerous smile curls her lips back.

She has her brother by his bad arm, twisting it so far behind him I'm surprised it hasn't already been dislocated. The other hand holds a knife to his throat with enough pressure that a small trickle of blood runs down his neck.

"Run," he gasps, his head tilted back from the blade.

I want to lunge for them. I want to tear out her eyes with my bare hands and rip her into strips like a wolf.

I don't dare move. I barely breathe.

"What desperate back alley did you dig her out of, brother? It was my understanding that not even the whores will have you." The ice of her voice splits further.

His watering eyes don't waver from me, begging me silently. *Please. Run. Please.* Over and over and over. I shake my head in time with his wordless mantra.

"It doesn't matter," she says flippantly, shifting her grip so the knife bites deeper. "Give it to me or I kill him." I wait for the plunge into icy depths now. Not even a hint of humanity made it through those words.

"Kill him, and I destroy it." My knuckles are white against the pendant, the tightness of my fist struggling to not shatter it. I would rather destroy it than let her touch it again, but I still hesitate.

"Destroy it, and I will kill you both." No part of her moves aside from her hand tightening around the hilt of the dagger. "Stop wasting my time. Set it down."

She we kill both of us regardless of what I do. Why wouldn't she? If I destroy it there is a chance Kedren will be able to get away while she's distracted. If I do nothing we both die here, so I have to do *something*.

I close my eyes and think. I try to make it look like I'm resigning myself to handing the vial over, but I'm trying to buy time. Time for Rend or Envir to come bursting into the room to save us. Time for me to have some brilliant revelation.

Tears roll down my cheeks. Her sharp, brittle laughter makes my hands, my whole body, shake. I won't let her take him from me, but I can't let her have the piece of my heart I hold in my trembling fingers. There has to be something I can do to protect us both.

It's your turn now.

The words flow around me like a summer wind. The scent of new growth and clean forest decay clears the sweat, stone and blood from my nose. The soft sound of leaves rustling in a breeze cuts through the bitter laughter like a gentle caress. Everything is suddenly still and alive all at once.

The trickle of blood from the prince's neck slows.

Daralyn's expression freezes between mirth and confusion.

Sap flows through yew branches. Water is drawn up through the searching stems of foxglove and my precious lily-of-the-valley. Roots bury into soil, reaching for that which will sustain them.

In the center of it all is the light radiating from between my curled fingers. The usually sedate flame churns violently within the walls of its glass prison. Tendrils of answering light course through the plants around me, pulsing with the beating of my heart.

This is what the flame is.

It's so simple, I can hardly believe I didn't know what it was until now. Maybe, somewhere inside of me I did, but now the truth burns through me like a drug. Like life. Like *magic*.

I urge the flame to creep around the confines of its cork. I send it dancing around my fingers and it sprays embers into the air. Daralyn's smug face shifts to curious wonder as threads of flame crawl up my forearm. As I siphon the fire from the pendant I will it into the rivers of life flowing throughout the room.

Daralyn tries to step back, pulling the prince with her, but jerks to a stop as a yew branch brushes her cheek. Another curls around the arm holding the knife. She tries to struggle against it, but it splits and weaves its way up and around her fingers. The needles are sharper than they should be. They leave tiny red scratches on her skin that swell and spread into patches of pink rash.

She tries to yank her arm free. I watch in stunned horror as the blade presses closer to the prince, but he throws himself away from her as the struggle with the branches distracts her. He tears his arm from her hold and falls toward me with a stifled moan.

Its difficult to break away from the sight of the princess being cocooned by wild shrubbery. The play of forest-green fire and freshly grown trees captivates me. I smile as the small, leafy needles start to make their way into her mouth and muffle her cursing. Maybe luck will be on my side, and she will die here, suffocated and poisoned by her own decor.

"Kedren," I breathe as he stumbles into my arms.

I take his face in my free hand and make him look into my eyes. His breath heaves and he shakes under my touch, his eyes wide and watering. I wonder how many times he's been that close to dying under her hand. The yew branches tighten in a violent spasm.

"You're alright. We both are." I tilt his chin up to check the cut on his throat to be sure he is actually alright. It has already stopped bleeding. I nod and move his head in a little nod as well. "You are going to be alright."

I switch what hand holds the pendant so I can take him by his uninjured side and lead him to the now open door. I hit the marble tile at a jog and drag him behind me. I would love to slip into the servant halls, but I would get us lost in that warren, and I'm not sure Kedren is capable of leading us anywhere right now. Down the hall it is.

My need for subtlety is gone. Daralyn knows my face. She knows what the fire does. She knows what I'll do for her brother. And, hopefully, she knows that I'll be the end of her. Because I know it won't be good enough for me to let anyone else take that job.

We take the steps two at a time. I refuse to let go of his hand despite my guilt about pulling him after me. I know he has to be in agony, but we can't afford to slow down.

Another set of stairs. Another hall. I retrace this path for the third time today, and I'm unreasonably shocked when I hear the sound of the crowd still buzzing from the center of the palace. It feels unreal that more time hasn't passed and people are still blissfully unaware of what their princess is willing to do for a power she doesn't even understand. That she killed the king they mourn. That she would have killed the prince.

The final sweeping stair leading to the entrance hall spills down into the heaving crowd. I'm ready to plunge us into the chaos when a familiar blur of auburn hair separates from the mass and rushes toward us.

"I lost sight of her, and I couldn't get away. I'm sorry. Fucking Dienna and Marlayne," Envir says in a rush while ushering us to one of the discrete servant doors. "Are you alright? What happened? Ked?" Apparently just noticing the blood, Envir latches on to the prince, tilting his head like I did.

"We're fine," I snap impatiently, urging him to keep moving, "But we all need to leave now."

"What happened? Where's Daralyn?" His head bobs between Kedren and me, but thankfully he takes the hint to lead us through the stone maze, and back to where Carolyn and our things should be waiting.

"I found the pendant. She threatened to kill him. I tried to kill her. Mixed results on both fronts," I answer Envir between breaths.

Kedren squeezes my hand tighter. He is pale and fights for each breath but keeps pace with us. We should stop so he can breathe, but none of us do.

It's no time and forever before we duck out of one of countless, identical doors into the mildly familiar hall of the prince's residency. Without stopping, I kick open the door to my room, snag my bag off the hook, and toss the leather strap across my chest. The familiarity comforts me, and I carefully replace the vial into its pocket, safe and protected among my clothes.

"Is Jyn here?" the prince gasps as we pass Envir's room.

"No. He's at our home in the city. I sent him away before we started looking just in case."

"Good," I take over the conversation before Kedren can gather enough air to speak again and slam open the door to his room, eliciting an undignified yelp from Carolyn.

She flies out of the chair she was reading in and immediately reaches for her own bag, slides the ancient book inside and hooks the strap over her head. "You have it?" she asks without slowing and buckles her borrowed sword around her waist.

"I have it."

"Excellent. No time to waste." Carolyn arches an eyebrow at Envir who is hovering around Kedren as if waiting for him to fall. Honestly, I can't blame him for thinking that.

"Oh. Right," he says, spurred into action by Carolyn's prompting.

I haven't stopped moving. I shift from foot to foot and pace at the door. We just got here, but it feels like an eternity. I keep thinking I hear people running down the hall, but it's just the hammering of my heart against my ribs.

Before Envir can finish donning the second bag, I'm out the door again, head swiveling from side to side. I pace uselessly when I realize I don't know where the hell I'm going. Kedren slips out behind me and starts off in the opposite direction I would have taken. Envir skips ahead of us while Carolyn falls into step with me. The gray walls blur around us as we hurtle toward the relative safety of the city.

We steal into the stables before I recognize where we are. A confused and startled guardsman shouts at us to stop before recognizing the men. I hadn't expected to have horses, but I can't say I'm upset about not having to run the whole way back to the Woods. I am upset that we don't hit the cobblestones at a gallop, but I understand the unwanted attention that would bring. Instead, we clop along sedately, blending with the horse and foot traffic flowing to and from the palace.

"Envir. Kedren. Get Jyn and go somewhere. Anywhere. Find Rend and go out to sea. Go climb a mountain. Anything but stay in the city or following me." I waited as long as I could before blurting out my intentions. I had hoped I would be able to duck away without them noticing, but it isn't like they don't know where I'm going. Best to deal with the inevitable push back here before they waste time following me.

"Excuse me?" Envir asks, surprising me. "We are getting Jyn, but we're coming with you. I'm not sending you back into that chaos without someone at your back."

"I will be there," Carolyn says calmly and nudges her horse to ride beside mine. "Two people can move faster and hide better than five."

"No," Kedren says, flatly.

There it is.

"I will not let you vanish into those Woods without knowing you are safe."

He looks so determined, even sweat-soaked and impossibly pale. The black of his shirt is too dark for me to tell how much he's bleeding, but the damage must be severe to cause this much of a reaction from him. Thankfully, the streets are functionally empty this far from the palace, because I draw my horse to an abrupt stop directly in front of him.

"First of all, you will not *let* me do anything." He tries to say something, but I throw my hand up to stop him. "Second, I will *not* let her use you against me again. She knows now. She knows what I can do and what I will do for you. And if-" I shake my head. "When they find us, I won't waste time worrying about them killing you. I can't."

Envir looks between us and sags visibly in his saddle. "She's right, Ked. You're not in any shape to go running through the forest dodging cultists, and we shouldn't make it so easy for them to catch all of us together. We're the only ones who know." He scrubs at his face briefly before urging his horse forward again. "I think I have somewhere we can go, but, Alyssia, I don't know when, or how, I will be able to get to you again. If something goes wrong..."

I don't take my eyes off of His Highness as Envir speaks, or as I reply, "We will be fine. We will do what needs to be done. We will see each other as soon as we can. We *will* find each other when it's done. But *please*, Kedren, do not follow me." I want to touch him one last time, but I'm afraid I would never let go. I want to fix whatever he did when he tore himself from Daralyn. I want to find some way to stop all of his hurting. But I have to leave. I have to trust Envir to do what I can't.

He doesn't say anything. He doesn't move. I wait for a long, painful moment, but he doesn't even acknowledge that he heard me.

"Take care, Envir. Of all of you," I say, quietly, as I nudge my horse into motion once more.

Carolyn and I turn as one to the west.

I don't look back.

CHAPTER THIRTY-FIVE

KEDREN

We are hardly out of the city before the moonless night makes it too difficult to continue. Envir and Jyn took an age to pack for our escape and attempt to fix my shoulder, despite my insistence that we not waste the time, but the delay serves my purpose well enough.

"I know this isn't what you want, Ked, but Alyssia is right. It isn't worth it for you to get killed over this." Envir is tying the horses to stakes in the ground while Jyn lays out bed rolls. No fire will be risked this close to the city.

I say nothing, not trusting myself to stay calm and not scream in rage and frustration over this betrayal. This infantilizing.

This abandonment.

I cannot decide if she has abandoned me, or I her, but I cannot stand it either way. Not knowing if she will be safe. Not knowing when, or if, I will see her again while I hide like the coward I am somewhere in the nowhere reaches of my own kingdom. I will not let this be who I am.

My chest hurts more than when I was first injured weeks ago. When I tore myself from Daralyn, the searing pain of tearing flesh blinded me against anything else for far too long. I can move my fingers, but anything else is intolerable, even for me. It is bound once again at Envir's insistence. Rage over my unending uselessness burns hotter then the wound. I am so tired of my life being a series of new pains and their accompanying disabilities. Now it is worse than ever. I have been hurt worse, but I have never had anything I truly needed to do. I could languish within my self-pity and pain with my books for weeks at a time while I healed. But now there is a woman I barely know taking my place in my fight against Daralyn. A woman risking her life for not only mine but so many others, and only because of a cruel, random twist of fate. A woman who sees me as nothing but a liability. A burden.

The fact that she is not wrong is what stokes the coals of my temper, but a tantrum would solve nothing so I keep quiet and go through the motions of settling for the night. Jyn and Envir speak softly, huddled together in the dark. The time I force them to be apart wounds both of them deeply, and it is something I frequently feel guilty about. I rely on that pain and their time apart now to prevent Envir from coming after me at least until he has seen Jyn safe.

I lay stiffly on my back and stare at the blackness of a cloud-dark night, waiting as long as I can to hear the even rhythm of sleeping breaths in the dark. When I can be still no longer, I roll up to my feet as quietly as possible, eyeing the bed roll for a moment, debating if it is worth repacking. Deciding against it, I pick my way slowly toward the slightly darker shadows of the horses.

Gritting my teeth against the effort of pulling myself into the saddle is the only thing that prevents me from cursing audibly when Jyn's quiet voice materializes out of the dark.

"He's going to be out of his mind when he wakes up, you know."

"I have to go," is all I can say.

"I know. I'm not going to stop you," he pauses to sigh. "Just be careful. For his sake, more than yours."

"Will you prevent him from following?"

"I will do my best, but you know how he gets."

"I know. Thank you, Jyn." I try to ensure he knows how truly grateful I am before I nudge the horse into a slow walk.

"Please don't make me regret this."

His whisper follows me into the darkness.

CHAPTER THIRTY~SIX

ALYSSIA

The old, familiar mass of tangled trees that form the entrance to Eklar call to me like a siren. It has been years since I have seen this particular tunnel open its bark-covered arms to me, and I'm more than ready to fall into its embrace. I have completely lost track of what time, or day, it is. Carolyn and I have been riding or walking since we left the city, stopping only long enough to deposit the horses in Curaria's pasture. Even on the path to the western village, which can fit several horses across for most of its length, it's still faster to walk. We are both stumbling over nothing by the time I push open the door to my parent's home. It's as dark inside as it is outside, but I find my way to my childhood bedroom by memory alone.

Waking up to a wet kiss on my forehead and someone shouting my name was not the experience I wanted moments after falling asleep, but here I am.

"Yes. Hello, Mama. It is I, your ungrateful daughter. Back from the abyss to finally grace you with my presence again," I mutter, reluctantly dragging myself back into the waking world and all of my problems. Before I can physically pull myself up though, she climbs into the bed and wraps her arms around me, hugging me close.

"The men who came with those guards told us what happened," my mother says sadly. She saw Inness as a granddaughter. I hadn't thought of what this loss would mean to her.

"I can't talk about it, Mama. I still have things I need to do." *Canopy Above, why won't the tears just stay in my damn eyes.*

"Carolyn mentioned that. I'm just so..." she sighs, squeezing me tighter. "I'm so sorry, my little Lys."

For a very long time, I let her hold me, stroking my hair while I will my eyes to dry.

The door slams, and we both jerk upright. My feet hit the ground before the echoes cease.

If they found me here already...

I scoop my bag off of the ground as I make for the door, digging through it for the pendant, now reattached to its cord and sling it around my neck, discarding the bag unceremoniously.

The living space is empty. Carolyn's books lay open on the table, but there is no sign of her.

"Carolyn?" I call out pointlessly, still running for the door.

My mother lags behind, calling for my father, "Sen? Sen, was that you?"

I burst through the door and scan the narrow walkway for a telltale flash of white robes.

There, around the spiraling curve of the stairs built along the trunk of the tree the house rests in.

"Carolyn! Carolyn, stop!" By the Trees, I'm so tired. "Where are you going?"

The snapping hem of her robes stay just at the edge of my sight as I chase her down the steps until we hit solid ground. She takes off toward the dense edge of the village, a straight shot into a thicket of tangled trees with gaps wide enough only for squirrels to squeeze through. I slow down once I know she won't get very far.

"Carolyn, what is happening?"

My usually abnormally stoic friend is breathing hard, shoulders heaving with an effort disproportionate to our jog. She spins around when I approach, tears in her eyes.

"Alyssia, it is all a lie." She chokes back a sob, failing to keep the composure she clings to.

"What is a lie, my heart?" I take her by the shoulder and draw her close to me.

"Kiv. Davor. The magic. Our power. All of it," her voice breaks. "Kiv was against the use of magic and had none of her own. Whatever it is we can do, it does not come from her. It would be an offense to her. We have been working against her true wishes for centuries. It is all a lie."

Carolyn's entire life has been devoted to learning the texts, facts, and history about Kiv. I thought she would have known everything there is to know by now.

"The relics we are looking for?" she crackles with a hysterical giggle. "They aren't just things he owned. He *created* them *from* magic. What she wrote doesn't translate well, but I think it means the essence of the world, whatever that is supposed to be. He stole it and made these pieces with them. She fought him with nothing but her sword," she sob-laughs again, "Because she despised his use of magic and she was powerless."

I hold her as she breaks into erratic crying. My mind races. If these relics are not just jewelry, but something made from some inherent power of the earth, what could they do? The Essence of the Woods could not be a better description for my flame. Is that what he used? Is there only the spirit of my Woods, or are there other magics like this? Different spirits? I start to ask if she knows, but stop myself. This isn't the time.

"She was my whole life, Lys," she cries into my shoulder. "I thought I knew everything about her. My *whole life,* I did nothing but devote myself to her."

"I know, my heart. I know. You did everything right. You couldn't know about this. Someone, at some point, made sure no one would when they hid it away. But she was still Kiv. She still stopped Davor. Not everything was a lie." I sure hope it isn't anyway, or that she will never find out if it is.

I pull her down to the soft, leafy earth to sit with me in the alcove of dense trees. She curls against me in a way so foreign and yet so familiar. How many times have our roles been reversed? How many times have I huddled in her arms when my world was coming down around me?

My heart breaks for her, but knowing these pieces hold their own power, separate from what the Davorists have, is an incredibly useful discovery.

The green-gray of twilight creeps into our den by the time she stirs in my arms.

"There was more," she says, her voice rough with crying. She pulls away so we can face each other. "She was talking about what they would do with the relics when they defeated him. I think this journal was from right before she died," she pauses for a steadying breath before continuing. "They were going to be split and taken back to the places they were made."

If there were multiple locations, it would make sense that they would have different properties. Different kinds of magic. That would also mean we would only be able to find one of the three in the Woods.

"I think the essence she is talking about is my fire. One of them, anyway. When I found it in the palace..." I trail off and draw my knees into my chest. "Daralyn had the prince with a knife to his throat, and when I thought we were truly fucked something happened." She looks at me quizzically, one eyebrow raised. "I could see the same light flowing through the plants in the room. I could control it." Her second eyebrow raises.

I close my eyes and breathe deep, focusing on the cool glass of the pendant against my chest.

It takes longer than I would like without the imminent threat of death looming over me, but eventually it comes. The deep calm and crisp green of the life all around me. It's stronger here, in the place it's meant to be, and I'm swept up in the overwhelming torrent of it before I grab on to one nearby thread and haul myself back to reality by its tether. It's the trunk against which I lean, massive and bright as the sun on a summer day. Its presence is magnetic. I want to explore its power, and my own, but it's not the most conducive to an easy display of whatever this is. I don't know if I could even shift something as large as that. Instead, I find a smaller thread. A straggly witch hazel bush on the opposite side of Carolyn sticks out to me. I smile, and slowly the shrub reaches for Carolyn, its branches winding up her leg loosely.

She jerks away from the touch, but the springy branches hold fast, and she gapes at me wide-eyed.

"It's how we got away, and why we had to get away so quickly. She knows what it is. And she knows I will fight her for it. With it."

"And that is why you made him stay behind." She looks at me with a different kind of sadness in her eyes. One for me, rather than herself.

I sigh again and bury my face in my hands. "Yes, but I can't deal with whatever that is and all of this at the same time."

"And what is that? Do you know?"

Instead of answering, I drag myself to my feet. The darkness blankets us more thoroughly now, and my stomach rumbles. "I have no idea. Not great for us long term I'm sure, but who knows how long my term has left?"

"Do not speak like that." She stands, holding onto my arm for assistance. "You have to surpass Arty. You promised." She manages a smile. I grin back.

"I forgot about that. I do have to outlive that bastard." I turn for the village. "I guess that's one worry put to rest."

"Only about a thousand problems left to solve." She smiles again, more strongly.

I groan, rolling my eyes up to the darkened canopy as we make our way back up the winding stairs to my parents' home. "Where do we even start?"

When I re-enter my parent's house, I do so with significantly more presence of mind than when I did last time, to a more traditional greeting. Both my mother and father push away from the table and race to see who is the first to hug me. As always, my father lets Mama win so he can wrap his arms around both of us.

"Is everything alright?" Mama whispers in my ear.

"I think it will be, eventually. She learned something she didn't expect, but also something that might help us."

With a final rib-creaking squeeze, I extricate myself and sit down at the table, where a simple meal waits for us. Eating will solve another of my many problems, and I think my parents may be able to help with yet another.

"Mama. Da." I sneak around a mouthful of bread, too tired to care much about manners. "If you wanted to find something as old as the ruins, where would you look? Not the lake. We already went there." I continue chewing while they frown in concentration.

They turn to each other slowly, their faces going through a range of expressions. It always amazes me how they can have whole conversations without saying a word. The older I get, the more it makes sense. My girls and I can say quite a bit to each other without opening our mouths, but their silent conversations are still impressive. They settle on a look of mutual foreboding. My father sighs.

"I don't know what you're looking for, but if it wasn't at the lake, the only other place I can think of like that is the Barrows," he says it so dourly the hairs on the back of my neck raise. "But I don't love the idea of you going out there. Alone, or otherwise."

I quirk an eyebrow. "I've been walking these Woods alone for years, what could possibly be out there I can't handle?" They exchange a *look* again, and I huff, "What?"

"It's dangerous. People who go out hunting or gathering get lost frequently." He glances at my mother again. "If they do come back, the tales they tell sound like Otherfolk ghost stories."

"You said it was important but," Mama frowns at me and squeezes Da's arm. "I don't think you should go."

"Dangerous and strange have been the general course of my last three weeks," I sigh, poking at the last remains of dinner. "What specific kinds of stories?"

Another look.

"Well. Usual Wood fare, I suppose. Strange creatures, shifting paths, whispering in the leaves, luring spirit fire. They claim the Otherfolk themselves call the Barrows their resting place."

"What is it with everyone? The Otherfolk aren't real. They're stories. Tales for children so they don't go wandering into the dark. They don't haunt the Woods. And I'm not one of them." My fingers tug on the cord around my neck, drawing it from my shirt. The calmly swirling green light radiates more brightly. "But the lights are real."

"Where did you take that from?" Da asks quietly.

The tone and the wording of his question makes me frown.

"I found it in a tree by some ruins first, and then in the building on the lake. Have you seen them before? If you give each other another *look* I'll scream," I add the last bit hastily when I see them start to turn their heads. It snaps their attention back to me.

"It has been a very, very long time." It's Mama who answers, looking at the table instead of Da. "You must have been too little to remember, but you were one of those that went to the Barrows and came back. You were always wandering away to explore, but I could usually find you right away. That day you just vanished. We couldn't find you for a whole day. The entire village went out looking for you. Artemicles was there as well, assisting with a sickness that was plaguing us. He's the one who found you at the edge of the Barrows playing with the lights. With *that* light." She points at the vial and shudders. "He decided to take you as his apprentice that day. It was years before you were old enough, but he said he would take you far away from that place as soon as he was able."

"Why?" I ask, slumping back in my seat casually.

Da slams his fist on the table, making me jump straight again. "Why? *Why?* Because that place almost took you from us. That's why."

"It wouldn't take me anywhere," I respond without hesitation. I know my Woods would never hurt me, now more than ever.

"You don't know that, but it's irrelevant. We don't want you going there again. It isn't safe." My father frowns at me and folds his arms over his chest.

"I don't think I have a choice," I say flatly. They know they can't actually stop me from doing anything. I've been out of their control for over twenty years now, but that doesn't mean I enjoy going against their wishes. "Mama said you knew a little about what happened and why the prince's guardsmen are here. About who killed Inness." I twist the cord with its green ribbon between my fingers, making the vial spin. "It isn't just about us or the Woods. It's so much more than that." I heave a frustrated sigh and lean back. "Trust me. I don't want to be doing any of this either. I just want to go home and have everything be how it was, but that isn't an option anymore, so here I am."

"Adline. Sen. She is not alone. I will be with her and the forest itself is with her. It is of dire importance that we find what we are looking for. If these Barrows are the only other significant landmark you can think of, we must try." Carolyn, quiet until now, speaks with calm command. Her steadiness gives me hope that perhaps not all of her faith is lost.

My parents still seem unconvinced, but they drop the subject. Without a word, Mama stands and starts cleaning the table. Carolyn follows her lead. My father and I still sit, staring at each other before he nods and stands, heading for the door. I follow him into the crisp night air. We wander in silence further up the spiraling stairs until we reach a sitting area nestled into a knot of the tree and settle onto an empty bench. I curl up against him as he pulls a pipe from his jacket pocket and packs it with my custom blend of fragrant and pungent herbs. His hair and beard are gray now, but he is still as solid as ever, and the familiar scents and ritual motions of the pipe filling and lighting soothes me.

We don't speak until each of us has had our first slow drag at the pipe. I let the flavorful, tingling smoke curl and roil around my mouth and slowly exhale it from my nose so the spicy, floral scent lingers there.

"It's really too much for me, Da," I breathe out another curl of smoke with my words and hand the pipe back.

A pause. An inhale. Another cloud of smoke. "Is there anyone else that can do what needs to be done?"

Pass. Breathe. Blue-gray smoke.

"I really don't think there is. Not for this part, at least."

He exhales slowly with a plume of smoke and a little cough. "Then you have to do it, and you have to survive it. Not just for your mother and I, but for Inness and Carolyn and Kyla and Rend and all of us in the Woods. I know what you do is sometimes thankless, but we need you. Even if it's just to find someone else to replace you before you leave."

I look at him from the corner of my eye, suspiciously. "Before I leave?" I hate when he knows things about me I don't.

"It wouldn't surprise me if you didn't go back after what happened, after what you lost. I wouldn't expect you to." Another pull, another breath out. "I will be proud of you no matter what you choose to do after this. There just needs to be an after."

His arm is wrapped around my shoulders. Tears roll silently down my face. If I keep this up, my cheeks will be carved like the Woods by the river.

"I don't know if I can have an after." I stop and swallow back a choking tightness in my throat. "I don't know if I want one. I just want to fix this and then lay down with Inness and let the Woods grow through me," I finish with a cracking whisper. I don't want to be saying these things. I don't want to be thinking them, but they have been lurking in the back of my mind in the same place I keep putting everything else I can't think about. The smoke blurs the boundaries, letting them leak through.

"You can always have an after, Little Lys. Just because you can't see the shape right now, doesn't mean you can't build something beautiful. You have so many hands to help you."

I sob into my Da's shoulder harder than I have since I was a small child.

It's very late when we walk back to the house, hand in hand. I'm once again wrung out like a wet rag and exhausted with a headache brewing between my eyes. But the blurring of my thoughts has turned pleasant and the scant, flickering lights of the village truly look like stars floating in the darkness. I let myself imagine falling into the sky, stopped only by the solid warmth of my father tying me to the earth below.

CHAPTER THIRTY-SEVEN

ALYSSIA

*S*wirls *of emerald race around me in a burning whirlwind with embers made of leaves raining down, green fire chewing at their edges. My boundaries are consumed until there is nothing left, and I become the spiraling storm.*

I am nothing but bone, pitted and brown, dirt filling the space my marrow once grew. Life thrives within me. Insects churn like my muscles once did. Small tendrils of roots lace through me like blood vessels, carrying what is needed to the plants that grew them so carefully. I am a thriving hum of peaceful activity.

Blood limned in red-streaked gold falls around me in a torrent. In waves. It burns when it touches me. When it pulls me under, I am a pyre. It is hot and heavy. Oily black smoke rises from its edges. I want to scream, but it fills my mouth, my nose, my eyes. Everything is red and gold and black and the waves slam against me so hard, the impact pounds sharply through my skull.

The pounding doesn't fade when I come back into my body, my mouth dry and my head throbbing in time to my heart. Disorientation takes too long to resolve as I piece together where I am and drag myself from the remnants of dreams I don't want to remember.

My parents' house. The soft light of morning under the trees. The smell of the kitchen fire and breakfast. The warmth of Carolyn at my back. The soft murmur of voices in the main room. Footsteps down the short hall.

"Lys?" Mama calls softly, peeking her head through the door. "There's someone here to see you." It's a statement, but I hear the question in it. I blink several more times trying to understand.

Who in the world would be asking for me instead of trying to kill me?

I groan and roll out of bed, tossing the pendant around my neck from its place on the side table. I hate not sleeping with it on, but I've developed a fear that I will break the glass and lose it again. This time for good.

The last dregs of sleep are violently shucked from my body when I see who waits for me, leaning tiredly against the open door frame, silhouetted by the morning light behind him.

"What, in the name of all the fucking trees on this earth, are you doing here?" Rage and fear and relief and outrageous indignation fight within me as I stalk toward the fucking prince, my fists clenched.

He flinches away from me as if I am about to hit him, which I haven't decided if I will do or not. He instinctively raises his hand in surrender.

"Lys." Mama is somewhere behind me, her tone a warning to stop being rude to guests in her home. I'm not in the mood.

"Not now, Mama." I don't break my advance on the prince, pointing at him violently then beyond him through the door. "You. Outside. Now." He tries to speak. I smile wildly, begging him to try me.

He shuts his mouth.

I slam the door behind us and stalk down the steps, boiling inside with the urge to push him off the edge or kiss him. Or kiss him and *then* push him. He follows in silence until we are nearly at the spot Carolyn and I were huddled in yesterday.

"Alyssia," he says quietly.

"No. No, Your Highness. I told you to stay the hell away from me." I twist around to face him. The necklace swings, trailing green light. "I can't worry about you. I can't deal with you being my responsibility right now. I have too much of that already."

"Stop it." He doesn't look at me, choosing to stare at his feet instead. "I am not asking you to protect me." He looks up, his gaze dark and intense in the leaf-shadowed light. "I am not asking you to save me, and I am not here to save you. But you cannot ask me to hide while you do not. You cannot ask me to wonder if my sister has slit your throat while I sit in a hole somewhere, safe and sound. You cannot ask me to not know if you are alive or dead or, even worse, captured by that bitch. You cannot ask me to do that. Not when you know she has carved what she is capable of into my body my entire life. Please do not ask me to do nothing but imagine what she could do to you. I do not care what happens to me, but I cannot bear that happening to you."

My body goes strangely still.

I feel the breeze shift through the undergrowth. I listen to the hum of the animals and the distant morning work of the villagers. I feel the soft forest glow of the fire flow through the vial and the veins of the plants around me.

"Why can you ask me to stand back and watch when something happens to you? Why can you ask me to watch someone put a knife to your throat *again*? Why do you get to ask me to wonder what she will do to you if she has you in her hands *again*? If I cannot ask you to do the same, why do you get to ask it of me? Why do you get to tell me to not care what happens to you, if what happens to me is all that matters? What part of any of that is fair?"

His hand goes through his hair right on cue. "What about any of this is fair?" He gestures violently around us. "What screams fairness about this path Daralyn has decided to follow and force us onto as well? None of this is fair, but I will not cower in fear because you do not want to be bothered by me. I know I am only an unfortunate obligation to you, but this is not about that. This is not just your problem, Alyssia. She has been my problem far longer than she has been yours."

The fire burning on my chest flares brightly as my temper rages inside of me. "You know, keeping you alive *is* an unfortunate obligation I have. One you keep *making* me have. If this isn't about me, then why don't you go fight her on your own ground? This *is* my problem because this is *my* home. You didn't know we existed a month ago. If you are so hellbent on dealing with her, take Envir and fucking deal with her. But since you haven't done that at any point in your entire life, I *really* don't see how this isn't about you asking me to watch you die so you can feel better about yourself when you do," I shout by the end, stabbing at the air between us with a pointed finger. I would like to take him by the shoulders and shake him until his head falls off, but if I touch him I'm afraid I would kiss him so hard we both taste blood.

His expression shifts so quickly I can't keep up. Hurt. Rage. Despair. Disappointment. Longing. He settles on some indistinguishable mix of all of them. "I did not come here to ask you to watch me die." He turns from me. "I came because I knew more surely than I have ever known anything that I belong here with you. Facing this together. I am pulled toward you whenever we are apart. I cannot ignore it. I do not *want* to ignore it." His good arm is crossed beneath the other when he turns back to me, hugging himself tightly. His eyes shine with the reflected glow of the pendant. "The last thing I want is to hurt you any more than I already have, but, Alyssia, I cannot be away from you and still think. Still *breathe*. I can do nothing else if I have to wonder if you are safe. There is not enough of me left for that. Please, Lys. I will fall to my knees and beg if it means I do not have to feel that helplessness."

Canopy Above.

"What are you trying to tell me, Kedren? That you what? Love me?" I throw my hands up and make a sound somewhere between a laugh and a sob. "We. Do. Not. Know. Each. Other. I cannot put enough emphasis on the fact that you didn't know my entire town existed a month ago, let alone me."

His mix of emotions slides toward anger, his voice rising ever so slightly. "We do not know each other?" It's his turn to laugh bitterly. "I know what it feels like to carry you as you shatter against me. I know what it looks like when the fire inside you forges something unstoppable from that very wreckage. I know that you will do anything you can to help anyone who needs you. I know that when I showed you the truth of me, you did not shy away or drown me in pity. You *saw me*. You see me still, in all of my brokenness, and yet here you stand. I know that you stick your tongue out when you think. I know that you hate running, but you can climb through your forest for days. I know you know more about this land than I could have imagined possible. I know you have friends that would do *anything* for you." He breaths out another bitter laugh and presses his hand against his chest.

"You know that I am a coward when it comes to my family, and you know that my only friend until three weeks ago was Envir. You know I do that stupid thing with my hair when I'm upset, or nervous, or trying to think, and it makes you smile when it's because I cannot handle being so close to you. Which then, of course, makes it worse."

"I have known many people my entire life and not known even a fraction about them that I know about you. I am not saying I do, but would it really be *that* unreasonable if I did love you? If I loved the way you look with leaves tangled in your hair? If I loved the steady skill of your hands when you stitch even your own wounds? If I loved the terrifyingly calm smile that curved your lips as you encased Daralyn in a tree? Is it really that hard for you to imagine that I may feel something for you after seeing all that I have seen? Why does it matter how long it has been when we have seen the worst of each other and I, the best of you? Why is it so hard to see that I desperately want to show you the best of me?"

He is so close that we would touch if I breathed too deeply. The tension that holds him back from me is stretched to breaking. It hums between us like the echo of his words. I want to scream and pound my fists against the space between us until I can no longer hear the truth of them in my own heart. I want to rage against him because I don't want to feel anything like love ever again. Because already, the thought of holding his lifeless body in my arms makes the world shake under my feet. I know that if I let them, his words would swallow me completely.

"I have already seen the best of you, you idiot," I breathe, trying so hard to keep some semblance of calm. "I saw it when you fought for me and my Woods without knowing anything about us. I see it in your gentleness despite everything you have faced. I saw it in the glow of moonlight and green flame as you sat across from me in my kitchen. I see it in the way you talk to your staff. I see it in the way Envir looks at you, and in the way you look at me. I see it in the way you stand against the person who has broken you over and over again for me. I see your best, and I really don't want to, because if I have to feel the blood of someone else I love flow over my hands, I won't survive. I can't be broken like that again. I need your hands to help me build my after, Kedren. I need all of my people to do that and, Canopy Above, you are one of them now." I blink to clear my vision and tears fall.

For the love of the Trees, I didn't want to do this now. I didn't want to acknowledge the truth of whatever this is between us. There is too much to do, and I can't let myself start feeling anything yet. If I let myself have this, I will have to deal with everything else as well. I want to explain that I can't do this right now and that I want him to take back everything he said, that I want to take back everything I said, but as soon as I can finally find the breath, a familiar shouting of my name interrupts me.

Not again.

CHAPTER THIRTY-EIGHT

ALYSSIA

I step away from Kedren and watch as his hand trails after me like there is a physical tie between us. I tuck my necklace beneath my shirt as I jog toward the sound of my name.

"Adean!" I call to catch his attention as he skips down the nearby steps. "What happened? Why are you here?" My heart races, and I scan him for blood, but he seems whole and calmer than he was when he found me in the library.

When he reaches us, he looks to Kedren first and nods. "I'm glad you made it alright. I was hoping to catch up to you, but you got here faster than I thought." The boy shifts from foot to foot. "A little while after you left, a couple of ladies showed up asking for you and someone who sounded like Lys. Nothing seemed that suspicious about them, but after everything it didn't seem right to just tell them, so I ran after you. If they were alright, I was going to tell my Da it was okay, but if not, we could lie about where you went."

The prince curses under his breath and visibly stops himself from raking his hair back. "What did they look like?"

Adean frowns in concentration. "Nothing special really. One had brown hair. The shorter one had lighter hair. Kind of pretty I guess, but mean looking."

"Thank Kiv, at least she couldn't be bothered to come herself. However, Dienna and Marlayne are unpleasant enough on their own." He looks from Adean to me and loses the battle to not scrub a hand through his hair. "They won't be alone though. If Daralyn is serious enough to send them, they will have cultists, and maybe even guardsmen with them."

Of course.

Forgotten, possibly very important childhood memory revealed? Check. Speaking out loud for the first time your desire to lay down and die? Got it. Having to confront your wildly inappropriate feelings for a man you just met? Yeah, that too. Why not confirmation that people who want to kill you and start a few wars are hot on your tail? *And* they're coming after you in force?

Perfect.

I would ask myself if today could get any better, but I'm absolutely sure it could get worse.

"Well, I hope for their sake, someone back home tells them where we are. I don't want to cause any more trouble for them." I rub my hands over my face and groan." But I also don't want to cause trouble *here*." I beckon for the boys to follow me back up to the house. "No time like the present, I suppose."

"Do you know where we need to go?" The prince follows me so closely I can feel his anxious energy radiating. I'm not sure if I am comforted by it or annoyed.

"I have an idea, at least. Really, I think it is our last option outside of just starting in the top corner and working our way down." I flap my hand in frustrated annoyance. "So yes. I will go with I know where we need to go."

When I pull the door open, Carolyn looks up from helping my mother set the table. The smell of food reminds me that maybe I'm so irritated because I'm hungry *and* functioning solely under extreme duress. Immediately, Carolyn looks between the prince and I with an eyebrow raised. I shake my head and insert myself into the breakfast routine.

"We'll have to go as soon as possible. Some people who are looking for us have caught up a little faster than I hoped. Although, it isn't like it's a surprise. They had a pretty good idea of where I'd be going, and there are only so many roads to follow out here." I sigh and sneak a piece of toast from a plate passing by me. "I feel like I will always be stuck wanting just a little more time," I mumble around bites. My mother is gaping at me, appalled. At least she isn't thinking about me running off into unknown dangers if she's worried about me chewing with my mouth open in front of guests.

Oh right. Guests.

"Mama, the kid poorly sneaking bread is Adean. He has kindly come to us from Curaria to tell us about our unwanted visitors." I hum for a moment, thinking. "Belar's son. I think you and Da know him."

She nods and smiles, passing him a plate of eggs to go with the crusty loaf he's chewing on.

"And the one who decided to interrupt my sleep," and probably the entire course of my life, "is none other than His Royal Highness, Prince Kedren D'raci. At your service I'm sure, and my extreme annoyance," I mutter with more bitterness than I truly feel. He is far too engaged in bowing with suspicious formality to my mother to notice my tone, however.

"It is my absolute honor to meet you." He has an incredibly charming smile plastered over his face, and his hair frames his beautiful eyes, and I find myself momentarily jealous of my *mother*.

"Adline," she provides helpfully with an actual blush, complete with coy smile.

I think I might prefer the cultists to this.

"Right. Well, Adean is going to stay here because I don't want him going back through whatever mess our friends might be making by himself, and I suppose the *three* of us are going to be headed to the Barrows as soon as we're fed." I swallow the eggs I'm working on and squeeze Mama's hand. "They aren't far, right?"

She frowns, obviously displeased, but also distracted by being introduced to royalty. "No. Perhaps a few hours northwest. It's a large area. I doubt you will be able to miss it, but your father can tell you more specific directions."

With a glance at my companions, I slide in close to Mama, pulling her attention to me and only me. My voice is as calm and confident as I can make it. "Mama. I will come back. I *will* come back to you and Da. The forest will not take me today. The forest's ghosts will not take me. The Davorists will not take me. *Nothing* will take me from you today." I squeeze both of her hands tight in mine and ignore the tears that are pooling in her eyes; light blue and just like mine. "I will not make you give me back to the Woods. I swear to you."

With a final squeeze of her hands, I stand and kiss her forehead. I don't look back on my way to my room to see her shaking shoulders, but I still know they do. Carolyn's voice hums low and wordless behind me as I throw myself unceremoniously on the bed, trying to pull myself together so I have some hope of keeping that promise.

A shift in the bed makes me open my eyes and look over. The prince looms over me, looking his usual concerned, serious self again.

"Is where we are going really that dangerous?" His hand rests on the covers, playing with the ends of my hair.

Without thinking, I move so my head rests in his lap. His face lights up as I do so, a smile softening the lines of his face.

"I don't think so, just a little extra strange." I shrug awkwardly. "But people say a lot of strange things about the Woods. They *are* strange." I close my eyes and let the rhythm of his fingers through my hair soothe me. "It isn't where we are going that worries me, but who we might run into on the way."

"Three can move faster than a group. You have your magic, Carolyn hers, and I have a more appropriate weapon for my current ability. We can lose them in the Woods, find what we need, and destroy it before they catch us."

He sounds so sure, I almost believe him.

"Speaking of your current ability, how bad is it?" I've been thinking about the state of his chest and shoulder since we parted ways. I didn't trust myself to treat it and leave him behind then, and I don't trust myself now. Especially now, after what was said. The idea of him shirtless and at my mercy is currently far too much for me to handle.

He doesn't respond for long enough that I open my eyes and look up at him, expectant.

Taking a deep breath in, he sighs out, "Bad enough, but I can deal with it."

"When this is all over, we'll fix it. I can make this right again, at least." I roll out of his lap and off the bed in one laborious movement. "But in the meantime, we'll have to do the best we can."

Back in the main part of the house, my mother has calmed down, and she and Carolyn have everything cleaned up from breakfast. Adean is nowhere to be seen, but he's probably out exploring his new surroundings.

"Carolyn?" When she turns, I offer her her bag. She dries her hands on a cloth before taking it from me. "Mama. I'll see you soon, but don't worry if it isn't as soon as you want. We might need to lead those friends of ours away from everyone. I swear I'll be fine."

She doesn't even look at me. She says nothing, just a small noise in her throat and a nod of her head.

I don't want to say goodbye either so I'm the first out the door.

As we take the winding path through the village, I consider tracking down my Da to ask him for directions, but the concept of saying goodbye to him seems worse than my mother. I let go of that notion and keep my mind focused on reaching the western gate.

The western *gate.*

I stop so suddenly, Carolyn runs into me, and Kedren makes it several strides ahead of us before realizing we've been left behind.

"They *are* gates," I shout, laughing, much to both of my friends' confusion.

"What are gates?" Kedren blinks back at me.

"The gates are gates! The openings into the villages we always called gates even though they are just open bits." I duck back around Carolyn and start running, shouting over my shoulder as I go, "It's how I can keep them safe. *I can close those gates.*"

I don't know how I know this, but I'm more sure than I have been about anything in quite some time. I've never really thought much about why our villages had such curiously dense walls of gnarled old trees. I always assumed the locations were chosen for their natural protection, but all three of the villages in the Woods are nearly identical, with only the gates to let people in or out. Until now I never had any reason to think they could be anything but naturally occurring. Until I learned what the spirit of the Woods could do.

Until I learned what I can do.

I just have to make sure everyone is inside.

Bolting toward the center of the village, I shout questions and instructions at villagers as I leap through shortcuts I haven't used since I was a child. I don't stop to see if my instructions are followed until I reach the center. Like in Cuaria, there is a Great Tree, slightly smaller than ours, but a towering central meeting area all the same. I catch my father, tools in hand, repairing a loose rail on one of the bridges leading to it.

"Da!" I shout up to him, my path taking me closer to the ground than not. "Da, get everyone inside the village gates. Make sure everyone is here." I spin to find my friends.

Carolyn is right behind me, but Kedren is looking dubiously at the vine we used to swing down here.

"Don't bother," I shout up to him. "You and Carolyn go look for Adean." I make an about face and see that my father has sent several of the men working with him running and is now making his way to me.

"What's your plan?" No nonsense, no questioning my bizarre request, just tucking his hammer in his belt and getting to business. I love my Da.

"The Prince thinks our friends are coming with a decent amount of force, and I'm pretty sure I can actually do something about it. I can make sure nothing happens here like it did before. I just need everyone inside the gates." The giddy joy from being able to do something that might actually make a difference makes me feel ten years younger.

I catch myself bouncing on the balls of my feet and force myself to settle. Da looks both confused and exasperated.

"That's wonderful, but what are you going to *do*?" His arms are crossed, and he's looking back and forth, craning his neck, either searching for the men he deployed or taking a mental note of anyone passing by.

"I'm going to close the gates."

He raises an eyebrow at me, exasperation intensifying. "We don't have gates."

I shake my head, the bouncing returning. "We do." I raise the vial so it dangles between us, " With this they *are* gates. I think this is how they were made, and I can use it to make them close. I know I can."

I'm not sure if I have convinced him, but he appears to be humoring me at the very least, no longer protesting.

I want to run for the east gate and start. Even from here, I can feel the flow of life crawling through the trees at the edge of the village. It's everywhere in the Woods, but it's more ordered, more deliberate in the walls, and I know I'm right. I know they were created by the will of people who came long before me. When I close my eyes and follow the burning rivers, I can see the shape of the break in the wall, and the denser, twisting, roots just beneath the surface of the earth, ready to be brought forth and shaped.

"Lys." A sudden touch on my arm pulls me back from the veins of cool fire. I blink and focus on my Da. "Everyone from the village is accounted for. I'll explain what is going on to them. You can do what you need to do."

There aren't many people living here, but I'm taken aback by how quickly everyone has been found. "I need one of the people I sent looking for Adean to come back, then I can."

With impeccable timing, Carolyn chooses this moment to start shouting my name from some hidden spot to the east, getting several repetitions in before finally appearing from around the curve of a trunk, Adean materializing a moment later.

"Lys, go. I could hear men and horses. They will be in sight at any moment. Go."

I started running the moment I saw Adean, and I'm already past them before she is done.

"Find the prince and meet me at the west gate. I'll be there as soon as I can."

Trees. How many are there if she could hear them that far out? The path to the east gate from the forest is fairly straight, we should be able to see anyone approaching at quite a distance.

It doesn't matter. I just have to get close enough to the gate to get it closed. The moment it comes into view, I clutch my pendant and will the tendrils of flames out and around my forearm, using their touch as an anchor and a guide. Without slowing my stride, I sink into the forest. I feel the breeze as it flows over my skin. I smell the bitter green of spring growth. I hear the sounds of leaves and the small rustlings of life. I can trace the path of the forest's essence through the air. Faint, trickling, sparks of green rushing and plodding and swirling and swishing like the currents of so many rivers.

Currents that I can control.

I'm not sure if my eyes are opened or closed as I approach the break in the wall. I can sense every roughened ridge of bark, every tickle of insect, every slow surge of sap. I pour myself into it.

My pendant is empty glass now. I'm wreathed in the distilled spirit of my Woods. It rushes around me like it flows through the trees and our bodies are one. The smallest shift of my hand. A tilt of my head. The rise of my chest with each breath. Each movement is heavy, heaving as the tangle of massive plants unwinds. The immensity of the weight, force, and will it takes to move each root, each branch, to its position threatens to pull me to the ground. I shake with the effort, and I nearly collapse from shock when I see the first mounted rider appear beyond the painfully slow gates.

Then a second.

Then a host.

When I can see the first two riders clearly enough to determine they must be Dienna and Marlayne, they see me as well, wreathed in green fire in the dim, canopy-filtered light, framed by the impossible knitting of a wall from nothing but trees.

They come at a gallop and eat the distance between us faster than my heart races.

Almost.

I'm almost there.

My hands are against bark now, and I press myself into the wood, begging for speed, dragging at the trees with my body and mind to make it move just a little faster.

I can hear the snorting breaths of their horses now. The golden, red-laced light of the Davorists' magic crackles at the edge of my vision.

I'm on my knees when the grating sound of a horse pulled up short rings in my ears, and the red lightning of cultist magic licks harmlessly through minute gaps in the wall. Eventually they may be able to carve their way through, but the trees are so old and full of their own magic, that the Davorist force barely damages the bark.

There is cursing and shouting behind the wall. I really want to stay and gloat, but I still have two gates to close before I'm done. I drag myself to my feet, half-crawling for several strides until I stumble into an unsteady jog for the north gate.

The second gate closes faster than the first, like the power in the walls needed to wake up after all that time asleep. The crashing clumsiness of the assailants in the Woods reverberates through the ground, overwhelming me with its chaos.

There are too many of them.

Fear rises in my gut for Cuaria, but I hold onto the hope that the women were more interested in finding me than harming them. The roots I'm urging to move rattle in time to my shaking, and the strong, steady currents begin to pull at each other at random. I stop to breathe. Close my eyes. Shut out the fear, and the noise of the approaching enemy. Focus. I must slide back into the steady rhythm of the Woods. I'm on my knees again. My fingers claw into the earth, rooting me to the forest, creating a bridge between my will and the trees.

When the job is done and the last piece of the gate has been shifted into place, I stay kneeling, digging into the soil. Panting, I gather the fire to me, as much as I can hold around me and as much as I can coax into the vial around my neck. My senses are filled with it. Burning with it. I want to consume it, for it to consume me. I want to lose myself in the web of vitality that traces the entire forest.

With a gasp, I tear myself away from the ground and force my eyes to see what is in front of them. I don't have time to lose myself like this.

One more gate.

Finding my feet is harder this time, and it takes several wobbling attempts. I feel like a fawn, tripping over my shaking legs as I stagger as quickly as I can through the village. I ignore everyone. I can feel them staring. I can hear them calling after me, shouting questions. But I can't stop. I can't make the effort to understand their words.

One more gate and they are safe.

One more gate and I'm significantly less safe.

I wish that I could hide within these walls with everyone else, but if the artifact is in the Barrows I've essentially led the cultists right to it. Which means I have to be on the other side when the gate closes.

Vaguely, I realize the village structures formed by the trees have been bending around me as I run, aiding me in my flight to the west, catching me as I slide from branch to root to ground in a dizzy haze of green fire and blurred homes until I finally drop down from one drooping, gnarled vine directly in front of Carolyn. She steadies me as I list into her.

"Let's go," I wheeze, gesturing at the path beyond the gate.

"Are you hurt?" The prince sweeps up to my other side, brushing loose hair from my face.

I push him away with more force than I should and fling myself through the open passageway into the Woods.

"I'm fine. We have to go. If I can't convince you to stay behind, Your Highness, get out here so I can close it off." I'm dimly aware that I'm shouting, but it seems like a secondary concern. Stomping hooves, booted feet, and crashing bodies pulse in shades of green inside my head.

Both of them rush out to stand at my back as I dive into the river of light once again. This gate, smaller than the rest for a path less traveled, closes even faster than the first two, but the weight of it crushes me. The noise of the cultist force barreling through the trees overwhelms me.

I fall back into my companions in blind flight from the spreading chaos of bodies approaching us, trying to clear my vision of the burning tendrils. "Go. We have to go," I gasp.

The prince catches me before I can fall, crashing through them and asks, "Which way?"

I fling my hand out to the northwest and follow the motion with the rest of my body, throwing myself off the path and into the trees. I'm still wreathed in creeping tendrils of green flame that grow brighter as I dive further into the Woods. Seeing with two vastly different kinds of vision makes me so disoriented, I close my eyelids and run through the trees with nothing but their light to guide me.

CHAPTER

THIRTY-NINE

ALYSSIA

I lose myself to the immensity of the forest while transversing it by the sight of the magic alone. Trying to organize the positions of all of the cultists, my friends, and my own immediate surroundings nauseates me. It's bedlam and the only thing that makes sense in the world. I can't hold it all.

With a startled cry, I trip over a loose stone I didn't notice in the fabric of the Woods, and my eyes spring open. Everything is so dull again. My ears ring in the stillness. Carolyn and Kedren are speaking, and slowly the sounds come back between fits of tinny whining. She grabs my arm as she climbs past me and drags me up with her.

"Are you alright?" she whispers.

I shake and nod my head at the same time, ending up with an awkward diagonal movement. "I don't know. It's so much." I scan the trees as we push our way through the undergrowth as quietly as possible. She looks at me like I may collapse at any moment. I can only hope the prince is far enough back to not notice my staggering. "It's fine. I'll be fine. How they are still so close behind us is the fucking mystery of the day, however. We should have lost them by now."

Carolyn frowns. "I have not been able to research it since you suggested it, and I do not think I can do anything about it now."

"It isn't worth the time to figure out," I pant.

"Stop," the prince hisses and grabs at my shirt.

The three of us slide to a stop at his warning a stride-length from the edge of a gaping gorge. He looks at me with an eyebrow raised, like he can't believe I didn't know it was there. To be fair, I can't believe I didn't know it was there either.

"Fuck." A tickle of swirling fire brushes against my skin, reminding me of the power I have. "I can make a bridge, but it will take time."

"Hurry," they say simultaneously, scanning the Woods.

There is only so much hurrying I can do. The magic here is unorganized, free and meandering, unlike the ordered lines of the gates, ready to fall into their true shape. I sink to my knees so I can dig my dirt stained nails into the ground once again. The ponderous groaning of long-sleeping roots seeps into me as they shiver awake. A shower of debris cascades into the depths of the ravine as the trees respond.

It's so very, agonizingly slow.

Too slow.

A wall of force slams into me. My vision is awash with stars. I'm torn from my hold on the ground. There is nothing but air beneath me.

Air and leaf-green fire.

I yank a collection of finer threads of light from the ravine wall. A web just large enough to catch me knits together as I plummet. I stop so suddenly, the air rushes from my lungs for a second time in too few days. I want to scream, but no sound passes my lips, just strangled gasps.

Shouting echoes down to me from above, and I finally drag in enough air to think. I close my eyes and concentrate on my surroundings to will the trees, vines, and my own body to climb back to the top of the gorge.

When my head clears the edge, I freeze, clinging to the makeshift ladder in horror.

The Woods are crawling with black clad cultists and armored guardsmen with bowmen who track the chaos from the edges. Several swing their aim to me when I appear.

Carolyn and the prince are surrounded, back to back, ferociously clutching their swords. Carolyn clearly doesn't know enough about the weapon to be of any real use, and Kedren isn't enough to stop the tide. Not one-handed and exhausted. Two cultists still lay on the ground near him, not moving, but there are far too many still standing.

What I don't understand is why I don't see the golden light of Carolyn's magic cracking the air, blocking the advance of the cultists blades or weapons of red-tinged gold that harry them.

Frantically, I reach out with my own magic, sending chaotic surges of will through the ground and into the peacefully dormant plant-life that creates the battlefield. As I rise, so do the structures I selected. Several assailants are tripped or trapped by their creeping tendrils, I'm too slow while spread so thin. They hack and tear at the greenery when they do not dodge it outright, but I don't dare lose myself to the vision of the Woods to hold them more tightly. I can't risk losing sight of my friends.

From the press, two women emerge in a sphere of flickering light. Writhing whips of sinister red and gold circle them like snakes, diverting any of my attempts at ensnaring them with dismissive ease.

"Enough," one of them drawls impatiently. Instantly, the men snap into order.

The circle around Carolyn and Kedren compresses as one perfectly aligned mass. It's painfully clear my friends were being toyed with before. Each of the archers on the fringes have their weapons trained on the central conflict as well, leaving me free of immediate danger.

"If I feel one rustle of leaf, forest whore, we start killing the extras," a lilting, feminine voice rings over the sudden stillness.

The deadly tips of blades advance a step closer to the throats of my friends. I throw my hands in the air, sending the rest of the wreathing flame back into the vial or down into the earth.

"Perfect," a slightly different voice says, and the swords surrounding my friends lower as one.

With a casual flick of her wrist, the shorter woman catapults a small orb of light toward Carolyn. She tracks its approach, and I plead for her to react, to grab for her relic and defend herself. To my relief, at the last moment, she throws her hand up in the familiar gesture of her warding.

The projectile punches into her chest, and she shouts as she is thrown to the ground. Her sword flies from her hand. Upon impact, the orb splashes into a mass of twisting ropes that coil around her, binding her hands behind her back. She writhes, bucking against the bonds. Her white robes blacken and smoke, and her skin reddens as the chains of light tighten around her. Burning.

The charred corpse at the lake stares back at me from my memory.

"Stop it! Stop! Stop!" I shriek at the women, my hands still raised helplessly.

Carolyn's screaming stops with a whimper. The wisps of smoke from her clothing dissipate in the breeze.

"It's hard to have a conversation over all of that noise anyway," the blond says.

"Speaking of noise." The second woman steps forward, and the rest of the men surrounding Carolyn and the prince fall back.

There is no one left between the three of us and the two of them. Kedren still grips his sword tightly, the blade pointed toward the ground, but steady. I can see part of him in profile, his feet planted, stance ready, back straight. His mouth is drawn into a tight line of pain and sweat runs down his face. He stands no chance against the lightning quick crack of the woman's whip. He brings his sword up to parry, but the weapon of light passes by the blade and coils around the wrist of his sling-bound arm.

I know what's going to happen as soon as the weapon makes contact.

I throw a sharp piece of the forest floor upwards like the thrust of a sword to cut through the sling and free his arm, but I'm too late. Kedren and I scream as one as the bones of his wrist snap, trapped between the binding of the fabric and the recoil of the whip. He's still braced for defense and jerks back from the lash instinctively, adding even more force to the attack.

He falls to his knees as the whip falls slack. Carolyn struggles to hers, spurred by his cry. The blond pulls against the glowing ropes binding her and she falls back with a grunt.

The two women loom over their captives, so alike in posture and expression, but so very different in everything else. One is tall with mousy, brown hair pulled back severely with sharp, bird-like features. The other is short and soft, and delicately pretty, with golden blond waves that cascade loosely around her face and shoulders. Both grip the ends of their red-gold chains in one fist and long, ornate daggers in the other.

Both smile like wolves.

"So pleased we could get everything settled," the blond says with a smile. She jerks at the chain in her hand making Carolyn twist uncomfortably.

"We have been so eager to meet you," the brunette continues.

"Ever since you tried to murder our princess."

"Committing treason for such a hopeless cause."

"A little forest witch rescuing our favorite princeling in peril."

"How could we not want to know what else she could do?"

"Sadly, less impressive than we thought."

"But there may still be something you can do for us."

Their sing-song back and forth gives me a headache. I stand with my knees bent, and my feet spread wide to steady myself, but I keep my hands up and out, clear of my necklace and free of flames. "Let them go or I won't do anything for you."

They laugh in disturbing, harmonized unison. I already want to kill them almost as much as Daralyn.

"That is not how this will work," the brunette drones as the chain she holds coils around Kedren's wrists, lashing his hands behind his back.

"We will be taking these two as," the blond continues, pulling herself and Carolyn closer together, "collateral." She smiles down at her, tracing the tip of the dagger along Carolyn's jaw.

"Our High Priestess will be fascinated to find out the famed Priestess of Drevda is broken."

"And Her Highness is always pleased to spend time with her dearest brother." A step and a yank, and she and Kedren are that much closer.

"But we might let you have them back, if you bring us what we've been looking for."

I want to protest. Claim I don't know what they're after. Tell them I would never give it to them. That I will destroy it. That I will destroy *them*. But while I hesitate, the brunette grins like she can read my thoughts.

She rips at the bonds holding the prince with significantly more force than I thought her capable of. His already ruined arm is pulled straight back. Just when I'm sure I will see it tear from its socket, she steps forward so suddenly, and with such violence, I stagger back, sending debris bouncing into the ravine. The chain of light has turned to steel in her hands. It is a coiled cage that traps his arm as she drives it with supernatural strength straight into the ground.

With his other arm still tied behind him, he has no chance to brace himself against the impact. He slams into the ground. I feel the collision through the earth, even without my magic. His head rebounds from the force long enough for me to see blood pouring down his face before the sustained pressure grinds him into the forest floor. A series of devastating cracks reverberates like breaking glass. His arm crumples like paper. I have never been so relieved to know someone was unconscious.

I can't even scream.

I can't even begin to reconcile what happened as something done to a living person. I separate the limb from the man in my head and cycle through how I could treat it. How I could set it. What books from the library I could use to help. Its just an academic exercise. It couldn't possibly have happened. Not to him.

I fall to the ground in a plume of leaves.

Carolyn is sobbing somewhere in front of me, and I wonder if she thinks he's dead.

He isn't. Yet.

Blood still pulses slowly from his mouth and nose. The forest floor must have been soft enough to stop the woman from killing him with a broken neck, but I can certainly see where Carolyn would be concerned.

"I will bring it to you," I say, my voice distant, hardly recognizable to my own ears. I don't want to listen to myself say what what I must. There can't be words for what I'm about to do.

"We thought that may be the case." She steps back from Kedren, letting the chain soften into red-sparking ropes once more.

"We will be waiting for you at the temple."

"If you hurry, both of them may still be alive, but we really don't know what the High Priestess will want with that one," the brunette speaks, but the blond tugs playfully at the bonds holding Carolyn, who cries silently now.

"And, technically, the prince was an accomplice to your treason, so we'll see what happens," the blond adds with a shrug.

"The temple is too far. Wait for me here. I know where it is," I lie, blatantly. "I can bring it to you now. Wait for me." What does it matter if I'm begging? The prince is starting to breathe in shallow pants, the blood on his face bubbles with each exhale. Consciousness must be returning. My mouth twists into a grimace, waiting for him to fully come to.

"You think we will wait for you here?"

"In your Woods?"

"Where your magic and that of the relic are strongest?"

"My dear, you are not that lucky."

"And we are not that stupid."

"We will be waiting for you where *our* magic is the strongest."

A low moan from the prince punctuates the women's words, immediately followed by him retching violently, choking as he breathes in blood and bile.

"Oh, none of that." She hauls him upright by his bonds so he is no longer in danger of choking on his own fluids. "No use to us as a hostage if you die in front of her."

"We would have to find the stupid thing ourselves then."

"And we really do not want to do that."

The blond pulls Carolyn to her feet while addressing me, "Well, what are you waiting for? Shoo!"

What can I say? It will be alright? I'll save them? Hang in there? It's all nonsense. Even if I could kill every single person here before any of us died, the prince will not be alright. Carolyn clearly isn't either. Burns and bonds aside, she has lost her magic.

So I don't say anything.

I make a running leap across the gorge, haul the net I made up to meet a second knitting together from the other side and land in a roll. I half-crawl, half-drag myself to solid ground and sprint into the shelter of the trees, away from the grating, harmonized laughter of the women holding my people's lives in their hands.

CHAPTER FORTY

ALYSSIA

I know I have crossed into the Barrows when I plunge suddenly into rivers of green. I plummet through the green-black soul of the Woods. I spiral freely through heavy, thrumming power like nothing I've felt before. The edges of my mind fray, unwind, and reform within the depths consuming me.

As quickly as it pulled me under, I am thrown back into my body. The particularly wild stories about this place no longer surprise me. Even though I have crossed into that realm on my own, I'm left shaken and unsettled in the wake of that torrent. I would have lost my mind just like those in the stories if I was taken under like that with no knowledge of what it was. You are stripped away there and only the Woods remain. It would not shock me that not everyone would be able to make it back.

The weight this place, even outside of that strange other version of the Woods, burrows into my flesh and nestles against the heaviness I carry. It both dulls and clarifies the grief within me. I want to lay down in the moss and let the slow, inevitable growth of the forest to take me within its embrace. I want to rest here like so many others before me. But

I can hear Carolyn's screams as the burning chains tighten around her as if she is next to me. I can still see the moment Kedren's head hit the ground. The matching, predatory grins of the women holding their bonds shimmer in the air before me. The soil pooled in the corners of Inness' eyes runs through my fingers as I try to brush her face clean.

Enough.

I force myself to see beyond the visions haunting me. I will find a way to protect my Woods and save those who can still be saved.

Deeper into the Barrows, the undergrowth thins. The ground begins to rise in frozen waves, painted with decaying leaves and wide, languorous strokes of twisted roots. The canopy is so thick that, despite it being midday, I feel as though I'm walking through twilight and into the night.

A night illuminated by emerald stars.

Flames burn in hollows, knots, and the bends of trees like torches lighting a path. They flicker over everything like the creeping blankets of lily-of-the-valley in our meadow or the grave markers in the yards outside of the city. I follow the illuminated path with fascination and awe.

Great stone doors begin appearing where trunks meet ground the closer I get to what must be the center of this melancholy grove. The bark that surrounds them form intricate, beautiful patterns. I'm entranced by the artistry of blending the works of man and nature that my predecessors had such delicate control of. My own awareness trickles out in increments, careful to not go too far lest I be dragged under again. Every moment I spend here is another Carolyn and the prince suffer. Already, I have spent too much time marveling at the wonders around me while the creeping stillness of this place makes my steps slow.

The tombs of these mysterious ancestors resonate with the pieces of me that want to give up and be taken by the earth. I want to pull open the heavy stone doors and lay my bones to rest beside those that already reside there. I wonder if lily of the valley would find me here and dig their roots into soil made rich with what remained of me. I wonder if I would find Inness distilled into spirit fire and dancing through the trees. I wonder if I would find peace.

Screams.

The bubbling of blood.

The broken shaft of an arrow.

There can be no peace for me. Not yet.

I rip myself away from the dark, peaceful recesses of hollowed out trees and back to the bloody violence that drives me. Right now I need to find the relic, rescue my friends, and stop the deranged princess from completing any more of her plans. After all of that, I can decide where I'm meant to be. Not before.

My dragging wander turns into a walk, then a jog, and finally a run. The lights in their hollows blur as I sprint through the winding, rolling mounds. Closer to the center, the lights grow brighter, the trees larger. The branches above me twist into arches until I'm bounding through a tunnel lit only by the flames of the forest. Then I stumble, blinking against sunlight filtering into a sudden clearing.

The area is dominated by one massive, earthen rise framed by roots the size of most trees that twist their way into the most magnificent, ancient ash I've ever seen. Crumbling stone pillars outline the remnants of a pavilion in the center of the basin. Broken stones and fallen logs alike are blanketed by moss and strewn about in huddled piles like burial mounds. Some, as I approach the soaring, carved stone doors embedded into the central tomb, appear to be the graves of long dead forest creatures. Off-white pieces of bone glow dully green with reflected, leaf-filtered light among the moss.

No.

I stop facing the doors.

The color washing the bone was too vibrant to be ambient light. It is bright and warm with the sun, free of the Woods' usual green twilight.

With sudden, unnamed fear, I slide my gaze back to the closest pile of moss covered bones.

It isn't there.

I turn slowly, scanning the ground. I must have remembered it in the wrong place, but it's nowhere to be seen. The broken pillars, now more threatening than beautiful, loom ominously. I imagine what could lay in wait behind them; the kind of creatures lost Woodsfolk would tell stories of. The kind of creatures that could be guarding the dead.

I catapult forward and slam into the earth, narrowly missing a crumbling mass of rocks. The world flashes black. I spit blood and leaves out of my mouth. Sharp, searing pain flashes brighter with each breath and movement. My breaths come fast and shallow, so loud in my own ears I almost don't hear the scraping stomps strides away from me. Almost.

With a desperate heave I lurch to my feet and stand face to face with the most horrifying, and most beautiful, thing I've ever seen.

A stag, larger than I thought possible, paws the ground with dull, black and gray, stone hooves. His head is bent in challenge, his antlers of bone and branch wider than I am tall. His flesh of moss, bark, and bone, ripples with dry huffs of air that only simulate breathing. Green fire bores into me from mismatched eyes. One a deep hollow of bone and the other a perfect replica of flesh sculpted from bark and moss.

I'm so enchanted by its construction of bone knitted with tendons of vine, muscles of roots, and plates of bark coated with patches of moss that I can't move. I don't feel the pain in my back or notice the blood still dripping from my split lip and bitten tongue. The flame-hearted mass of bone and flora, a construct of pure life and lingering death, consumes me.

A roar echoes off the basin's walls.

Primal fear fills my limbs with blind, scrabbling urgency. I dive to one side in an explosion of pain and leaves as the stag thunders past me, his antlers catching my thigh with a glancing blow. I'm up again with the instinct of prey and bolt for anything that could be considered shelter. A hill of collapsed rock, a way up the walls, anything to protect me from the wood stag and whatever horror released that bestial cry.

Before I can find any kind of safety, I sprawl across the ground once again. A scream tears from my throat and bright blood pours down my leg. Another bellow answers from right above me. I kick at the ground in jerky fits, trying to escape the claws of an over-sized bear.

It's a bear made of the same bark, bone, and raging green fire as the stag. A great swathe of ribcage is exposed to show more of the forest's flame burning where the beast's heart should be, pulsing in time to my own of flesh and blood.

I scream again as its paw slams down onto my leg and pierces my calf with one claw. It drags me closer. My fingers tear at the ground for any kind of purchase. I desperately haul, drag and heave myself away from it. Still, I am dragged inexorably forward.

I'm all animal fear and pain when I kick myself free just before its jaws can sink into me. I push myself back like a crab sliding in sand and leave a trail of my blood in the dirt. I flatten myself to the ground an instant before the stag's antlers pierce the air where my body was. It crashes into the charging bear instead of me.

The bone-jarring impact of the two creatures gives me enough time to scratch out my bloody escape. I sob and rake at the wall of rock, root, and earth for some means of escape while the glow of my necklace washes over shadowed crevices.

My necklace.

I stop scraping at dirt and dive headfirst into the spirit of my Woods.

I don't fear the depths this time. I gather fistfuls of the threads around me, then armfuls, as I plunge boldly through it.

Splinters of bark scrape at my face as the claws of the bear tear into the dome of woven Woods I pulled around me. Its roar of frustration makes my ears crackle. Bits of wood rain down on me as the bear continues its relentless attempt to force its way through my shelter. Several points of the stag's antlers thrust between small gaps when it charges. The structure groans and shifts as it tries to thrash its way free.

Chaos ravages me. The Woods flicker between reality and burning blackness. The visions of my people return louder then ever, their screaming echoing inside my head louder than the creatures in front of me. The thought of being shredded by beasts of my own Woods before I can save my people makes me spit bile as well as blood.

I'm only an apothecary from a small village that nothing ever happens to. I'm not a hero or a queen or an Otherfolk. I'm just a regular woman.

A woman of the Woods.

A girl who danced with the ghosts of the forest.

The memory of me as a small child lost in the trees cuts through the pandemonium. But I wasn't lost like my parents suggested. I was following my heart deep into the leafy undergrowth. The trees were so large to my tiny body, they didn't even register as trees. They were the walls of the world. Columns supporting a sky of green. I don't know if I had seen the true sky yet, or if it had always been the leafy underside of the canopy, but the Woods were all I knew. They were all I needed to know. I remember the stone doors nestled into trees like portals to other worlds. I remember the green flames dancing around me, following me, leading me. They were part of me and I was a part of the Woods.

Enough.

Crumbling bits of the wall I cower against scatter as I push myself to my feet. The branches surrounding me shed broken pieces in large chunks, but the destruction holds no fear for me now.

The fire that burns in them burns in me too.

The soul of the Woods is my soul. The blood of the Woods is my blood. I have always been a child of the trees. My heart has always belonged to the people who buried their dead in tree hollows and light their final paths with undying flames.

This path will not be the last I walk, but it will blaze brighter than the sun.

I let the remnants of my cage fall apart in a shower of bark and wood that does not touch me.

The beasts buck and rear. They tear at the air between us, but they come no closer. I slowly close my hands into fists while I seek their burning hearts within the essence of the Woods. They rage like wildfires in the dark, but I burn brighter still.

CHAPTER FORTY-ONE

KEDREN

Flashes of white and red stab the space behind my eyes between periods of blessed blackness. There is no fear. I feel no horror or revulsion. There is only the intermittent oblivion and the grinding of my bones like grains of sand under a boot heel. I know I am on a horse only because the sway of it is frequently the cause of my jarring return to my body. My left arm hangs lifeless and full of fire at my side. I cannot even register the pain, only the violent sickness it causes. The blood occasionally draining from my mouth and nose comes back up with monotonous regularity. With every choking retch I slide back into the blackness, prevented from falling to the ground by the bonds strapping me to the saddle.

There is no night. No day. No time. There is nothing but the molten shards of what was once my left side. I am unconscious enough that I still have the voice to groan fitfully when I am not. That is, until the glaring, too bright sun is replaced with the nauseating flicker of torchlight. Then there is not even enough left for that.

My arms are chained above me. My body hangs heavy against the bonds. Blood soaks everything. I cannot tell if I am wearing clothes, or if I simply cannot see my skin through it . Daralyn's voice comes to me in waves. I am no longer sure if any of this is real, or if I am alive at all. I laugh but only bubbling red spit comes out. What more can she do to me if I am already dead?

The long, drawn out screams of the priestess pull me from the restless void somewhere above my corpse, or body, or whatever that mess is that lays broken and bleeding on the stone floor. My focus does not last long, however. Her screams are usually followed by a strange tingling as Daralyn takes a blade to me and collects the blood in a small, black bowl.

I think I spit in her face as she leans close, an act of defiance I was never capable of when I was alive. That must mean I am dead. I could never stand up to her in life. She would not let me, and I was always so afraid. Afraid of her. Afraid of pain. Afraid of the looks and the laughter when I tried to explain what happened. I am not afraid anymore. How can I be afraid knowing there is someone who brushed the hair out of my eyes like Envir does for Jyn? How can I be afraid when someone took me as I am, and how I want to be, despite how fucked up I actually am? How can I be afraid when I love someone this much? No. There is no fear now. Only peace. Only her.

A flash of red-edged light and searing pain radiates down one leg after my small act of rebellion. From my place above my body, I can see the leg now sitting at an odd angle. It does not matter.

Nothing matters.

My body will rot here in this tomb, and Alyssia will be free. Safe. Away from all of this. Able to destroy the relic and ruin Daralyn's plans. It is out of my hands now. Well. Hand. I am not sure that deserves a plural anymore.

I always knew she would kill me. I have known that since I was very, very small. I do not know if it was the first time she broke me, or the tenth, or the hundredth, but I have known for such a long time that her cruel touch would be the last I ever felt.

Only, I did not expect the afterlife to hurt this much.

CHAPTER FORTY-TWO

ALYSSIA

The tomb wakes as I enter. Torches of green come to life in circular succession around the walls, illuminating the chamber in a wavering, ghostly glow. It's smaller than I thought, more intimate. Breaks in the torches allude to other passageways, other tombs, but this is the only room I need.

In the center are two ornate altars made of stone and tree, atop of which lay golden, resinous caskets. I approach them slowly. My fingers trace the smooth, luminous surfaces as I walk between them. I've seen insects trapped in amber, the crystallized sap preserving their bodies in transparent gold. But how could I have imagined this? Humans in perfect preservation, sleeping in beds of forest jewels.

It's haunting. Beautiful.

There is a man and a woman, their hands crossed over their hearts. The woman is much older, her gray hair reflects yellow-green in the filtered flames, and worn lines of wrinkles trace her fair skin. That they're royalty is no question. Their embroidered clothes, their presence here, the gold circlets of branches that lay on their brows, and the brilliant emerald ring encircling the woman's finger all point to their importance.

The ring.

That ring is why I'm here. Dread fills me over my need to disturb this woman's peace. The relic would be safe here, protected by beast and amber. I could find some other way to save my friends. I could tell the princess I couldn't find it or that I destroyed it. But would it end? Would they kill all of us, regardless? Would they burn my Woods to the ground to find it?

I study her face to attempt to sear it into my memory. I trace the soft bow of her lips, the long sweep of her lashes, the deep lines of cheeks used to smiling. It looks like a face that would forgive me for what I'm about to do. I hope it is, anyway.

Only when I'm sure I will never forget her, the swirling flames begin to gather along my forearm. Tendrils lick at my fingers and spark against the amber beneath them. The ring ignites in response. Cracks of green splinter across the surface of the perfect, seamless crystal. Tears of remorse seep into the channels as I weep for this woman I don't know.

I sob because I've been forced into thievery because I can't see how to save my friends without it. Splinters of amber cut my hand as I press through the shattered surface. The body within glitters with the broken stars of her resting place before the long-dead skin begins to dry and crack. By the time I reach the ring, the hand it rests on falls into its component parts. I shake the golden band to dislodge the bone stuck inside. Centuries of preserved majesty disintegrates into dust at my feet. My sorrow falls onto the ash like rain as I slide the ring onto my shaking finger.

My mind and body are wrenched apart. The Essence of the Woods is a conflagration that would consume the sun and the relic devours me. I am embers, burning with the chaos of a storm I can't fathom. The flames fill my lungs and seep beneath my skin and the trees take root inside of my bones, and I am no longer human for one blistering, eternal moment.

—

When I become reacquainted with my mortality, I have no idea how much time has passed. The forest outside the chamber is dark, and the blood on my clothes is dry and flaking. My wounds ache, but don't cripple me as they should. I scramble to my feet in the pile of grave dust and amber and break for the Woods.

Renewed rage boils under my skin and flames wreath its surface as the doors swing ponderously shut behind me. A crown of sun-burnished green burns across my brow, the blazing afterimage of the one left behind on the broken altar. Never again will I stand idly by as people bleed and die for me. I am the wrath of an ageless Wood. Those who cross me will know the power of it.

I am not the hunted.

I am not the deer bounding away from their pursuer.

I am the hunter.

I am the bear who will take her payment in blood and fear.

If they're too cowardly to meet me in my arena, I will eat the earth between us and destroy them in their own.

The guardians of the Barrows supplicate themselves before me as I approach. The bark along the back of the bear ripples as I swing my leg over it, forming itself to my body. The fire around me merges with the fire in her, and we are of one mind. One purpose.

We run. We gallop. We *consume.*

I collect the spirit of the Woods as we careen through the Barrows until I'm clothed in its light. The trees are a shadowed blur. The gorge that nearly ended me isn't even a thought as we bridge the gap without breaking our stride. The pool of the prince's blood is a dark stain in the twilight that breathes fresh life into the coals inside of me.

The road between the villages is the fastest way through the forest. The gates I labored so hard to raise part like curtains before me, retreating to their place under the earth as I pass through like the echoes of a storm. Time warps around me. I pass through the gates of Curaria before I have left the thoughts of Eklar behind. I'm bathed in the starlight of the open plains before I can lament the dark emptiness of my home within the great tree. I race the sun as it rises over the horizon. I fly through the western gate of the capital to the shouts of startled guardsmen.

The further from the Woods I get, the more of my own fire I feed into the construct churning beneath me. By the time its wood-and-bone claws chip the cobblestones of city streets the only flame that clings to me is that of the crown. Still, we run. We pass the Prism and the library as I trace my way through the streets on the paths most familiar to me.

Backed against the northern wall of the city, the sprawling Davorist Temple darkens a side street with its imposing stone facade and twisted, black iron gates. The bear lands in a satisfying and destructive slide through a bed of flowers on the other side of the fence, pieces of it shedding as it shudders to a halt. The power holding it together wanes quickly in the stone-walled prison of the city.

Instead of fighting its dissolution, I use it. The barely coherent pieces of the construct creep, and climb, and mold themselves to me like armor. I lift the massive head to my own, strips of it flaking away as it transforms into a helmet. It hides the ferocity of my gaze behind mismatched bark-and-bone eyes and frames the sharp curve of my mouth with even sharper teeth.

Coils of root and vine wrap themselves around my arms and legs. Plates of hardwood and bone protect the softest parts of me. Ribs curve, claws protrude, moss softens, vines grasp. I am rage, and fear, and a thing of legend made real. Right now, I am the Otherfolk Queen I have been so adamantly denying, and I will make these cultists be eaten by trees.

None come bursting forth from the ornate front doors, and the lack of a welcoming party concerns me. If little time has passed, I'll relish the advantage of surprise. If I am too late, and they're already dead, no one here will survive me.

But they are alive. They must be.

I stalk up to the heavy, double doors and press my palms against the smooth surface. A questing trickle of my awareness tells me they are barred from the inside. With one small effort of will, the bar of wood shatters into splinters. I lean in and shove the doors wide, the bear helm's rictus grin matching my own.

Two cultists begin shouting before I clear the doors. I silence one with a quick thrust of my hand. The coiled root wrapped around my forearm is a snake-quick spear. The blood from the man's throat soaks into its dry bark as it wraps back up my arm. The other, a woman, has a leash around her neck. I drag her to her knees at my feet.

"The princess expects me. Where is she?" I reduce the pressure of the vine wrapped around her throat so she can speak. The slack seems to make her think I'm less serious, despite the blood soaking the floorboards next to her.

"If you have brought her what she needs, she has no use for you alive," the woman sneers.

If she isn't going to be helpful, she isn't worth my time. Others are getting closer from up the stairs and down the hall stretching from the entry. I squeeze my hand into a fist and choose the hall. I lose the sound of her head hitting the floor within the rhythm of pounding footsteps echoing behind me.

The corridor is long, but narrow. At least it feels long, clogged with milling bodies. The cultists and guardsmen can only come toward me two at a time. I move through them with quick precision, disposing of them with the same efficiency I harvest my plants.

Bright, arterial blood paints the shining wood floors red and slick. Cultist magic hammers into me from both directions. I don't fight it. I allow my body to follow the momentum. Flashes of pain erupt through my torso and my legs as I weave through their assaults with fluid, dancing steps.

The stream of people trying to kill me and take the stolen ring from me, clings to me like creeping vines and slow me down. She can't have me though. She can't have it. She can't have *them*.

A cultist, apparently without magic, makes the mistake of touching me. I twist and lock my hand around his forearm in a fond greeting as mayhem spirals around us. His eyes go wide when they meet mine through the shadows of the helm. I send silk-thin threads of rapidly growing roots through his veins until they tangle in his heart. I let go and step over him as he drops to his knees, digging at the weeds taking root in his chest.

I don't count the bodies I leave behind me. I don't listen to the shouts and moans of pain. I don't choke on the metallic scent of blood in the air. I don't slow when I reach the doors at the end of the hall. I do slam those doors behind me and seal them with a wave of magic that melts the wooden doors into their frames. It isn't perfect. The doors are light and won't hold against any significant force, but it will buy me time.

Time I'll need to deal with the swarming mass of robe- and armor-clad assholes milling about in this mockery of a temple. Even in its ruinous state, the forest temple held majesty a hundredfold more significant than this mausoleum of a room. The shapes are all similar, but everything here is sharp, rigid, and too crowded. The columns rise stiffly to curved buttresses that look like ribs. Wooden pews stand in straight rows like soldiers marching toward the altar at the far side. Mounds of melted candle wax emerge from every surface like seeping pustules.

There is no tattooed High Priestess or cruel princess. No sign of those I'm here to free. Just pawns. Not even the unsettling combination of Dienna and Marlayne wait for me.

I have to be missing something.

It's difficult to think straight with the constant annoyance of blades, orbs, and other various weapons of red and gold light nipping at my edges.

Catching a cultist whip with my forearm before it can wrap around my neck distracts me entirely. I brace myself and heave against the line, pulling the man at the other end off balance and sending him stumbling into an armored guard.

I don't have time for this.

I dodge forward, passing a guard who takes a wedge out of the pauldron on my shoulder. I reel sideways. The hit sends me crashing into the first row of wooden pews which, conveniently, was what I was aiming for. The moment the ring makes contact with the bench, I let go of my questionable control over the power contained within it and plunge into the world of black and green.

The pews are empty shells, vessels ready for life but so long removed from the ground, they do not carry their own. With the relic pressed between us I can remind them of what they once were.

With a nauseating effort, I bring both of my worlds into focus. The same sense of ethereal slowness I experienced when I discovered this power descends. A leaf-rustling wind sweeps through the room, bringing with it the scents of a summer day tinged with woodsmoke. I mark the positions of everyone in this room and ignore the jarring impact of something against the doors.

With one slow, controlled exhale I drop to a crouch, my fingertips resting on the stone tiles. The pews take root at my touch. Thick tendrils rush beneath the floorboards toward each of the sluggish bodies creeping toward where I kneel.

Time surges back to normal with the thunderous crack of a dozen bark-skinned tentacles bursting through board and stone, impaling or ensnaring every body inching toward me. Killing is not my goal here, I simply need to move without them holding me back, but I will not mourn those who are lost.

I sway to my feet, bleeding and scoured raw by the magic. I'm exhausted beyond pain or empathy, my world narrowed to one goal. I turn from the closest cage and it's bleeding, gory ornament. It is the guardsman that took a piece of my armor, his sword trapped mid-swing by knotted ropes of wood, half his face replaced with gore-soaked bark. He won't tell me what I need to know. The next closest is a weakly struggling cultist, the bonds of my creation cutting roughly into her soft flesh. The red-lightning sparks of her lesser magic sizzle harmlessly against them.

"Tell me where they are, or you die broken and slow," rough and low, this voice is hardly my own.

The cultist spits in response.

With the flick of a wrist, I press a sharpened piece of her bonds against her stomach.

"My job is to keep people alive," I say flatly, stepping closer, "and I'm rather good at it. How long do you think I can keep you alive, while also killing you?"

The wooden barb sinks further into her, and I sense the slight pop of resistance as it breaks the skin. She is sweating now, but to her credit, she doesn't scream. She bites her own lip bloody.

"Tell me," another incremental push. "where they," another, "are."

Hissing, spitting breaths spray the bear's face with blood and saliva, but as I slide the root through greasy layers of fat toward her intestines, she speaks in choked pants. "A door. Behind the altar."

"Perfect. Thank you." I bare my teeth at her and on a delusional whim, pat her cheek with one bloodstained hand. Heading toward the altar, I look back and consider removing the spear from her insides but her flaring nostrils and haggard breathing reminds me of Inness' last breaths. I feel an odd sense of pride to know my apprentice faced death better than the adults who killed her.

Laying my palm against the back wall, I unravel pieces of the root coiled around my forearm. Much like I did with the man in the hall, I send the tendrils out, probing for cracks in the stone. Knowing it's there, the hidden door is easy to find and its latch is easy to trigger. The section swings inward.

A long, narrow, poorly lit set of stairs plunges into subterranean darkness. My injuries pulse with pain and my muscles shake from fatigue as I stand at the top staring down with the greatest reluctance, but I refuse to wade through horrors only to be defeated by a staircase.

The echo of a scream erupts from the abyss. I dive after it, slipping on the worn edges of steps and catch myself on torch brackets and gaps in the wall. The pain in my back is worse than when I fell into the lake, my knees grind together every time I miss a step, heat radiates from my thigh and calf. It feels like I'm breaking apart step by plunging step, but even if all that's left of me is bones strapped together by the will of the Woods, I will make it to the end of this.

That was Carolyn's scream.

She, at least, is still alive.

CHAPTER FORTY-THREE

ALYSSIA

The scream cuts off abruptly. I hit the last step just as a cultist appears to investigate my clumsy descent. I don't hesitate to slam an elbow in their face and duck past them.

How many of these bastards are there?

When I slide around the dusty corner at the base of the stairs that hides the main room, I choke on bile, a scream, and a gasp all trying to escape me at once.

Where the room upstairs was a miniature, half-realized copy of the Forest Temple, this underground space is a vast, macabre tribute to a horror beyond my imagining. Bones, both human and animal, create detailed patterns embedded throughout walls and columns of carved stone. The reek of blood and vomit threatens to overwhelm me. I cover my mouth with one hand and breathe shallowly. The room is designed to draw the eye to one central point. A point from which I can't look away despite my desire to be looking anywhere else. Four columns of bones arch upwards and meet in the center above a large, plain altar that looks more like a dissection table than anything else. Distillation equipment opaque with burnt black residue, half-burned cones of incense, pools of melted candles, and a number of unclean surgical tools sprawl across the surface. Loose pages are scattered throughout and spill across the floor.

It all pales in comparison to the people arranged like some horrible painting.

Daralyn and the High Priestess recline on plush, upholstered chairs, a game of cards spread on an ornate table before them. They look up as one over glasses of wine and smile.

They are flanked by my nightmare.

Chained to a column on the left is Carolyn, her white robes are crimson and gray with blood and filth. They are slashed into formless ribbons around her, her pale skin exposed in gory stripes of blood and cloth. Her arms are bound above her head, just high enough that she must kneel awkwardly. Fresh blood trickles down her forearm from a cut in her wrist.

She is a paragon of health and wellness in comparison to the prince.

Hanging in the same manner from the opposite column, I barely recognize him. His hair, soaked in sweat, blood, and vomit clings to his swollen, bruised, and bloodstained face. His shattered left arm hangs from the manacles in a surreal, liquid way that makes me gag. He is shirtless, the shreds of it decorating the ground around him, and it exposes the horrible, bruised swelling and deep, wet gashes that have taken over his entire left side. His right leg sprawls under him in an angle that is not possible. I can't tell if he's still breathing. I don't know if I want him to be. Not through this.

It takes no more than a heartbeat after I slide into the room to see all I need to see. The inferno of my outrage threatens to pull the entire chamber down around us, but I force the sudden, roiling mass of deeply buried roots to stop their shifting before it brings the whole building down around us. Fire burns in wild rivers across my bark-armored body. I clutch the ring in my fist like it is one of Rend's knuckle dusters, but instead of a punch, I throw the magic behind one of the gathered plants I have snaking beneath the stone and send it striking into the chair Daralyn occupies so casually.

She moves like she can read my thoughts. Darting to the side, she draws a blade of red-soaked gold out of the air and shaves off a piece of wood that got too close. Before the chair hits the ground, she's running.

And she has magic.

A hail of red and gold spikes pelts me from the Davorist priestess. One vambrace quickly morphs into a shield that catches most of them, their red-lightning tips a finger-width from my face. The barrage doesn't stop. More piercing spines fly at me, some licking at exposed flesh like burning tongues. The princess is dodging madly toward me, her body low to the ground and her blade nimble. I can't catch up to her with the ponderously slow roots, not while I'm also trying to stop the priestess's projectiles.

I want to sink into the power of the ring again, but I don't know how to control it. I can't risk losing myself to it and becoming useless. I can't abandon Carolyn to this. I can't leave the prince in their hands. I trip, distracted by the devastation of Kedren's body and sheer exhaustion. I land hard. Jolting pain courses through my battered ribs, but I manage to throw my shield between myself and the princess' downswing. The blade shears through the wood like soft wax until I focus all of my effort on maintaining its shape. I have nothing left to counter with. I extend my second vambrace as much as I can to block the relentless spears from the priestess. My whole body shakes with the effort to keep the princess at bay. She still advances.

"Lys!"

The shout startles all three of us. The princess' blade slips as she jerks around to search for the source. The priestess' projectiles swing wide of their mark. In the confusion of the echoing exclamation, I roll out from under Daralyn and rise to one knee. All of us look to the narrow entrance, and I could weep with relief. With her bloody, double-bladed ax held loose and ready in one hand, Rend runs toward me. Envir is close behind her, longsword shining red in the torchlight. I try to call out and move to throw myself between him and Kedren's broken form. I want to spare him that sight so badly, I lurch to my feet and lunge toward them, princess and priestess be damned.

I'm too slow. I'm always too slow.

The wail that escapes Envir pierces my heart so violently it tears a sob from me. I brace myself against my knees to stop from crumbling to the floor.

Daralyn has no such empathy, but thankfully, neither does Rend. Her ax swings up to catch the edge of the princess' blade before it can tear into my exposed back. I have just enough presence of mind to move; shaking, gasping, sweating, and bleeding, but moving.

Envir runs to his prince's side, his sword forgotten in his hand. I wish I had the time to join him, but my attention is required elsewhere.

Daralyn is losing ground against Rend's vicious swings, so I turn on the priestess. She retreats behind the altar, and I haul a sharpened piece of root toward her from beneath the stone floor. I'm, once again, too slow. An easy sidestep and a quick slash of her own magic cuts my weapon off at the base. I press on, ripping pieces of wood out of the earth with each step. Biting. Slashing. Unswayed by failure, they appear faster and faster as I find a rhythm.

"I think that's far enough, forest whore."

"Call off your dog."

"Or the priestess and the ponce join the prince."

Materializing from the shadows, Dienna and Marlayne quirk small smiles. The blond has Carolyn by her hair, a long knife pressed against her chest, the brunette has Envir in a magical bond, strung up next to his best friend's shattered body, a matching knife poised at his throat.

I raise my hands, palms out. "Rend. Stand down."

Stopping so suddenly makes me stagger, sick with a tiredness I've never felt before. I can't think straight, but I've already failed twice. I can't afford a third.

Rend is a shoring force at my side as I frantically conjure some plan while I watch Daralyn, the priestess, and the hell twins for any hint of sudden violence.

"Just give me the ring," Daralyn trails off with a frown, "Whatever your name is." She waves her hand, and the magical blade she holds winks out of existence. "You've already cost me my assurance of an unbroken royal line," she says while she kicks at Kedren's sprawled legs before leaning against the blood stained altar. "I would sincerely like to wash my hands of this and move onto the next step if it's all the same to you."

I have one last plan, and it's worse than a gamble.

"It appears that I have no choice." I take a step forward and shake my head sharply when Rend starts to follow. Envir makes a strangled sound of protest, but I ignore it. It isn't like he can stop me. "You win, Daralyn. Just call off *your* dogs." I twist the ring off my heat-swollen finger. "Step forward, I'm not getting that close to all of you."

Canopy Above. Please let this work.

When the princess clears the columns, and stands over my last line of defense, I flick the ring to her.

I slam my mind into the relic, ready to tear the waiting wall of twisted roots through the stone and straight into her.

My world erupts in white fire before I ever get the chance.

Discordant waves of screaming voids consuming each other beat at me from every side. I can't separate reality from the havoc tearing apart my mind.

A flash of red-gold light cuts through a chaotic tangle of roots I must have pulled up during the bedlam to reveal a scene of mayhem drowned out by the roaring in my ears. Pure gold light flares into life to one side, only to be swallowed by snaking shadows. A shattered knife falls to the ground in front of Carolyn. The bonds holding Envir dissolve, and he immediately goes back to the prince, pointlessly trying to ease some of the weight off of his bound wrists. Dienna and Marlayne drag Daralyn back into the shadows behind the altar. The princess' mouth is open in a silent scream, and she claws at her head; a feeling to which I can relate. The priestess stoops low before fleeing after the others. The blinding world fades to black.

I roll onto my knees, coughing up who knows what, and send a cascade of debris clattering to the ground. I'm too busy retching to put anything together. Even sound is disjointed with voices and high-pitched ringing interchanging too rapidly for me to understand words.

I don't need words to know the priestess took the ring.

I trip through chunks of wood and bark, tear the skewed helm from my head so I can see, and stumble toward the altar before Rend starts making sense.

"Lys, stop!"

I obey and take the opportunity to think about what I'm doing in relation to what I can see and hear.

Envir cradles Kedren's head in his lap and brushes his filthy hair out of his bruised face. He's crying, looking up at me and shouting nonsense.

"Alyssia," his voice breaks into stuttering sobs, "He's alive."

I can't stop looking over my shoulder into the shadows that swallowed the princess. I still edge backwards, itching to run. The need to reclaim the ring and tear the princess into shreds eats at my gut.

"Lys," Rend shouts at me again as she frees Carolyn from the chains holding her, "What do you think you are going to do against them?" She lowers her gently to the ground.

"I have to stop them, Rend. I have to." I can barely stand. The flame in my pendant is a mere candle flicker. I refuse to recognize Envir mumbling over Kedren's body that everything will be alright.

Nothing is alright.

They have the ring. Inness is dead. The prince is dead. Countless people will be dead because of this. Because of me.

"Lys. You can't do anything about them, but you can help me do something here." Rend gestures between Carolyn and the prince's body.

The prince's very, very shallowly breathing body.

He's actually alive.

Fuck.

Thoughts of the ring evaporate as I watch his chest rise and fall with shuddering irregularity. I push past the gaudy chairs, knocking into them and shoving them out of my way.

"Alyssia," Envir calls, panic edging his voice, "I don't know what to do."

I hesitate, suspended between the two columns, torn between who I should go to first. The prince obviously needs me more, but Carolyn is Carolyn.

I stagger toward the men only when Rend adamantly waves me off, and I half-fall into Envir's outstretched arm.

"Let's see what we can do to fix some of this, alright," I say with shaking softness as I swing my leg over to straddle the prince, very careful to not touch him. I breathe deeply, my eyes closed, and erect a wall between my heart and my mind so I can look at him without falling apart.

His face is bruised and swollen. His striking, sharp-lined nose is shapeless and crusted with blood. What little unmarred skin remains is pale and slick with sweat. His breathing is fast, shallow and irregular, hissing softly over cracked lips. His left shoulder is swollen and locked awkwardly out of place. His arm is shattered with the jagged ends of bones pressed tight against his skin. Long, shallow cuts trail down his forearm. More bruises bloom around his ribs. His right thigh is swollen and bent. He's cold and his pulse is rapid and thready.

"A Kivaran physician might be-"

"N-no," Kedren convulses, his face contorted in pain. "No more." He breathes in jerking gasps like the ghosts of sobs. "Pl please." Another violent shudder rips through him ruthlessly. "End it."

Envir and I freeze, straining to hear and then wishing we hadn't. I should sit back. I should let Envir be the one to lean in and comfort his lifelong friend. It would be selfish to take this moment from them. But I'm desperate for my failure to stop Daralyn to mean something.

To mean *him*.

To mean seeing his soft smile again while he runs his fingers through my hair, and to hear him begging to know what would be wrong about loving me.

So, I'm selfish. I lean so close I can feel the heat of his swollen cheeks against my skin, and I tangle my fingers in his hair to hold his head gently.

"I'm sorry, Your Highness," I whisper for only him to hear. "But I told you, you can't ask me to sit back and watch you die. I need you to fight to be with me again, but this time, I'll fighting too." I brush my lips against his forehead before sitting back. Envir stares with tears in his eyes and one knuckle between his teeth. I nod and keep my gentle hold on the prince as he writhes against pain I can't begin to imagine. "Any extra time spent in the city or the palace is probably not the best idea, so physicians might not be the way to go. But we need to take him somewhere. I really can't do anything here." Everything is covered in dirt and wooden wreckage. The empty sockets of skulls bore into me from every direction. Dim torchlight wavers in a mockery of visibility. The metallic reek of blood and rust assaults me.

"If we can move him, we can go," Rend says, suddenly looming over me and supporting a somewhat-standing Carolyn. "The *Lady* has been ready to sail since you all vanished after the funeral. The princess threw a truly royal tantrum, and it seemed prudent to have an escape route ready."

"Bring me that flat piece over there. We can't move him like this."

Rend lowers Carolyn gently to the ground and retrieves the large piece of my armor left intact by the splintering impact between Daralyn and I.

My ears are still ringing from the unfathomable cacophony created by that collision. Whatever it was.

When Rend returns with the board, I reluctantly remove myself from my position hovering over the prince and set the piece of wood near his less injured side.

"Envir. Rend. Lift him just a fraction, so I can slide this under him." Back to business now, sweeping the grave dirt that is my insides under the rug of my lifetime of training.

The prince doesn't make a sound as he's moved, but he's still conscious. The fingers of his right hand dig into my thigh, making the job of sliding the soon-to-be-litter beneath him more difficult, but it's not like I'm going to begrudge him the inconvenience.

"I don't see how that's going to help us." Rend squats next to me casually, blood-soaked but unruffled, arms draped over her knees.

"Patience, my friend." I muster an upward curve of my mouth for her before sitting down with my knees drawn to my chest. I block out as much of my surroundings as I can and let my mind brush past the glow at my heart and reach outwards. Small tendrils of fire swirl like wisps of smoke in the aftermath of my wildness. I gather them like draws on a pipe. They come slowly, but I breathe deeply, gathering them to me steadily.

The image of how I want the board to form under the prince is perfectly clear in my mind. The flames sink into the wood beneath him, and I mold it carefully under the curves of his body. Ridges and valleys form around him, and smooth, curved handles extend from either end. I collect as much of the remaining free magic back into my vial until I'm too tired to snatch the errant shreds.

"I suppose that answers a few of my questions." Rend exhales heavily and stretches her way to standing. I don't even want to open my eyes, let alone follow her. My body feels like it was replaced with lead. "You can answer the rest of them later because I want to get out of here. I feel like I slipped into hell when I wasn't looking." She grabs me under my arms and hauls me to my feet, holding me as I sway, reordering my legs to obey me. "Head or feet, D'luane?"

I help Carolyn stand, both of us pitifully unsteady and clinging to each other to keep upright.

"Head. If anyone tries to stop us, I'll take care of it."

"After you, then." She nods, and they position themselves.

I hold my breath as they straighten and start toward the exit of this garish place. When he doesn't start screaming, I release the breath, knowing I did the best I could. Carolyn and I shuffle after them, careful to avoid tripping over wreckage.

Perfect and strange among the destruction, the bone-white eye socket of my helm catches a reflection of wavering torchlight. I change our course to collect it.

CHAPTER

FORTY-FOUR

ALYSSIA

Wading through the carnage, my carnage, keeps a steady stream of bile in the back of my mouth. I'm able to swallow it back down until I stumble over something heavy and loose in the entryway. The wide eyes of the first woman I killed meet mine briefly as the head I kicked rolls across the floor. Thankfully my stomach is empty of anything but its native juice, and my rib-straining gags produce hardly more than a voluminous spit.

"The first severed head is always the worst," Rend says with teasing sympathy.

"I'm sure I'll keep mine about me next time," I say dryly, wiping my mouth on the back of my hand.

"You two are disgusting," Envir rasps, voice wavering as he picks his way through the bodies and blood that litter the floor. There is more now than when I made my way through.

Rend and Kedren are the only two unaffected by the butchery. The prince would likely be less casual about it if he weren't otherwise so occupied with not dying.

Someone closed the doors after I made my way through them, so I drag Carolyn and myself in front to pull one of them open. It's so much heavier now that I'm not crashing through with supernaturally augmented fury.

"Lord D'Luane?" a deep voice asks from the other side of the door I hide behind. "What's the meaning of this? What's going on?"

"Attempted murder of the prince, a Priestess of Kiv, and civilians, and you are just waiting on the porch? None of you heard anything?" He pushes forward impatiently, and I lose sight of him around the door. "Get out of my way or I will implicate you in the death of His Highness as well as negligence of duty."

"We have orders, Lord D'Luane. None of the guards are allowed in the temple or the library unless-" a sharp intake of breath cuts off him off as he sees the prince. "Who is responsible for this?"

I pull Carolyn and I around the edge of the door so Envir doesn't have to find the most politically expedient answer. "Princess Daralyn. Her ladies-in-waiting and High Priestess D'Brae are accomplices. With the greatest misfortune, they're all still alive. They fled into an underground tunnel beneath the building that you should probably go investigate." I gesture toward the open door behind me with the bear helm. "Don't mind the mess."

We stagger down the stairs after the others without a backward glance. Two of the loitering guards split from the small, seething mass of them to flank Envir. The way their helmeted heads keep swiveling toward Kedren indicates they must be some of his men, or, at the very least, not exclusively Daralyn's.

Our path through the city is slow and convoluted. Envir and the guards take us through alleys and side streets, attempting to avoid notice. I don't dare to look away from His Highness long enough to suggest a better way to the docks. I'm too busy monitoring his obviously increasing distress. Twice, we are forced to duck behind corners while the guards disperse crowds. The fact that the men escorting us aren't taking us to the jail is a testament to their disloyalty to the princess, but it's only a matter of time before someone else realizes that Envir, Rend and I are responsible for not a small amount of murder. I'd rather not be in the city when that happens, and our sluggish pace grates at my already ragged nerves.

We make it to the busy harbor, finally, and the guards slip back into the streets after a murmured exchange with Envir, trusting our safety to the anonymity of the busy docks.

"Lys, do you see the *Lady*?" Rend asks, her voice raised over the shouting and haggling even though we are right next to each other. I follow her eye line and scan the port for her distinctive sloop, the *Hooded Lady*.

"I see her." The figurehead of a cloaked woman, her face lost in the shadows of her hood, clutching her own naked body in modesty or pleasure is completely unmistakable for anything but Rend's *Lady*. "This way."

Carolyn leans on me more and more, and I stagger under our combined weight, but I force a way through the crowd, Envir close on my heels. Turned heads and hand-hidden whispers follow us, space opening around our ungainly, dramatic burden. I should care more about the rumors we could start if anyone recognizes Envir, but at this exact moment, all I care about is the easier passage through the crowd and the rapidly approaching salvation of the *Lady's* gangplank.

"Shoen!" Rend barks in her most resonant captain's voice. "Up and out. Now!"

A shirtless man in wide, black trousers tied tightly at the ankles, jumps from his uninterested repose on a dock post and darts up the gangplank shouting Rend's order for those on deck. We follow with increased determination now that safety is at hand.

"You two will take my quarters. There is no way he'll make it below decks, and it has the most room to work."

Envir heads toward the door beneath the quarterdeck, not waiting for direction. The *Lady* may be unique in her details, but she has a fairly standard layout, so he will know his way around from experience with his family's ships.

Her quarters aren't wildly impressive, but I know the dimly lit, low-ceilinged room well and love them dearly. I breathe in the salty, wood and sea scent of it, spiced by a new, lingering hint of incense. Cenna is stretched across the low, built-in bed that takes up most of the curved aft end of the room, and a sudden sense of possessive jealousy ripples through me. As Envir and Rend carry Kedren past me my envy evaporates. I guide Carolyn into a side chair and follow them.

Cenna rolls to one side in her catlike manner, making space for the prince.

"Don't move him, I'll do the same as before."

Rend arches her eyebrow at me. "Can you and still function after? You almost blacked out last time, and you need to actually fix him now."

"And you aren't doing anything with that mess on this bedding,"

Cenna mumbles as she stands, slinking toward the door. "I will send for an old sailcloth and the ship's medical supplies. Do not let all of that blood get on my things, my oasis."

The gore covering the four of us is, admittedly, extensive. I don't bother answering Rend, she can see the truth as well as I can feel it. Instead, I peel the remainder of my armor off and stack it in an out of the way corner. My shirt and boots follow but one look at the sticky, blood and dirt soaked pant leg, I decide those can stay on for a little longer. I'm glad I went with the black ones this time, though, they make it easier to ignore. Rend and Envir stretch out their hands and shoulders, and by the time I'm down to my blood-stained stays, crew members have arrived with a wide piece of sailcloth and a collection of leather cases.

Everything and everyone gets shuffled around, set up, and ready for me in an organized milling of ants in the tight space. When it's time to transfer Kedren to the bed, I worm my way between the crowd to be anxious from a better angle.

"Be careful," I mutter, unhelpfully, as they make ready to move him.

"Thank you for the professional insight, Lys. I was ready to toss him like a bag of grain. What would I do without you?" Rend says flatly before nodding to Envir.

As one, they lift him the barest fraction, and I hurriedly slide the board out from under him. He groans when my back is turned, and I spin to face him. His breathing is so fast and shallow that his skin has turned shadowy blue around what I can see of his mouth.

I grab at the last crewman as he passes. "Boiled water please, as much as you can get to me quickly."

I dig through the recesses of my knowledge for everything I can find about traumatic injuries; bone setting, extreme blood loss, soft tissue damage. It isn't as much as I would like, and I curse myself for becoming complacent instead of always striving to learn more. I lay the things I will need from the cases out on the desk at the front of the room. The implements line up like soldiers ready for my orders.

Rend startles me by speaking low and sharp directly into my ear, "I need to get this ship out of the harbor, Lys. Are you alright here? Do you have everything you need?"

"Once my water gets here, I'll be ready to start. Go. We can decide where exactly we'll be going after I'm done."

"Once you're done you're going to sleep, and *then* we can decide where we're going," she says with a light kiss on my forehead before ducking out onto the deck, barking instructions before she shuts the door behind her.

To my surprise, Cenna is still in the room with us, looking over my arrayed collection with interest. "I can attend to the priestess if you would like to start with His Highness right away. Her injuries do not appear to be complicated. Just filthy," she says in her warm accent, glancing between Carolyn, me, and finally, over her shoulder toward Kedren. "That is not something I am equipped to remedy."

"I'm not sure it's something I'm equipped to deal with either," I murmur before taking a quick breath in and snatching scissors off the desk. "But yes, please. If you don't mind seeing to her, it would be very helpful." I look back to Carolyn, half curled into an upholstered arm chair, her face pinched tight, but her chest rises and falls in a deep, even rhythm. "Tell me if you run into any problems," I say absently, already taking the three strides to Kedren's side.

Envir sits beside him, holding his uninjured hand in his lap with both of his, running his thumbs gently over blood stained knuckles. "Alyssia..." His deep blue eyes are glassy with tears, and his words come out choked. "Is he-" a sob stops him. "Fuck. Is he going to be alright?"

"I won't let him leave us without one hell of a fight. That's all I can give you." I take a deep breath and start unbuttoning his boots.

"I can help with that."

"You're helping now. Stay there."

Cenna's low voice rumbles softly behind me, talking gently to Carolyn while Envir cries quietly. The smell of sweat, blood and dirt drowns out the salt and spice scent of the familiar room, and the change in the rolling of the deck tells me we have left the mooring. All of it is secondary noise. My attention is only for the man beneath my shaking hands.

Carefully, I remove his boots, struggling with the one on the broken leg for longer than I would like as it gets stuck on the swollen limb. I don't try to save his trousers, cutting them away quickly and depositing the ruins on the deck along with everything else. My detachment threatens to crumble as the pit of my stomach burns in retaliation against the sight of him naked and broken beneath me.

"And this is where it gets worse." I toe the bucket of water at my feet forward and slip back to the desk for a bottle of the alcohol soaked sutures and soap. I scrub my hands and soak them in alcohol, ignoring the burning of my cut palm.

I start with his mouth since he isn't actively bleeding anywhere. The wet cloth traces his cracked lips slowly, the warm water loosening dried blood. The faint pink line of a cut along his cheek surprises me when I wipe the area clean. It seems like years ago when I sat before him, cleaning this small wound, my fingers tracing his sharp features with hypnotic fascination. Now his cheekbones are bruised and swollen. I prod them gently, looking for breaks. Something feels wrong with the one on the left, but nothing shifts under my touch so I move to his nose.

"Alright. First one, Your Highness."

With brutal efficiency, I press through the swelling, closing my eyes to focus on the feel of it as it is and how it should be. He flinches back from my touch, but Envir and I work together to hold his head steady as I forcefully manipulate the small bone back to some semblance of its correct position with one steady push. It won't be clean when it heals, there are too many pieces, but I do my best.

A small sound escapes him, and Envir and I both make nonsense soothing sounds.

"I know, Your Highness. I know. I'm sorry, but it's only going to get worse from here."

The next noise he makes sounds suspiciously like a laugh. Envir must think so as well, because he smiles and wipes sweat from Kedren's forehead with a strangled laugh of his own, "My brother, this is the last time you will have to survive her. You can do this."

My hand makes fist, squeezing bloody water from the cloth down my forearm. "Never again," I hiss through tight lips. "I swear it on the Trees. She will die before this happens again."

Envir looks up, frowning, but he nods and returns his attention to whispering comfort to his prince.

Tending to the rest of him takes time. Broken ribs shift under my fingers when he breathes, cuts gape and ooze. Washing and stitching the more superficial injuries is a slow and careful process, and my tongue presses into my lip in deep thought while I work.

When I finish, I get up with a creaky sigh and quickly wipe my hands clean before I cross my arms and frown at my surroundings.

Problems have solutions, you just have to make them.

My face softens at the memory of another saying of Arty's. I change my frown from one of hopelessness to concentration. I will make a solution, I just have to figure out how.

I keep drifting back to the pile of discarded armor, studying the pieces I made with passive consideration as I try to make a plan for the rest of the prince's treatment. I blink, and a tired smile ripples across my lips.

Snatching two pieces from the collection, I turn back to the bed triumphantly.

Envir looks up quizzically, but I wave him away with one chunk of wooden armor and settle onto the bed. I straddle the prince and try to forget the memory of these same thighs shaking with the need of me as I ran my hands along the lines of them. Now they shake with pain and blood loss as I lay the strips of wood across the top of his leg and just above his knee. I'm far to tired to manhandle everything back into place on my own, so I'm making a solution. I lean over and rest one hand on each piece of wood. The light is soft, but it flows from my necklace and down my arms and into the waiting material steadily.

The relatively flat pieces of armor mold into bands around his leg before growing branches that weave together and toward each other. When they met in the middle, they press together and begin to lengthen the prince's leg until it's straight again. I'm vaguely aware of the his weak twitching and soft groaning, but keeping control of the magic takes too much of my focus to let that distract me. When I finish the makeshift traction brace it extends below his knee and above his hip. I roll off to one side to lay on my back, my eyes closed and my knees drawn up.

"Is he still breathing?" My voice is calmer than I expect.

"Yes," a long pause. "Yes. I think he's finally out."

"Good."

"Will you be able to continue, Forestwalker?" Cenna asks softly, sounding unusually demure.

As the only person here who spends any significant time in a forest, I assume she's talking to me. "You couldn't stop me."

She doesn't say anything, but the bed shifts with more added weight. I open my eyes and crane my head back, looking for Envir. He moved at some point in the proceedings to cradle the prince from behind, much like he did the night I cleaned that cut on Kedren's cheek.

"Switch with me," I say to him, already crawling toward the head of the bed.

I pile pillows into the alcove the bulkhead makes and shimmy in carefully as Envir slides out the other side. Our bodies relax together. His head rests in the crook of my shoulder, and I bend my knees slightly to support us both. A hint of warmth radiates from him. The corner of my mouth turns up slightly.

"Hand me another piece of that armor, would you?" I ask Envir, who has taken up looming off to the side.

He complies quickly and without the questioning glance from earlier.

I repeat the same process, more or less. The damage here is more intricate and requires more slow attention than brute force, but it's still exhausting. I run my hand across his shoulder, tracing the path the branching wood travels, guiding it to reshape as I go. My fingers slide downward and the branches follow. They spread and twist, pull and push as they do, slowly putting the prince's arm back together under my touch. I rest my cheek against the side of his head and close my eyes as I gently rest his arm across his stomach, the bracing branches following to keep it in place.

When I finish, it looks as if he is being absorbed by my Woods, much like I wanted to be not so long ago. Holding him with both arms wrapped loosely around his waist, his body heavy against me, his breaths coming suddenly easier; returning to the Woods, to Arty and Inness, no longer seems like such an important thing to do.

CHAPTER FORTY-FIVE
ALYSSIA

I feel like I drank far too much questionable liquor, fell out of a tree, the tree fell on me, and the whole lot was then wrapped up and thrown into the ocean. I steel myself for what I might find, open my eyes slowly, and blink in the dimness of Rend's bedroom with hair that's not Rend's or mine in my mouth. Another bleary blink, and the past collides violently with the present.

Everything hurts or is tingling with the sharp numbness of having spent an unknown amount of time sleeping, half-sitting and trapped by the not-quite-dead weight of the prince. Someone covered us with a blanket at some point, making me suffocatingly hot, but I know he needed it.

His good arm holds onto my thigh firmly, despite his injuries. I smile and wince, as he just so happens to be very close to digging his fingers into the gashes there. My arms around his waist feel strong, rhythmic breaths that reinforce my cautious hope. I press a gentle kiss against the top of his head.

"I believe it is time to upgrade you from Otherfolk Queen to Forest

Goddess, Alyssia." His rough, cracking whisper of a voice makes me twitch in surprise, which causes him to groan, and then both of us to laugh in quick succession.

"Only if you join me in my divinity, Your Highness," I say into his hair, my hands tracing along the uninjured parts of his body, reassuring myself that he truly lives, "Because no mortal should have survived that."

"I remember someone I love asking me to fight when I was so desperate to finally die." His hold on me tightens. "So I fought." His voice drops even lower, "I will never leave you to fight alone."

"I wasn't alone," I say quickly. He has to be delusional with pain still, casually mentioning that he loves me, so I don't acknowledge it. "Envir and Rend came to our rescue, and Cenna helped once we got to the *Lady*." I place my hand on top of his and run my thumb against his knuckles. "I let them go. She has the relic. I couldn't stop her. I'm sorry." The tightness in my chest at that confession threatens to crush my lungs.

He squirms, pushing himself up enough to free me and nods to the side. "Lay next to me, please."

Slowly, I disengage from my place beneath him and help him lay back against the pillows, pain tightening his face. I curl up next to him, careful of his leg, and hug his arm, lacing my fingers between his.

"Do not ever be sorry for not dying. Nothing is worth that, not even killing her." His eyes are bright and hard, framed by the deep purple shadows of his broken nose.

"How many will die because I couldn't stop her? I was the only one who stood a chance, and I couldn't, not even with Rend and Envir. I couldn't stop her, she took the ring, and it's my fault. I made the wrong choice." I start crying, and I don't bother trying to stop. I've accepted it as inevitable by now.

"What else did you do before you found us?" he asks, quiet, steady, and dreadfully solid despite everything. "How many did you fight through? Had you slept? Eaten? How many of them were there? The High Priestess? Daralyn? Dienna and Marlayne? When did Vi and Rend arrive? How much did they do?"

"I don't know. I don't know. None of it seems real. I fought ghosts, and destroyed something ageless, and fell into another world. I waded through blood and bodies to find you." My eyes squeeze shut against the memories. "They came when I needed them the most. They saved me and gave me a chance, and I lost it."

"For Kiv's sake, Lys, stop." He tries to roll onto his elbow to look down at me, but falls back. "*Fuck.*"

I sit up instead, and brush the hair from his face. "I really wouldn't try that. I don't know if you noticed, but you've been in better shape."

He glares at me before taking my hand in his. "You are one woman. Magic or not, you are one person. Not four. Not invincible or immortal. We got out alive because of you. I am alive because of you. Not Rend. Not Vi. You." He looks me over, and nudges me to turn so he can see my back. "And you are hurt," he says, sternly. I'm grateful he can't see my leg under the covers. "You were a village physician weeks ago, not a warrior. You have done more than anyone could have asked for from Kiv herself, and you have done it well. So stop. We will deal with the situation as it is now. You cannot keep going thinking *any* of this is your fault. It will make you reckless."

That makes me snort, even though I don't think he was trying to be funny. "First of all, I'm an apothecary, not a physician. And secondly, you're the last person who should be calling me reckless, Your Highness."

"I am the best person to call you reckless, it is my specialty, after all," he huffs a strained laugh, and I settle back into him, this time with his arm around me and my head resting on his chest.

"Does this hurt too much?"

Another breathy laugh, "Everything hurts more than I have ever hurt in my life, and I have a considerable amount of experience to compare it to. At least this time I have you." He tilts his head down to kiss my hair, and I trace my fingers along the cage of branches holding his body together. He sighs and melts back into the pillows. "Is Carolyn going to be alright?"

I lift my head to search for her, but don't see her curled in the chair she occupied. "She must have gone below. She's pretty cut up, but nothing life threatening."

"I am glad." The brushing of his fingers against my arm slows as he drifts off again. "I would have been unable to forgive myself if anything had happened to her."

"And you tell me to not blame myself?"

He's asleep before I finish speaking.

—

The next time my eyelids flutter open, it's to dramatic whispering coming from the direction of the door.

"Just ring a bell next time, folks," I groan and peel myself away from the mutually sweaty embrace between the prince and me.

"Oh good, you're awake," Rend chimes, striding into the room, ducking beneath the low door. Cenna, Envir, Jyn, and Carolyn all spill in after her, crowding the small space, but also bringing a wide grin to my face. "Did His Highness make it, or do you have something for me to add to the altar?" She's smiling, knowing I wouldn't be smiling back if I'd been sleeping on a corpse.

"I have not died quite yet, despite my best efforts," the prince mumbles tiredly. He tries to sit, so I slip my arm around him, shifting pillows and helping him up. His arm wraps around me tightly before I can pull away.

"Excellent news, Your Highness. I would've been out of a job if you had your way," Envir says, sitting on the desk, his arms around Jyn, who is leaning on the edge in front of him.

Carolyn curls into the armchair again, looking tired and pale, but alert. The most jarring aspect of her appearance is the fact that she's wearing some of Rend's spare clothes instead of her robes. I don't know if I've ever seen her in anything but white.

Rend and Cenna slide onto the other side of the bed, sitting at the foot of it.

"We figured it was our turn to do something useful," Envir starts, his chin on Jyn's shoulder, smiling stupidly at Kedren and I, "So we put all of our heads together, and we think we made a plan."

"While you slept. *Allegedly*." Rend winks dramatically at us and the silver ring in one eyebrow glints in the soft light. I roll my eyes, but Kedren laughs.

"I am incredibly honored that you think I am capable of anything *but* sleep right now."

"I'm incredibly impressed you are able to breathe right now, so honestly, I'd believe you are capable of just about anything." She smirks at me. "And Lys can be *very* gentle."

My cheeks grow warm, and I want to kick her, but I know it would hurt me more. Memories of the two of us not sleeping in this very bed flare to life. I shove them back into the box they belong in before I ignite with embarrassment, lust, jealousy, indignation, shame, or a combination of all of the above. Kedren's arm tightens around me, and I hope he can't feel my racing heart.

I clear my throat with unnecessary force, "Anyway. About that plan you're all so proud of?"

"Right," Rend says, twirling a lock of Cenna's hair, who drapes over her like a possessive cat that stares at me with gleaming green-gold eyes. "Before His Highness needs another...nap."

My urge to throw something at her must be written all over my face because she laughs harder.

"Our biggest problem is that we don't know for certain if Daralyn is still going to the North, or if her plans have changed after your meeting." Jyn's calm, reasonable voice slides in under Rend's loud cackling, returning order to the congregation. "So we have decided it's best to split our forces. For that reason, and for your safety, we thought it would be best if you two were," he hesitates, eyeing Kedren particularly, "Elsewhere."

"And," Rend takes over again, "you have passage through the Goddess Gate. It doesn't buy entrance for many people, though, so the less of us that plan to land on Alsairdian soil the better."

"The Goddess Gate?" I ask curiously.

"The coin on your necklace," she sighs, "Of course those cryptic bastards didn't explain it. I don't know how they work, I just know how to use them and what they do. They get you to the Edantai's private harbor, the safest place to dock in that whole country. Toss it into the water at the right spot, and we'll be good to go." She smiles again, running her fingers absently through Cenna's hair, giving Kedren a wry look. "And to save us all some trouble, I'll be depositing both you and His Highness on that shore. I have no desire to have to keep him tied down in my quarters, and we came to the unanimous conclusion that would be the only way to keep him away from you. Grievously injured or not."

Envir snorts, and it isn't entirely with good humor.

"I cannot say you are wrong, or that tying me down would be enough. I would not tolerate being an entire continent away from her." The prince's hand slides up my arm as he speaks.

Jyn, of all people, smiles knowingly at Kedren, and his hand on Envir's arm tightens briefly.

"I will also be staying in Alsairdia with the two of you," Carolyn's rich voice wafts to me from her corner of the room. "Someone needs to watch over you, and I am also too curious to stay away. I never imagined having an opportunity to learn about this land."

"And I will be making the long overdue journey to visit my esteemed father with the rest of them," Rend groans, gesturing to the others.

"What does Oran have to do with any of this?" Curiosity is replaced with confusion.

"Right, I guess that hasn't actually come up has it?" she laughs, a little nervously. "What's my full name, Lys?"

"Sybella Vangariad Rend?"

"What's the name of Ardjan's King?"

I stop to think, trying to remember what that man's name is. Ayamar's politics barely register for me, and Ardjan is even further outside of my notice. The name of their King is not really on the tip of my tongue.

The prince makes a strange, choking sound, however, and answers for me.

"Vangariad Renvald."

"Correct. And I'm named after my father. My actual father." She spreads her arms out wide, dramatically. "May I introduce you to the bastard daughter of King Vangariad Renvald of Ardjan?"

I actually throw a pillow at her this time.

"Excuse me?" I ask shrilly. I try to modulate my tone but it's no good. At least I manage not to yell. "Have you known this this whole time? I've known you for over half of my life, and this is just now coming up?" I thought I knew everything about her.

"Well, it wasn't relevant until now." She at least has the good sense to appear abashed. "Oran Rend is my father as far as I'm concerned, but the King and I know of the other's existence and always have. Cenna will likely need some muscle in her corner to get that lot of snow-mad hooligans to listen to reason. I happen to be particularly well-suited muscle for this occasion."

The cat-like princess' lilting voice rolls over Rend's smoothly, deftly taking control of the conversation. "We intend to keep them from falling into the trap of war Daralyn is planning. Water willing," she pauses dramatically while I gape at them in stunned, incredulous silence. "And we plan to find the third relic."

Her perfectly bowed lips curve into a devious little smile, her revelation distracting me from Rend's.

"The third relic? What about the second? What do you know about them?" I ask sharply.

"More than you," She isn't overtly rude, but a flicker of temper rises in me all the same. "Like exactly where the second is, and general knowledge about the third. According to Carolyn, we know essentially the same about how they were made, and when they were taken home."

"Where is the second?" Kedren asks slowly, sleep already over-taking him again.

Cenna removes the golden circlet from her hair and slides her fingers across the delicate, embossed details at its center. A piece of it falls away with a click, revealing a deep blue gemstone glowing with the light of roiling flame.

"Here," she smiles again, this time ruefully. "You were not the only one keeping secrets, Kedren."

His arm around me twitches as he reaches to cover himself, even though hardly any of his scars are visible through bandages and the creeping network of roots. Everyone has seen them now anyway, and he knows it, but his instinct to keep himself hidden is strong. I wrap my arms around his and squeeze. Canopy Above, I want to strip the skin from Daralyn for making him live with this fabricated shame, and my ill will towards Cenna raises another notch for acknowledging them.

"The crown has been in my family since it was returned after the issues over here were resolved. We keep the the Heart of the Sea safe within the Empire." I open my mouth to interrupt, but she continues without hesitation. "And yes, I had my suspicions of what your vial was, but I cannot manipulate it anymore than you could mine. Besides, it looks like you figured it out just fine. The third relic is made from the essence of fire from the northern mountains, so that is where we will look after or during peacekeeping with Rend's hooligans."

Knowing where the relics are, and already having one of them, is incredible. Knowing I'm not going to be the one looking for the last fills me with guilty relief. "Well, its nice to finally wake up to some good news, for once." I stretch out my aching leg, aware of the fact that I really need to do something about it sooner rather than later. "How long until this plan unfolds, and can I eat before then?" I don't remember the last time I ate, and my stomach aches with it. Everyone laughs, and I'm grateful for the break in the dourness.

"It will take three more days, give or take. You've already been asleep for nearly two." Rend disentangles herself from Cenna and acrobatically rolls backwards off of the bed. "And yes, we can all eat. I'll see what's ready."

I scramble inelegantly after her, having to sternly detach the prince's hold on me. "I can help. I need to move a little."

"You really don't have to, Lys, you look awful." Rend raises a critical eyebrow in my direction and chews on one of the rings in her lip.

"Thank you. But really, I'll feel better once I get up," I say. I'll also feel better once I clean the holes out in my leg, but I leave that part out. As it is, I hide a stumble when I put too much weight on it, turning it into an awkward lurch to catch myself with an arm around Rend's shoulder. "Let's go."

CHAPTER FORTY-SIX

ALYSSIA

"So, how bad is it?"

Rend and I sit side by side on a bench on the mess deck while I try to soak the crusted fabric off of my skin with hot water. A jar of suture silk stands ready at my elbow.

"I honestly don't know, I was a little busy at the time," I hiss out as I peel the crusted fabric from my skin, trying to inspect the damage in the dim light. Frustration and irritation wash over me despite the fact that I made sure to eat something before I started. Usually that helps more. I lower my leg back down and scrub at my face.

"It seems like you've been busy for a while." She wraps an arm around my shoulders, pulling me close despite my feeble protest. "Carolyn caught me up, for the most part, when we were coming up with the plan." She rests her head against mine. I breathe in her familiar scent and wish we could go curl up in her bed together like we used to. "I'm so sorry, my dearest. You know if there was anything else I could do for you, I'd do it. I will do it. I'm so sorry I was gone so long this time. If I had been here..."

I shake my head under hers, cutting her off. "No more what-if's from any of us. Including me. It gets none of us anywhere except worse off than where we already are." I take a knife from the table to the pantleg just above the first rake of claws and cut it off. There's no point putting the extra effort into working around it.

"Fire and Sea, Lys. Is that *moss*?"

"It does appear to be, yes." I blink dumbly at the three long cuts across my thigh, running my fingers over the soft, fuzzy green I thought was dirty, dried blood.

"What in the fuck is it doing there?"

"You know, I have absolutely no idea." With a sense of surreal curiosity, I twist my calf into view, and sure enough, matching tufts of mossy green peek out from both sides of the through-and-through hole in the meat of the muscle.

"How do you not know?" Her clipped, awed horror is unusually funny to me as I pick at the resident moss.

"I just don't. There were a few instances where I sort of lost touch with the world at large. It's a reasonable assumption it creeped in during one of those."

Absolutely fascinating.

"Should you do something about it?"

"Oh, most definitely. Magical mystery moss or not, those all need to be closed. I'm not waiting for that mess to come together on its own." I start picking at it, matted clumps of it coming off in blood-clotted pieces. It hurts. "And I am going to need you to distract me while I do it, because, Canopy Above, it does not feel great."

"But you ignored it up until now? There is a hole straight through you, and there is a plant growing in it," She says so incredulously, I laugh.

"It's been a long few weeks, Rend. I've gotten really good at ignoring things." I breathe hard between clenched teeth as I pick clean the second laceration.

She sits in silence for longer than I would like before leaning back against the edge of the table, her knees spread wide.

"Do you remember the day I got the *Lady*?"

I look over my shoulder and catch her staring at the ceiling, hands behind her head.

"I remember the general concept of it, and it involving a lot of Kyla's not-so greatest work."

"There was quite a lot of that, yes," she sighs, looking down at me with a sad smile. "Do you remember how excited we were? Both of us?"

"Of course I remember. Your own ship? How could I forget what that felt like?"

"I got her for us, Lys."

I rip a large sheet of the moss with one startled jerk and curse loudly. Taking a deep breath, I focus extra hard on removing all of the little pieces, taking the excuse to not look at her. "Why? And why didn't you tell me?"

"I always thought if I had my own ship, my own crew, you would be a part of it. Come on as the ship physician, learn to really be a sailor. Be with me." She pauses, but I don't dare look back at her. "I think I did tell you that night, but I can't be sure if it was real or if I've imagined it so many times I remember it as a memory. I have a lot of pride, Lys, too much to beg."

"I thought you always asked me to stay just to be cute. I thought you knew I couldn't leave my work, and that I was only running away with you because I knew I wouldn't have the time soon," I say quietly as I focus on my task, almost preferring the tearing pain of it over the conversation.

"You never asked me to stay with you."

The uncharacteristic hurt in her voice is enough to drag my eyes up to hers.

"What would have been the point, Rend?" I sigh and stop fiddling with my leg. "You wouldn't have stayed, and if you had, you would've been miserable. Why would I ask you to make that choice? You belong to the sea, just like I belong to the Woods. I've known that our whole lives."

"Will you ask him to stay?"

I blink at her, waiting for a smirk to bely the joke, but she remains serious. "Rend, I'm in the middle of planning a murderous coup against the princess. If I succeed, he's going to be King."

"And when he asks you to stay with him?"

"I would tell him no. I don't belong there." I go back to cleaning out the moss, moving to the hole in my calf, trying not to think too hard as I push the bits of it through the other side. "Besides," I groan as I catch a chipped nail against the wet inside of the wound. "He would need heirs, Rend."

Even if I was younger, I haven't had my courses since I was a teenager. Overdosing on every contraceptive remedy, poison, or preventative I knew about after the first time I had sex with a man took that option from me. That was long before I knew enough about anything to have the kind of knowledge I had or the access to the things I had access to. Oh, to be young, and so very stupid again. I shake my head and start washing the wounds to stop my mind from turning to Inness.

"Lys." The apology in her voice makes me cringe.

"Don't. You know I made my peace with that a long time ago." I tip the alcohol from the suture jar over the open wounds to out the rest of the moss and try not to scream. "What are you going to do if Cenna asks you to stay?"

"You know as well as I, that won't come up." She grips my shoulder to steady me before I start stitching. "But like you said, I belong to the sea, and she will be an empress. That's an even more unlikely pairing than you and a king."

"I don't know, the Empress and the Pirate Queen? It has a certain ring to it."

She snorts derisively.

I pinch the first cut closed as neatly as I can and start to sew.

"It isn't the prince's name, but I do have someone to add to your altar." A significantly less personally heartbreaking subject change seems like the most prudent way to avoid an emotionally, and physically, painful silence. "Envir's little sister, Laenry of the Wild Seas." Her hand squeezes my shoulder as I bite my lip against the sharp, pricking pain of my needle. "He said she would've loved my Woods, but she was a child of the sea. I think she belongs here, with you."

"Consider it done. I didn't know there was a second D'luane brat. It will be good to have her here."

"You can show him the shrine, and learn more about her on the way north," I suggest, quiet again, torn between enduring the work on my leg in silence, or talking about a subject that hurts even worse: leaving her. Again, and again, and again.

"I don't love leaving you down here alone." The *without me* remains unspoken, but I hear it in her pause. "But I'm going to do my best to make up for not being there for you. I'm going to try to fix this before it has time to become your problem again." With a final squeeze of my shoulder, she stands, not letting me reply. "Do you want me to deal with the crowd in the room while you finish up and take a minute?"

"Please, and thank you. For everything." I laugh unexpectedly, pulling the spider silk through my leg.

She pauses in gathering the meal we promised everyone else ages ago. "What?"

"Everything. This is all so stupid, and backwards, and out of control.

Everything is just so wrong. There was moss growing in my leg, and I didn't even notice. I let an insane person have a weapon that can possibly devastate entire towns to save a man I met a month ago. I'm about to land on the beach of a country who hasn't been seen by the outside world in centuries." I laugh again, looping another translucent suture. "What am I supposed to do, except laugh?"

I bury my face in one hand while the other holds my flesh together by a literal thread.

"We just keep going, Lys. As we always do." She kisses the top of my head. "Take whatever time you need."

My leg comes together in neat rows of stitches while Rend disappears up the steep steps to the main deck.

The stairs hurt when I finally limp my way up them, but I make my way to the quarterdeck with minimal, mumbled cursing. The white froth of the waves mirror the churning of my thoughts. I lean against the rail of the ship and stare into the water.

"Lys?" It's Carolyn, anachronistic clothing and disheveled black hair be damned, it's her. Bloodied and exhausted, just as I am, but alive. Here. With me. "Do you want to be alone?"

"Not without you." I open my arms and wave her over. "I'm so sorry, Carolyn."

"It was my choice. I knew what I was no longer capable of," she says with the smallest of shrugs. "Besides, I am sure the nightmares will stop one day." Sliding into my embrace, she rests her head on my shoulder.

"Physically, are you alright?"

"I am. I do not know how, but I am." She sighs, melting into me further. "Or at least, I will be."

"I think it was Kiv, or whatever it is you have always called her power. Something protected you from a knife to the heart. I didn't see it clearly, but I do know that."

She frowns at the horizon. "Perhaps. Perhaps it was something else entirely. Either way, I am here today. Despite everything, or perhaps because of it, we are still here to protect the world from what is to come."

"We will. I'll feel her last breath for what she and her people have done to me and mine. I won't let that go."

"I will not be taken again. Helpless and emptied of everything I am. I will not."

"I know." My leg aches, and I'm tired and unsteady, but the ocean air and Carolyn at my side does wonders towards reviving me, "No matter what happens, I'll be there for you. We'll do this together."

"I know." Her arms squeeze tighter, and I let her familiar touch wash over me. Thoughts of Rend, our lives before this, and the quiet peace I had carved out for myself tumble around like the waves.

I don't know how long we stand, leaning against the railing of the *Lady*, arms tight around each others waists, but eventually I sigh and tilt my head to speak, "Will you really be alright?"

"Will you?"

"Do we really have a choice?"

Her head nestles into my shoulder. "No. I do not think we do." A breath. Two. "We will be what we need to be, Lys. For everyone."

I want to ask about what we need, but I know that doesn't matter for us. It never has before.

She pulls back slowly, brushing my cheek as always, a small lift to the corner of her mouth. "We should both get some rest. Who knows when our next chance may be?"

"You aren't wrong." I pry myself off the rail after her and follow, limping down the steps to the main deck.

I watch her disappear below, leaning against the door to Rend's room, not wanting to turn my back on her ever again. When the top of her head vanishes, I slide into the dim room like a thief, not wanting to wake the prince if he's sleeping like he should be.

The murky silhouette of Envir, sitting hunched over on the edge of Rend's desk, feet on her chair, startles me. The sliver of bright sunlight from the open door catches his attention, and he turns to me briefly before returning to stare at the bed. Slipping around the desk, I rest my hand on his shoulder. He covers it with his.

"I hate having to choose," he whispers. "But I can't leave Jyn. Not like this. Not now. I don't know enough to feel like he would be safe without me. I can't live like that." His fingers tighten around mine. "But how am I supposed to leave him? I have *never* left him. And the last two times he's slipped away, he's almost been killed." His free hand curls into a fist. "I thought he was dead this time. I can't live with that thought, either."

"I know." My grip on his shoulder tightens. "I didn't believe you when you said he was alive."

He pulls me around to face him, taking both of my hands in his. His eyes are red, but dry, and they capture mine in a startlingly intense gaze. "I'm trusting him to you, Lys. You are the only person I have ever even considered saying that to. I need you to know how important that is. How important *he* is."

I want to pull away, look anywhere else but into his eyes that shine like Cenna's relic. I want to flee while shouting over my shoulder that I can't promise to keep him safe, that I have no idea what I'm doing. I'm only one person who has fallen into a world she knows nothing about, and I can't be held responsible for anything, let alone him.

But none of that is precisely true, and I know it.

I know nothing *but* helping people. It has been my entire life since I was ten. The only difference now is the scale.

"I will do everything in my power, and more, to keep him safe, Vi. I will fix this." I try to smile encouragingly and squeeze his hands. "Fixing things is what I do."

He jumps down from the desk and pulls me into an embrace so tight my ribs creak.

I don't flinch from the sharp pain that radiates from my myriad of bruises. I hug him back, even tighter, until he releases me.

"I owe you everything," he whispers.

"You owe me nothing. All of us are in this together now. We're all just doing what we can."

"Thank you, Lys." He kisses my forehead softly and slips out of the room.

I'm left alone with a sleeping, broken, prince who has confessed his love to me in the twilight-dim bedroom of my past love, on a ship traveling to a land I know nothing about while I'm full of cracked ribs and stitched up holes.

By the Trees, I'm tired.

I sway with the rocking of the ship as I make my way to the bed, crawling onto it from the side furthest from him, trying not to disturb his sleep. He reaches out for me anyways, tugging at my arm until I'm close enough to feel the heat of his body. It guides me like the draw of the stars when you are lost at sea, and I give into it. I curl against him, mindful of his injuries, but less so than I should be. I wrap one arm around his waist, tucking myself into the embrace of his good arm, my cheek resting against his chest once more.

He kisses the top of my head, and his body relaxes under mine. "Thank you."

"For what, Your Highness?"

"Giving Vi what he needed to let go. He needs to be with Jyn instead of always picking up after me." His thumb trails across my arm, light and slow. "He deserves the break, and you have no need to feel beholden to your promise, either. I know you did not ask for any of this, and I will not add to your burden. You do not have to take care of me."

If I was the tiniest bit less tired, I would pull away and glare at him, but I'm too comfortable be bothered. I give him the smallest pinch at the crest of his hip instead. "It's far too late for you to stop being my burden now. And I didn't ask for any of this, but it was given to me so I won't run from it."

I won't run from you.

I almost let it slip, but I bite my lip against the words.

"You truly are a goddess that this world does not deserve. That I do not."

"Go to sleep before I kick you in an attempt to bring you to your senses."

He shakes with silent laughter but doesn't respond.

CHAPTER
FORTY-SEVEN
ALYSSIA

"Alyssia."

I stop rummaging through the spare clothes Rend provided to look over my shoulder at the prince, who is frowning and struggling to pull himself up.

"Yes?" I ask, annoyingly innocent.

"Stop that. What happened? Are you alright?"

Snorting, I turn back to picking clothes for us to wear. "I'm fine."

"What happened, Alyssia?"

His clipped, demanding tone causes my already brewing irritation to boil over. Nearly three days of sleeping and watching him suffer in the cramped quarters has me more than on edge. His new found attitude, while significantly more deserved than mine, has me ready to start screaming.

I kick through the mess I've made on the floor to pick the bear helm out of the pile of discarded armor, and toss it onto the bed.

"That's what happened." I yelp in surprise and throw out a hand to steady myself as the ship rolls unexpectedly.

I don't elaborate, and he doesn't say anything. He turns the helm around in his good hand, pausing when he sees the gouges taken out of the wood. I go back to the pile of clothing and peel myself out of the remains of my cut apart trousers. Somehow I had avoided him seeing the angry red gashes down my leg until now, but my luck ran out. I replace the pants as fast as I can with a pair of the wide-legged trousers many of Rend's crew wear in a violent shade of burnt orange. A loose, sleeveless shirt in undyed linen gets thrown on over my head to hide the bruises on my back before I steel myself to approach the prince, a nearly identical pair of pants in a deep, blood red draped over my arm.

"I learned what power is, and what it can do," I say flatly as I tear back the covers and begin dressing him, ignoring his protests. "It took awhile, but I got the point eventually."

Despite my irritation, I dress him carefully, trying my hardest to not cause him any unnecessary pain. When I'm done, I turn to the board he was carried in on at the remaining pieces of armor. I pick up the board to get it ready for him to be moved again.

"No." Kedren's voice startles me. "I will not be carried out of here. Not while I am conscious and capable."

The dumbest, open-mouthed gape splits my face. "You and I have vastly different concepts of capable."

"A crutch or a cane will be fine," he says with an unusually imperious lilt of command. His good leg is drawn up and the helm balances on his knee. He's still frowning at it. He continues darkly, "I know what my limits are."

For some reason, I don't think he's talking about physical limitations.

As much as I would love to continue arguing until I say something I would sincerely regret, I roll my eyes and mutter, "Fine."

Manipulating the wood and bone comes easier again now that I'm not so exhausted. Embracing the the flame is calming and I breathe easier as I sit with the materials from my Woods. The crutch for His Royal Pain in my Ass is simple and quick. I toss it aside with a sharp snort and go back to working. I take my time making the armor this go-around. I put my frustration, uncertainty, and restlessness into its creation.

I'm tired but infinitely less annoyed when I finish. The new pieces laid out before me still glitter with small rivulets of green fire running through the lines of bark, and they are as beautiful as the first were utilitarian. The bark itself makes patterns of flowers and vines, the forms of small bears hidden within the swirling lines. The only thing that remains unchanged is the helmet, still resting on the prince's knee. That I leave as it is, gouges and all.

The door opens as I stand, fighting back a groan so the prince doesn't start his admonishments again.

"Alyssia, Rend wants you." Envir's auburn hair glints bright and coppery in the morning sun shining behind him.

"Perfect. Have fun with that." I jerk my head toward the prince before swiping my helmet from his knee and picking up the rest of my armor by the awkward armful.

Envir starts shouting just as I close the door behind me.

"Trouble in paradise?" Rend calls down from the quarterdeck, and I glare up at her.

"How would I know? When's the last time I was in paradise?" I haul myself and the ungainly pile of armor up the steps to her, and drop them in a heap I can trap against the rail with my shins. "Did you actually need me, or were you rescuing me?"

She nods to the starboard bow just as the ship lists to port, opening the view to land. My eyes widen, and I lean eagerly against the rail like it could help me get a better view. Sheer cliffs crowned in rich green crumble to rocky seas and soar to distant, tiered heights as far as I can see. They are broken only by the rapidly resolving form of a woman's head carved into the cliff, er mouth gaping wide. Trailing up and behind her is a series of similarly massive stone heads, each with open mouths spilling white-laced waterfalls from terraced cliff walls painted with the deep green of clinging plants. The first is some kind of large cat, the second is too distant to make out details.

"We approach the Goddess Gate." She smiles a wide, excited smile and strands of her black and white hair whip around her face. "I need the coin, and I thought you may want to see it before we got too close."

"What? I don't see any docks." I still hang over the rail, marveling at the mossy, vine-covered, sculptures, my armor forgotten at my feet.

"Why would I ruin the surprise? Just get the coin off of your necklace. We have a good wind, and it will be time to pay the toll soon enough."

The closer we get, the more I can see, and the more cowed by their size I become. Blooms of brilliant color cling to the statues in tangled, flowering masses. The detail carved into the stone is breathtaking and so realistic it's as if a giantess simply settled in for a bath in the sea mid yawn, the ridges of her delicate eyebrows becoming homes to falls of creeping foliage and strange, colorful birds. Reluctantly, I look away from the masterpiece coming into focus so I can remove my necklace and begin working at the twine knotted through the coin's square center.

Wearing it constantly through water and battles and everything else that has happened has matted the fibers of the string together. I pick at it with increasing annoyance. Staring at my hands for so long makes me grimace. Dirty, broken, peeling nails expose raw nail beds. Cuts, bruises and red, cracked skin mar my already age-worn hands. So steady and sure in my practice, they shake against the twine. *Canopy Above.* I'm tired. I'm scared out of my damn mind, and I have never been further out of my depth.

Good thing I know how to swim.

The knot finally comes free as I tear at it with renewed determination, and I slide the coin free, tossing it to Rend. "Sorry, we've been through a lot together. Didn't want to let go, apparently."

"I figured. I could've helped, but it seemed like you two needed a chance to say goodbye." She winks and flicks the coin into the air. The dull black metal absorbs the light instead of reflecting it before being snatched back by Rend's quick hand.

"Finish getting dressed and come up to the forecastle with me." She flips the coin again as she skips down the steps and melts into her crew amidships, clapping shoulders and pointing out slack where there should be none, or vice versa; small adjustments that ease the ship toward the open mouth of the stone passage.

I follow her advice and start sliding armor on. I make small adjustments to the wood as I settle the pieces over my body like it's already second nature. It's seamless and beautiful. Roots twist across my chest and back, attaching pauldrons decorated with claws to the breastplate with flexible tendons of new growth. Ribs slash across my own, the smallest of hers wrapping around my whole torso. The fit is perfect, the material is light, and my body hums with the resonance of the fire coursing through it. I feel strong and terrifying, despite everything, and I haven't even settled the fearsome helm onto my head yet.

Keeping that in hand, I trail after Rend, my new-found fierceness faltering slightly as my leg almost gives out on the stairs. I climb up to the forecastle with most of my dignity intact and join her at the bow, ducking around the forestay sail.

"You look good in armor. Avenging apothecary suits you."

She grins, and I roll my eyes, but her praise pleases me as it always does. I regain some of the pride my limping stride took from me.

"I would have rather not had to find that out about myself, but I'll take what I can get right now." I pop my foot up to take weight off and lean over the rail. "So, what are we waiting for?"

"We need to be fully within the gate before we toss the coin into the water. Then the fun begins."

The wait isn't a long one.

Sailing through the statue's open mouth is surreal. The ship feels small, swallowed by the cavernous size of the gate, plunged into the twilight darkness of light reflected from water. Teeth hang above us like stalactites. I'm struck by the detail. They are not straight, ideal approximations of teeth. I can see the slight unevenness where one massive canine sits too close to its neighbor. The ridges of the roof of her mouth are waves of shadow, and beneath us in the clear, blue-green water, more darkened shapes hint at the existence of her lower jaw. The tunnel of her oral cavity concentrates the wind, and the sails of the Lady snap sharply before the crew can respond and trim them accordingly. The ship shudders with increased speed, and we burst into the bright sunlight of a narrow, cliff-walled bay headed by a roaring waterfall.

The moment the bowsprit touches sunlight, Rend hurls the small, dark coin as hard as she can over the water, its tiny splash barely perceptible as it sinks beneath the surface.

The roar that follows is deafening.

Water surges aft-ward and the ship raises on the wave as the massive mouth behind us *begins to close*. I tighten my grip on the rail and swing my head wildly from side to side, but the crew of The Lady are undisturbed, manning their lines and posts as normal. Traces of sea life and salt stain the cliffs around us. This is meant to happen. But it happens so quickly.

We race up the waterfall, and the change in elevation makes me nauseous, my stomach trying to stay at sea level, but I can't look away. Rend plunges into the thick of things, shouting orders so fast I can't follow them, but the ship stays steady, fighting the current and the wind to stay far enough away from the sides of the narrow channel. The screaming mouth of a massive wild cat looms over us, spewing the water that draws us ever closer to its uncannily real teeth.

"What in the absolute hell?"

Envir pops up from behind a sail. I add a louder curse to the litany of lesser ones pouring out of my mouth.

"The Goddess Gate, apparently," Cenna purrs while ducking out from behind a sail. "It's a lock," she continues, leaning casually against the rail despite its heaving. "Albeit, on a much larger scale than I have seen before. We use them in the canals in Ecadaes."

Even her cool, unflappable demeanor slips as the ship surges closer to the second gate, individual strands of the cat's fur standing out in algae-coated relief.

I've never questioned Rend's ability to sail a ship, but the wild rocking of conflicting wind and current and the rapidly approaching second gate, narrower than the first, has my knuckles white against my ragged skin.

"D'luane! If your landlocked ass still knows how to work a line, get down here!" Rend's shout breaks through the noise, and Envir doesn't hesitate. He shoves his sleeves past his elbows and leaps down to the main deck, running to the ropes she points to.

I can't decide if I want to stay above and watch us crash into the massive statue, or if I want to go hide somewhere down in the hold where I may as well be the first to drown when we smash to bits.

Morbid curiosity wins the day, but I at least move from the bowsprit and its sails, staying as far out of the way as I can. Cenna retreats more fully and disappears into Rend's quarters. A smug little smile playing across my lips until, that is, another rumbling, grinding sound splits the air and shakes the ship.

The jaws of the cat's head are collapsing together. Canines pierce the water's surface in a slow and ominous crawl upwards. The opening narrows with every passing breath. I can't see how we will be fast enough to clear the barring presence of the lower jaw.

"Any time now, Cenna," Rend shouts over the noise of the gate closing.

I turn when I hear her.

The stern erupts in a column of pure blue fire, spiraling upward in an intricate dance before plunging into the water. Where I expect steam, sprays of swelling waves crash against the hull. The ship jumps forward, picking up speed faster than any wind could account for.

Rend is shoulder to shoulder with her helmsman, both of them heaving the wheel against the clashing currents, keeping the ship as straight as they can as we careen through the gate.

"Clew the main sail. Cenna, slow us down."

Blue fire burns along the gold of Cenna's crown. It flows around her like silk. It licks at the edges of the waves around us. She moves with slow, deliberate grace and the sea obeys her.

I turn back to see what fresh horror awaits through the second gate, and I'm not disappointed. The next section of the lock is narrower than the first, like the gate itself, and the water rises in rushing waves around the stone bodies of towering, robed women, their smooth gray hands flung skyward in praise, or pleading, as the waterline creeps steadily upward. The swirling of their robes and their faces of open-mouthed worship turn desperate as the water rises swiftly to consume them. Just like the gates, these statues unsettle me in their perfect imperfections. Life frozen in stone.

I want to reach for them and take their over-sized hands in my own to save them from this fate they have suffered so many times before. The fear in their eyes reflects in my own as I suddenly shake at the memory of being lost in that same dark embrace.

A wave laced with blue fire breaks against the hull. It flings me back as the ship barely escapes the reaching grasp of one of those stone hands. Another wave of fire and sea crashes over the port side. The tack of the ship corrects itself, angling its way safely through the drowning statues and toward the third gate.

Narrower still, I'm not sure if the *Lady* will fit between its viscous fangs. Long and thin, they trail from the upper jaw until they split the rushing fall of water.

It's a snake. The fangs protrude from the slim, angular head of the deadly reptile, stone scales smooth and glistening with algae. Its beady eyes burn with white-purple light from beneath ridged brows. I scramble back, slipping on the wet deck, away from its waiting maw, afraid that it's about to slither free of the cliff to swallow us whole.

It stays firmly sealed within the stone as we rise inexorably toward it. The ship is fully wreathed in the swirling blue fire now. Sails, rudder, and magic all work in concert to keep us centered. I don't breathe as we barrel into the shadowed cavern of the snake's mouth. The hull of the *Lady* passes so closely between the stone fangs that I could reach out and touch them if I was foolish enough.

I'm on my ass on the deck, panting and fighting a burbling, hysterical laugh from escaping, staring up at stone venom sacs as we pass through the gate and into the sun. The rumbling of the stone closing behind me is nothing but a buzz vibrating through the rush.

It's the smallest gate and the last.

Walls of lush, deep green jungle create a perfect, small basin that fills with just enough of the water crashing against the closing stone to send the ship drifting into a still lagoon nestled between two branches of the mighty river that feeds the treacherous Goddess Gate. A massive structure of stone and the same strange black metal of the coin spans the entire lagoon and both sides of the river, connecting each bank to an elaborate, if small, man-made harbor complete with docks suitable for ships even larger than Rend's. Although how they would make it in here is beyond me.

As suddenly as the chaos began, everything is calm again. Not still, but no longer frantic. The crew readies the ship to dock, trimming sails and whatnot, but the liquid fire has vanished. The spray of magical waves has dried in patches of flaking salt across my wooden armor. The grinding of stone has quieted, and Envir stands above me, hand outstretched, shirt soaked in sea and sweat, a smile plastered on his face. His eyes still burn with excitement.

I take his hand, hot and rough with rope burns, and pull myself to my feet.

"I'm not sure I would be going back that way if you told me it would solve every single one of my problems immediately," I wheeze, the fall to the deck making the muscles around my bruised ribs clench tight.

He laughs, not letting go of my hand until he knows I'm steady. "You could have stayed below deck. I'm not sure the ride would have been much smoother, but at least you wouldn't have almost fallen overboard."

"Next time I'll be sure to do just that," I huff and scoop my helmet out of a tangle of ropes it lodged itself in. "And I didn't almost fall overboard. I fell backwards, the opposite of over."

He makes a mocking sound of agreement before skipping back down to midships to look for more sailing excitement, but the excitement has dulled into ordered maneuvers as the *Lady* sails close enough to the dock to throw out heaving lines to waiting dockhands.

"Are you ready?" Disheveled and sweaty, but just as flushed with excitement as Envir, Rend is at my side again, watching the procedures out of the corner of her eye.

"Not particularly, considering I have no notion of what to be ready for." I shrug, the claws on my pauldron waving up and down in a way that makes both Rend and I snort with laughter.

"Nice, *paw-ldrons* you have there," Rend cackles between laughs, sending us both further into fits of giggling.

As the gangplank touches the dock, she throws her arms around me, lifting me from the ground in an embrace so tight I swear I can hear the armor creak. Our laughter dies.

"We will find each other again soon, my heart," she murmurs into my ear before setting me down.

Leading me by the hand, she takes me to the main deck where Carolyn waits, dressed in all black, her white bag slung across her chest. Her fists are clenched at her sides, and her mouth is a thin line. Her sleeveless shirt shows the stark white of bandages covering her forearms with more hidden beneath the fabric, but she still stands tall and strong. Determined. Ready. A swell of confidence fills me at the sight of her. The earth may shake beneath us, but our foundation will not falter as long as we still stand.

Beyond her, moving mostly under his own power despite everything, stands the prince with Envir at his back. I want to stay mad at him, but my resolve crumbles as he pauses to dip low and push a lock of his hair behind his ear without letting go of the crutch he rests against.

An irrational compulsion to run to him engulfs me, but my hand still entwined with Rend's holds me back. My time to hold on to her has long since passed, but I never could let her go. Not really. Being back on the *Lady* and having her within my grasp makes it even harder than when I'm alone and merely dreaming. It's impossible, really, but a flash of Cenna's hair streaming behind her in waves as wild as the sea sends a sharp knife through my heart.

I bring Rend's knuckles to my lips and kiss them fiercely. When I raise my head, her smile holds the same realization as mine. No words are needed when she squeezes my fingers one last time and steps back. Our hands separate slowly, one finger at a time.

There is no point in looking back. She will always be there for me when I need her, as I will be for her. Where I need to be now, however, is in front of me, not behind.

I don't run to him, but I do walk rather quickly.

The prince and I speak over each other when I reach him, our bodies as close as they can be without touching.

"I'm sorry."

"I am sorry."

We both smile. I see my own relief reflected in him. I want to ask if he's alright or if he needs help, but I nod at the gangplank instead.

"May as well get it over with," I sigh.

I begin to step to the side, but he leans down. I stop and tilt my mouth to his. Our dry, cracked lips, still tasting of iron and salt, meet for a kiss that anchors me more surly than any ship. When I step back we nod with matching resolve. Carolyn falls in at my other side with a brief touch to my cheek and a sharp adjustment to the bag across her chest, the gold of her relic catching the sun as she moves the strap.

I slide the bear helm over my head at the last minute and smile beneath its teeth.

If I must face yet another unknown, another trial, another step toward ending the woman who has taken so much from me, I will do it as my fiercest, truest self: armored in bark and bone, and stained with the blood of those I love, standing side by side with those that remain.

List of Content Warnings

The Forest and the Flame includes difficult themes. The following list includes what the author has identified, but it may not be comprehensive to each individual.

- Child abuse
- Death of a child (on page)
- Death of a parent
- Explicit sexual content
- Explicit depictions of violence and gore
- Infertility

Acknowledgments

This project never would have started, let alone reached this point, without an entire community (lovingly) yelling at me to keep going. Light, my first and loudest cheerleader, my partner in chaos, my light in the dark. Thank you. With everything that I am. Thank you. For Lotus, my editor-in-chief, my necessary slap-in-the-face expert, what can I even say? With your talent for editing and your belief in me, you helped me build this project into something I can be proud of. You built me into someone I can be proud of. Bea/Alcatraz/partner in crime, unknowingly the start of it all. Thank you for dragging me along into the book club of insanity. Thank you for the purple pen treatment. Thank you for dealing with me for so many years. Thank you Zephyr (L.E Teetzel) for dragging me kicking and screaming through the final steps. Your help with formatting and your wealth of knowledge about the technical side of publishing truly made it possible for me to even dream about seeing this finish line. To all of my alpha, beta, and every other Greek letter readers (looking at you Drachen, Whisper, and Analog), it's you who carried me through this strange and wild ride.

It takes a village, and I have the absolute best village you could ask for. Coyote, Harvest, Jabs, Bond, Dive, Becca, Alexis, Alyssa, Jackie, Katelyn, Nick, David, Rachel, and Mike, thank you for believing in me, as a writer and as a person, and for making me who I am today.

And saving the best for last...

Thank you, the reader, for giving this book a chance. Thank you for walking into this world with me and letting me show you around. I hope it helped you believe in your own magic and the magic in the world around you.

About the Author

S.C Wolf is a dreamer stuck in the American Midwest. The corn-field hostage situation is only made tolerable by her family of five cats (and one husband), and the fact that she can travel pretty much anywhere and end up in the arms of a friend. She's only been writing for real since 2023, but it was quickly obvious to her that this is what she was really supposed to be doing the whole time, despite the fact that she claims she's quitting every two weeks.

Join her on
Instagram at: s.c.wolfauthorx
Website: scwolfauthorx.com